A SPECIAL EXCERPT

Beneath me, the bridge seemed to swing from one side to the other; I had to maintain white-knuckled grips on the ropes to prevent this, and I could feel my fingernails digging into the meat of my palms after only five steps. The groaning planks beneath Petras's feet less than two yards ahead of me did not help settle my unease.

I closed my eyes and listened to the rushing water below, the sound of the wind rustling the palm fronds and the rhododendron leaves. Last night's sleep was hard and dreamless: I dreamed now, imagining I was floating high above the earth, no bridge beneath my feet, just the air and the babbling river, white and frothing, and the swaying fronds that were so big they looked prehistoric—

The line at my back went taut. My eyes flipped open, and I told Petras to slow down as I glanced behind me. Shotsky, taking up the rear, was moving too slow.

"You gotta step it up a notch, man," I called to him.

"This pace feels about right," he said. I did not like the quaking in his voice.

"Shotsky, the slower you move, the longer you'll be on this bridge. Do you understand?" I turned to look at him.

He nodded but did not increase his speed.

"Shotsky," I said again, and that was when the plank beneath my foot snapped.

The world blurred as I rushed downward, feeling the jagged edge of the busted plank tear my cargo pants. Reflex caused my hands to spear out; I grabbed one of the vertical ropes, which briefly arrested my fall yet caused the bridge to pitch on its side. I heard Shotsky moan and saw John Petras bound toward me. The busted plank was at eye level. What looked like blood seeped into the wood. My blood? I had no idea.

"Hang on!" Petras shouted.

The rope was slick with moss; I lost my grip and felt the world pull me toward its center.

With all this gear on my back, I'm going to drown, I thought. A second later, I felt the concussion of striking the surface of the water. My bones rattled in my skin. For a moment, I thought I had somehow missed the river completely and hit the embankment, and I was now splayed out and broken on the jagged white rocks covered by a mat of fronds.

But then I felt the icy waters claim me, seeping into my clothes and attacking my flesh, and I couldn't see a damn thing. I was fucking blind, and I was drowning, blind and drowning.

PREVIOUS ACCOLADES FOR RONALD MALFI'S SHAMROCK ALLEY

"This is a bottom-of-the-ninth, two-out, grand slam home run of a book . . . *Shamrock Alley* is a novel that demands to be read and Ronald Damien Malfi is an author to whom attention must be paid."

> —Lorenzo Carcaterra, author of *Sleepers* and *Chasers*

"This is a gripping thriller, similar to the novels of Gerald Petievich, the Secret Service agent turned author, but with more emotional and moral depth. The author's previous books have garnered him acclaim and a small but devoted audience; this one could easily lift him into the mainstream."

> —David Pitt, *Booklist*

A NOVEL OF SURVIVAL

THE ASCENT

Ronald Malfi

MEDALLION
P R E S S

Medallion Press, Inc.
Printed in USA

DEDICATION:

For my parents and grandparents,
who taught me to never stop climbing.

Published 2010 by Medallion Press, Inc.

The MEDALLION PRESS LOGO
is a registered trademark of Medallion Press, Inc.

Typeset in Adobe Garamond Pro
Printed in the United States of America
Title font set in Cacavia01

Library of Congress Cataloging-in-Publication Data

Malfi, Ronald Damien.
The ascent : a novel of survival / Ronald Malfi.
   p. cm.
 ISBN-13: 978-1-60542-067-7 (alk. paper)
 ISBN-10: 1-60542-067-0 (alk. paper)
1. Self-actualization (Psychology)--Fiction. 2. Mountaineering--Fiction. 3. Psychological fiction. I. Title.
PS3613.A4355A93 2010
813'.6--dc22
                          2010008942

10 9 8 7 6 5 4 3 2 1
First Edition

ACKNOWLEDGMENTS:

Having never attempted to climb a mountain, I must confess to a certain degree of ignorance—both in the act of climbing as well as the undertaking of writing a novel centered on such a subject.

The following books helped me in the writing of this novel: *No Shortcuts to the Top: Climbing the World's 14 Highest Peaks* by Ed Viesturs with David Roberts; Jon Krakauer's breathtaking *Into Thin Air: A Personal Account of the Mt. Everest Disaster*; *Chris Bonington's Everest* by Sir Chris Bonington as well as Bonington and Charles Clarke's *Everest: The Unclimbed Ridge*; *Everest: Alone at the Summit* by Stephen Venables; Ian Baker's astounding *The Heart of the World: A Journey to Tibet's Lost Paradise*; and a countless selection of Let's Go travel guides.

Thanks also to Helen A Rosburg and the folks at Medallion Press, particularly Lorie Popp for her priceless editorial assistance, and Kerry Estevez, who has guided me like a Sherpa through this publishing terrain.

PART ONE

THE GHOSTS WE TAKE WITH US

CHAPTER 1

1

I WASN'T THERE WHEN IT HAPPENED, BUT I CAN SEE
it nonetheless: the Italian countryside, cool in the stirrings of an early
summer that promises not to be too overbearing. Clouds sit motionless in the bluest of skies like great seagoing vessels. I imagine the lush,
sloping hills spilling into the scenic valley, the grass aquamarine and
populated by a dazzling array of thimble-shaped purple and yellow
flowers. There is a rutted dirt road, just wide enough for a single
vehicle, which winds around the hillside like a satin ribbon.

The vehicle appears first as a glinting beacon over the farthest
hill. The stillness of the afternoon vibrates with the grinding of gears
and the rumbling of tires. I imagine the vehicle to be an old motorcar,
something from the 1920s, with a convertible top stripped away, rubber
matte running boards, headlamps like snare drums.

David is behind the wheel. I dress him in ridiculous driving
goggles, racing gloves, a worn bomber jacket. The only thing missing
is a silk scarf flapping behind him in the wind.

Hannah is in the passenger seat. She laughs, and I can see the
glitter of her teeth, the faint parenthetical lines at either side of her
mouth. Her hair is short, curling just at her jaw, and appears the

color of new copper in midday.

When the car strikes something in the road—an errant tree limb or a large stone—David jerks the wheel, and Hannah's laughter dies. I watch the motorcar swerve off the narrow, gouged road and rumble over a grassy knoll. The vehicle crests an embankment, and in that moment, it seems plausible that it will come to rest at the zenith of the embankment, seesawing precipitously on its undercarriage but secure.

Instead, it clears the embankment and barrels right over to the other side where it teeters motionlessly in the air for what seems like both a millisecond and a millennium at the same time. The motorcar tips forward and plummets to the mountainous terrain below, then erupts at the bottom in a dazzling belch of fire.

This image runs through my mind over and over as I lay dying.

2

AT LEAST, I THOUGHT I WAS DYING . . .

My eyes fluttered open, yet I could not see. Pure darkness surrounded me. My hand splashed through the freezing water until it fell on the cylindrical shell of the flashlight. I cracked it against my palm a few times until the light winked on. The beam illuminated a wall of limestone a mere two feet from my face. I was in a cavern chamber of sorts, sprawled out in several inches of water. Eleven hundred feet below the surface of the earth, I was overcome by disorientation.

I tried to sit up, but a searing pain shot through my left leg and blossomed like an explosion in my stomach. I turned the light toward one of the cavern walls and closed my eyes until my respiration was once again under control.

The foolishness in coming out here alone was suddenly all too apparent. It went against the tenants of the trade. *Always go exploring with a partner; always tell people where you're planning to go so they know when to expect your return.* Stupidly, I'd done neither.

"Fuck," I uttered, my voice echoing all around me.

I reached down and felt the cut in my left leg, the jagged serration of my shinbone projecting through the tissue and the fabric of my pants. I refused to shine the light on my wound, refused to look at it. My ignorance kept me anchored to sanity.

I directed the beam along the walls of the cave. The light reflected and refracted off the frozen javelins of ice. At one point, the beam fragmented into a rainbow prism, and I tried to hold it there, unmoving, while I caught my breath.

It was cold, but I was sweating through my anorak. I adjusted the couplings—metal hooks digging into my waist—and wiped my brow with one shaky hand. I glanced up. The ceiling of the cave pressed close to my face. I could see the calcium deposits, the shimmering constellations of mica embedded in the rock. I found the narrow hole, too—the hole I'd carelessly fallen through just moments ago—and that was when my flashlight died on me again.

Absolute darkness.

"Come on, you son of a bitch . . ."

I slapped the flashlight a few times, but it wouldn't come on. Seconds passed, but it felt like hours. The pain in my leg seemed to intensify in the darkness, its throb in synchronization with the pulsing, vinegar threads of burst blood vessels behind my eyelids. I was beginning to breathe my own spent breath; it was coming back at me like reverberations off the cave walls. How much air was down here, anyway? How much time before I bled out?

After a time, I realized I could make out the paleness of my hands in the darkness, which meant the darkness was not absolute after all. Squinting, I discovered the suggestion of light issuing from a coin-sized opening somewhere far above my head. I did not know if this was actual daylight or just its reflection off a frozen, glossy spire. It was like trying to weed out reality in a hall of mirrors.

The flashlight came to life in my hands, startling me. I aimed the beam into the hole where the light dulled to a milky nothingness. The fall could have been twenty or thirty feet, but I couldn't tell for sure. The flashlight's beam fell upon vague indentations in the walls, which might serve as handholds, but the passageway itself looked dubiously narrow. How in the hell had I managed to fall down such a tight shaft?

You came down that way, I told myself. *You can climb back up.*

Taking a deep breath, I attempted to stand on my one good leg. My thighs, which had been soaking in the stagnant, icy water, were practically numb. The shaft was narrow enough to lean against and keep pressure off my wounded leg, although the mere act of readjusting its position sent fireworks up my spine. I gritted my teeth so hard I nearly ground them to powder. Still, I raised myself on one leg, easing my head and shoulders into the hole in the cave ceiling. I heard the fabric of my anorak ripping and the metal hooks on my belt scraping against the stone. Each exhalation brought my breath back in my face. The opening was snug enough to disallow my arms to pass through; panic shook me as, for one terrifying second, I felt stuck.

Then somehow I managed to free myself and push through. Halfway up, the flexing of my muscles caused the space to tighten around me, and I froze with one hand pinned against my chest. The hand holding the flashlight was still below, too bulky to work its way through the narrow mouth of the hole, so my vision was dependent upon the minimal amount of light issuing from somewhere far above me.

My injured leg refused to straighten out. It would be impossible to climb the shaft without straightening the leg. Trying not to think about it, I attempted to slide my hand back down, but it wouldn't budge. I was stuck.

Jesus . . .

I started thinking about my SUV, and that was always a bad sign. My metallic green Jeep Cherokee was parked maybe thirty yards from the main road, visible only to those who might actively been searching for it. Not that anyone would be searching for it. I'd heard enough stories from spelunkers to know that when you started wondering if your car was visible from the highway, you were already in too deep. You'd bought the farm, as the saying went.

But I was panicking. I wasn't thinking.

Five years old, I thought. *Swimming lessons. Dad kept telling you to put your head underwater, put your head underwater, put your head underwater. Deep breath and put your head—*

"Underwater," I whispered. I said it not to hear the word but to release the last bit of air in my lungs, narrowing my chest in the process.

The rock loosened around me, and I was again able to move my hand. I thrust it upward and slapped a numb palm against the wall of the shaft, groping for one of those handholds I'd spotted. My fingers slipped into a groove and gripped it. Something caught in my throat. I thought of skeletons blanketed in cobwebs. I was able to rise on the tips of my toes and snake my other hand through the maw, spilling white light from the flashlight straight up through the narrow tunnel. Everything smelled of sulfur.

It's not sulfur. It's chlorine, I kept hearing in my head. *This is no different than swimming. You're swimming. This is swimming in a pool; can't you tell?*

I could tell. I could tell, all right.

The flashlight fell from my hand. I heard it clatter against the rocks as it dropped, pulling the light with it. It struck the water with a hollow, plastic sound. An instant later, I was awash in blackness again.

This is swimming. This is swimming—

I realized I hadn't taken a breath in quite a while. I took one now, my lungs aching and my chest expanding, pressing hard against the stone all around me. The constriction was too great. I couldn't catch a full breath.

It was the fear of dying alone in the dark that set my body in motion. I proceeded to scale the wall, my fingers seeking out niches in the wall to hold on to, the muscles in my arms and shoulders straining as I hoisted myself off the ground without the assistance of my legs. The tunnel was too narrow to bring a knee up; my legs hung uselessly below. My broken left leg felt as if it were rigged with coat hangers and packed with broken glass.

I gripped a ledge above and felt space open up behind my shoulders. The tunnel was widening. *This is swimming. This is swimming.* I managed to raise myself up farther—

My hands slipped, and I anticipated the fall before it actually happened. But when I crashed to the bottom, the pain in my injured leg was potent enough to send my mind whirling . . .

I stood at the end of a long pier watching a Ferris wheel pull slow rotations in the oncoming dusk. Something tickled my throat, and I coughed into my hands. People shouted from the boardwalk, and when I looked in their direction, I was shocked to see many of them pointing at *me.* I cupped my hands to my mouth and coughed into them again. This time, however, I coughed up the head of a daffodil, glistening with spittle in my palm, and I stared at it with wonder—

And then I'm there once again, standing off in the distance, admiring the green, sloping lawns of the Italian countryside. As soon as I realize where I am, I see the motorcar speeding around a curve in the road. I wave my arms as it approaches, pleading for the driver to slow down.

I stood in a room of darkness as a figure approached. How I was able to discern the figure's shape I did not know, but as it drew nearer, I sensed a radiance from it, and there was an anticipation in my chest.

Then my eyes opened to the blackness of the real world.

Here, I thought. *I'm going to die down here.*

The pain had ushered me into blessed unconsciousness. Upon awaking, I felt the numbness of my left leg—the frightening *absence* of it—but it was no longer that drilling, incomprehensible pain.

I was on the ground, icy water all around me. I knew I was awake and lucid, but I refused to move. The flashlight was dead, probably destroyed when I'd landed on it, and I didn't care. This was it. I was watching the motorcar launch over the hillside, and I no longer thought about broken legs or my Jeep Cherokee.

There was someone else here with me.

The feeling was unmistakable. When I was a child, my mother used to gather me in her lap and rake her long fingernails down my bare back. She would carve designs, designs I was required to guess—a turtle, a lion, a skyscraper. Seconds before her fingernails ever grazed my flesh, I could sense their approach, could feel them coming like a twinge in my spine, a tickle in my tailbone. This feeling was like that: a sense of impending certainty of the presence of another.

"I'm dying," I said. Although I could not be certain if I spoke these words aloud or not . . .

—*You're not,* Hannah said.

I felt my heart leap in my chest. I wished for light by which to see her, but there was no light here. This was a tomb below the surface of the earth.

—*Get up,* she said.

"I *can't,*" I managed, certain this time of the words forming in my throat and hearing the way they croaked forth and came back to me. "Can't . . . move . . ."

—*You can't die down here,* she said.

There were other words, too—words that made no *verbal* sense, no *vocal* sense—but they were dedicated to forcing me up from the frigid water.

I didn't see the hand come out of the blackness above; instead I *felt* it. Again, it was similar to my mother's fingernails on my back, causing goose bumps and sending shivers down my spine. I knew the hand wasn't actually there—that I was feeling it only in my mind—but the sense of it was enough to cause in me a surge of power, of strength, of celebration.

My arms were over my head this time, a smarter approach. My fingers fumbled and grasped a set of niches in the wall. Using my renewed strength, I hauled myself off the stone ground and out of the freezing pool of water in which I'd been sitting. This movement caused fresh agony to bullet up through my left leg. I could feel it everywhere throughout my body, igniting every single nerve ending and causing my teeth to gnash. Still, I continued to raise myself into the hole above my head, using only my arms and my one good leg.

The narrowness of the hole permitted my elbows to bend to a maximum of perhaps thirty degrees, merely bowing out and not truly bending at all. There was nothing more I could do about this; the walls of the channel pressed hard against the points of my elbows, and I was once again breathing in the heavy dust.

It took all my strength and concentration to release my grip on one of the handholds I'd secured and to swing momentarily like the pendulum of a clock. My free hand shot straight up, providing more room in the tunnel in its wake.

Then I was able to bend my other elbow just a bit more, drawing my face closer to where one hand still gripped the handhold. I could feel the tendons in my body, as tense as violin strings, quaking in unison. Yet I was able to raise my free hand higher into the darkness above. It slapped against the stone far above my head with numb satisfaction. The fingers immediately slipped into another groove.

Overzealous, I pulled myself up too quickly and was instantly rewarded with a blinding, delirious pain as my exposed shinbone, rising into the hole, cracked against the lip of the crevasse. The blackness was overcome by a dazzling display of fireworks—explosions of all color—and I thought maybe I had died and was boiling in a vat of molten lava in the deepest depths of hell.

—*Up.* Hannah beckoned. *Up.*

I could have let the pain engulf and destroy me, but I allowed it to fuel my aggression and will to survive. I didn't care if I ground the exposed bone to yellow powder against the walls of the shaft. I was going to climb out. The pain made me determined.

I continued to climb to the wan light. I didn't know how long it took me to reach the chamber above and to let the fading daylight course down on me fully through a rent in the ceiling of the cavern—

it could have been minutes or hours. When I finally climbed out of the crevasse onto stable ground, I passed out.

3

FLASHES OF CONSCIOUSNESS FLITTED BY LIKE dragonflies. Whether or not I was actually dreaming, I could not be certain because when my eyes unstuck, I was somehow out of the cave itself and in the open desert, watching lizards lap water from kiss tanks with vibrating black tongues and feeling the pre-evening heat clinging wetly to my body.

I crawled in the dirt toward an immense outcropping of stone, suggestive of the undulating, skeletonized backbone of some prehistoric animal. Again, I fell into unconsciousness.

This time when I awoke it was night. The moon was a fat pearl shimmering behind a stretch of clouds like pulls of dirty wool. The air was frigid against my skin. I blinked several times, trying to remember where I was and how I'd gotten here.

When I tried to stand, my body refused to cooperate, and I was sent sprawling to the dirt, agony coursing through the marrow in my bones. I glanced down and saw the horror that was my left leg—the blackened, soaked trousers and the ghostlike glow of the bone in the moonlight—and vomited into the sand.

I wasn't sure if I passed out again or if I switched over to autopilot, but the next thing I remembered was leaning against a wall of stone, the heavy limb of a tree under one arm as a makeshift crutch, and squinting into the distance. The sky was a velvet canopy of stars. Around me, the cacophony of nature—the twitter of insects, the screech of birds, the howl of wolves, the cumulative chatter of all things wild—was nearly deafening.

I peered across the vast white flats of the desert, searching for the highway. I could see no headlights of passing vehicles, nor could I locate the vaguely orange sodium glimmer of a distant civilization. The surface of the moon couldn't look less desolate.

Hannah stood about twenty yards ahead of me. In a simple white cotton dress, her hair bobbed short as I'd often imagined it, her skin pale to the point of near translucence in the light of the moon, she appeared to hover like a spirit several inches off the ground. And of course she was a spirit—Hannah was dead.

"Hannah," I breathed, my throat abraded and raw. It hurt just to breathe let alone speak. God only knew how long I'd been without water.

She turned and walked—no, *floated*—to a craggy hillock of stone, disappearing around the other side. She said nothing, and she was too far away to see her expression, but I was certain she wanted me to follow her.

Leaning on my makeshift crutch, I hobbled toward the hillock, pausing only once to catch my breath and allow the feeling to shift back into my numb left leg. There was no more pain. I was beyond pain now, which was good for the moment, though I knew such numbness was a bad sign in the grand scheme of things. The leg was going dead. Also, hypothermia was beginning to set in. All the signs were present—the profuse sweating while simultaneously shivering, the blurring vision, the lethargy I felt with each tedious step I took. I wanted to curl into a ball and close my eyes. In fact, that might have been my fate had I not spotted Hannah—

That's not Hannah, a voice spoke up in my head. *Hannah's dead.*

Hannah appeared on the other side of the hillock, staring straight at me. As I lumbered forward again on my crutch, she turned and headed through a veil of low trees.

I pursued this visage through the trees, using their outstretched branches as support, and if it wasn't for the peripheral sight of Hannah's white gown in the darkness, there but not wholly there, I would have surrendered to the sheer weight of my exhaustion before ever passing through the trees into a vast clearing.

But it wasn't a clearing at all. It was pavement. I was standing in the middle of the highway.

4

I NEVER MET THE MAN WHO EVENTUALLY STOPPED to collect my broken husk off the side of the road, propping me up in the backseat of his car and shuttling me to the nearest hospital, but the doctors later assured me that he was a very nice guy who wished me well.

CHAPTER 2

1

MARTA CORTEZ CAME AT THE END OF THE WEEK, looking pretty with her hair pulled back and her naturally tanned face fresh and without makeup. She hummed to herself, and the sound was pleasant enough to instantly brighten the entire apartment.

"Look at you." She sighed, pausing in her long-legged stride. "You're in one of your bitter moods."

"How'd you get in? I thought I locked the door."

"Don't be so combative." She practically swished through the apartment, her arms burdened with brown grocery bags and a swinging leather purse, and went straight for the kitchen.

I was on the deck, the balcony doors open, watching the distant glint of traffic creeping across the Chesapeake Bay. I maneuvered my wheelchair around and thumped over the rubber threshold stripping of the deck into my apartment. Even with the breezy summer air filtering in, there persisted the underlying stink of stale sweat and old, musty books throughout the place—a smell I'd once found comforting, the way some people find libraries comforting, though which recently alerted me to my own hermitic lifestyle. With the exception of Marta's weekly visit to bring me groceries and play the occasional game of backgammon or chess, my tiny Annapolis apartment entertained no visitors.

"This place is a mess," she said, emptying the bags of groceries into the refrigerator. "Can't you clean up a little?"

"It's homey," I retorted, surveying the room. Clothes clung like foliage to the sofa, while towers of paperback novels and DVDs teetered on nearly every available flat surface, including the leveled shade of a lamp— a potential fire hazard. A half-empty bottle of Macallan scotch, along with an assortment of used rocks glasses and champagne flutes, stood atop a stereo speaker. Empty food containers from various local delivery joints had cropped up like tiny civilizations seemingly overnight. In particular, a carton of reeking Chinese food balanced on a collection of DVDs that in turn perched atop a mountain of books on the coffee table in the middle of the room: a cumulative testament to just how pathetic I'd become. "Anyway," I continued, ignoring the mess, "I'm still getting the hang of this chair. It's hard to get around and clean up."

"I thought you were on crutches now."

I glanced at the pair of crutches propped in one corner of the room, a ratty old Hawaiian shirt draped over one of the cushioned supports. "Ask some of the neighbors, and they might attest to seeing a man in his late thirties, skin pasty, a bad dresser, stumbling around the lobby on a pair of crutches from time to time. But they'd also no doubt relay the embarrassed and frustrated look on the man's face."

"You're an asshole, Tim," Marta said matter-of-factly. Then, some musicality coming to her voice, she said, "I got you a surprise."

"Oh yeah? What is it, a housekeeper?"

She appeared in the kitchen doorway, looking almost seductive in a pink halter top and a pair of too-short black shorts from which her brown, coltish legs seemed to slide like shafts of daylight. Marta and I were friends and had never dated. Although one night several years ago after spending a few hours getting hammered at a Main Street bar, we'd returned to this very apartment where, midway through watching a Coen brothers movie, we'd kissed. The kiss transitioned into clumsy groping, resulting in Marta bare-chested on my sofa, me on top of her with one hand down her pants—which was the exact position we woke up in the next morning. We were mutually humiliated, and I hadn't kissed her nor seen her breasts since that night.

She crossed the room and tossed a DVD case in my lap.

"*Rear Window*," I said. "Hysterical. Don't let anyone ever tell you that you've got a lousy sense of humor."

"Did you see the boats?" she said, returning to the kitchen.

"What boats?"

"They're gearing up for some big race. People from all over the country are in town. You should see the size of the boats down at Ego Alley."

Ego Alley was what the locals called the downtown dock, where all the silver-haired, retired Annapolis moguls coasted by on their enormous boats, their chests puffed out, while bikini-clad, amber-skinned women decorated the decks. If one were to look closely at these men, it was almost possible to spot a fan of peacock feathers sprouting from their asses.

I piloted my wheelchair back onto the deck, snatching the bottle of Macallan as I went. Sure enough, I could make out a cluster of white sails farther down the shoreline. Uncorking the bottle, I brought the scotch to my lips and took a quick swig. Marta had stopped reprimanding me for drinking while on pain medication, knowing damn well I'd sooner give up the meds than the whiskey. When she caught me now, she would only shake her head like someone who'd just heard of a terrible automobile accident on the news.

It had been six months since the incident at the cave and four months since the last of my surgeries. The result was a steel plate and a dozen or so stainless steel screws drilled into the bones of my left leg. Such things were beyond the assistance of simple pain medication; such things were beyond mere *pain*.

"Is this a new one?" she called from inside.

I craned my neck to find her standing in the vestibule, holding an envelope.

"Another one from New York?"

"They're always from New York," I reminded her.

"You didn't even open it."

I took another drink from the bottle and watched a pair of Jet Skis carve white tracks of froth across the surface of the bay.

Marta came up behind me, fanning herself with the envelope. "Can I open it?"

"Be my guest."

She tore open the envelope, depositing a pigtail curl of white paper into my lap, and read the contents of the letter out loud. She'd gotten only partway when she stopped reading and said without humor, "What's the matter with you? These guys are making a great offer. They want to fly you out and discuss it. Oh, shit. What's the date?"

"Don't really know."

"Damn it. They wanted you to go out *last week*. You missed it."

I shrugged. "Doesn't matter."

"Right," she said. "Nothing matters. This letter doesn't matter and neither do any of the others that came before it. There's a stack of them in a shoe box under your bed, you know."

"I thought you threw them away."

"Why would you think that? You never asked what I did with them, and I never told you."

"Why are you making a big deal about this all of a sudden?"

Marta crinkled the letter into a ball and dropped it in my lap. I could tell, even without peeling apart the ball, that it had been typed on expensive paper. Probably watermarked, with an upraised crest in the header.

"Because it's been too long," she said, slipping into the apartment. "Too much time has gone by, and you haven't done anything to get back on track."

I turned the wheelchair around and followed her inside. "It was never my intention to get back on that track."

"Well, you need *some* track. This place is a dump, and you're running out of money."

That much was true. Since the accident, I hadn't been able to teach at the college. I'd attempted to provide students with an online seminar for the semester—something I could teach via the Internet and a digital camera three nights a week—but I was not a very good lecturer. And it was next to impossible to teach an art class over the Internet. Fortunately I was able to take a sabbatical while I recuperated, and I'd spent the past six months watching DVDs and in the evenings crutching from bar to bar through downtown Annapolis.

"I told you," I said, not knowing if I'd ever said these words to her or not, "I can't do it anymore. It's left me."

"Are you so sure? When was the last time you even *tried* sculpting something?"

"Before the accident, I was sculpting every day in class—"

"I don't mean at the college. I mean for real, in real life. Not something that takes you fifty minutes to mold out of clay. I'm talking about the kind of sculpting you used to do before I knew you. The work that made you happy and got your face on the cover of that magazine you've got framed . . ." She glanced at the empty square of wall beside the front door—the spot where a crooked little nail jutted erect, suddenly so obvious I was surprised she hadn't noticed earlier. "Why did you take it down?"

"It accidentally fell and broke," I said. This was only partially true.

Seemingly defeated, she flopped onto the sofa. She looked like she wanted to hit me. Instead, she shook her head, something like a coy smile teasing the corners of her mouth. She brought her hands up and rested her chin on them. A spray of freckles covered her arms.

"Let's play," I said, placing the bottle of Macallan on the floor. I started setting up the chessboard that sat on the coffee table between us.

"No." Marta stood.

"What?"

"I've got a date."

"No shit?"

"You always sound surprised."

"I always am. Who is he?"

"He's no one you know."

"That's not what I meant. What does he do?"

"He's a bartender."

"Maybe I *do* know him."

"Ha. Seriously, he's just a nice guy, nothing fantastic. But I'm not getting any younger."

"So you're thinking a bartender's the way to go, huh?"

"Cool it. I'm watching my life tick by." And for whatever reason, this statement caused something to turn over inside her—that much was evident by the change in her expression—and she cocked her hip and looked at me from beneath her brow. "What the hell possessed you to explore the cave on your own that day?"

In all this time, she'd never asked the question. Right now my answer was a long time coming. "Guess I was just looking for something," I said, continuing to set up the chessboard. I would play by myself if I couldn't convince Marta to stay.

"Looking for what?"

I shrugged. "Can't answer that."

"Can't? Why not? Someone holding a gun to your head? Or is it some vast government secret?"

"The latter one sounds cool. Let's go with that."

"Christ, Tim. Sometimes you're just goddamn impossible."

I almost told her about Hannah right then—about how it was Hannah's ghost that had helped me out of the cave and beckoned me toward the highway. I would have never found that highway on my own, and I surely would have died in that cave if not for Hannah.

But I kept my mouth shut, not wanting to discuss such things, because that story was connected to another story, a *current* story, and I didn't want to tell that one at all. Given the physical and psychological stress my body had been under at the time of the accident, seeing Hannah's ghost was easily explained away. Her image was a figment of my imagination, summoned from the depths of my memories to the forefront of my world while in a state of excruciating pain and the onset of hypothermia. I could have claimed to have been led from the cave by Elvis, and it could be blown off with a subtle grin and a wave of the hand. That wasn't the problem. The problem was where the story led me—to the here and now—and how such claims were no longer dismissed as easily.

Because since the accident I'd seen Hannah in my apartment. Most recently, three nights ago, standing outside on the balcony . . .

"What's wrong?" A furrow creased Marta's brow. "You look frightened all of a sudden."

My palms were sweating. I swallowed and my spit felt granulated, like sand. When I spoke, my voice cracked as if I were going through puberty all over again. "Guess I was just thinking back on the whole thing."

"It must have been horrible. But it's over now. You escaped. You're alive."

I cleared my throat. "Stay. Just for one game."

"Stop it." She came and kissed the top of my head. It was such a motherly act that I felt a pang of nostalgia for my childhood. "I have a date and I need to go. I'll stop by and see you tomorrow, okay?"

"Unless you get lucky tonight. You know how sharp those bartenders can be. By the way, tell him I said hello, whoever he is."

"You're a regular riot. There're fresh cold cuts in the fridge. Try to stay out of trouble."

I winked.

She left.

2

WHEN NINE O'CLOCK ROLLED AROUND, I WAS STILL thinking of Hannah. The apartment had grown cold and dark, and the air that came in through the balcony doors carried with it the gritty scent of the Chesapeake.

I sat in my wheelchair and watched the first hour of *Rear Window* until my memories got the better of me; I began to trick myself, believing I saw Hannah in the periphery of my vision. Once, as Jimmy Stewart looked out across his courtyard with a telephoto lens, I thought the face of the leotard-clad dancer in the opposite apartment bore Hannah's face. This was stupid, of course . . . but I still reversed the DVD and paused it on that frame nonetheless.

After a time, I rolled out onto the balcony with the Macallan. It was good scotch; I approved of the cozy chateau emblem on the label. I sat and drank, watching the sodium lights twinkling farther down the stretch of beach toward downtown. Directly over the water, which was now a vast blanket of darkness, stood the Bay Bridge, bejeweled with the countless headlights of automobiles.

I'd lied to Marta earlier when I said I thought she'd thrown all those letters away. I knew very well she'd tucked them inside that shoe box under my bed. I'd gone through them a number of times since, though not with any sense of remorse or regret at having missed the opportunities. In fact, I felt very little emotion when I looked at them, except maybe for a sense of anchoring, of stabilizing, the way a ship gets tied to the docks when it growls into port.

They were letters requesting my services as an artist and a sculptor. Usually they came from multinational conglomerates and faceless corporations throughout the country's major metropolises, requesting some titanium twist of modern art for their marbled courtyards. Or some board member I'd never heard of from a company of equal anonymity would pen a letter, explaining he'd read such and such an article and would love to have me chisel the bust of their CEO in granite, something they could prop on a pedestal in their lobby.

Over the past few years, these requests dwindled dramatically but not to the point of extinction. The latest—the one Marta had read this afternoon on the balcony—was from a textile company in Manhattan. The company's vice president was infatuated with the number three, the letter explained, and it was this man's desire to hire Timothy Overleigh to design a wrought-iron numeral to be displayed in his office. His reasons for choosing me were appropriately threefold: the magazine on whose cover I'd once been pictured was called *Three Tiers*; I was once named the third best sculptor in young America by the *Washington Post*; and lastly because of the sum of the letters in the abbreviated form of my first name.

I finished off the last of the Macallan and was feeling pretty good. When I squinted, the lights along the shore blurred and spread out in a greasy smear. The chill from the strong breeze caused my injured leg to ache. I turned the chair around and, thumping over the rubber doorjamb, rolled back into the apartment.

Hannah stood across the room, mostly hidden in the dark.

My breath caught in my throat. I felt the empty liquor bottle slide from my hand and strike the floor with a hollow thud. Suddenly I forgot all about the pain in my left leg. Unable to move, I sat frozen in the wheelchair, staring across the room, trying to dissect the shadows to better view my wife.

"Hannah." It came out in a breathy whisper, the sound of it—the foolishness of it—forcing rational thought to override my panic. She wasn't there, of course. She was dead. Hannah was dead. She was—

I watched her move along the far wall, an indescribable shifting of depth, until she reached the section spotlighted by the moonlight coming in through the balcony doors. I anticipated her coming into relief the moment she crossed that panel of bluish light . . . but she never did. She vanished before she reached it, dispersing into granules of dust in the darkness.

"Jesus," I uttered, my voice choked and nervous. I forced a laugh; it came out as a bark.

I decided to get the hell out of the apartment for the night. My eyes locked on the pair of crutches leaning in one corner of the room. It was not difficult to maneuver on the crutches, although they certainly provided less comfort than the chair, and I quickly rolled over to them and dragged myself out of the wheelchair while leaning against the television for support. I winced as I carelessly banged my left leg against the credenza, a million fireworks exploding before my eyes, then took a number of slow, deep breaths as I situated the crutches into the sockets of my armpits. Upright, I balanced precipitously for a moment before lunging toward the front door.

My apartment was in walking distance of downtown but not crutching distance, so I had the building's doorman wrangle me a cab. It was a feat getting into the cab's backseat, even with the assistance of the doorman and the cabdriver—both of whom spoke little English and looked as though they may have hailed from the same South American country—but I was soon shuttled off and deposited at the city dock.

It was a beautiful night, and the streets were alive. I could faintly hear live music issuing from a number of the closest taverns and beyond that the distant growl of boat engines. The bars along Main Street would be packed at this hour, and I was not in the mood to have my leg bumped by drunks in Navy whites, so I hobbled down an alleyway to seek out a more reclusive haunt hidden from summer tourists.

The Filibuster was as reclusive as one could hope for. A narrow, redbrick front fitted with iron sconces, boasting none of the typical Annapolis fanfare in its windows—goggle-eyed ceramic crabs or miniature rowing oars crossing each other to form an *X*—the Filibuster was easy to miss if you weren't looking for it. Brom Holsworth, a retired Department of Justice prosecutor, owned the place ever since I could remember. Inside, it was musty and dark, the walls adorned with yellowing photographs of disgraced Washington politicians, many of whom Brom helped to disgrace.

Tonight, as expected, the bar was only mildly populated. I nearly collapsed on the closest barstool and, leaning my crutches against the wall, let out a hefty sigh.

The bartender was a nice enough kid named Ricky Carrolton. His face seemed to light up when he saw me. "Been gone so long, I was beginning to think you jumped off the Bay Bridge."

Something about his comment bothered me. "Downtown's more crowded than usual," I said quickly, trying not to let my discomfort show. "What's the deal?"

"Regatta race starts tomorrow morning. Didn't you read today's paper?"

"I only get the Sunday paper."

"We've even been getting some of the stragglers all the way down here." As Ricky spoke, he fixed me a whiskey sour. "Out-of-towners, most of them. All the hotels are busting at the seams. Good for business, though, I guess."

"How's Brom?"

Ricky set the drink down in front of me. "Laid up with the gout." He nodded toward my crutches. "When are you gonna get off those? You seem to be moving around better."

"I'm biding my time."

"Doc keeps giving you pain meds as long as you're a cripple, huh?" Ricky said, laughing. "I dig it."

A hand fell on my shoulder.

I turned, expecting to see someone I knew, but this man was a stranger to me. Perhaps one of the out-of-towners Ricky had just spoken of.

"Your name Timothy Overleigh?" the man asked. He was

a large, barrel-chested behemoth, with grizzled white tufts of hair spooling out from beneath his mesh cap and pepper-colored beard stubble covering the undulations of his thick, rolling neck.

"Who wants to know?" I retorted.

The man jerked a thumb over his shoulder toward a darkened corner of the tavern. "Guy in the back," he said, turning his rheumy eyes from me so he could scan the collection of liquor bottles that climbed the wall behind the bar.

I peered across the room and could make out the shape of a man seated by himself in a corner booth. The lighting was too poor, however, to get a good look at his face.

"Oh yeah?" I said. "He say his name? It's a bit of a hike for a guy on crutches, particularly when he's not comfortable with the idea of leaving his drink behind."

"Didn't say no name," grumbled the man, who sat two stools down and lit a cigarette.

Over the past several weeks, I'd become rather adept at using one crutch. I did this now, holding my drink in my free hand, and made my way to the darkened corner.

As I approached, the man's features seemed to materialize out of the gloom. He was a good-looking guy, in a somewhat ordinary sort of way, with high, almost feminine cheekbones and a small slash for a mouth. His eyes were large, deeply set, and black like a bird's. He had long black hair pulled back into a ponytail.

He lit a cigarette and grinned with just one corner of his mouth. Then I recognized him—not fully enough to recall who he was but enough to know I had seen that grin before.

"It *is* you," he said, the cadence of his voice equivalent to a low, breathy gasp. "I looked up and thought, shit, that's Tim Overleigh sitting over there, his leg all fucked up. And I was right."

"Holy shit," I uttered, realizing who he was.

"Holy shit, indeed," said Andrew Trumbauer, his one-sided

grin widening.

In disbelief, I mumbled, "Last time I saw you—"

"We almost died," he finished.

3

I FIRST MET ANDREW TRUMBAUER IN A WHOLE other life. I can still picture him coming out of the ocean and strutting toward Hannah and me, this strange creature whose skin is so pale it is nearly transparent. His scarecrow-thin body beaded with seawater, his bare feet dotted with white sand. That grin overtakes one corner of his mouth, cocking it upward into an almost comical gesture of aloofness, and he raises a mesh bag of dog biscuits. He's got a pair of goggles around his neck, the band pulled so tight it appears to be choking him, and he is so horridly, morbidly pale I imagine I can see his skin start to sizzle and turn pink, then deepen to red as he approaches from the other side of the beach.

4

I SAT DOWN IN THE BOOTH ACROSS FROM ANDREW, still somewhat shaken.

"You remember, don't you, Overleigh?" he said, his voice remaining low and breathy. The way the shadows played off his face, he was a patchwork of dark hollows and blaring white flesh. My name sounded comfortable coming out of his mouth, too, as if no time had passed between us. "How we almost died?"

"Of course." The words were automatic—I had no idea what he was talking about. It occurred to me that the last time I saw Andrew Trumbauer was at Hannah's funeral three years ago.

"That was something," Andrew muttered, blowing smoke rings toward the ceiling.

"No, wait," I said. "What are you talking about?"

Andrew frowned. It was a grotesque gesture, his face too thin to accommodate it properly. Instead, the corners of his mouth seemed to sink to twin points, and his chin wrinkled into a walnut. "You don't remember?"

"No, I have no—"

Then it all came rushing back to me: leaving the funeral service in the gray, rain-soaked afternoon, Andrew behind the wheel and me in the passenger seat, Andrew turning at the last minute as the power line snapped, spitting fire as it whipped the ground, the car nearly running over the downed line . . .

"The power line," I said, my voice distant. I'd almost forgotten about it, the other events of that horrible day overshadowing all else.

Andrew leaned back in his seat, a look of satisfaction overtaking that vague little frown of his. Something glittered in his eyes that caused me to turn my gaze down at my drink.

"I'm sorry," he said after the silence between us grew too long. "That was a shitty thing to bring up right off the bat like that."

"It's okay."

"You look good," he said.

I smirked. "Liar. I know I look like shit."

"What happened to your leg?"

I told him about the caving accident and admitted that it had been foolish to undertake such an excursion alone. "The bone came right up through the skin. I was a mess. I'm just lucky a car happened to stop after I made it out to the highway. Was probably the only car around for miles."

"Talk about luck," Andrew said, although he didn't seem too impressed.

"Six months later," I went on, "and I've learned my lesson. For the time being."

"Thing about lessons," Andrew said, "is that there's always a new one to learn."

I bummed one of his cigarettes and said, "What the hell are you doing out here, anyway, man?"

"Regatta race."

"You're in it? Get the fuck outta here. You have a boat?"

"Not my boat. I'm one of the crew."

"You can sail?" But I knew this was a stupid question. Andrew Trumbauer was one of those guys who did everything from hiking the Grand Canyon to rafting down the goddamn Nile.

"Don't tell me you've never gotten involved in the race yourself," he said, thankfully ignoring my question. "You live down here, don't you? You're an adventurer at heart. Doesn't take those crutches and a busted leg for me to see that—I *know* you. And you've never sailed the Regatta?"

I shrugged. "Been a busy few years."

"That's a sad excuse. What's the craziest thing you've ever done?"

I considered this. After Hannah's death and the disappearance of my artistic talent, I'd submerged myself in the world of extreme sports—skydiving, spelunking, white-water rafting. But I knew nothing I said could compete with anything Andrew had done. So I said, "I once ran out to get my mail in the middle of a downpour without my rain slicker. It was risky, I know, but that's just the kind of guy I am."

Andrew smiled. This time the expression looked more human. "You still sculpting?"

"Actually, no. I gave it up."

"You make it sound like you just quit smoking."

"No, I still do that from time to time."

Andrew's smile died. "Wait—you're serious, aren't you?"

"As a heart attack."

"Jesus, man, why? You were brilliant."

"It's . . . it's a lot of mitigating factors. Complicated bullshit."

"Life is full of complicated bullshit. Yours is no different than anyone else's."

I felt my heart flutter. For some stupid reason, I said, "I see Hannah."

Andrew stared at me with an intensity that made me uncomfortable. "What are you talking about?"

"Forget it." I waved a hand at him.

"Tell me."

I sighed, watching a group of older men shoot darts. After what felt like an eternity, I said, "You'll think I'm crazy, but I believe she's been haunting me."

"How's that?"

"I first saw her that night in the cave." I explained how I'd gotten free of the cave and found the highway, following what I thought was Hannah's ghost. I didn't know if I expected Andrew to laugh or clap me on the shoulder and tell me I needed psychiatric help, but he did neither; he merely watched my lips move while I talked and never interrupted. "After that, I kept seeing her in my apartment. Out of the corner of my eye. But every time I turn to look, it's a coatrack or a pile of clothes. And every time I flip the lights on, she vanishes." Once again, I waved a hand at him. It seemed a sane gesture, one I was required to do in relaying such a bizarre story. "It's stupid, I know. But it's been bothering me."

"Why?" said Andrew.

I didn't know quite what he meant. "Because it's fucking unnatural."

"No." He fluttered some fingers before his face. "I mean, why is she coming to you now? She's been dead for three years."

"Never mind," I said. "It's all in my head. I'm dealing with a lot of shit about her death."

"Maybe it's a warning. Like she's trying to tell you something from beyond the grave."

"Or maybe it's that I've been spending too much time alone with my thoughts."

"And back in the cave?" he said, cocking one eyebrow.

"Back in the cave I was in agony, and I was nearly hypothermic and dehydrated and whatever else you can imagine. I could have imagined I'd been rescued by Bigfoot, and it would have seemed perfectly natural at the time."

Andrew sighed and rubbed at his upper lip with an index finger. His eyes never left mine. "You're such a realist. You remember all that crazy shit we used to do?"

I nodded. I remembered it well.

"Realism will be your downfall."

I snorted and said, "That makes no fucking sense."

"Everything makes sense. Listen," he said. His voice had adopted a less breathy tone. "I believe in fate. And I believe fate had me run into you here tonight."

"Why would fate go through the trouble?"

"So I could apologize."

His words surprised me. "Apologize for what?"

"For all the time we lost after Hannah's death. For disappearing for three years. And for siding with her in the separation."

I glanced away and watched the smoke coil up from the tip of my cigarette. "It was only fair. You were Hannah's friend, too. And I was an asshole. I was fully to blame for the split."

For whatever reason, I waited for Andrew to tell me that wasn't the case, that both Hannah and I were equally to blame, but he didn't. If he had, it would have been a lie. Hannah leaving me was *my* fault, not ours.

"Have you ever heard of the Canyon of Souls?" he asked. It was like something straight out of an old movie—particularly the way he leaned over the table and whispered to me in a conspiratorial tone. "Have you?"

"No."

"It's a canyon, an ice canyon, slick like a buffed flume, that runs under the earth, and no one on this planet has ever been able to successfully traverse it from one end to the other. Hell, no one's ever even *seen* it. *No one*, Tim."

I felt a frozen finger touch the base of my spine. Suddenly I was no longer sitting here in the bar; I was back in my apartment, watching the molten shadows shift in the darkness from across the room. I was back in the caves, too, with my leg all fucked up and the stink of my own inevitable death filling my nostrils. I thought of Hannah's hand coming down through the opening in the cave's low ceiling, hoisting me up. Of Hannah's visage appearing through the desert trees, beckoning me toward a road I could not see . . .

"No one," I heard myself echo.

"I've done a lot of shit. I've been all over the world. Look at this." He rolled up one sleeve and revealed a puckered, shiny panel of flesh along his forearm, roughly the diameter of a tennis ball. "You know what did that? You have any idea?"

"No idea."

"Bull's horn. Gored in the streets of Pamplona. Shit, I've eaten the hearts from live snakes in Vietnam while drinking shots of bile. I've seen the wildest sex acts you could image in the remotest parts of the world—shit with donkeys and mules and some unbelievable thing called the 'elusive transplant.' That stuff's old for me now. I'm going big-time." He winked, and I thought I could hear his eyelid snap. "I'm going to touch the other side."

I surprised myself by laughing. "That's cool. Seriously."

"I've got everything set," he said, leaning back against the red vinyl cushion of the booth. "I want you to come with me."

For some reason, I had been expecting this. "You're crazy. You've always been crazy. I can't compete with that."

"What's the matter? You broke your leg so now you've given up on life? That's disgusting. Hannah would be disgusted with you."

The mention of her name stung me. "I'm in a different place now."

"What were you doing in that cave by yourself?"

It was the same question Marta had asked me earlier. However, this time I found it much harder to avoid giving an answer. "I wasn't thinking. It was stupid." I chewed ravenously at my lower lip. "Where is this Canyon of Souls, anyway?"

"Nepal," he said. "The Himalayas."

I brayed laughter. "You're out of your goddamn mind."

"The whole thing will take a month. You're experienced—you've been ice climbing, and you're familiar and comfortable with the equipment."

"I've got a busted leg."

"Fuck that," said Andrew. It was his turn to laugh. "It's not until next year."

"I'm a teacher—," I began.

"No, you're not. You used to be an artist who gave up art. You used to be an athlete, but now you've apparently given that up, too. So what's left?" His eyes were frighteningly alight. "What's next?"

My response came out small, strangled. "I . . . don't know . . ."

He pressed his lips together until they turned white and bloodless, his nostrils flaring. I briefly wondered who had been more afraid in Pamplona—Andrew or the bull.

"Remember that first night in Puerto Rico? Remember what it felt like to fly?" he said finally.

I finished my drink and crushed out my cigarette. "I could never keep up with you. Never."

"Neither could Hannah. But she tried."

5

ANDREW CONVINCED ME TO STAY FOR A FEW MORE drinks, and there was no further talk of Nepal or the Canyon of Souls. There was no further talk of Hannah, either, which was just fine by me. We tossed darts, drank Maker's Mark, and pumped countless quarters into the jukebox, Andrew favoring the Creedence Clearwater Revival songs. After a while, I'd lost all inhibition and was feeling no pain. I felt I could slam my injured leg in a car door and laugh.

Around midnight, after returning from the restroom, I found our booth empty and the tab paid. There was no sign of Andrew; it was like I'd imagined the entire evening. I staggered over to the bar and asked Ricky if I was dreaming.

"Ain't dreaming," he said, "but you're pretty darn well sloshed. I'll call you a cab."

Back at my building, I opened the door to my apartment and hobbled into the stale-smelling little box without bothering to turn on any lights. If Hannah was here, crouching in the dark, then I'd just let her be. Anyway, I was drunk.

I stumbled into my bedroom where I peeled off my clothes and crawled beneath the blankets on my bed. The bedroom window was open, and a cool breeze stirred the curtains.

As sleep drew nearer, my thoughts clashed into one another. At one point, I was crawling through a tight space, the walls hugging my shoulders and forcing my head lower and lower until my chin pressed against my breastbone. There was shallow water on the ground, freezing my hands and soaking through the knees of my pants, causing my teeth to chatter in my skull. I crawled, not knowing where I was going or even where I was.

Then I struck a wall—the end of the tunnel—and fear began to suffocate me. I tried to back up but couldn't. I attempted to turn around, but the chamber was too narrow. Claustrophobia settled around me like a warm, wet blanket.

I'm going to die down here. I'm going to die down here. I'm going to die down here—

I awoke with a scream caught in my throat, the sound of a distant boat horn bleating in the night. The curtains still undulated in the night's breeze.

I ran one hand over the mattress and realized I'd wet the bed.

CHAPTER 3

THREE MONTHS AFTER OUR CHANCE MEETING AT
the Filibuster, I received a package from Andrew. It arrived in a wooden crate the size of a footlocker, delivered by two burly men wearing harnesses and fatigues. It was early November, but the men glistened with sweat, both of them panting in synchrony while I signed their clipboard. I felt obligated to offer them each a glass of water. They accepted without hesitation, and I listened to the click sounds their throats made as they drained their glasses in about three seconds flat.

"She's a heavy mother," said one of the men. He had a deep scar along one side of his black face, the skin itself looking like the coagulated film atop pudding that's been sitting out too long. "What is it?"

"I don't know," I said. There didn't appear to be a return address on the little slip that came with the crate nor anywhere on the crate itself.

"Thanks for the water," the man with the scar said, and they both plodded out of the apartment, leaving the door open.

I shut the door and scrounged around the hallway closet for my largely unused toolbox. I located it buried beneath a mound of winter coats but frowned upon opening it. Unless I was able to coax the wooden crate open with a few thumbtacks and a bunch of old washers,

I was out of luck.

Like a lion stalking prey, I circled the crate, wondering what could be inside. My leg was fully healed, and I'd ditched both the wheelchair and the crutches long ago, but I swore I felt a twinge of pain in my left leg. It was a dull ache—nothing serious but enough to remind me of what had happened in the past year.

It occurred to me that I had my old sculpting equipment in my bedroom closet. I hadn't messed around with that stuff since I'd given up sculpting—since Hannah's death—and I'd all but forgotten about it. But sure enough, as I climbed a footstool and pawed through the cluttered mass of old books, blank VHS tapes, a pair of Adidas running shoes, and threadbare sweaters, I located the hammer and chisel.

A moment later, I stood like some mythological god before the crate with my hammer and chisel—God of Lame Legs, perhaps—and located a seam in the wood. I drove the chisel into it and heard the wood stress. Then I brought the hammer down on the chisel's hilt, driving it deeper. The wood split. I felt a stupid, childish enthusiasm overtake me.

After a few more strikes of the hammer, the front panel fell away from the crate. Styrofoam popcorn spilled out and pooled around my feet in a cascade. What stood inside the crate caused me to blink, as if to realign my vision.

It was a massive chunk of granite, a perfect rectangle, perhaps three feet high and two feet wide and at least eighteen inches deep. The granite was dark brown, speckled with glittering mica and textured, multicolored stone.

There was a piece of pale blue stationery folded once over and taped to the hunk of stone. I plucked it off and unfolded it. A single sentence, inked in a child's undisciplined handwriting, read:

Never take your talent for granite.
—A.T.

It took me a few seconds to realize the initials stood for Andrew Trumbauer—a connection I would have never made had I not seen him only three months earlier and because something about him and our chance meeting still resonated with me.

Two days later, when Marta stopped by for our ritualistic evening of board games and movies, the hunk of stone was still in the middle of my apartment, three-fourths of the wooden crate surrounding it. Though I'd attempted to clean up the spilled Styrofoam popcorn, there were many pieces on the floor, some having been flattened by the treads of my sneakers.

"What in the world is this?" she marveled, peeking into the crate with her hands on her knees.

"It grew there," I said, "straight up through the floor."

"Tim . . ."

"Okay. Then would you believe a bunch of elves delivered it in the night?" I didn't know why I was being difficult. Perhaps I just didn't want to talk about Andrew Trumbauer. Because to talk of him was to talk about Hannah George, and Marta Cortez knew nothing about my wife except for the fact that she'd once existed.

Suddenly I saw elation fill her eyes. She all but clasped her hands over her chest. "Tell me this means you're sculpting again."

I went into the kitchen and poured Maker's Mark into two tumblers, then added some sour mix. I stirred both drinks with my finger.

"An old friend of mine mailed it to me," I said finally, returning and handing Marta her drink.

"I can't tell when you're being serious anymore."

"I'm serious. It showed up two days ago."

"Two days?" She looked incredulous. "And it's just been . . . sitting here?"

"It's a giant slab of rock. I'm not really sure where to put something like that in a tiny apartment without fucking with the feng shui."

"What kind of friend mails you a hunk of rock?"

"One who's both independently wealthy and overly eccentric."

"Interesting." She grinned. "Is he single?"

"He's not your type."

"Why's that?"

"Well, for one thing, he's probably off in Uganda for the next six months."

She rolled her shoulders and sipped her drink. "You know I don't like to be smothered."

I stood beside her, studying the slab of stone. "I just need to figure out how to get this thing out of here."

"I'm assuming it was sent to you for a reason."

"Is that right?"

"So you'd start working again."

"My sabbatical is over in the spring."

"Not *that* work."

Still gazing at the stone, I said, "Maybe I'll call the college art department, have them pick it up. I might get tenured for a donation this big."

But by the following Wednesday, with midweek ennui settling around me, I found myself seated on a stool before the column of granite. I'd liberated it from its crate. Together, we stood in the center of the living room, a crystalline frost building up against the windows, my hammer in one hand, my chisel in the other. I sat staring at it, locked in unspoken dialogue with this ridiculous chunk of rock in my living room. The top of the column was buffed flat and smooth. It could be a podium for a potted plant, an art deco stand for a decorative vase. It could be anything, and I needn't touch it at all. Not at all.

With a single stroke, I hammered off one corner of the slab. A spark flickered, and the triangular cut dropped to the floor and bounded under the sofa. The muscles in my arms felt weak; the strike, which by no means had been forceful, reverberated through the marrow in my bones.

I laughed.

2

I WAS TWENTY-SIX AND ON MY HONEYMOON WITH Hannah in San Juan when I met Andrew Trumbauer. It was our third day on the beach, and Hannah and I had just finished snorkeling and were laid out on towels in the sand when Andrew came out of the sea. I paid him no attention at first, but as he drew nearer, I saw something akin to a skeletal smile break across his face, causing the corners of his mouth to push his cheeks into sharp points. There was something radiant about him, a confidence in his walk. He headed directly for us.

"Holy shit," said Hannah. I thought I could see this strange man mouthing the same words at the same time, as if Hannah were providing the soundtrack of his voice. "I don't believe it."

Andrew's shadow fell across us, and he dripped water on my legs. He carried a mesh bag of dog biscuits used to feed the fish when snorkeling, and I couldn't turn away from his grin. His teeth looked preternaturally bright.

"Andrew!" Hannah shouted, bouncing off the towel and into his arms. She was laughing hysterically as she kissed him quickly on the cheek—a jab, really—and beamed over at me. "This is totally insane!"

"Indeed," I commented, not knowing what I was required to say. "My head is spinning."

"Andrew, this is Tim, my boyfriend."

"Husband," I corrected.

"Oh!" She laughed. She looked so beautiful and dark. It was before she cut her hair short, so she was very feminine. "Oh, God, we were just married a few days ago. I'm still not straight with anything."

"I'm Andrew Trumbauer," he said, grinning an awkward grin and driving his knees into the sand so he could shake my hand. His pale chest glistened. A string of cobalt-colored lapis hung around his neck.

"Tim Overleigh."

"Andrew and I went to college together," said Hannah.

"Good old JMU. I was the loser friend all the pretty girls took pity on," Andrew said, still grinning.

"Not *all* of them," said Hannah. "Most hated you."

And then Andrew did something that caused my testicles to crawl up into the cavity of my pelvis: he winked at me.

"So true," he said. "Most everyone hated me."

Later that night we all had drinks together at a local dive, and Andrew waited for Hannah to stagger off to the restroom before practically crawling into my ear and whispering, "I've got something I want you to try."

"What's that?" I was expecting him to offer to sell me weed, speed, pain pills—whatever the going pharmaceutical trend on the island.

"Flying," he said, which only reinforced my expectation. "You up for flying?"

"Sorry to break it to you," I said, "but I've flown before."

"Yeah?"

"All through college and every once in a blue moon on weekends." I lifted my drink and nodded at him from across the table. "Alcohol's been my airplane for the past year or so."

Andrew laughed, and I immediately doubted its authenticity. It was too brash, sounded too forced. He was shirtless across from me at the table, his skin sunburned and painful to look at, the twin pink discs of his nipples resembling engorged pimples.

I went on, "And Hannah, of course, doesn't necessarily appreciate—"

"I was asking you. Not Hannah."

"No thanks."

"Think about it. You're in good shape." As he said this, he

seemed to appraise me.

Not knowing what being in good shape had to do with shooting a few lines of coke or whatever, I could only laugh with some discomfort and wait for Hannah to return from the restroom.

That night, after a huge dinner and slow, lethargic lovemaking, Hannah and I fell asleep in each other's arms. The windows of our small grotto opened on the water, and I woke when the sounds of distant quarreling echoed up from the beach. I listened for a very long time, staring at the darkened ceiling, while I rubbed my foot against Hannah's.

"Hmm," she muttered. I couldn't tell if she was awake or not.

I leaned over and kissed her cheek, brushed her hair off her face.

She smiled faintly without opening her eyes.

"I'm going out for a ride," I said.

"Hmm."

Outside, as I had done for the past three nights, I rolled a bicycle from the grotto shed and led it across the property to the roadside. The resort grounds were fastidiously maintained and accommodating; the streets beyond were dark and winding, where fast cars with missing headlamps sped, their radios blasting, and chickens loitered in squalid, feathered heaps in the culverts. On foot, I would have been concerned traversing the unlit byways of the island, certain that I'd run into unsavory characters up to no good. On bicycle, however, I blew by the hordes of shifty-eyed locals and was able to avoid the few automobiles whose drivers found it amusing to attempt to run me off the road—a dangerous scenario given "off the road" would mean plummeting nearly fifty yards over an embankment to wooded forests or rock quarries below.

I rode now on the snaking, single-lane roadway that wound up the mountainous terrain. The moon was fat and blue, so close I could nearly count the individual craters on its surface. My heart rate rose, and I could feel the sweat breaking out on my forehead and across my back. One mile, two miles, three—straight to the top of the world.

From this vantage, I could see one full side of the city, including the lights of the cruise ships docked at the harbor. I hopped off the bike and set it down in the reeds. It was impossible to gauge my height, what with the darkness fooling with my perception, but I knew I was high. Even my breathing, which I'd maintained at a regular pace while riding, was a bit labored at this altitude, although I wondered if that was only in my head. I could faintly hear calypso music and beyond that the squawking of phantom chickens.

Through a line of dense trees, I spotted dim lights issuing from the windows of clapboard houses along the cusp of the cliff face. Still somewhat unsure of myself, I stepped through the trees into a clearing. The closest house—a hovel, really, like something you'd see in one of those commercials where they ask for money while showing kids with no shoes muddle through sewage—was fronted by a screened-in porch. Large flaps of screen had been torn away and hung down like triangular wedges of pizza, and small birds darted in and out of the openings. Tallow light spilled from a single lamp beside the doorway. I heard the sizzle-pop of an electric bug-zapper firing somewhere nearby.

I sat on the porch steps and wiped the sweat from my brow. In front of me, my shadow stretched out along the brown grass, framed in a glow of dancing yellow light. Around me, the stalks of candles flickered. Many unlit candles littered the ground. Some even protruded from the mouths of discarded liquor bottles, and others were clustered together in clay pots. I retrieved a waxy yellow candle from one of the pots and held it above the flame of another until it grew malleable and dripped melted wax onto the grass. I proceeded to mold it into a sphere and elongate the sphere into a slight oval. My thumbs created the impression of eye sockets. With one fingernail, I carved out a mouth, then formed the fullness of a pair of lips around it. I don't know how long I sat there sculpting before I heard the door open behind me.

"Well," said Andrew, "you showed up after all."

I really didn't know why I'd come. I wasn't interested in getting whacked out on drugs, and I had even less interest in spending any more time with Hannah's college friend. Still, I'd come to the very spot Andrew had told me to, and not knowing why bothered me more than actually being here.

"I feel like you summoned me," I said, tossing the ball of wax aside and standing. The second the words were out of my mouth, I regretted them. It sounded like an admission of sorts, like I was granting him power over me.

Andrew smiled his queer smile. He was wearing a loose-fitting cotton shirt, and the hem of his floral-patterned shorts hung below his knees. He stood barefoot at the top of the steps, looking at me. "I'm glad you came. Are you ready to go?"

"Go where?"

"To fly."

I nodded toward his ramshackle house. "I just assumed we'd . . . you know . . ."

"Come on," he said, bounding down the porch steps and brushing by me.

I followed him through the trees, the leaves so dense above my head that they completely blotted out the moonlight. When we broke out onto the reedy precipice that overlooked the city, just a few yards from where I'd dropped the bike, Andrew turned away from me, placed both hands on his hips, and leaned back at a curious angle. I heard his spine pop.

"You live in that house?" I said.

"I've been here for about eight months. I've got a place in New York, too. My old man was filthy rich. He owned an oil company. When he died, he left it to me. Then I smashed it to pieces and sold it to the Japanese."

"So what do you do?"

"Whatever I want," he said, shrugging. He didn't have to look at me for me to realize he was smiling.

"Where are we going?" I said after a while. The urge to hop on my bike and pedal the hell back to the grotto was suddenly overwhelming.

Andrew extended one arm and pointed off to the right.

I followed his arm but could see nothing except for the edge of the cliff. "Yeah. Funny. Flying, huh? Is that what you meant?"

"It's what I *said*, wasn't it?" He turned, grinning at me from beneath a partially down-turned brow. His eyes seemed to glitter in the moonlight. As I watched, he stripped off his shirt and tossed it in the reeds.

"I thought you meant something else."

"Like what?"

I shook my head. "Forget it."

Andrew began unbuttoning his shorts.

"Whoa," I said, holding up my hands. I may have even taken a reactive step backward. "Hey, man, you're barking up the wrong tree . . ."

Andrew chuckled. "I'm not a fag, if that's what you're worried about."

"So you only get naked with straight guys?"

Andrew dropped his shorts and stood there stark naked. His paleness was severe and nearly translucent. I thought I could make out his heart strumming through the wall of his chest. There was a small tattoo etched across his upper left thigh.

He winked at me, perhaps playing up to the homosexual undertones of the situation. "Look at that city down there," he marveled, glancing over the ridge to the cluster of huts below. "Look at those lights." He exhaled with enthusiasm. "Beautiful."

He pivoted and tromped through the reeds to the farthest side of the cliff. Beyond, the moonlight dazzled on the surface of the water.

Closing my eyes, I could still see the enormous face of the moon floating like an afterimage behind my eyelids.

"Such is the way to immortality," Andrew said. In an instant, he was gone, having flung himself over the edge of the cliff. For a moment, he seemed to hover in defiance of gravity, his legs pressed together and his feet pointed, his arms outstretched like the wings of some great bird. Then he disappeared, carried below the face of the cliff and out of my line of sight.

My breath caught in my throat as I ran to the edge of the cliff. I braced myself for a gruesome sight—Andrew's pale, reed-thin body tumbling down the rocky mountainside—but what I saw was his ghostly white form sailing out across the darkness as if flying. He grew smaller and smaller until he struck the water in a perfect dive, slipping beneath the dark surface with hardly a splash. As the ripples spread and faded, I counted several seconds beneath my breath until the white orb of his face broke through the surface. Even from this distance, I could tell he was grinning.

"How was that?" he shouted, his voice borne on echoes rising through the valley.

I felt like a fool. I'd come here under the pretense that we were going to smoke some pot or maybe do a few lines of coke, failing to take Andrew's comment about flying in its literal sense.

Andrew pulled himself from the water and scampered up a winding, sandy roadway that trailed to the top of the mountain. It took him nearly two minutes to reach the summit, and by that time, I was yanking my rented bicycle out of the reeds by its handlebars.

"Where are you going?" he asked innocently enough.

"Back to the grotto."

"But it's your turn."

I laughed. "I don't want a turn."

"You're not afraid of a little midnight cliff diving, are you?" Had the question been proposed by anyone else, it would have sounded derisory; with Andrew, however, it sounded oddly sympathetic, as if he felt some deep, inexplicable sorrow for me.

"You're out of your mind," I said.

"The sad thing is that you're passing up what might prove to be the most exhilarating ten seconds of your life because you're scared to try."

"They could prove to be the *last* ten seconds of my life."

Andrew ran his hands through his hair. His body, oily and slick, glistened in the moonlight. Several times I found myself staring at his genitalia and had to force myself to look away.

"Don't lie to me," he said. "You came here tonight because you thought you'd be getting high, right?"

I shrugged. "So?"

"So you have no problem shoving shit up your nose, losing all control of your senses, and burning the fucking septum out of your face, but you won't dive off a cliff." He snorted. "Fuck you, Tim."

"Hey." I held up one hand—a traffic cop stopping a line of cars. "Listen, man, I—"

"This is your one chance not to fail yourself," Andrew said.

And for whatever reason, that resonated with me. *Don't fail yourself*, I thought, stripping out of my clothes. *Don't walk away from this chance.*

It was stupid. Perched birdlike on the crest of the cliff, the cool night breeze stimulating my naked flesh, I took a deep breath, and as one single thought blazed like a neon sign outside a speakeasy—*You're going to make your wife a widow on her honeymoon*—I pushed off the ground and let the air cradle me and carry me swiftly to the sea.

Hours later, just before the sun rose, I snuck inside our small rented grotto and slipped beneath the sheets next to Hannah. She sighed and rolled over, draping a warm arm across my chest.

I stared at the ceiling, mottled with incoming daylight, listening to my heart throb in my chest. Wired, I could not close my eyes.

"Where've you been?" Hannah whispered, still half asleep. Her voice startled me.

"I met up with your friend Andrew." I couldn't help but grin. "He took me flying."

I felt her smile as she pressed her lips against my ear. "Oh, the cliff-diving thing."

The remainder of our honeymoon was punctuated by intervals spent with Andrew. He took us to various hole-in-the-wall bars, the best places for drinks on the whole island. The drinks were all heavy with rum and decorated with slices of rubbery fruit.

"Do you think they call these drinks cocktails because all the fruit hanging over the lip of the glass looks like the feathered tail of a rooster?" Hannah said at one point.

We dream-waltzed through lush lands, past fenced-in yards populated by suicidal-looking chickens and land crabs captive in pens, which ate nothing but grain in order to cleanse the badness from their noncomplex systems before becoming meals. In parts, it was a city of somnambulists: the shambling, drunken-eyed swivel of puppet necks outside every whitewashed tavern with pictures of naked young girls pinned above the bar showing gap-toothed smiles. Saw-toothed, spade-shaped flora waved at us at every turn. The skeletons of rusted automobiles snared in mountainous ruts, the green veiling of trees, fences of fronds, and all the wet and dark places that smelled of some indeterminate amphibious odor.

On our last full night in San Juan, after a bout of acrobatic love-making, I left Hannah curled up in bed and met Andrew at one of his favorite bars by the bay. A number of empty glasses stood before him on the bar, and when he turned to look at me, his eyes were like the headlamps of an eighteen-wheeler.

"It's your last night, Overleigh." A tannin-hued hand clamped down on my shoulder. The glow of the gas lamps prompted shadows to caper across his face. "Tonight will be the flight of all flights."

We'd spent every evening jumping blindly from cliffs along the bay. This night, however, we taxied across the island, the looming silhouette of the Sierra de Luquillo now at our backs, and were dropped off at a slope of beach covered in dark, reflective stones. To our left, a sheer cliff, black as a thousand midnights and like the rampart of a *castillo*, rose into the night sky.

As the taxi lumbered away through the brush, I gazed at the wall of rock. "Where's the path to get up there?"

"There is no path. We climb."

"Are you kidding me? That's impossible."

"Nothing," Andrew said, removing his sneakers, "is impossible."

I took several steps backward, still staring at the vertical face of the cliff, until my feet were lapped by the surf.

"Take your shoes off," Andrew said. "It'll be easier to dig into the rock. Besides, there's too much moss on these stones. The soles of your sneakers would slip right off."

"You're out of your mind—do you know that?" But I was already following Andrew's lead, pulling off my shoes and tossing them farther up the beach and out of reach of the surf. "We're both gonna die here tonight."

"No." Andrew stood beside the face of the cliff, his hands planted on his hips, looking straight up. His white linen shirt was unbuttoned and billowed in the cool breeze. "Not tonight."

The climb began slow and arduous. There was little talk, as much of our concentration was limited to the climb. Finding hand- and footholds was tough at first—the niches were either too small or the protruding fingers of stone too thick—but I soon got the hang of it. Halfway up the face of the cliff, I could feel the muscles straining at the back of my legs, my heart galloping at a steady pace, and the ebb and flow of my breath coming in syncopated rhythm.

Only once did I pause to glance over my shoulder, and that was when I nearly lost it. The world tilted to one side, and the tremendous expanse of water, black like velvet covered in glittering jewels, seemed to rush up and claim me. My muscles tensed.

An instant later, Andrew's fingers wrapped around my wrist. "Don't look down."

"Yeah." I directed my eyes back against the wall of rock. Closed them briefly to recalibrate. Opened them.

"Never look down. Come on."

He ascended steadily and I followed, shinnying ratlike up the vertical face. Still, the top seemed very far away.

"She's a good girl," Andrew said as I came up beside him. "You're a lucky guy."

"Thank you. And, yes, I am."

"Would it be . . . ?" He paused, swinging out to grasp an overhanging finger of stone. He pulled himself up, his toned legs following. "Would it be too much of a cliché if I were to threaten you with her well-being? You know, the jaded male friend locking horns with the new guy?"

"It would be a cliché," I said, "but I appreciate the sentiment. I love Hannah very much."

"I would hope so." He climbed faster now, his arms working like machinery, the tendons in his ankles popping with each pivot of the joints.

Something flashed within me, sending a jolt of adrenaline coursing through my system like a fire through an old warehouse. I kicked it into high gear and matched Andrew inch for inch. Together we pulled the cliff down into the earth and brought the summit closer to our fingertips.

"You've got . . . a lot of willpower," Andrew breathed.

Beside him, I said, "What's the matter? Can't you keep up?"

"I'm keeping up . . . just fine . . ."

Gritting my teeth, my fingers growing numb, I advanced up the face of the cliff but could not outdistance him. Goddamn it.

"Takes . . . a man . . . to make it to the top," Andrew said.

"I know what it takes," I growled. My arms quivered; my muscles ached. Still, I climbed. "Would it be too much of a cliché . . . to have me beat you to . . . the top?"

"Never . . . happen," Andrew wheezed. Amazingly, he began to climb harder and faster, leaving me in his wake. It was almost preternatural. He clambered up the side of the cliff, issuing grunts and groans as his muscles surrendered under the strain.

I refused to surrender. I pushed myself, feeling the burn throughout my body, that great warehouse conflagration no longer a detriment but rather a source of energy—*use the pain*. I could see nothing but the top of the cliff just a few feet above: my goal.

"Shit," Andrew groaned.

We both climbed over the cliff at exactly the same time. My heart like a jackhammer in my chest, I didn't pause to collect my breath. I scrambled quickly to my feet and, like lightning arching toward the earth from a bank of clouds, tore out across the grassy plateau toward the opposite end of the cliff.

Andrew was right beside me, his bare feet smashing potholes in the dirt. He let loose his linen shirt, which was lifted by the wind and carried out across the bay. I peeled off my T-shirt and tossed it into oblivion, still running. Our finish line was the opposite end of the plateau; the winner would be the first to sail over the abyss. I pushed harder, passing him. The bastard might be able to beat me in climbing, but he wasn't going to outrun me. Not by a long shot—

"Coming up on you, Overleigh!" He suddenly appeared beside me, a locomotive of white, ghostly flesh, his legs pumping like pistons through the reeds.

I could feel the sweat freezing on my skin, could feel the icy pull of tears trailing across my temples. The edge of the cliff rushed to meet me. With one final strain—a grunt, a childlike cry—I leapt over the edge just milliseconds before Andrew. Arms flailing, legs cycling through the air, I gulped down fresh oxygen and held it in as the frigid waters rushed up at breakneck speed to swallow me whole.

An hour before daylight, I climbed into bed beside Hannah.

"Hmm," she moaned softly.

"He's a strange guy," I said.

"Are you talking to me?" Her voice was groggy with sleep. "Are you some stranger in my bed talking to me?"

I rolled over and kissed up and down her ribs, her neck. Hannah told me I smelled like the ocean, and I promised her that I'd already showered.

"Just how friendly were you two in college, anyway?" I asked after a while.

"Who? Andrew?"

"Who else?"

"In other words, you're asking if we slept together?"

"I would consider that pretty friendly, yes."

"I thought you were stronger than that."

"What does that mean?"

She groaned. "Why do men always insist on dredging up the past?"

That was answer enough.

CHAPTER 4

1

SHAKING, TEARFUL, I AWOKE ON A MATTRESS
sodden with sweat. The weight of my body, coupled with my perspiration, had cultivated a sinking Tim-shaped pit at the center of my mattress. The tiny bedroom seemed to close in all around me, making it difficult to breathe. For a split second, just before my eyes adjusted to the darkness, I swore I could see Hannah floating on the ceiling, her white cotton gown—the type of gown I'd imagined since childhood all the angels of heaven to wear—rippling along the ceiling like the sails of a ship.

2

"I'D LIKE YOU TO SEE SOMEONE," SAID MARTA.
A marimba band performed on the beach, and in the early spring evening, the sound carried all the way up to my apartment. I walked out onto the balcony, a Dewar's and water in my hand, and watched them. Despite the mild temperature, I was sweating through my work clothes, which were powdered with dust. The April breeze did very little to cool me off.

Marta appeared in the doorway, arms folded. "Are you even listening to me?"

"You're exaggerating."

"This is not the apartment of a healthy man."

I continued watching the marimba band for a while, though my mind was on the aborted creation in my living room: a statue that was not fully a statue, a creature that refused to be brought to life. I'd spent months trying to summon my old talent, but it had proven futile. And the futility led to self-loathing. In the intervening months, I'd grown to despise Andrew Trumbauer for shipping me the hunk of granite; what had no doubt been a thoughtful gift had in my own brain been bastardized into a snide, deliberate mockery—Andrew's way of pointing out my weaknesses. I was unable to create—had been since Hannah's death—and that half-assed abortion in my living room was the proof.

Disgusted, I gulped down the last bit of bourbon, then chucked the tumbler onto the beach. It didn't disrupt the marimba band, but a few kids who'd gathered around to listen to the music glared at me as if I were Count Dracula sizing them up from the parapets of my castle.

I heard Marta sigh and stomp back inside. I followed her, rubbing my bleary eyes with the heels of my hands. She gathered her purse from the sofa and tossed an empty McDonald's cup into the trash.

"Where are you going?"

"Out," she said, a harsh finality to her voice.

"You can't break up with me," I told her. "We aren't even dating."

"I can't keep seeing you like this. It's breaking my heart, and you won't do anything to fix the problem."

"So what do you recommend I do?"

"Get the fuck out of this apartment and start living again." She gestured toward the statue in progress. "This . . . thing . . . isn't living. You're stunting yourself. I never met Hannah and don't know a damn thing about her, but if you're going to—"

"Stop it," I said.

"What happened to her? Tell me what happened."

"No."

"Well, whatever it was, you need to get over it. Unless you want to die in this apartment." She shook her head. "You need to let go."

"Stop," I said again, though there was little force in my voice.

"*You* stop," she said, softening, and leaned in to kiss my cheek. "*You* stop. Okay? Or you'll die, too."

As she reached for the doorknob, I said, "It's my fault she died. We were married, and I was too caught up in my career to give her what she needed. I felt the marriage breaking apart, but for whatever reason I didn't try to stop it. So she left. She met a linguistics professor named David Moore, and they went to Italy. Then their car drove off the road and crashed. They were both killed." The words had come from my mouth like a locomotive; I hardly took a breath.

Marta's hand never left the doorknob. Finally she turned toward me. There was concern in her eyes, and her eyebrows were stitched together. She looked like she wanted to cry, but she was too strong for that. It suddenly occurred to me that I was the weak one. "That is not your fault."

"It doesn't matter what you say. You can't change how I feel."

"I know," she said. "That's the problem."

After she left, I tore the kitchenette apart looking for alcohol, but there was none to be found. Out of the corner of my eye, I saw a shape move, but when I turned to look at it, there was nothing there except the refrigerator.

I stepped into the living room, where the hunk of granite stood, chunks of stone littering the floor, while powdered debris coated every available surface. I took a deep breath, inhaling the stone-dust particles that floated like motes in the air, and studied the unfinished sculpture.

The body was recognizable as female, but the face looked nothing like Hannah's. The cheekbones were too high, too sharp, and the brow was too dramatic and severe, almost Cro-Magnon. I'd spent the entire winter hammering and chiseling away at the stone, whittling it down to the framework of some unidentifiable woman. Looking at it, I felt a sinking in the pit of my stomach. There had been a time when in a single afternoon I could have taken a hammer and chisel to a lump of rock and carved fucking Mount Rushmore.

But it wasn't just the sculpture. It was Hannah, too. Because lately I saw her everywhere. It had become so constant that I started to doubt my sanity. Once, hustling down the stairwell of my apartment building, I thought I heard her laugh. I paused and stared up through the spiral mesh of stairs and caught a glimpse of someone retreating over the balustrade—a woman, no doubt. Hannah.

She was also in my apartment, and there was no getting around that. At night I would wake up to the sensation of her arm slipping around my waist or the feeling of her warm breath against the nape of my neck. These things were enough to drive a man crazy.

Maybe I was going crazy . . .

A poor diet and a constant urge to jog through the streets of Annapolis caused me to lose considerable weight. And while I felt stronger and healthier than I had in a long time, I could simultaneously sense something rotting away inside me. I couldn't blame Marta's reluctance to hang around; I had become a shadow of myself.

Disgusted by the sculpture, I laced on some tennis shoes and went downstairs to the lobby to retrieve my mail. I rifled through the stack of standard bills, advertisements, and requests for donations. Only one letter stood out—in a plain white business envelope, the return address somewhere in Australia. It was from Andrew Trumbauer. The envelope was weathered and scuffed. Someone had stamped his boot across its front; the impression of the sole was clear, a formulaic matrix of clovers and wavy lines.

Just seeing Andrew's name with the return address was enough to cause something small and wet to roll over in my stomach.

I carried the mail over to the Filibuster, where I ordered a glass of scotch and occupied the same booth Andrew and I had sat in eight months earlier. I drank the scotch, getting up to go to the bathroom three times before the drink was finished, my hands shaking, my face flush with fever. My reflection in the spotty bathroom mirror was gaunt and terminal, and I thought about a book I'd once read about a man waking up on a city bus with no memory. Suddenly I prayed for no memory, but I couldn't stop picturing that old motorcar driving off the cliff, David behind the wheel, Hannah in the passenger seat . . .

I had two more drinks before I opened Andrew's letter. It was written in the same childlike handwriting he had used in the note that had accompanied the hunk of granite months earlier.

Stop fighting old ghosts, Tim. Please come.
—A.T.

"Son of a bitch," I muttered.

Included with the letter was an airplane ticket to Kathmandu.

PART TWO

THE GHOSTS WE LEAVE BEHIND

CHAPTER 5

1

THE AIRPLANE TOUCHED DOWN AT TRIBHUVAN International Airport in Kathmandu after a connecting flight in London followed by several hours of nauseating turbulence. I tried to sleep, but it was useless. I'd only accomplished the type of half-sleep that recalled my days of falling asleep at my desk in high school, where every sound around me was incorporated into my dreams and boiled down to nonsense.

After the plane had landed and I gathered my bags, I hopped on a tram that climbed through brown villages. From every direction, I could see the mountains, enormous and capped in bluish snow. It was early November, and the villages were celebrating the Hindu versions of Christmas—Dashain and Tihar, according to the magazine article I read on the plane. We passed through Kathmandu, and I was slightly disappointed to learn it was a small city just like most small cities around the world, corrupted by industry and modernization. There didn't appear to be anything magical or spiritual about it.

I hadn't spoken with Andrew since our chance meeting at the Filibuster. However, approximately one month after I'd received the airline ticket, another letter bearing Andrew's name appeared in the mail.

This time the return address was from Miami, and the letter itself was more detailed. Andrew outlined the items I was to bring and included a few hand-drawn maps of the surrounding villages and the name of the lodge where I'd be staying. He had already booked my room.

At first, his presumption provoked in me a childish stubbornness, and I quickly became resolute—I would not go on the damn trip. I couldn't just pick up and leave everything behind on a whim, could I? Yet despite this determination, I never threw away the airline ticket or the follow-up letter.

By midsummer, the apartment was suffocating me. I couldn't finish the sculpture, and Hannah's ghost had become unrelenting. The first week in August, I couldn't get the smell of Hannah's perfume out of the place. I even had it fumigated, which seemed to do the trick for two days . . . until that aromatic lilac smell crept through the walls and soaked into the furniture. By that time, Marta was long gone; her refusal to set foot in my apartment was steadfast, although I would meet her occasionally for lunch at the City Dock Café. I told her about the smells and how it was becoming hard to breathe in the apartment. I told her, too, about Andrew Trumbauer and the airline ticket to Nepal.

"Is there any doubt what you should do?" she told me one afternoon. We were at the café, eating club sandwiches and knocking back mimosa after mimosa. "You once lived for this sort of thing."

"My leg," I offered.

"Is healed. It's been over a year. And you're out running five, six miles a day. Physically you're in good shape. Mentally, though . . ." She rolled her shoulders, and her small, pink tongue darted out to nab the teardrop of mayonnaise at the corner of her mouth.

She was right, of course. That hollowness continued to spread through me. At the end of each visit with Marta, I found myself fearful to return to my apartment. And I hated myself all over again for being such a coward.

As the tram bumped along, I leaned over to the man next to me—an Indian fellow with streamers of white hair sprouting from his large, brown ears—and asked him if he had ever heard of the Canyon of Souls.

He responded, but in his language it meant nothing to me.

2

FORTY MINUTES LATER, THE TRAM LET ME OFF AT the lodge. It was cool, not cold, and I slid the zipper of my jacket down. The air smelled smoky. The sky was dense and gray to the east, but the west was a vibrant blue, uncorrupted by clouds, and the sunlight glittered like fire on the frozen peaks of the distant mountains. Down the valley stood the monsoon forests, heavily green and like a canopy over the land.

My room was small but adequate, furnished in alpine furniture and with a full wall of windows that faced a stand of evergreens and a dilapidated shed. Two young men helped carry my bags to the room, and I paid them in rupee I'd exchanged at the airport. I proceeded to unpack with the lethargy of someone submerged in water. Exhaustion weakened my muscles and brought my eyelids lower and lower. Finally I succumbed and climbed onto the bed where I napped for a few hours.

When I awoke, the wall of windows was black. I took a long shower, then dressed in a pair of cargo pants and a long-sleeved cotton shirt. I grabbed the book on George Mallory I'd brought, then crept out into the night.

The lodge was comprised of one main building and several smaller four-bedroom units scattered in no discernible fashion about the property. The buildings looked run-down and forgotten, but I could tell they weren't cheap. This trip must have cost Andrew a fortune.

I entered the main building and crossed the lobby to an iron stairwell that wound down to a subbasement. It wasn't a bar per se but a small eatery, poorly lighted, with a bar along one wall and large wooden tables and chairs spaced out along the floor. At the far end of the room, a fire blazed in a stone hearth.

There was no alcohol at the bar. A dark-skinned woman with horrible teeth served me a mug of hot tea, which I carried over to the fire. Situating myself in one of the sturdy wooden chairs, I thumbed through my book while sipping the tea. It was scalding hot and tasted like pine needles. My mouth watered for some liquor.

As I read, a few people shuffled in and out of the room. They whispered in a language I couldn't comprehend. A few times I craned my neck to see them; their shadows, amplified by the proximity of the fire, danced along the stone walls.

I returned to my book, skipping all the way to the final chapter, which described Mallory's demise on Everest's north face. I felt a twinge of claustrophobia, and I couldn't help but recall that night nearly two years ago when I'd almost died in that cave in the Midwest.

Andrew's voice popped into my head—*What were you doing in that cave by yourself?*—and it was simultaneously Marta's voice as well. A good question.

Someone appeared behind me. When he spoke, his voice startled me, and I sloshed some hot tea into my lap.

"It's a good book," the man said. He had a low, meaty voice.

I looked up and found he was less bulky than his voice had me believe but in good shape. His face was sunburned and creased with ancient gray eyes, though he looked about my age.

"Course, you skip to the end like that and you miss all the details."

"How'd you know I skipped to the end?"

He sat in one of the empty chairs and held his hands up to the fire. "You were on the tram with me from the airport this afternoon. I noticed by your bookmark you were only about halfway through the book. Unless you're a speed-reader . . ."

I closed the book. "No, not a speed-reader. Just a cheater.

Caught red-handed."

"I'm John Petras," he said, extending his hand. "But just call me Petras. No one save for my mama calls me John."

I shook his hand. It was a firm grip. "Tim Overleigh."

"Where you from?"

"Maryland."

"Wisconsin, myself," said Petras. "Land of cheese."

"Are you here with a tour?"

"Nope, no tour. I'm here for the same reason you are."

I grinned, thinking he was putting me on. "And what's that?"

Petras returned my grin and said, "Because Andrew Trumbauer told me to come."

3

MY EXPRESSION CAUSED PETRAS TO CHUCKLE. IT was a rumbling sound, reminiscent of an eighteen-wheeler barreling down an empty desert highway.

"How do you know Andrew?" I said.

"Ice climbing. Canadian Rockies. We were in the same group. There were about fifteen of us. Spent a good two weeks in the hills, then spent another week getting drunk in Nova Scotia."

I was still confused. "I mean, how'd you know . . . ?"

Still grinning, Petras said, "I heard you ask the man on the tram about the Canyon of Souls." He scratched behind a large, sun-reddened ear with one massive hand. "Ain't many folks come out here searching for the Canyon of Souls. Hell, most have never heard of it."

"I've never even heard of it myself."

"See, this place, it's practically Disney World for mountaineers, climbers, the whole lot. Even the amateurs come in their guided tours to say they've set foot on Everest or took a piss on the Khumbu Icefall and watched it freeze. I know this because I'm usually the guy guiding the tours. These people don't care about making it to the top of anything. Most of them wouldn't know a crampon from a tampon." He pointed to the book in my lap. "There are very few George Mallorys left in the world. What's become important to folks is being able to *say* they've done something. The *doing* it part . . . well, that's just what has to happen in order to tell their friends. There's no heart in it, no spirit. And these people sure as hell ain't here to cross the Canyon of Souls."

"So why are *you* here? What's so special about the Canyon of Souls for you? Or is it just because Andrew Trumbauer mailed you a plane ticket?"

Petras's gaze flicked toward the fire in the hearth. After a moment, he said, "I guess it's because it's never been done before. No one's ever crossed it. Few that I know of have even bothered to try. The place, it's not in any of the guidebooks or maps. Few care. Forgive me for cribbing Sir Edmund Hillary, but I'm doing it because the damn thing is there to be done."

"That's a good answer," I said.

"So how about you? What made you drop everything and run the hell out here?"

"Unfortunately my reasons are a bit more complicated."

"I hope I don't look stupid to you," Petras said without any emphasis or insult. I could tell it was only his way of imploring me to open up.

"I didn't mean it that way."

"I know. But you see, you and I are getting ready to trust each other with our lives. This little adventure ain't gonna be no walk in the park. So before I put my life in the hands of another man, I like to know why that man's putting his life in mine. I find comfort in what makes a man tick, and I sure as hell like to know why someone would do such a crazy thing." He smiled warmly and his eyes twinkled. He couldn't have been more than thirty-five, but there was something fatherly in that smile. "I just want to know we're not dealing with a death wish or something here is what I guess I'm saying."

I ran my thumb along the rim of my teacup, then set it on a small table beside my chair. "I used to be an artist, but my talent died along with my wife. So I'm here because I'm hoping to find something that'll get my life back on track. It's no death wish coming out here. The death wish would have been to stay home."

Petras nodded. "Fair enough. It's as good a reason as any I've ever heard. Better than most, probably." His eyes narrowed. "You know, you look awfully familiar. Any chance we've met before?"

"Doubt it. I'm pretty good at remembering faces. I've been on a couple of magazine covers a few years ago. Did several sculptures for some important people."

"Well, then," Petras said. "You were more than just an artist. You were *successful*."

I shrugged. "Depends on your definition of success."

"And," he added, grinning, "your definition of art."

Smiling, I rubbed my upper lip with one finger. "What is it about him?" I asked in a quiet voice, as if I were talking to myself. And perhaps I was. "What is it about Andrew Trumbauer that gets us all jumping just because he tells us to?"

"I'll admit I don't know him that well," said Petras. "In fact, I was pretty surprised he asked me to come out here. In truth, we didn't particularly like each other near the end of our expedition together."

"He's a tough guy to understand."

"We're all tough to understand. Especially to ourselves. That's why we do stupid stuff like this. Didn't you figure that out yet?"

I leaned back in my chair and watched the fire dance in the hearth. "There's quite a bit I haven't figured out about myself yet," I said, and it was like an admission.

4

THE TEMPERATURE HAD DROPPED CONSIDERABLY
while Petras and I talked in the lounge. Walking across the wooded
clearing toward my cabin, my hands stuffed into the pockets of my cargo
pants for warmth, I could smell the smoke from nearby chimneys and
the alpine scent of the wilderness around me. *I've never seen a darker
night*, I thought, pausing to stare at the blanket of stars. There were
full clusters of them, too many to count.

I mounted the steps to the cabin and was about to reach for the
door handle when a large shape materialized at one end of the cabin,
causing me to freeze. I heard the boards creak beneath the man's
considerable weight as I tried to make out his features. But it was too
dark; I could only discern wide shoulders covered in a wool coat and
a whitish face dense with a heavy beard. I couldn't see the man's eyes.

"Can I help you?" My voice shook.

"You are one of the Himal climbers?" the man said, his voice
deep, his English laden with a dense regional accent. "Your party
leaves at the end of this week for the Canyon of Souls?"

"Who are you?"

"You must not go to the canyon," he went on, ignoring my question.
"To do so will mean great disaster for your party. The canyon was
not meant to be crossed. Do you understand?"

"No, I don't. How do you know about me? How do you know
where we're going?"

"My name is Shomas. I live in the village. I am often hired to
navigate climbers through the Churia Hills. I know this land very
well, as I know the climbers who come here to conquer it." He took a
step out of the shadows, illuminating his face with moonlight. He was
hardened, his forehead and cheeks a patchwork of creases and ancient
scars, his eyes steely beneath an extended brow. "I know your party
is planning to cross the canyon."

"I appreciate the concern, but we'll be fine."

"It is a canyon not meant to be crossed. If you do not listen to me, you will find this out firsthand."

I opened the door. Warm, milky light from the hallway spilled out. Shomas's face was once again cast into shadows.

"Thank you," I said, "but I've come a long way to just turn around and go home."

"Do not be a fool," Shomas cautioned, his voice steady and without inflection. "Do not be the foolish American. I have seen many of them in a short time already."

"Good night," I said and quickly pitched myself through the door, closing it behind me. I hustled down the corridor to my room, glancing over my shoulder to see if Shomas would be bold enough to follow. But the door remained shut, and by the time I entered my room, I was breathing heavy, as if I'd just run a marathon.

A cold breeze froze the sweat on my brow. Across the room, I noticed one of my cabin windows was open; the gauze curtains billowed in the breeze. Looking at my bags, which I'd stacked in a heap at the foot of the bed, I realized they'd been looted while I was out.

CHAPTER 6

1

TWO DAYS LATER, ANDREW SHOWED UP, HIS FACE sunburned, his hair short, his eyes aglow with eagerness.

I spotted him when I paused to catch my breath and feel my pulse in the clearing near my cabin. I'd just come from a ten-mile run along the stretch of roadway that wound around the base of the hills. Since my arrival, I could sense tremors threatening to overtake me, like a psychic foretelling an earthquake in Asia. I hadn't had a drink in several days, and the sharpness of the world struck me like sudden daggers.

Andrew, dressed in neon orange snow pants and a Windbreaker, stood at the opposite end of the clearing, a pair of binoculars around his neck. Grinning, he opened his arms as if to hug me, despite the fact that he was nearly twenty yards away.

I approached, still catching my breath (I was not used to running for long distances at this altitude and had suffered a minor nosebleed somewhere around the seven-mile mark), and was quickly folded into Andrew's embrace.

"Can you believe places like this still exist in the world?" he said. "It's enough exhilaration just standing here breathing."

"It's beautiful, all right."

"The flight out was good?"

"It was horrible," I said, "but at least they didn't lose my luggage."

"Did you have a chance to meet the others?"

Aside from John Petras, I'd run into Michael Hollinger, a tattooed, well-built, introverted Australian who'd received an airline ticket and an invitation from Andrew in the same cryptic fashion as both Petras and I had.

We met last night during dinner at the lodge—a meal of stewed goat and an eclectic selection of wild vegetables that I was quite certain had not yet been cataloged by mankind. I must have looked overtly American in my Gap button-down and American Eagle corduroys because he approached my table and introduced himself. I invited him to dine with me, and we ate and talked for several hours. Hollinger knew Andrew from time spent in the Australian outback. For six months in their early twenties, they'd lived together with two aboriginal women in a hut built of fronds while subsisting on marsupials hunted with bows and arrows.

"A couple of the guys," I told Andrew. "John Petras and Michael Hollinger."

He winked. "Good guys, yeah?"

"When did you get in?"

"This morning. I'm jet-lagged like a motherfucker."

"Listen," I said, "I need to talk to you about something."

"It'll have to wait." He scanned the sky, one hand shielding the sun from his eyes. "I'm on the hunt."

"For what?"

"For whatever's out there." Andrew placed the binoculars to his eyes and took a series of steps backward. Gravel crunched under his Timberlands. "Tonight," he said, still examining the sky, "in the main lounge. The food's on me. All the guys will be there. I'll make an appearance to go over the itinerary. We'll leave at the end of the week."

He pivoted in the dirt and stalked toward the woods, the heavy binoculars still at his eyes. I watched him weave through a stand of spindly trees until he was nothing more than an orange neon dot getting lost in the woods.

Asshole, I thought.

Not for the first time, I wondered what the hell I was doing here. The answer I'd given Petras that first night in the lounge was true enough—that I had been slowly dying in my little apartment back home—but that didn't necessarily mean I had to come here, did it? There were plenty of other interesting places on the planet, many I'd already witnessed. I could have gone anywhere. But now I was here in Nepal, preparing to scale a mountain. With Andrew fucking Trumbauer.

As I walked to my cabin, I couldn't help but recall that evening in San Juan when he and I jumped off the cliff into the shocking black water below. I also remembered how Hannah had pressed her warm, little mouth against my ear after I told her where I'd been. "Oh," she'd said, "the cliff-diving thing." It was our honeymoon, yet I'd remained awake in bed for maybe half an hour, wondering if she'd ever gone naked cliff diving with Andrew.

"Fuck this," I said now, not wanting to deal with those old thoughts, those old feelings. After all, it was the reason I was here.

I opened the door to my room slowly, as if anticipating a burglar, ready to split my skull with a crowbar, hiding behind the door.

For all I knew, this wasn't too far from the truth; I was still concerned about the open window from two nights ago and the fact that someone had gone through my luggage. I'd assumed it was a robbery, but nothing had been taken . . . which, in a way, bothered me even more.

Why would someone break into my room and rifle through my belongings if not to steal? It made me think about James Bond movies and how bad guys always planted venomous snakes and deadly scorpions under his pillow or in the pocket of his bathrobe. At first, this notion caused me to grin, but then I thought of Shomas, the mysterious hulk who'd materialized outside the cabin on that very same night, preaching about danger and turning back. James Bond, indeed . . .

But no one was here. The windows were still closed, and my luggage was just how I'd left it. While this helped calm my heartbeat, it did little to soothe the shakes I could feel rumbling up through the core of my body. I needed a drink. Bad.

I decided to shower and take my mind off my withdrawal. The water wouldn't get hotter than lukewarm, which was fine by me, because by the time I stepped under the spray, I was sweating like a hostage.

2

ABOUT TWO HOURS LATER, I WATCHED AS A caravan of nomads rolled through the clearing on horse-drawn carts. They reminded me of the old paintings in high school history textbooks of the carpetbaggers traversing the flatlands of a blossoming new country. There were children among them; they shouted and laughed and hopped down from the carts to sell vegetables to whomever they could.

I felt a lower eyelid tremble. The withdrawal shakes were coming, all right. *Easy,* I willed it. *Easy now, boyo.*

As I watched the caravan, a man appeared above an embankment. He was deeply tanned with feathered yellow hair and wraparound sunglasses. He carried a backpack over one shoulder, and his strides were long and well defined.

The children hurried over to him, proffering their goods. The man smiled, exposing what appeared to be—at least from what I could see while standing on my cabin porch—two rows of perfect white teeth. The man tousled the hair of the nearest child, then lightly slapped the underside of the child's hand that held a plump, red tomato. The tomato hopped into the air, and the man snatched it before it could fall back into the child's hand. He nodded at the young boy, and even though he was wearing those wraparound sunglasses, I got the distinct impression he winked at him, too.

As the children looked on, their giddy playfulness fading, the man's two rows of perfect teeth reappeared for an encore performance before disappearing into the fat skin of the tomato. I could almost hear the snap of the bite and the patter of the juices down the man's chin.

The caravan continued down the roadway. The children, collectively expressionless, stared at the man for several moments before catching up to the carts. I could still hear the clop of the horses' hooves and the creaking of the wooden carts after the caravan disappeared over the embankment.

"Howdy," the tomato thief said, tipping me a salute as he strode toward the main lodge. "You from the States?"

"Yeah."

"You look like a Trumbauer experiment." If this was meant as some sort of joke, I was not in the mood.

"If you're hungry, they've got a pretty decent menu in the lounge downstairs," I commented.

The man paused and slid his sunglasses halfway down the bridge of his nose. Crystal blue eyes seared me. "I'm Chad Nando. From Miami."

"You fly out here from Miami or just steal a boat?"

Grinning, he tossed the tomato at me.

I caught it, more out of reflex than skill. My fingers sank into the juicy skin.

"This is going to be an interesting little adventure," he promised.

Indeed, I thought and watched him walk into the lodge.

3

THERE WAS LIGHT MUSIC COMING FROM THE lounge, something prerecorded and full of percussion, and I smelled steamed meats before I actually entered the room.

Petras leaned against the wall outside the lounge, examining his fingernails while clinging to a pint glass of something dark and frothy.

"Please tell me that's a beer," I said, saddling up to him. Laughter boomed from the lounge, and I peered into the room. A group of men crowded around a single table filled with plates of steaming food. *Thangkas*—Tibetan scrolled paintings—hung above them from the rafters.

"No such luck," Petras grunted. "It's supposed to be some kind of local juice, but it tastes like motor oil. Want some?"

"I'll pass." Scanning the table and the rest of the lounge, I couldn't locate Andrew. I asked Petras if he'd shown up yet.

"Haven't seen him. Hollinger saw him earlier today. He told me to come here tonight, so I did."

"You meet the rest of the guys?"

Petras stared at the dark liquid in his pint glass. "They all seem okay. Except maybe for that Nando guy. He's got a big mouth and likes to hear himself put it to use."

"I watched him wrestle a tomato from some homeless Nepalese children earlier today."

"You okay, Tim?"

"Sure," I said, suddenly aware of Petras's eyes all over me. "Why?"

"You look . . ."

"What is it?" I urged.

He shrugged. "It's nothing. Your hands, that's all. They're shaking."

In truth, I felt like shit. A hollowed-out husk, a rubbery mockery of a man . . . "I'm sweating, too," I commented nervously, thinking—for whatever bizarre reason—that this statement might lessen the tension of our conversation. It didn't.

"You on something or coming off it?" Petras wanted to know, his voice level and baritone.

I forced a chuckle. "Are you kidding? What in the world would—?"

"Only two reasons a man shakes like that." He seemed to consider his own words. "Well, maybe three reasons, but I wouldn't concern you with the third. Just two reasons, and they're both cause for alarm."

I felt some semblance of camaraderie with Petras, so I didn't lie to him. "I've just recently quit being an alcoholic, you might say."

One of his carved-in-stone eyebrows raised. "How recent?"

"Fairly recent." I forced a grin and felt like an imbecile. "Since I arrived in Nepal, actually."

Petras gulped down a mouthful of the oily drink, his gaze leaving mine for a second to scale the opposite wall, which was laden with stuffed animal heads. Without looking at me, he said, "Normally I'd say I'm not your father and whatever you choose to do is your own business. As a rule, I stand by that type of thinking. But as I said, come the end of this week, my life—if you'll permit me an overstatement—will be in your hands. I thought I was clear on this the night we met."

"Jesus, you don't have to worry about me. I swear to God I'm good to go."

Petras stuck out his lower lip and nodded with the lethargy and commitment of someone acknowledging his guilt to a jury of his peers.

"Please," I said, immediately disliking the whininess of my voice. "Please don't make this into something it's not."

"No, I won't." His steely eyes shifted back in my direction, and I thought I felt them sear my soul with one glance. "You've got a good heart and a healthy spirit. And I believe you may need this journey more than me." He cocked his head toward the doorway and added, "More than any of those guys, really."

"Thanks."

"Come on," he said. "Let's get some food."

4

WE ATE UNTIL WE WERE FULL, AND THEN WE ATE
just a little more. There were six of us in all, excluding Andrew who
hadn't shown up yet: Petras and me, of course; Michael Hollinger,
the quiet Australian; the loudmouthed Chad Nando from Miami,
whose voice carried a bit louder and a bit edgier than the rest; a gray-
eyed, muscular black man from Ohio named Curtis Booker, who'd
been in the Marines but needed to be prodded for a long time before
he'd talk about it; and lastly a surprisingly flabby guy named Donald
Shotsky who looked to be in his late forties and whose craggy face,
replete with acne scars, resembled a tic-tac-toe board. Shotsky had
the perpetually rheumy eyes of a career alcoholic, and the calculating
little man inside me assumed the chunky little bastard had a bottle or
two stashed in his cabin. A good friend to have, no doubt.

"First molehill I ever climbed was the Mount of the Holy Cross in
Colorado," said Chad, who had been dominating the conversation for
most of the evening. "I'd just turned nineteen and was with my older
brother, Alex, and some of his friends. Me being a novice, the plan was to
scramble up the North Ridge—fifty-six hundred feet in over eleven miles."

Curtis nodded. "I know it. Marked by a white cross of snow you
can see for miles. Ideal for extreme skiing."

Chad snickered and shook his head. "Yeah, well, I had no idea.
Wasn't about to punk out, you know, so after some arguing, it's decided
we'll climb up that vertical part of the cross, the Cross Couloir route, and
then ski straight down the way we came. So we get geared up—man,
there must have been six of us that day—and we weren't even an hour
into the climb when I lose my footing and drop straight over a sheer face.
Course, I was tied in, but that didn't prevent me from swinging out over
a ravine like a human yo-yo or some shit, the world blurring in front of
my eyes. I squeezed that goddamn line so tight it cut through my gloves
and caused stress fractures on the palms of my hands."

Hollinger whistled.

"I swing out," Chad went on, "and sure as shit, as if in slow motion, I see a fist-sized blade of rock coming right for my face. I brace my feet in front of me to catch the wall, but I'm swinging with too much force now, and I've got to keep some spring in my knees, not locking 'em, otherwise I'd break my legs on impact—"

"Or push the buggers up into your rib cage," suggested Hollinger.

"No shit. And, see, all this is going through my mind as I'm swinging toward it, which is why I say it was like in slow motion. Probably could've sang the whole goddamn theme song to *Gilligan's Island*, seemed to be so much time." Chad snorted and ran a hand across the top of his head. Then he pointed to a vague indentation below his left eye. "Rock struck me here, shattering my cheekbone. My eye was like jelly in the socket and filled up with blood. The force of it knocked me unconscious, too, but overall I guess I was lucky. Less than an inch higher and I'd be sporting one fancy little eye patch."

"Jesus," Donald Shotsky said in a breathy whisper.

"Split my pretty face like a Halloween pumpkin." Chad shrugged. "Somehow they get me down and bring me to Alex's truck. But Alex, who's panicking like a son of a bitch right about now—I know this 'cause it's just about the time I come to, sprawled in the backseat with a blood-soaked towel holding my face together— he gets lost on the trails going back to the interstate. First town we come to is Holy Cross City itself, which is nothing more than a ghost town, an old mining town with a few dilapidated cabins and mining boilers scattered around. Not a soul in sight and certainly no hospital. Then, because God tends to fuck with the hopelessly panicked, one of the truck's tires blows out."

Everyone groaned, myself included.

"So we're stranded in the middle of fucking nowhere and my face is goin' all spongy and Alex starts slamming his hands against the steering wheel. Everyone's looking for signs to I-70, but there's nothing but forest and run-down cabins. Then someone starts shouting out the window at some dude passing by. Figured it was one of the ATV bucketheads we'd seen cruising along Mosquito Pass earlier in the day. But this fucker turns out to be a goddamn *Indian* from some tribe in the Ute Mountains, scrounging for recyclable cans and bottles or whatever down here. He comes over to the truck and pops the hatchback and stares at me like I'm an alien species of wildflower he's thinking about smoking. He's not even wigged out by the blood, and there was a lot by now.

"Bastard climbs into the back with me and peels the bloody towel from my face. He was a big son of a bitch, and his skin looked like dried tobacco leaves. I remember thinking he was Mexican because he wore one of those wide-brimmed hats with the little *cholo* balls dangling from the rim. He placed his hands on either side of my face. He smelled like piss and whiskey, and for one freaky second, I thought he was simply gonna pop my head between his palms like a fucking overripe tomato.

"'Can you see me?' he asks. I must have responded because he then says, 'I want you to look directly into my eyes. I want you to tell me what color are my eyes.' So I'm looking real hard at his eyes, but I can't for the life of me tell what color his eyes are. For a moment, one of his hands slips off my cheek, and I think I feel my head expand, ready to come apart. 'What color are my eyes?' he says again, and he follows this up by stuffing a foul-tasting thumb into my mouth. I'm too out of it to buck him off, so the thumb goes rooting around my mouth, and when it finally retracts, I think I can make out the color of the old Indian's eyes. But then something weird fucking happens, and he's no longer *got* two eyes but just one *single* eye, right smack in the center of his face. Like what do you call those fucking things . . . ?"

"Cyclops," Petras offered.

"Yeah, right. Cyclops. And I'm focusing on this single eye, and I can clearly see the ridge of brow above the eye, the hollow pocket it's sitting in, the whole nine, man. I mean, the bastard morphed into some Cyclops right in front of me, and looking into that one eye was like looking at a hypnotist's pendulum, 'cause I'm suddenly feeling nothing but cool, calm, and relaxed. By the time Alex finds the highway and gets me to a hospital, I'm as content as an old dog after a big meal." Finished, Chad slapped a palm on the tabletop. The plates and glasses jumped. "Now how do you boys explain something like that?"

Hollinger said, "You'd lost a lot of blood, mate. You were hallucinating."

"Wasn't no hallucination."

"Peyote," suggested Petras. "That's why he put his thumb in your mouth."

"Brother," Chad said, "I've juggled my share of psychedelics. His eyes *changed*."

"Nonetheless, it was unfortunate they couldn't fix your face," Hollinger said.

We all laughed, none louder than Chad, who saw it fit to bray laughter.

I crept to the bar to order another glass of the oily, black liquid we'd been imbibing all evening. It tasted like sweat wrung from gym socks, but it was all they had. And, anyway, I needed to keep pouring it down my gullet to keep my mind off the shakes.

"Speaking of psychotropic drugs," Chad went on, "where the fuck is Trumbauer?"

"You'd think he'd show up, seeing how he put this whole thing together," Curtis said as he leaned back in his chair, two chair legs off the floor. He'd hardly spoken all night. The sound of his voice was like the tolling of a great and distant bell.

"Oh," howled Chad, "this is fucked up. We've been summoned from around the fucking world, right? Check us out. He calls and we all come running."

"How do you know Andrew?" Petras asked Chad.

Chad's eyes narrowed. "Any of you guys cops?"

"Go to hell," growled Curtis.

Chad shrugged. "We met in Colorado one winter, working the slopes. I helped him move some cocaine across the country in fish."

Michael Hollinger sat forward, smirking. "Fish?"

"Salmon." Chad smirked back. "Cut 'em open and pack 'em in ice and ship 'em all over the country. He knew a guy who knew a guy who wanted to move some powder. We packed the fish full of coke and sent them on their way. And that's how I met Andrew Trumbauer."

"Motherfuck," said Shotsky. "That ain't true."

"Sure as shit," Chad promised.

"How about you, Shotsky?" Hollinger said. "How do you know Andrew?"

"He saved my life," Donald Shotsky said matter-of-factly. "Five weeks in the Bering Sea, a ship called the *Kula Plate,* we're hoisting the little clawed monsters on board one pot after the next. I could see the dollar signs in my eyes, like a fucking cartoon character. I'm there and Andrew's there and maybe eight other guys on deck, plus the engineers and the captain.

"Third week, just as a storm's coming through, we're bustin' our asses to get everything pulled before we have to close up and pull everything below deck. Like an asshole, I get one of the ropes twisted around my ankle as we're tossing one of the crab pots back overboard. And these are big fucking pots, the size of Volkswagens, heavier than shit. It goes over the side, and the line goes taut. I feel something bite into my ankle, and the next thing I know I'm on my belly, dragged across the deck and slammed into the railing. Lucky for me Andrew was close by. He cut the line before I went over. Otherwise there'd be some other fat slob sitting at this table talkin' right now."

"Jesus, that's some story." Hollinger turned to Curtis Booker. "And you?"

Booker said, "You jump out of enough planes, climb enough

mountains, you eventually hear about Andrew Trumbauer. Three years ago, I put together a climb in Alaska. Andrew was one of the guys who signed up for it. Never met him in person, but I knew who he was. I agreed to take him on—there were about fifteen of us—and thought everything was set. But he never showed up."

"Sounds like Andrew," remarked Chad. "Good old reliable Andrew . . ."

Curtis grinned. "I thought about doing the same to him on this trip, actually."

"Why didn't you?" I said. For some reason, the notion of screwing over Andrew appealed to me.

"Because I'm too goddamn excited to cross the Canyon of Souls. Anyway, old Andy probably made a wise decision skipping out on my little exhibition." Curtis lowered his voice and said, "I lost two men in the death zone on that climb."

"The death zone?" Shotsky said, his voice suddenly shaky.

"Fuck, man," Chad interrupted. "You've signed up to cross the Canyon of fucking Souls, and you've never heard of the death zone."

Chad was an asshole, but he was right: Donald Shotsky hadn't done his homework. Beside me, I could almost feel Petras cringe.

"The death zone," Curtis explained, "is the place high on a mountain where you don't get enough oxygen. We had oxygen tanks for the summit climb, but at twenty-six thousand feet, the human body goes bad real fast."

"Are you kidding me?" Shotsky said. Both his thick, red hands were plastered to the tabletop, and I noticed a fine glimmer of sweat breaking out along his brow. "There's a motherfucking *death zone*?"

"Both guys died of edema," said Curtis. "Was the worst climb I ever made."

"Will we be climbing into the death zone?" Shotsky wanted to know. "I mean, how high are we going?"

"It's in the middle of Godesh Mountain," Petras said. "It's a difficult climb, but the Canyon of Souls isn't as high as twenty-six thousand." He shot me a glance, and I waited for him to wink. "I don't think so, anyway," he added. The wink never came.

"You afraid your heart's gonna give out up there, Shotsky?" Chad said, running a hand through his bleached hair.

Shotsky waved a hand at him. "Fuck off, snow bunny."

"Because I ain't gonna drag your rigor mortis ass back down the hill; that's for damn sure," Chad went on. Had they been friends, Shotsky would have most likely continued to wave Chad off. But they weren't friends—they'd just met this evening, in fact—and it was evident Chad's words were irritating Shotsky. "Or maybe I'll just ride you down like a sled," Chad added, oblivious to Shotsky's growing agitation.

Shotsky's face creased. His hands balled into fists on the table. "How 'bout I ride *you* like a sled, fuckface?"

"Cool it," Petras said.

"Whoa." Chad balked, throwing his hands up in surrender. "I didn't mean nothing by it, bro. I'm cool. Just making light of the whole thing." His gaze swung in my direction. "Right, Shakes?"

Something snapped inside me. I sprung across the table and grabbed a fistful of Chad's sweater. With my free hand, I struck him on the left cheek, which caused his head to jerk to the right. I refused to release the hold on his sweater even after his chair tipped and spilled him to the floor.

"Hey, hey, hey," Petras muttered into my ear. His big hands were on my shoulders, prying me off Chad. "Ease off, Tim. Ease off."

Finally I released my grip and allowed Petras and the others to drag me across the table.

Hollinger bent over Chad and asked if he was all right.

Chad laughed and scooted against the wall, his eyes locked on mine. I found myself praying for his nose to start gushing blood—somehow I thought that would make the scene all the more dramatic—but that never happened.

"Nice," he called to me, grinning. "Got a hell of a swing there. Guess this is amateur hour, huh?"

"Asshole," was all I could muster. Petras was still holding me back.

Andrew appeared in the doorway, smiling down on us like the Creator Himself. "Very nice display," he said, applauding. "Glad to see you boys playing nice together. I'm sure there exists a more than suitable quote about men growing up into boys or something like that, but I don't know any."

"He started it," Chad barked. A second later, he must have realized how childish it had sounded, because he chuckled.

"I can't let you ladies out of my sight for one second, can I?" Andrew said, folding his arms and leaning against the wall. "How's the food?"

"Ain't the food that's the trouble," Shotsky growled.

"Tastes like the padding of my sneakers," Hollinger commented, perhaps in hopes of diluting the tension, "but at least it's hot."

"The food's purifying," Andrew said. "I want all of us to be cleansed and ready for the climb. No smoking joints, no alcohol, no greasy cheeseburgers."

"God, I could use a joint," Shotsky said.

The guys laughed. Even Chad seemed to loosen up.

"It's the air up here. The altitude is different. Makes us act crazy, like a bunch of psychopaths. But we'll be okay, won't we?" When no one answered, Andrew repeated, "Won't we?"

"Sure," said Petras, and all heads turned to look at him. He was by far the most imposing figure among us.

"Here's the deal. I've already been in your rooms. I've left some equipment for each of you. Everyone is responsible for their own equipment." Andrew surveyed the group, as if in anticipation of revolt. "There'll be a bus outside the lodge this Saturday at six in the morning to take us into town. We'll pick up whatever else we need before heading out to the Valley of Walls. From there, we'll have a team of Sherpas take us through the pass to the base of the Godesh range. It'll be a full day's hike. We'll climb to the first plateau and establish base camp. We'll spend one more night there before leaving the following morning to climb. It's a steep climb, and we'll be going alone, just the seven of us, for several days."

"Lucky seven," Curtis muttered.

"You all need to be rested and prepared for strenuous conditions. If you get sick or feel you can't make it once we've begun, it'll be up to you to either establish sanctuary and wait for us to return or make it back to base camp on your own. If you wish to enlist the help of anyone else to carry your ass down to camp, just keep in mind that no one here signed up for this journey with the hope of sitting in a canvas tent for two weeks, sipping hot chocolate and listening to their iPods, while the rest of us climb. You're all here because I have faith in each and every one of you." A disconcerting smile crept across Andrew's features. "We're going to be the first team to cross the Canyon of Souls."

This sparked an eruption of cheers and applause from the group. I couldn't help but smile, either . . . while deep in the recesses of my brain I recalled the fire behind Andrew's eyes that night in San Juan when, stark naked and pale in the moonlight, he leapt off the cliff and into the black night air.

Abruptly Andrew turned and walked out of the lounge.

"He's leaving already?" I whispered to Petras.

"He's a strange dude, all right," Petras said, rolling his massive shoulders.

I hustled out of the lounge and up the winding iron stairs to the main lobby of the lodge. Andrew was zipping up his jacket and heading toward the doors.

"Hey," I called.

He paused and swung his head in my direction.

"Got a minute?"

"What's up, Overleigh?"

"You're not gonna stay and chill out awhile?"

"What are we, in college or something?" Again, that curious grin of his appeared, and his eyes narrowed. "Did that sound abrupt? God-damn, I can never tell how I'm going to sound until the words spill out."

"Listen," I said. "Do you know a guy named Shomas? Big guy? Local?"

"Never heard of him."

"He stopped me outside my cabin to warn me about climbing Godesh. Said it was a canyon not meant to be crossed. He seemed pretty adamant about it."

"Come on. It's local superstition. He's probably some guide who's pissed he didn't get the job."

"Well, yeah, he said he was a guide . . ."

"Then there you go."

"I think he broke into my room, too."

"What are you talking about?"

"When I went back to my room, someone had gone through all my stuff. I thought maybe someone had robbed me, but nothing was taken."

"Then what's the problem?"

The problem is nothing was taken, I wanted to say. *The problem is that big behemoth had been in my room rifling through my luggage . . . and didn't take a single thing . . .*

"What was he looking for?" I said. "If he didn't take my money and my valuables, what the hell was he looking for?"

"Jesus, what's wrong with you? You're shaking like a tuning fork."

"Forget it. I'm fine."

"You're sweating, too."

"Never mind."

"Look," he said, placing a hand on my shoulder. Inwardly I cringed. "If you've got something missing, report it to the lodge. They get thousands of travelers here every year; they won't stand for theft scaring away the tourists. But if nothing was taken, then consider yourself fortunate that you scared the guy off before he could rip you off. Simple as that. What more do you want?"

It was a fair enough question. I had no idea what more I wanted. I wanted Hannah, and I suddenly wanted to be back in my tiny Annapolis apartment, but I couldn't say those things to Andrew. Not at all.

"Forget it," I said finally. "I guess I'm just exhausted."

"Get some rest. You need to be in pristine fucking condition by Saturday."

"Yeah."

"And quit fighting. This ain't boxing camp."

"Right."

"Now get to sleep." He squeezed my shoulder, then marched out of the lodge, turning up the collar of his jacket as he went.

CHAPTER 7

1

SATURDAY MORNING I GOT UP A FEW HOURS before the sun had time to rise. Knowing I would not see another shower for several weeks, I languished beneath the lukewarm spray of my shower until the water grew cold. Then I climbed out and toweled myself off while staring at my blotchy reflection in the full-length mirror behind the bathroom door. I was in good physical condition, yet my eyes quickly found the one haunting flaw on my body: the ragged, brutal, puckered scar running along my left leg from just above the ankle to just below the knee.

Momentarily I was overcome by claustrophobia, thinking back to how I'd almost died in that cavern beneath the earth, my shinbone jutting through a serpentine tear in my flesh. And with the claustrophobia came vertigo; I scrambled for the toilet, where I closed the lid and dropped on top of it, catching my breath.

But it wasn't all about the claustrophobia. It wasn't all about the memory of the caves. It was the drinking too. The withdrawal. And in a way it was Hannah . . .

She hadn't returned to me since my arrival in Nepal, which comforted me to some extent, making me think I was probably doing *something* right. And now, so many thousands of miles away from home, her haunting my apartment seemed nothing more than a dream, something my overactive and whiskey-pickled mind had conjured up. On the morning of the first day of our climb, Hannah was nothing more than a sad memory.

Back in the room, I dressed quickly in fresh clothes and a lightweight anorak. My bags were piled by the door, along with the gear Andrew had delivered to my room—a walkie-talkie; a miner's helmet with the flashlight affixed to the front; a pickax; several blue vinyl flags, the kind one might see hanging above a used car lot; and a steel canteen with my name engraved on it.

I dragged my stuff out to the cabin porch just as a low rumbling could be heard over the horizon. Moments later, twin headlamps pierced the darkness. The bus shuddered into the clearing between the cabins, coughing gouts of black smoke from its exhaust pipe. I entertained serious doubts that it would be able to transport us a mile down the road let alone into the city, what with its rust-peeling shell and four tires that were practically running on the rims.

"She's a beauty, ain't she?" someone called off to my right. I looked and saw Chad strutting toward me, a backpack slung over one shoulder. "We should get a bottle of champagne to christen her."

"No chance it's got seat belts, huh?" I replied.

Chad snorted. "What's a seat belt?"

The bus doors shushed open, and dark-skinned teenage boys spilled out. They chattered to each other in a language I didn't understand and quickly surrounded Chad like aliens deciding whether or not they should beam him aboard the mother ship.

"Hey, guys," Chad said as they quickly relieved him of his backpack. They carried it to the bus. "Jesus, I feel like Arnold Schwarzenegger among a bunch of hobbits. Look at these people."

At the next cabin, Petras appeared on the porch. Bundled in a winter coat and thick gloves, he looked twice as large as usual. He raised a hand in my direction, then disappeared back into his cabin, only to return moments later dragging a duffel bag by its straps.

After all our gear was systematically loaded onto the bus, we gathered outside the main lodge in anticipation of Andrew's arrival.

"Let's smoke 'em while we can," Chad said, pulling a cellophane pack of cigarettes from within his jacket. He shook some into his hands. "Who wants one?"

Everyone except for Petras grumbled in agreement, and we held out our hands. Chad lit the smokes one by one with a silver Zippo.

Closing my eyes, I inhaled deeply and felt the smoke fill my lungs. I was aware of a barely noticeable grin creeping across my face.

"Might be a stupid question," Shotsky said, sucking the life out of his own cigarette, "but did anyone think to bring, like, a gun? You know, for protection."

"From what?" Chad said.

"Anything. Whatever's out there."

"I got this," Petras announced, producing a five-inch hunting knife with a pearl handle from his belt.

"Jesus," I said.

Petras turned the knife over in his hands. "Yeah, could kill a bear with this thing."

"No bears where we're going," Andrew said, appearing beside the bus. He leaned against the grille, silhouetted by the headlights. The sun hadn't risen yet. "Just people. Sorry to disappoint, but it's just us, boys."

"Fair enough," said Chad. "Let's get a move on, shall we?"

Andrew smiled. "Let's roll."

We piled onto the bus and trundled along the dirt road for forty minutes before we reached the city. I had anticipated returning to Kathmandu, with all its intricate temples and bustling marketplaces, but this was a smaller city—a remote Buddhist village—situated at the foothills of a mountainous forest. The homes and shops looked like log cabins, void of any distinguishing markings. As the sun came up, I could see chickens and goats in the streets and young children pulling rickshaws through the mud.

"Where the hell are we?" Curtis whispered in my ear.

"Looks like purgatory."

"If this is purgatory, I'd hate to see hell."

The bus stopped outside a long, concrete building, pressed close to the ground and surrounded by rhododendrons.

When the doors whooshed open, Andrew stood at the front of the bus. "Anyone want some Taco Bell?" He stared at the rest of us, imploring.

We all just stared back.

He broke out into a laugh. "Just kidding. Sit tight. They'll load up the rest of our stuff."

Sure enough, more young boys stuffed crates and boxes into the cargo hold beneath the bus. Men in flowing maroon robes watched from doorways and porches, smoking elegant, long-stemmed pipes.

Chad swooped down in the seat in front of me, beaming like a pair of headlights. "Listen, Timmy, I was all wired up the other night. No hard feelings, right?" He held out a hand.

"Sure," I said, gripping his hand, then dropping it like a wet rag.

"Excellent, man." Chad hopped up and sauntered toward the back of the bus.

"The guy's a blatant asshole," Curtis said, staring straight ahead.

"I wouldn't have pegged him for the apologetic type."

"Despite what just transpired, I don't think he is." Curtis glanced over his shoulder, perhaps to check on Chad, then turned around. "I'd watch my back if I were you."

"Duly noted." Which was when I happened to catch Shomas moving through a crowd of vendors in the cluttered marketplace. I noticed him in profile, but it wasn't until he turned and glanced at our bus did I recognize him fully.

"Jesus Christ." I jabbed a finger at the window. To Curtis I said, "That's the guy who broke into my cabin."

Curtis leaned across my lap and looked out the window. "Which one?"

"Son of a bitch." I shoved Curtis aside. He called after me, but I was already off the bus and sprinting across the street. I followed Shomas's hulking shape through the crowd, his clothes the color of sawdust and easily lost in the confusion. He turned a corner behind one building—or at least I thought he did—and when I pursued him, turning that very same corner, I was alone. The land dipped into a gradual valley where yaks grazed in a field far below. I must have miscalculated; had Shomas turned this corner, there was no place for him to hide.

And why hide? Did he even know I was following him?

"Hey," Andrew said, startling me with a hand on my shoulder. "What the hell are you doing?"

"I thought I . . . I recognized someone."

"Got a lot of friends out here, do you?" There was no humor in his voice.

"Sorry."

"Run off like that again and we'll leave your ass."

"Okay. Sorry."

"Get back on the bus."

When I reclaimed my seat, Curtis thumped an elbow into my ribs and muttered, "The hell got into you, man?"

"Something doesn't feel right," I said before I fully understood what I was saying.

"What do you mean?"

"I don't know. Never mind."

"You losing it already? Because we ain't even on the mountain yet."

"No," I told him and wondered if it was the truth.

2

BY MIDDAY, THE BUS LET US OUT AT THE CUSP OF
a dense forest. Two Tibetan guides in full regalia waited for us. It was as far as the bus could go, so we all emptied into the mud and strapped our gear to our backs. Andrew spoke briefly with the guides in Tibetan, while Petras and I tied bits of leather around our exposed calves and neck to keep the leeches off.

"Do you understand any of it?" I whispered to Petras, still keeping one ear on the dialogue between Andrew and the guides.

"Very little. My Tibetan is shaky at best. Something about a river, following a river. The Valley of Walls is farther than Andrew originally thought."

"What's the Valley of Walls?"

"I don't know. They keep saying . . ."

"What is it?" I pressed. "What?"

"*Beyul,*" he said.

"The hell's that?"

"If it's what I think it is . . ."

"What is it?" I pressed on.

Before Petras could answer, Andrew clapped. "We've got a few days' hike ahead of us, gentlemen. The Valley of Walls is farther than I thought."

Petras and I shared a glance. This time he did wink at me, and I said, "Nice translating, chief."

Our backs and shoulders burdened with gear, we tromped through muddy ravines while following the two Tibetan guides and cutting swaths through the hemlock with large knives. Andrew remained close to the front of the line.

By late afternoon, the forest opened onto a sprawling mountainside dotted with ferns. The air was clean and scented with pine. Ahead in the unreachable distance, seeming to float unanchored to the earth, the crests of the snowcapped mountains rose like the humpbacks of sea beasts. A trail of white stone led in a gradual slope to a distant valley over which an enchanting mist hung suspended.

"There it is," Petras said at my side, pointing at the line of snow-capped ridges on the horizon. "That's where we're headed."

I was not intimidated by the distance. In fact, I was invigorated at the sheer prospect of it all. My feet ate up the earth, covering the distance without difficulty, and I was hungry to keep moving even as a smoky twilight settled over the valley.

We crossed the valley and migrated through dense trees. In the oncoming dark, monkeys chattered and howled nearby, and I frequently heard other animals—bigger animals—burst through the underbrush no more than fifteen yards away. Yak herders waded through a small stream and smiled at us with toothless mouths. They bent at the water's edge and cleaned mud off their hands.

As the moon climbed, we came to a low-running river, no wider than a four-lane highway. We paused while our guides shared words in low voices and tested the current with stalks of bamboo.

After a few moments, Andrew turned to us and said, "We cross here. Once we're on the other side, we'll move through the trees. There's another clearing just up the embankment. We'll set camp there tonight."

I took off my boots and secured the bands of leather about my legs. Touching a toe to the surface of the water caused icy tremors to course up through the marrow in my bones.

"Latch on," Andrew said, tossing me a length of rope.

"Are you kidding?"

"I know it's shallow and there's hardly a current, but we're not taking any chances. You okay with that?"

Not taking any chances? I thought. *Is this the same guy who once stripped off his clothes and dived blindly off a cliff?*

"No problemo, amigo," I intoned and hooked the rope through

a clamp on my belt. I fed the remaining length of line to Petras, who did the same, and continued to pass it along to Curtis, Chad, Shotsky, and Hollinger.

We crossed with little difficulty. At the opposite bank, after un-latching ourselves from Andrew's rope, we surveyed each other for leeches before climbing back into our boots and ascending the vast, wooded incline toward the next clearing.

Farther down the line, Chad began crooning Sam Cooke's "Chain Gang." When no one joined him after several minutes, he lost interest in singing and proceeded to mutter to himself beneath his breath.

This caused Petras to chuckle—he was right at my back as he did so; the sound was unmistakable—and in turn caused me to grin and laugh.

Soon Curtis began belting out the song, his voice much stronger and more disciplined than Chad's, and this time the whole company, with the exception of the two Tibetan guides and Chad, chimed in.

"Come on, mate!" Hollinger prodded Chad from the back of the line. "Sing on, now! We know you know the words!"

Chad joined in, adding the "ooh" and "aah" when required. All in all, it was a surprisingly adept rendition.

When we reached the summit of the clearing, the moon was full in the sky, larger than I had ever seen it. Wisps of clouds drifted seem-ingly close to the ground—so close I felt I could reach out and touch them. The air was thin and cool, and my lungs were still acclimating, but I felt alive and rejuvenated.

His hands on his hips, Andrew wolfishly surveyed our surroundings and said, "We camp here and leave tomorrow at first light."

I dropped my rucksack and erected my nylon tent. Beside me, Petras did the same, humming some obscure tune under his breath. The Tibetan guides established a fire at the center of camp, using bamboo stalks and dried rhododendron leaves for kindling, and began cooking brown rice and beans in a cast-iron pot. The smell was instantaneous.

After peeling off the extra layers of my clothes, I slipped away from camp and passed through low-hanging moss where I urinated on a patch of saxifrage. From this height, I could hear the rushing of the river and see its meandering tendrils glittering like slicks of oil beneath the shine of the full moon. Beyond the hills, the tendrils convened into a single strong-flowing current that dropped perhaps one hundred yards beyond the valley into a steaming, misty gorge.

Hannah would have been speechless, I thought, feeling a dull pang deep inside me.

Back at camp, the Tibetan guides were doling out mugs of brown rice and fat red beans.

I claimed a mug and shoveled a spoonful into my mouth. I hadn't realized how hungry I'd been until I swallowed that first spoonful.

"Here." Hollinger handed me a tin cup. "Careful. It's hot."

"Thanks." The cup warmed my hands, and the tea tasted like basil.

Hollinger nodded and walked over to his tent. Grinning, he planted an Australian flag outside the tent door, then peeled off his sodden boots and proceeded to rub his toes on a straw mat.

I looked across the plateau and tried to make out the distant mountains, but it was too dark to see anything that far away. I could see Andrew standing on the precipice, his hands still on his hips, gazing out over the valley. He was briefly silhouetted against the moon. It was impossible not to think of that night in San Juan . . . which inevitably made me think of Hannah. I chased the thought away.

Petras sat down beside me, busy with his own bowl of beans and rice. "You've got some stamina."

"I'm still wide awake. I could go another ten miles." Truth was, as long as I was active and exerting energy, I didn't think about drinking. Now, sitting here in the dark while the world slowly wound down, I felt my tongue growing dry and fat and that old urgency causing my throat to convulse reflexively.

"Save it for tomorrow," Petras advised.

"Hey," I said. "What was it you were going to say earlier today? About the guides and Andrew? You'd heard them say something—"

"*Beyul*," Petras said, staring into his bowl. I heard his spoon scrape the bottom.

"What is it?"

"It means 'hidden land.' They're believed to be places of middle existence between our world and the next. Some lamas have spent their lives seeking out these places, interpreting the *beyul* to be a sort of paradise, a Shangri-la. Others believe it is where the earth is weakest, where our world is physically capable of touching the next. Many others think these hidden lands are not meant to be found and that the spirits—or nature itself—will prevent travels from uncovering their locations at all costs. I once read a book by a lama who said he was guided for a full year by a female spirit—what he called a *dakini*— in search of a *beyul* hidden beneath a glacier. He never found it, and he nearly died of exposure in the process."

"That's unfortunate," I said, yet my mind was still echoing with the concept of a female spirit, the *dakini*. "After a whole year with nothing to show for it."

"On the contrary," Petras said. "He was one of the lucky ones. You see, most lamas who set out to find a *beyul* die trying to find it. Or they simply vanish and are never heard from again."

"Yeah?"

"And sometimes," Petras continued, "you may be standing in the heart of the *beyul* and never even know it."

"Why's that?"

"Because you aren't attuned to it. Your spirit isn't ready or capable of accepting it."

Jackals howled in the distance. I jerked my head and could see the wreath of mist rising over the plateau. It was nearly impossible to make out the trees below, and the winding, glittering river I had witnessed less than thirty minutes ago had now vanished.

"Is that where we're going?" I asked. "The Canyon of Souls? Is that supposed to be one of these *beyuls*?"

"I honestly don't know. And as far as we're concerned, I don't think it matters."

I barked laughter and shook my head. "You're fucking with me, right?"

"It's the truth as I know it, anyway." He motioned in the direction of the two guides, who were asleep under a canvas lean-to. "I believe that's what our buddy Andrew was discussing with them earlier this afternoon."

"How do you know all this stuff?"

"I've been out here before. A few years ago, I came by myself and spent nine months with a rucksack over my shoulders. Spent many nights in the Western Hills, in Pokhara, and made friends in Thamel. It was a good way to clear my head, and back then I needed my head cleared. It was a rough time, but I guess we all go through that at some point." Petras faced me. "You all right?"

"Yeah, why?"

"You've been rubbing your leg the whole time. You get hurt?"

I was massaging the scar on my left leg. It didn't hurt; it had just become an unconscious habit. "No, I'm fine."

Across from us, Chad whipped out a harmonica and began playing some unrecognizable tune. Someone laughed, and someone else— possibly Shotsky—told him to shut the hell up and where did he think he was, the old West? Right on cue, Chad told his heckler to go fuck himself. Again, laughter from some disembodied voice.

I sighed, smiling and shaking my head. "This is going to be a long couple of weeks."

Petras leaned over and squeezed my shoulder. It was such a brotherly gesture that it caught me off guard and rendered me temporarily speechless. "Get some sleep," he told me.

I watched him rise and shamble over to his own tent, the bonfire causing shadows to dance across his broad shoulders.

After he disappeared through the flaps of his tent, I shifted my gaze out over the grassy plateau, black and still in the night, to the waning fire. Beyond the fire, I could see Andrew. He was perched on a large outcrop of white stone, his legs folded beneath him, his back facing the moon. He looked lost in meditation.

CHAPTER 8

1

IT WAS NOON, ACCORDING TO SHOTSKY'S WRIST-
watch, and on the third day of the hike when we reached the bridge
spanning the cliffs. It was an unsteady rope bridge, like something
out of an Indiana Jones movie, suspended at least five stories over a
chalk white river. Great fronds waved along the riverbank, but they did
not fully conceal the display of jagged white stones, slick with lichen,
that hugged the wet earth.

Chad tossed a rock over the side of the cliff; we all watched it plummet to the frothing waters below. Chad whistled but didn't say anything.

Once again, Andrew spoke with the guides. It had become his
custom to pull them aside and speak in hushed tones whenever the
spirit struck. This hadn't bothered me at first, and it wasn't until I
heard one of the guides say something to Hollinger in crude but un-
derstandable English that I began to feel uneasy about their discus-
sions in Tibetan. I thought of Petras's story about the *beyul* and how
some secret places were never meant to be disturbed. This, coupled with
the fresh memory of Shomas and how my room had been ransacked, did
not sit well with me. It seemed none of us knew much about the Canyon
of Souls. It wouldn't be unlike Andrew to lead us into danger.

"We cross here," Andrew said.

The guides were already securing lines to the moss-slicked rope handholds. The bridge wobbled unsteadily as they did so.

"They're sure this bridge will hold?" Curtis said. He eyed the wobbling bridge as dubiously as I had.

"It'll hold. Besides, we'll lose too much time climbing down and trying to cross the river."

"He's playing loose and fast," Curtis muttered as we secured our gear.

"But he's right about losing time if we had to climb down and cross the river," Hollinger said.

"That bridge don't hold," Curtis said, "we all might be in that river, anyway."

One of the guides went first. He traversed the slotted wooden planks with seemingly no difficulty, the palms of his small hands just grazing the ropes at waist height.

"Thirty-three seconds," Shotsky commented, staring at his watch. "From one end to the other."

"Yeah," I said, "but he moved damn fast."

"Thirty-three," he repeated, ignoring me. "What's thirty-three seconds?"

Chad laced up his boots at the edge of the cliff. "Don't tell me you're actually afraid of heights, Donald."

Shotsky scanned the length of the suspended bridge. "What can I say?" His voice was small, and I could hear the dryness in his mouth when his throat clicked. "I needed the job."

Andrew crossed second. He moved confidently and without concern. At the midpoint, he paused and called to the rest of us, "It's a sturdy bridge." Twice he stomped his boot against the planks; both times we all winced collectively. "We don't need to go one at a time. Space it out, leave about ten or fifteen feet between each of you. It's strong enough."

"Strong, strong," echoed the guide who'd remained on our side of the bridge. He pulled at one of the ropes to bolster his authority. Judging by his urgency, I assumed this had been the guides' suggestion from the beginning and was most likely the essence of their discussion with Andrew.

"Later, mates," Hollinger said, moving up from the back of the queue. He proceeded to cross, both hands gripping the ropes. His steps weren't as certain as Andrew's, but he moved at a decent pace.

Moments later Chad stepped onto the planks. "I'm next."

"Wait a couple seconds," I told him. "Give Hollinger more space."

"He's got enough," Chad said, seizing the ropes. He tested their bounce by shaking them, which caused the guide to scowl and wave his hands.

"Hold up." Petras dropped a hand on Chad's shoulder. The force must have been harder than it looked, because Chad swung his head around, his eyes wide as saucers. "Tim's right. Wait a second."

Chad slipped on his mirrored sunglasses and wisely kept his mouth shut.

"Okay," Petras said once Hollinger had covered a sizable distance. "Go."

Chad moved onto the bridge.

I glanced over at Shotsky. He was watching every step Chad took with mounting distress. *You've got to be kidding me*, I thought. I gripped a fistful of his parka. "You okay?"

His gaze bounced from me to the bridge, me to the bridge. "Doesn't look too safe. I'm maybe the heaviest guy . . ."

"Here," I said, setting my pack on the ground. I unwound a spool of line and ran it through one of the grappling hooks at my hip. I extended the line, latched it onto one of Shotsky's hooks, and tied it off in a figure eight. I tugged on it and it was strong.

Shotsky laughed nervously. "So this means if I fall, you'll fall, too, huh? Kill the both of us instead of just me, right?"

"You can go back," I said, my voice low. "You don't have to be out here if you don't want to do this."

"Yes," he said dryly, "I do."

I was about to ask what he meant when Petras clapped my shoulder. As I turned, he intercepted the line from my hands and ran it through two hooks on his harness.

"Thanks," I said, but Petras had already turned away.

Curtis followed Chad. We waited for Curtis to go beyond the bridge's midpoint before Petras stepped onto the bridge. Shotsky may have been the most overweight of the bunch, but John Petras, with his massive frame and shoulder span, was by far the heaviest.

From where I stood, I could hear the planks creaking beneath Petras's boots. There wasn't enough rope length between us to provide the requisite fifteen feet, so as the slack on my rope picked up, I moved onto the bridge. I glanced at Shotsky over my shoulder and said, "Thirty-three."

"Thirty-three," he echoed and audibly swallowed a lump in his throat.

Beneath me, the bridge seemed to swing from one side to the other; I had to maintain white-knuckled grips on the ropes to prevent this, and I could feel my fingernails digging into the meat of my palms after only five steps. The groaning planks beneath Petras's feet less than two yards ahead of me did not help settle my unease.

I closed my eyes and listened to the rushing water below, the sound of the wind rustling the palm fronds and the rhododendron leaves. Last night's sleep was hard and dreamless: I dreamed now, imagining I was floating high above the earth, no bridge beneath my feet, just the air and the babbling river, white and frothing, and the swaying fronds that were so big they looked prehistoric—

The line at my back went taut. My eyes flipped open, and I told Petras to slow down as I glanced behind me. Shotsky, taking up the rear, was moving too slow.

"You gotta step it up a notch, man," I called to him.

"This pace feels about right," he said. I did not like the quaking in his voice.

"Shotsky, the slower you move, the longer you'll be on this bridge. Do you understand?" I turned to look at him.

He nodded but did not increase his speed.

"Shotsky," I said again, and that was when the plank beneath my foot snapped.

The world blurred as I rushed downward, feeling the jagged edge of the busted plank tear my cargo pants. Reflex caused my hands to spear out; I grabbed one of the vertical ropes, which briefly arrested my fall yet caused the bridge to pitch on its side. I heard Shotsky moan and saw John Petras bound toward me. The busted plank was at eye level. What looked like blood seeped into the wood. My blood? I had no idea.

"Hang on!" Petras shouted.

The rope was slick with moss; I lost my grip and felt the world pull me toward its center.

With all this gear on my back, I'm going to drown, I thought. A second later, I felt the concussion of striking the surface of the water. My bones rattled in my skin. For a moment, I thought I had somehow missed the river completely and hit the embankment, and I was now splayed out and broken on the jagged white rocks covered by a mat of fronds.

But then I felt the icy waters claim me, seeping into my clothes and attacking my flesh, and I couldn't see a damn thing. I was fucking blind, and I was drowning, blind and drowning.

2

I AWOKE BESIDE THE RIVER, PETRAS'S FACE IN MY own. He had one thumb holding up my eyelid. I blinked, and he let go and took a step back.

Behind him, Donald Shotsky stood with his hands fumbling

over one another, his eyes bugging out. "On his neck." His voice sounded like it was issuing from the far end of a long, corrugated tunnel. "See it? What is it?"

"Leech. Big sucker, too." Petras peeled it from my neck and briefly examined it between his fingers. It was the size of a man's index finger. He chucked it into the underbrush.

Then the shakes started—the cold had permeated my clothes, freezing them to my body, the water causing them to cling like flesh.

"Can you hear me?" Petras asked.

I nodded.

To Shotsky, Petras said, "We need to get him out of these clothes."

I passed out.

3

LATER, THE SKY A MISTY GRAY AND THE SUN veiled by long streamers of clouds, I sat before a blazing fire. I was dressed in Michael Hollinger's clothes, which weren't exactly a perfect fit, and my teeth chattered in my skull. We still had several hours of daylight left, and Andrew had wanted to put them to good use. He was irritated and anxious at the mishap on the bridge, and I watched him pace back and forth along the brush, oblivious to the rest of us.

Petras brought me some *tsampa*—roasted barley ground to sticky flecks—and hot tea.

"The hell happened, anyway?" I said, grasping the tin cup of hot tea in both hands, savoring its warmth.

"You must have hit a weak board in just the right way."

"And I didn't pull you two down?"

"I reached the other side and secured the line around a post just before you fell."

"And Shotsky?"

Petras grinned wearily. "Lucky bastard got his foot tangled in one of the bridge's suspension cables. Just like that story he told about the crabbing boat when Andrew saved his life."

"Pudgy bastard's got a flare for that," I commented but with no disdain. "He's okay?"

"He's fine. How about you?"

"Never better."

"Your head still hurt?"

I frowned. "My head?"

"Gashed it pretty good."

I suddenly became aware of a dull throb at the center of my forehead. When I touched the spot, I felt the split in the flesh and the sting of my fingers upon it. "Nice," I muttered.

Petras shrugged. "You were an ugly bastard before. Doesn't change much."

I nodded in Andrew's direction. "He pissed?"

"Says we're close to the Valley of Walls. If we don't lose too much time here, we can reach it by nightfall."

I rose with some difficulty. My body was sore and unsure of itself. "Then let's go."

"You should give yourself some more time. Fuck Andrew Trumbauer."

"He's not my type."

Petras didn't protest further.

I carried empty bottles down to the river with Hollinger and Curtis and filled them with water, adding drops of iodine for purification. Back at the fire, someone had opened my gear and laid out my belongings to dry. I repacked it all and was ready to set off again in under an hour. The guides killed the fire, and we climbed a ravine to the next plateau in silence.

At the crest of the plateau, the land far below was dotted with tiny pagodas. Tendrils of smoke drifted lazily from huts pressed against the foothills. Yak herders watched us as we descended the other side.

In oncoming dusk, we dipped through a stone channel and found ourselves staring at the Himalayas, ghostly and blue and seeming to hover off the ground, in the distance. The range was spectacular in its grandness, its solidity, forcing even the most atheistic of mankind to pause and contemplate the existence of the divine.

At the end of the valley, foothills rose to touch the faint stars. The fields gave way to sand and crushed rock. At the front of the line, the guides once again spoke to Andrew in their native tongue. Like the other conversations, this one started out like a conspiracy in hushed tones and subtle gestures, but as it progressed, it was evident Andrew was becoming agitated. His voice rose. The guides adjusted their packs and began walking in the direction of the village we'd passed only an hour or so ago.

"What's going on?" Curtis wanted to know.

"They're leaving," said Andrew. "This is as far as they'll go."

"I thought you said we were close to the Valley of Walls," said Hollinger. "You said we would reach it by nightfall."

"It's just beyond these hills," Andrew said, surveying the terrain ahead.

"Then why did they leave?" Hollinger pressed.

"Because they're superstitious," Andrew said calmly, his voice once again quiet and restrained.

Under my breath I asked Petras if he had understood any of what the two guides had said.

He considered for a moment, then turned his head away from the others and said, "They believe the Valley of Walls to be one of the levels of the *beyul*, the outer level to the Canyon of Souls. They won't set foot in the valley."

"Why not? It's not just superstition, is it?"

"Not to them," said Petras.

Andrew slung his gear over his shoulder. "Doesn't matter. I know where I am from here."

"Great." Hollinger scowled.

"The Sherpas will already have camp set up," Andrew continued.

"They'll take us to the Godesh base in the morning."

"Do you blokes get the feeling he's making this up as he goes?" Hollinger said to Petras and me, then walked away before we could answer.

I rolled my eyes and Petras shrugged.

We continued through the pass, the foothills looming on either side, as the twilight faded to a deep, resonant blackness.

CHAPTER 9

1

THE VALLEY OF WALLS WAS JUST AS IT PRO-
claimed to be: a narrow tract of land flanked by the gradual slopes of
jungle and the sheer stone of the foothills rising high above the trees.

The entranceway into the valley was defined by a rising crest of
rock on either side of the stone path, like sphinxes bowing together
to form an archway. The floor was comprised of busted shale slats
and powdery white rock between which tall, spindly weeds sprouted.
Immense boulders had come to rest at random, wreathed now in age-
old moss and dressed in fallen garland, and what looked liked tomb-
stones jutted up periodically from the earth. The valley itself had once
been a river fed by a mountaintop glacier, but that had been many years
ago before the glacier disappeared and the riverbed dried up.

We lit electric lanterns and followed Andrew. The walls seemed
to narrow and close in on us until we were hiking single file down a
sloping flume. As I passed one of the tombstone-like edifices, I swept
my lantern across its face. Monastic prayers were carved into the stone.

"It's a spiritual place," Andrew said, his tone hushed and reverent.
Somehow I'd found myself beside him at the front of the line. "The
Yogis say there is always the scent of roasted barley."

I inhaled deeply but could smell nothing except the alpine scent of the distant trees.

Ahead, the prayer stones grew increasingly large, positioned at seemingly intentional angles. Soon it was like traversing through a maze. In the light of our lanterns, our shadows grew to hideous size on the stone walls. I pressed my hand to one of the prayer stones—it towered several feet above my head and must have been about fifteen inches thick—and traced the intricate carvings. I'd first thought the "walls" were the rising foothills on either side of the valley. I realized now that I'd been wrong.

"It's amazing," I breathed.

"Few have been this far," Andrew said. "I can only imagine what else is in store for us on this trip."

"The guides," I said. "They were afraid to come here."

"Bad juju. Nothing to worry about. They saw your little accident at the bridge as an omen."

"What if it was?"

Andrew merely glanced at me and kept moving.

In the distance, firelight flickered in the darkness. It was the Sherpas. They'd come from the neighboring village, hired by Andrew to set up camp in advance. As we approached, the frying electric smell of our lanterns was overpowered by the scents of stewed meats and boiled tea leaves. The four Sherpas were dressed in heavy maroon robes, their faces white and ageless in the firelight.

"It's like the pilgrims meeting the Indians for the first time," Chad mumbled and received Hollinger's elbow in his ribs.

The Sherpas said nothing for the entire evening, though they made us very comfortable and brought us more food than we were prepared to eat. Exhausted, I set my gear down between Shotsky and Petras and peeled my sodden boots from my feet with relish. Rubbing the feeling back into my toes before the crackling fire, I could feel the events of the day already begin to drain from me.

Shotsky appeared with a steaming cup of tea and some bread. He folded himself neatly onto a straw mat and tore into the bread with vengeance.

"You doing all right?" I asked him.

"Sure. How about you? You almost bought the farm today. Good thing you thought about tying us all together like that."

I winced, working a particularly painful knot out of the bottom of my foot. "Good thing you were nervous about crossing."

Donald Shotsky smiled and nodded, his eyes reflecting the bonfire.

"You said something about needing this job," I said after a few moments of silence. Around us, the stone walls laden with scripture cast rectangular shadows on the valley floor. "Back at the bridge. Remember?"

"I guess."

"What did you mean?"

"I mean, I needed the money." He tore at another piece of bread and washed it down with tea. "You think I'd be here otherwise?"

"Hold on. You're getting paid to be here?"

Shotsky sensed my change in tone. He shot me a sideways glance. "Of course. Isn't he paying you?"

"Andrew?"

"Who else?"

"How much?"

Shotsky seemed to consider whether or not this information should be shared. After too many drawn-out seconds, it looked like he was ready to self-combust. He said, "Twenty thousand dollars."

"Motherfucker," I whispered.

"Why else would I come? For the goddamn scenery?" Shotsky said. Then added, "Why would *you* come?"

"Probably because I'm a fucking idiot," I groaned and pulled my socks back on.

Chad, Hollinger, and Curtis were playing cards beside a couple of lanterns when I walked past them twenty minutes later. Petras was taking care of personal business in the nearby woods. The Sherpas had cautioned him to carry a knife in case a bear or wild cat came sniffing around. Petras only nodded. I noticed his pearl-handled hunting knife jutting from his belt.

The Sherpas huddled together in one tent, inking long swaths of parchment and murmuring to themselves. Their tent smelled of incense and burning grape leaves and exuded an intense heat, as if the under-the-breath praying generated physical energy.

Andrew was off in the distance by himself, secluded in shadows, meditating. As I approached, my boots crunched the stones to dust beneath my weight, but Andrew did not turn around. I stood there for several minutes, staring at the back of his head, watching the slow, dilatory rise and fall of his respiration, before I felt like a fool.

"Is this something new?" I said.

"What's that?" he said, not turning to face me.

"This meditation thing. This praying. I thought you were agnostic."

He dropped his head. After a moment, he stood and rolled his sleeves up his arms. His face looked almost see-through in the moonlight. The square cut of his jaw was dressed in three days' beard growth.

"Did you pay Shotsky twenty thousand dollars to come on this trip?"

"Yes." There was no hesitation, no emotion.

"Why?"

"Because he wouldn't have come otherwise."

"And why was it so important that he come?"

"Because," he said casually, "that's the point of this whole thing, isn't it?"

"I don't understand."

He shook his head. "It doesn't matter. It's not necessary that you understand."

"Did you pay anyone else?"

"No."

"No one?"

"No one else. Just Donald."

"So why is everyone else here?"

"The same reason you are."

The thing was, I could no longer remember what my reason had been.

"Do you think this is a game, Tim?"

"I don't know."

Andrew smiled. "Neither do I."

"Shotsky shouldn't be here. He's a fucking novice. He's scared of heights for Christ's sake."

"Donald Shotsky nearly died on a crabbing boat in the Bering Sea," Andrew said, his voice turned up a notch. "Since then he's been living in a one-bedroom shithole apartment in Reno. Last I spoke with him, there were men looking for him because he owed them money. Bad men. So I offered him this job. He comes out here; he gets twenty thousand dollars. Enough to keep those bad men at bay for a bit longer."

"And what do you get out of it?"

"Why are you suddenly so accusatory?"

"Because something doesn't feel right. Something doesn't make sense."

"I think maybe you hit your head hard on that fall from the bridge."

"Don't give me that bullshit, Andrew. I asked you a question. Shotsky gets the money; what do *you* get?"

"I," he said, "get Shotsky."

I shook my head. "What do you mean?"

Andrew sighed. He bent and gathered up the mat on which he'd been meditating and rolled it into a tube. "I didn't save that man's life on that boat so he could have it taken from him by a bunch of Vegas thugs. After that accident on the boat, if he was too much of a coward to go back to work, to work like a man, then I'm going to help him overcome that fear." He grinned, and it was the old devilish Trumbauer grin. "I'm going to save his life again." He tucked the mat under one arm and stepped around me, heading back toward camp.

"Then why am I here?" I called after him.

Andrew paused. I expected him to face me, but he didn't. I didn't need to look at his face to know he was still sporting that horrible grin.

"Same reason," he said and walked away.

2

IN MY DREAMS, I SHUTTLE THE MOTORCAR OVER

the sloping lawns of the Italian countryside. Hannah laughs from the passenger seat. She is not the Hannah from real life—not the woman I was married to a million years ago—but rather she is the Hannah from my dreams, my nightmares. Her hair is short, and she wears a lambskin jacket and pantsuit. I grip the steering wheel, a silk scarf flapping in the wind. I am David, the man Hannah fell in love with after she left me. Or perhaps the man she fell in love with while she was still with me, still my wife. None of that was ever clear.

I'm not going to mess things up, I shout over the engine, the wind.

Yes, you are, she says, and she doesn't need to shout.

I've got a second chance, I say. *I'm going to make things right. I'm going to fix things for us.*

You can't, she tells me.

Why not?

Because I'm dead, she says. *And because we are flying.*

I imagine cliff diving with Andrew and how I soared naked through the air, suspended for a million eternities, before crashing down through the black, icy waters. Flying, flying . . .

What do you mean we're flying? I say.

Hannah—the Hannah from my dreams, the *dakini,* not the real Hannah—faces forward and says, *Look.*

I look and find the ground has vanished from beneath the motorcar. We are careening over a precipice, suspended in air, a pair of cliff divers, the engine groaning and the wheels spinning without traction, and the chrome headlamps glinting in the sun.

3

IN THE MORNING, THE PROXIMITY OF THE GODESH Ridge was overwhelming. The Valley of Walls lay at the base of the range, the earthen path that was once a river carved straight through a pass where it disappeared. The Sherpas said the drop had once been a beautiful waterfall, something witnessed by generations long gone. It was dry as bone now.

The mountain itself was tremendous, twisting and bulging at its foothills like slaps of clay stacked atop one another to dry in the sun, its peak obscured by cloud cover. With the waning darkness still toward the west, two of the Sherpas led us through the arid pass, their sandal-clad feet kicking up tufts of white dust. They spoke perfect English when they wanted to, but mostly they kept to themselves.

Half a mile through the pass, I could see where the rutted, dried riverbed ended at a sharp drop. Far below stood the jagged pincers of exposed, sun-bleached rocks. I could easily imagine this as a waterfall, and the quarry below still held the shape of a basin, although filled with boulders and lush with plant life. While I watched, a flock of giant black birds took flight, calling shrilly to one another.

Our group continued along the base of the foothills, winding farther and farther away from the Valley of Walls, which was now situated directly below us. From this vantage, I could see all the stone walls and how the valley itself curled slightly like a monkey's tail. From this distance, the arrangement of the walls seemed nearly prophetic, something akin to crop circles or the looming statue heads on Easter Island. I tried to derive sense from the pattern, but it meant nothing to me. And perhaps that was how it was supposed to be.

We trekked through a series of stone portals wreathed with lichen, constantly ascending at a gradual incline. There was very little to grab onto here for support, and as the incline grew steeper, my back strained and I leaned closer toward my knees. A few of us skidded in the dirt, launching cascades of tiny stones down the face of the mountain.

I couldn't help but look up as I climbed. The clouds were wispy but in copious amount, and I still could not see beyond the first summit. It was impossible to judge the distance. Yet each time we wound around the passageways (once, even entering a cave which smelled of kerosene that emptied out on the opposite side of the foothill), a new plateau would appear closer and closer above us.

"You hear that?" Curtis said, appearing at my side. He started climbing slightly faster than me. "What's that sound?"

I listened. "Sounds like . . . running water . . ."

We reached the first of many plateaus to see a waterfall clear across the valley spilling into a forested gorge. Through its mist a rainbow projected, and I could see more of those great black birds swooping down toward the water for food. If this were a movie, it would be the part where the orchestrated music would kick in while the director of photography panned the camera for the breathtaking panoramic. For us, we were content to pause in our ascent just to watch and take it all in. Even Andrew, who'd seemed to be in a bad mood all morning, leaned against the crags, arms folded, and observed the spectacle in absolute silence.

By lunch, we had crested a ridge of fir-lined rocks that overlooked the entire valley. No longer could I make out the Valley of Walls nor the tiny huts and pagodas of the villages through which we'd passed. Here, we were utterly alone. There could have been a thousand of us, and each one of us would have been alone.

The Sherpas distributed cuts of burlap on which they piled steamed rice, boiled leaves, and cubes of grayish meat. Andrew wolfed his food down, then vanished through the trees, either to take a leak or continue with his meditation. The Sherpas read books and ate very little, though they continued to stoke the small fire.

I set my food down and trotted off toward the trees. After I'd urinated, I crept deeper through the firs until I made out Andrew's shape on the other side of the brambles.

"Not much farther," he commented as I approached. He was staring at the face of the mountain, running one palm along its surface. "We'll set base camp on the next plateau and bed down for the night."

"How far up is it?"

"Depends. If we keep spiraling along the path, it'll take till nightfall. If we go straight up, we'd save some time."

"It's steep."

"It's doable. And there'll be steeper along the way."

"Are we in some kind of hurry? To save time, I mean."

Andrew rubbed his forehead, then turned to me. I felt him scrutinize my entire body. "How's your leg, the one you broke?"

"It's holding up."

"And your head?"

"Fine. Just a little ringing in the ears."

"Listen," he said, looking hard at my eyes, "I'm glad you came. Means a lot. I'm sorry I've been distant out here, but . . . well, there's been a lot on my mind."

"Anything you want to talk about?"

"Not really. Not now, anyway. Maybe later." He cast another glance toward the invisible mountaintop. "Let's worry about setting up base camp first."

After lunch, it was decided we would continue winding our way to the top by sticking to the path. Whether or not my brief conversation with Andrew had anything to do with his decision, I didn't know. Only Chad suggested we climb straight up, but the Sherpas had no interest in scaling the vertical face of a mountain.

It took four hours to reach the summit. We were all exhausted. The air was much thinner and colder, searing my lungs as my inhalations grew deeper and deeper. I dropped my gear in the fronds and pulled my shirt over my head. The cool air against my sweaty flesh felt exhilarating.

"We'll set up base camp here," Andrew said. There was a smear of dirt across his right cheek. "We've got twenty-four hours before we start the ascent of the south face."

"I can't see the top," Chad marveled, looking up with one hand shielding the sun from his eyes despite the fact he was wearing sunglasses. "There's a mist hanging low on the next ridge. Cloud cover's heavy over the first buttress, too. Looks like rain."

I poured a splash of water from one of the plastic water bottles into a cupped hand, then lathered my bare skin—arms, chest, stomach, shoulders.

"You still jonesing?" Chad asked me.

"You starting up again with this?"

"Don't be so quick to jump down my throat, Shakes. I'm offering to share with you."

"Share what? You got a bottle of bourbon in that pack?"

"Not quite." He withdrew a cigar vial from his belt and unscrewed the cap. A joint the width of a thumb slid partway out into the palm of his hand.

"I take it that's not a Swisher Sweet," I commented.

Chad grinned. "One toke and it'll feel like someone put your head on backward."

"I'll pass."

"You sure? I'm lighting this fat fucker up as soon as the sun's down and the fire's going."

"I'm sure."

Chad shook the joint back into the vial and replaced the cap. "Anyway, you're welcome, Overleigh," he muttered and strode away, his heavy boots crunching the gravel.

The Sherpas coaxed a sizable bonfire from a nest of branches at the center of camp, while the rest of us set up the large canvas tent that would serve as our communal shelter. It was approximately the size of a carport with reinforced plastic sheathing for windows and a floor of double-ply tarpaulin. It was hardly tall enough to permit any of us to stand without stooping over, and we quickly ran out of corners to stash our personal gear.

By nightfall the Sherpas had prepared a fine meal of hot vegetable broth, freshly baked bread, and boiling green tea, which we all devoured in silent reverie. With the darkness came the cold; while the tent kept the wind at bay, the most heat was generated outside by the large bonfire. I took a seat on the ground, sipping my third cup of hot tea, to warm my feet at the base of the fire. Petras's looming shadow fell across me, followed by Curtis's, and they both sat on either side of me.

"Cheers, boys," I said, raising my cup and taking a sip.

"Not to tell tales out of school," Curtis said, "but you guys catch the way old Shotsky was huffin' and puffin' coming up the ridge today? I thought the poor bastard was going to keel over at one point."

"He won't make it," Hollinger opined, coming up behind us. "There's no way."

Curtis slid a slender black finger beneath his nose and turned his gaze toward the fire. "What's he doing here, anyway? He's not a climber. He's a goddamn greenhorn. Should be hoisting crab pots onto a boat in the Arctic."

"Let him be," Petras said. "He's here for his own reasons. Just like we are."

I thought about telling the guys that Andrew had paid Shotsky to be here. In fact, I opened my mouth but decided against it at the last minute.

No one except Petras noticed; his eyes narrowed, but he didn't say anything. After a moment, he turned and looked at the fire.

Curtis's face soured. "You can be as polite as you want to, Petras, but fact is fact. And fact just might be someone'll have to hike back down to base camp when the poor bastard cramps up or suffers a heart attack or stroke or something."

"Men will surprise you," Petras said.

"Shit," said Curtis. "I know *that's* true."

As if summoned by the sheer mention of his name, Donald Shotsky materialized on the other side of the bonfire. His face glowing in the flames and shadows dancing across his features, he grinned a big, stupid grin and raised a hand at us. "Hey, guys."

We mumbled and nodded at him.

He came over, followed by Chad. God knew how long he'd been lingering close by in the shadows.

Chad slid his cigar vial off his belt and unscrewed the cap. "I feel—," he began but was interrupted by a growl of thunder.

We all looked up, mouths agape. In the distance, above the cover of low-hanging clouds, bleached blue light flared and resonated in the filaments of our retinas.

Chad summoned an even wider grin and proffered the fat joint. "As I was saying, I feel the need to perform an age-old unifying ritual with you boys, passed down from generation to generation, going back all the way to the first huddle of stinking cavemen who sat in mud up to their balls, pissing on their feet."

"Look at the size of that thing." Hollinger laughed.

"It's primo, all right." Chad produced a Zippo and ran the flame around the twisted tip. Then he popped the other end into his mouth, lit the joint, and inhaled with gusto. The bonfire was not strong enough to mask the smell of the marijuana.

"Didn't Trumbauer say something about keeping us pure?" Curtis said, accepting the joint from Chad. "No liquor, no cigarettes, no fatty foods."

"Technically," Chad offered, "this is none of the above."

Curtis exposed his very white teeth. "Technically." He pulled a long drag, holding the smoke between his forefinger and thumb like an old pro.

"Where *is* Andrew?" I asked.

"On the other side of the far hill," Shotsky said. "He's mediating or something. Wanted to be alone. I didn't realize he was such a religious son of a bitch."

"Had a dream last night," Hollinger said. The joint was pinched between two of his fingers now. "I was alone and stumbling around in the dark. We'd gotten separated in a system of caves halfway through the mountain. I could hear the lot of you talking through the walls, but your voices echoed all over, and I couldn't pin you down. And every time I went in the direction where I thought one of you blokes might be, I walked smack into a wall of stone. So I kept feeling around the walls, thinking that if I ran my hands along the wall, I'd eventually follow it out into the open. But I realized I was in a tiny enclosed chamber made of icy cold stone, and there was no way in and no way out. As if I'd just appeared in a bubble of rock."

"It's a Freudian sex dream," Chad chimed in. "Means you're shooting blanks."

"Go to hell."

"I'm serious, mate," Chad insisted, executing a fairly decent Australian accent. "Means the old skin boat ain't shuttling passengers to Tuna Town."

The joint made its way to me. I considered it, then declined. I was expecting grief from the others, but no one said anything. Petras took the joint from me and examined it with the scrutiny of a Philatelist holding an old postage stamp up to the light. Then he leaned forward and handed the joint to Chad.

"Well," Curtis said, "my daughter told me not to come."

"Oh yeah?" Shotsky said. "How old is she?"

Curtis took a worn leather wallet from his BDUs and fished out what appeared to be a school photograph of a young girl with frizzy braids and two missing front teeth. "There's my baby girl," he said, passing the photograph to the rest of the crew.

"Adorable," Petras said, nodding.

"Her mother still in the picture?" Chad wanted to know.

"She is but not with me. Lucinda lives with her mother in Utah most of the year. I get her every other holiday and two weeks in the summer."

"Bummer, man," said Shotsky. "She's a cutie."

"And a handful." The picture returned to Curtis. He held it close to his face, smiling warmly at his daughter who was currently on the other side of the world. Then he kissed the photograph and slid it back into his wallet. "G'night, baby girl."

Lightning once again blossomed beyond the veil of clouds overhead, followed by a peal of thunder so close I could feel it in my bones. A second later, we were caught in a thunderous downpour. The rain hammered down in sheets, striking like icy spears. We scrambled to our feet and quickly grabbed what gear remained scattered around the drowning bonfire and tossed it into the tent in assembly-line fashion.

I heaved a backpack toward Petras and glanced behind me over the craggy hillock. The Sherpas pulled hoods over their heads and vanished like ghosts into their own shelter.

"Where's Andrew?" I shouted. The rain plastered my hair over my eyes and pooled into my mouth. "Petras! Petras!"

Another whip crack of thunder and the entire mountain illuminated like a pillar of fire. The storm had snuck up on us out of nowhere. I glanced up, shielding my eyes from the needling rain. The clouds above were black as roofing tar and slowly drifting counterclockwise in a vague circular shape.

I turned and cupped my mouth with both hands. "Andrew! Andrew!"

A shape darted across the campsite: Chad. I could make out his bright neon parka even in the dark. He trampled the steaming, blackened heap that had moments ago been the bonfire and sprinted toward the hillock. I followed, cognizant of Petras shouting my name as I ran.

"Where is he?" I huffed, skidding to a muddy halt beside Chad.

"Don't see him." Chad was farther up a gradual incline, peering over the ridge to the cupped pool of rocks below.

I waited for the next lightning strike, hoping it would reveal Andrew below, unharmed.

"I don't think—no, wait. Wait—" Chad took a step forward, and the crest of the ridge broke apart. His arms pinwheeled, and he bowed backward. Then he pitched forward as his feet fell away beneath him.

I grabbed a fistful of his parka just as a mudslide broke across the ground quick as a serpent. "Chad!"

He went over the edge, dragging me forward. My chest slammed against the rock as the cascade of mud pooled into the cuffs of my cargo pants and washed over my body. My arm seesawed over the broken crest of the ridge, the sharp rock slicing my flesh. I groaned and sat up, mud splattered and freezing, and grabbed a second handful of Chad's parka. He was heavy as hell; I could feel the tendons straining in my arms.

"Tim! Tim!" It was Petras, his voice nearly in my ear. I felt his hands slide beneath my armpits and wrap around my chest, his hands coming together in a death grip. My breath was squeezed out of me as Petras pulled me against his chest.

"Don't let go," I moaned, not sure if I'd actually managed to speak the words or not.

In a flash of lightning, I caught a glimpse of Chad's terrified eyes staring at me from over the ridge. He seized my arms with both hands, but the rainwater made it impossible for him to get a secure grip. His cheeks were quivering. For one horrifying second, as another bolt of lightning lashed out overhead, I thought I could see his skull through his skin.

"Come on!" I cried, trying to pull him up. "Come on, Chad!"

"Don't fucking drop me, Shakes," he said, his voice quavering.

"Don't you fucking drop me."

"Won't happen," I promised. "Get one of your feet up."

The pain ratcheted in my arms and shoulders as he swung toward the face of the cliff and tried to dig his boots into the rock. But like a cartoon character, his legs only cycled wildly in the air, pushing him farther from the face of the cliff and back out over the abyss.

Hollinger and Curtis were suddenly at my side, feeding a length of rope down to Chad over the jagged ridge.

"Watch your footing, guys," I cautioned them, my breath coming in gasps and wheezes. "The ground's turned to mud."

Hollinger pointed to the rope and shouted to Curtis, "Don't let the rope floss the rock, mate! It'll rupture."

Curtis dived forward and grasped the rope in gloved hands, his head two inches away from my own. I could see the deep trenches in the mud that his knees had made as he slid across the incline. The trenches quickly filled with water.

"Grab the rope!" Curtis shouted to Chad.

"He's slipping," I said through clenched teeth. I couldn't tell if anyone had heard me. "I'm losing him . . ."

"Come on, Chad!" Curtis continued. "There! There! It's in front of your face, man!"

"Use your feet," Hollinger yelled.

My hands were numb; I could no longer tell if I was still holding on to Chad's parka. I closed my eyes, my teeth chattering, my arms quaking. My chest was going to burst at any second. The breath whistling up my throat was the breath of a volcano.

The rope went taut.

"Here—here—" Curtis pitched forward as the top of Chad's sopping head appeared over the crest of the ridge. "Gimme your hand—"

One of Chad's hands swung around and clamped down on Curtis's elbow.

Curtis grabbed Chad by the seat of his pants.

How the hell is Curtis not falling? How is he not toppling right over the ridge?

"Heave!" Curtis hollered.

A moment later, Chad sprawled on top of him, both of them covered from head to toe in black mud. There was a second rope tied around Curtis's waist. I trailed it with my eyes toward a forked tree where Donald Shotsky still held the other end of the rope, both his feet planted against the bifurcated tree trunk.

Petras loosened his grip but didn't let go. He yanked me away from the edge of the cliff, as if to simply release me would send me shooting like a rocket out of the abyss . . . and given the adrenaline burning through my body, I might have done just that.

"I'm okay. I'm okay," I huffed.

Petras released me fully as Hollinger patted the top of my head like I was a child.

"Me, too," Chad wheezed, pulling himself off Curtis. His pale face was streaked with mud, his eyes blinking away the rainwater. Somewhat unsteadily he got up on his knees and gripped his hips with jittery hands. "Saved my life, Shakes."

I nodded like a fool. I didn't know what I wanted to say.

"Come on," Petras said, clapping me on the back. He caught one of my elbows and helped me to my feet. "Before the whole lot of us catch pneumonia."

Soaking wet and freezing, I wiped the hair out of my eyes. Lightning struck again, followed by the locomotive clang of thunder, but it was creeping over the valley and away from the mountain. The rain was beginning to let up now, too.

Andrew appeared in the lightning flash. He was perched on the crest of the ridge no more than twenty feet away, his eyes like hollowed black pits, his mouth a lipless slash. I could tell he was looking straight at me. I thought about going over and shoving him and asking where the hell he'd been when Chad nearly plummeted off the side of the mountain, but something in the way he just *sat* there staring in the darkness stopped me.

Petras shook my arm. "Come on. Let's get in the goddamn tent."

I followed him, feeling Andrew's eyes on my back the entire time.

CHAPTER 10

1

—OPEN YOUR EYES.

The acrid stench of burning fuel, of melting rubber . . .

—Tim, she said. *Open your eyes.*

2

MY EYES OPEN TO A RAGING INFERNO. I CAN FEEL the fire ravaging my flesh, charring me alive. I glance down and see that my hands are on fire. Through the flames I discern the suggestion of my bones, blackened and like tree limbs bound together by string.

—Tim . . . The rasping voice—hardly a voice at all—summoning me.

My eyelids disintegrate, and my skin sloughs like melting wax off my skull.

—Tim . . . Hannah's body, twisted like a corkscrew, matted with dirt and blood, so much blood. She raises a mangled hand in my direction. Her legs are on fire.

I grab her hand, then her other hand, and pull her away from the burning vehicle. Her legs leave streaks of fire in the dry earth.

Don't die, I beg her. Don't die on me, Hannah. Please.

She smiles. Her face is a black pit, a coconut smashed with a hammer and streaked with crimson gore. That mangled hand comes up again and touches my face. My skin slides off into her bloodied palm. Something hard and spiny rolls over in the pit of my stomach.

No, I plead. No, Hannah.

—*Tim,* she says. *Open your eyes.*

No—

—*Open your eyes.*

3

MY EYES OPENED TO INFINITE BLACKNESS. I WAS on my back, my hands folded across my bare chest, breathing hard. I blinked. It took several seconds for me to realize where I was.

I eased up on my elbows, the sounds of collective snoring amplified in the canvas tent. Sweat matted my hair to my head; I could almost feel heat rising off my flesh. It was difficult to breathe, the air in the tent stale and motionless. I peeled the flap of my sleeping bag off my nude, sweaty body and pulled on a pair of clean sweatpants. I negotiated through the dark to the zippered tent flaps, which I opened as quietly as possible, and crept outside.

The air was bitterly cold. My nipples hardened instantly, and my sweat froze on my body. I shivered and rubbed my hands along my forearms while I felt my testicles retreat into the cavity of my abdomen. The rain had moved on across the valley, taking with it the angry-looking thunderheads that had hovered over our camp just hours ago.

Something moved in the darkness ahead of me: a flitting shape, large and alive, hardly visible through the trees.

"Hannah." My voice was no louder than a harsh whisper.

The shape continued on through the trees.

Barefoot, I walked across the camp through freezing puddles

of mud and frost-stiffened reeds. My left eyelid began twitching. "Hannah . . ."

The shape crossed the veil of trees. It paused as the sound of my voice reached it. Then it proceeded up the gradual incline that was the ridge's pinnacle. I watched the figure slip out into the open, lighted now by the soft glow of the moon. It wasn't a human figure at all.

It was a wolf. Its pelt shimmered silver blue in the night. As its eyes turned toward me, curious of my presence, they glowed like floating, pearl-colored orbs. I watched it, my breath caught in my throat. I could feel its eyes boring into me. Then, with casual disinterest, it turned away from me and padded silently up the incline. I watched it until it disappeared over the ridge like a ghost.

"Tim." It was a man's voice.

I jerked my head around quick enough to crimp the tendons. A liquid hot pain spread across the side of my neck. Andrew stood behind me in a pair of faded chinos and a wifebeater. Half his face glowed with the light of a full moon.

Andrew raised both hands, palms facing me. "You okay, man?"

"You scared the shit out of me," I uttered, finding my breath.

"You out here looking for someone?"

"Just collecting my thoughts." Had he heard me calling Hannah's name? "Did I wake you?"

"Wasn't asleep."

"Where were you?"

"The tent stinks like sweaty men," he said with a smirk. "Just needed some fresh air."

"No," I said. "I meant, where were you earlier tonight when Chad almost bought the farm? We could have used the extra pair of hands."

After the incident, we'd all gathered in the tent where we collectively stripped our clothes and washed the mud and filth off us with fresh rainwater. Andrew had appeared during the process, and

I'd fumed as he crossed into the tent and peeled off his own sopping clothes. I'd thought some of the others might start attacking him, bombarding him with questions, but that didn't happen.

Chad had talked a mile a minute about how he'd almost died, grinning and clapping us on the back. He recounted what had happened to Andrew without seeming to realize Andrew had been missing. Only Petras noticed my unease with Andrew, but he didn't say anything. Apparently I had been the only one to see Andrew watching all that had transpired from his perch on the ridge. I considered mentioning this to Petras but decided against it.

"I was taking a leak," Andrew said now. "I didn't even realize anything had happened."

"Okay," I said, my fists clenching. "Cut it the fuck out. Chad was on that ledge because he was looking for you. If I hadn't followed him and grabbed his coat as he went over the side, we'd be scooping him up off the rocks down there and carrying him home in our canteens."

One of Andrew's shoulders rolled. "What would you like me to say? It's a scary thing, but this isn't exactly a trip to the zoo. We're all grown men. We know what we've got ourselves into."

"I *saw* you." I took a step toward him. "I saw you sitting on that fucking ridge, watching the whole thing."

"You're wrong. Calm down."

"Don't fucking tell me to calm down. I saw you sitting there."

Andrew sighed and raked a hand through his hair. He looked caught between a laugh and a sob. "I was taking a piss on the other side of the hill. When the rain hit and the mud started pouring down the side of the hill, it became too slippery to climb up. And when I *did* climb up, you guys had already pulled Chad over the ridge. It was all over before I could do anything."

"So you just sat the fuck down and watched us?"

"I was exhausted from climbing through the mud."

I glanced away from him in the direction the wolf had gone only moments before. "You were gone for a long goddamn time just to take a piss."

"I told you. The rain and the mud—"

"Before that," I said, glaring at him and taking another step closer. "You'd disappeared long before that. The rest of us were bullshitting by the fire, and you were off gallivanting." My fists were shaking, and my vision began to blur. "What the fuck's going on here?"

"Go to bed, Tim."

"Answer me."

"I said—"

"Who do you think you are?" I growled. "Don't tell me what to do. I swear to God I'll flatten you right here."

"This was a mistake." Andrew threw his hands up. "I thought you were ready for this. It's my fault. The whole goddamn thing was a mistake. When the rest of us take off for the first pinnacle, you can go back to the valley with the Sherpas. They'll take you to the roads that lead back into town. You can get a bus from—"

I hit him in the face. It was a poor, clumsy punch, but it hit with solidity, and I could feel Andrew's jawbone through his cheek and against my knuckles.

Andrew stumbled backward seemingly more shocked than hurt, a hand up to his jaw. His eyebrows knitted together, creating a vertical divot between them, and he didn't take his eyes off me.

"I told you not to tell me what to do," I said quietly.

Andrew's gaze shifted to the fist that had struck him, which was still balled at my side. His face was expressionless. "Okay, Tim. Okay. Maybe I deserve it. Maybe I've been distant and aloof and removed from the whole damn thing, keeping all you guys in the dark. So, yeah, maybe I deserve it. I'm sorry."

I wanted to tell him to shut the hell up, but my body refused to cooperate. I sat on a large white stone and pulled my legs under me.

I kept my eyes locked on Andrew for fear that if I looked away he might vanish into the night.

"You said you'd left us in the dark," I said finally. "What haven't you told us? And no more games."

Andrew took a deep breath and sat down beside me. "That maybe we shouldn't be here." He chuckled. "All right, you caught me. I wasn't just taking a piss tonight."

I stared at him.

"I was praying," he said. "Meditating. Trying to lock into the power of the land. The power of the gods."

"Meditating," I repeated. "You don't believe in that stuff."

"That doesn't matter here."

"Why shouldn't we be here?"

"Because there are a lot of people who think no one should climb the Godesh Ridge," he said. "You can forget about the folklore, the campy stories, or even the facts—the men who've died trying. You can't deny those things, but that's not all of it. Fact is, we're some big-time violators for coming here. The Godesh Ridge is sacred, a holy land, a temple not to be pursued, not even by the monks, the Yogis. No one. And the same holds true for the Canyon of Souls."

I thought about Shomas, the hulking man who'd been waiting for me that night outside my cabin and whom I'd chased—or imagined I'd chased—through the streets of a rural village days later.

"A *beyul*," I said, which seemed to catch Andrew's interest.

"Where'd you hear that?"

"Petras. You're familiar with the term?"

"Sure."

"Is that what this canyon is? A *beyul*? A hidden land not meant to be found?"

"I suppose."

"That's why the guides turned back after the bridge," I said. "That's why they wouldn't lead us into the Valley of Walls."

"The Valley of Walls is considered a gateway to the ridge and the first in many stops along the way to the Canyon of Souls. There are others, too—the Sanctuary of the Gods, the Hall of Mirrors—and many of the indigenous people of this area will not corrupt the land with their presence. Simultaneously they believe we're corrupting it by being here. To them, we're no different than a band of grave robbers."

He gripped my shoulder and squeezed it. It was a gesture very unlike him. "I meditate to maintain a connection with the land and to show my respect. Please don't let that weaken your trust in me to lead this mission. I haven't lost my mind, and I haven't dragged you all into something I can't handle."

"We shouldn't be here." I cast a wary glance at the sky. It was as clear as lucid thought. The moon hung fat and yellow, larger than I had ever seen it.

"You never struck me as the superstitious type, Overleigh." He was back to using my last name, and I was helpless to remember the day we first met in San Juan. This caused me to think once again of Hannah . . .

"Has nothing to do with superstition," I corrected him. "I know for a fact that we've pissed off at least one of the locals from Churia. I met him, and he didn't seem too happy with our little crew."

"Don't let that bother you."

"And then there's Donald Shotsky."

"What about him?"

"For one," I said, "the fact that he'll never make it. He's been struggling already, and we haven't even started to climb. The man's never climbed anything more strenuous than a flight of stairs in his life."

"We've already discussed Shotsky. I've explained it to you."

"You've explained your deranged reason for wanting him out here, but that doesn't make it right."

Andrew chuckled and repeated the word *deranged*, as if it were the punch line to a joke.

"Make me a promise."

"Yeah? What's that?" Andrew said.

"Promise me you won't break him. Promise me that if he can't make it to the end, you'll cut him loose."

"I'm not holding a gun to the man's—"

"So then promise me you'll let him off the hook if he feels he can't finish this."

Andrew's fingers drummed on his knees. "All right, if *he* feels he can't finish . . ."

"And that you'll give him the money."

His eyebrows froze in twin arches above his eyes. He said nothing.

"The twenty grand," I went on. "Promise me."

His eyes narrowed, and he clasped his hands in his lap, staring at the blackened heap of carbon that had been our bonfire earlier this evening. "And if I don't promise?" he said, not looking at me.

"Then I walk. Right here, right now—tonight. I'll pack my shit and head back to the valley. You flexed your muscles a few minutes ago and told me to do just that, but I know that's not what you want. You're here to make us all better, to fix what you think is broken in us, just like you said. Despite what you said, you don't want me to leave. You very much want me to stay."

I was working off a hunch, not quite sure *what* Andrew wanted. For one moment, I thought he might actually tell me to pack my stuff and leave. But when he faced me, his eyes somber and ancient, I knew I had called his bluff. Relief washed through me.

"Twenty grand's a lot of money," he said offhandedly.

"Not for you. Won't put a dent in your wallet." I knew this was true; after all, he'd paid for the whole goddamn trip.

"Why do you care, anyway?"

"I guess I don't want another death on my conscience."

Andrew's expression softened. "Been thinking about her tonight?"

"You mean Hannah," I said. It was not a question. And he didn't need to ask it. "I guess so. She's been on my mind a lot lately."

"Mine, too." He smiled wearily. He looked like he could close his eyes and fall asleep right here. "She was something else."

"Yes, she was." I laughed nervously. My vision was starting to blur.

"Okay," he said. "You've got a deal on this Shotsky thing. Against my better judgment, you've got a deal."

"Good." I shook my hair down in my eyes and pawed at my mouth with one hand. "Christ, I could use a fucking drink."

"Then take one," Andrew said and stood. He stretched his spine, the tendons popping in his neck and back. "Don't stay out here too late, bro. Get some sleep."

I said nothing more to him. He didn't seem to care or even notice. He strutted back to the tent, pausing to urinate over the side of the ridge for what seemed like twenty minutes. For someone so concerned about being in touch with the land, it seemed a rather vulgar gesture.

4

ANDREW'S COMMENT DIDN'T REGISTER WITH ME until I awoke maybe an hour later back in the tent, the tendrils of a passing dream still tickling my chest. I rolled over and blindly groped for my pack until I found what I was looking for.

It was the canteen Andrew had placed inside my cabin before departing on this trek. Sitting up on one arm, I unscrewed the cap and brought the canteen to my nose and inhaled.

Bourbon.

What the hell is going on here?

I was still pondering the meaning of it before I had time to consider what I was doing. Two swigs from the canteen and the bourbon seared my throat and exploded in the pit of my stomach like a car bomb, its warmth spreading through me like the serpentine tentacles of some nonspecific cancer.

PART THREE

THE GODESH RIDGE

CHAPTER 11

1

THE ONES THAT WERE FOUND WERE PRACTICALLY
unidentifiable. Hardly human, they were fragile, blue-skinned husks
whose eyes had frozen to custard smears in their sockets, whose
mouths were textured with colorless sores and frozen in a grimace of
torment and pain.

Typically they were wrapped in layers of clothes, tattered and
faded and solid as planks of wood. Others were found nude, fooled
by the onset of hypothermia where their skin burned and sweat dim-
pled their flesh even in the freezing temperatures. There was one
story about a man frozen solid to the wall of an ice cave, glazed like
a donut by a two-inch sheen of ice. His hands were sheared clear of
the wrists as rescuers attempted to hammer the corpse from the ice,
the blood within frozen to a dark purple slush.

Others returned defeated. Frostbitten, starving, anemic, and delirious from high altitudes and snow blindness, they staggered back
into base camp like petrified zombies, their tendons hardened to
broomsticks, their hands hooked into claws or molded into flippers.
These were the lucky ones.

Lastly there were the ones who were never seen again. The

disappeared. Separated from their groups or foolish soloists with no perception of mortality, these poor bastards were fated to slip down mile-deep crevasses, tumble off a shaky precipice, or become swallowed up by a sudden avalanche. Occasionally search parties would locate articles of their clothing or uncover evidence of what had presumably befallen them—a broken anchor halfway up the face of a cliff or a length of rope with a frayed end swaying in the cool wind over an abyss—but their bodies were never found.

What gear that was eventually recovered told a tale of frantic last moments: utensils scattered about rocky formations; pots and pans half filled with glacier water purified with iodine tablets; boots tossed in snowdrifts; vinyl flags staked in erratic patterns in the mountainside. Some left behind claw marks in the ice.

These were the stories that fueled the myth of the Godesh Ridge. I did not doubt them—I had heard similar ones about much of the Himalayas that I knew to be true—but I did not pay them much mind, either. I'd done my fair share of research in Annapolis while I was still debating whether or not to join Andrew and his crew in Nepal. These stories circulated the Internet like high school rumors. Despite the myth that surrounded the Godesh Ridge—the fact that it was a Nepalese hidden land or John Petras's *beyul* and quite possibly haunted—the stories were no different than any other mountaineering story found in a book or in a copy of *National Geographic*. I paid them little mind.

However, as we began the ascent up the southern face of the mountain, the stories returned to me in all their gory detail. In my mind's eye, I could see the frozen bodies with white, rubbery skin coated in a slick mat of ice, the scattered assortment of hiking gear melting impressions in the snow, the random boot jutting footless from a bank of powder.

It wasn't fear that brought these thoughts back to me. It was the bourbon from last night finally filtering out of my system. I'd downed half the canteen before screwing the cap back on and rolling over, my stomach burning with the calming roil of booze. My hands had stopped shaking, and my vision, even in the darkness of the tent, seemed to clear. Outside, I could hear the powerful wind barrel down the chasms and stir the trees along the edge of our camp.

Now in the light of a new day, I was going through withdrawal all over again.

The brown earth and whitish reeds graduated to snow midway through the afternoon. An hour after that, the snow was already several inches deep. I paused at one point and cupped a handful of snow, which I brought up to my face, wiping away the sweat and dampening my hair. Our group had paired off in twos, except for Petras and me who'd taken up the rear of the line to keep Shotsky company; in the lead, Andrew and Curtis appeared to be about a quarter of a mile ahead of us. They looked like small, colorless stones poking out from the snow.

"Good idea." Shotsky dropped to his knees and massaged handfuls of snow against his face. "God, that feels good!"

"You hanging in there?"

"Yeah," he said, planting both hands into the snow and resting on all fours. I could see vapor billowing from his mouth with each exhalation.

"Don't leave your hands in the snow too long," I cautioned him. "Or your knees."

He was in shorts, as were Petras and I. When he stood, which required some assistance, I could see his thick knees were fire engine red and dripping with melted snow.

"Jesus," Shotsky said, running the back of one hand along his forehead. "I'm sweatin' like a whore on Judgment Day."

"Come on," I urged him and was immediately tossed a glare from Petras.

We continued up the incline. To our right, huge black rocks rose out of the snow like smokestacks of a sunken ship on the floor of the ocean. By late afternoon, the sky had opened. The winding, serpentine backbone of the Himalayas was visible straight through to the horizon, great blue vestiges whose arrangement appeared to be preordained.

"Look there," Petras said at one point. He shook my arm lightly, while Shotsky staggered close behind us. "That's Everest."

Even from this distance it was tremendous, dwarfing the other mountains that surrounded it. Clouds encircled its midsection like the frozen rings of Saturn.

"You trying to beat some record, Tim?" Petras said.

I glanced over my shoulder. "Huh?"

"You're walking too fast. You're going to burn yourself out before nightfall."

"No way."

"It's not a race."

It was the shakes—I could feel them coming on again sooner than last time. The past half a mile the only thing I could think about was the canteen half filled with bourbon stowed inside my pack. Even looking across the reach to the haunting stretch of Mount Everest, it was all I could think about. Movement was the only thing that kept the shaking at bay.

"Man's like a bullet," I heard Shotsky wheeze behind me. I didn't bother to turn and look at him.

You have to kick this, I told myself. *There's no way you'll finish with your mind on a flask of booze. Dump it out in the snow. Do it now. Do it.*

I wouldn't do it. I *couldn't* do it.

"You better keep a good pace, Tim, unless you want to reopen that scar on your left leg," Petras said. He was keeping stride with me now.

"I'll be fine."

"How'd you do it?"

I hocked a wad of yellowish phlegm into the snow and said, "Caving. Fell through a ravine in the dark. Bone came through the leg. I was stupid. Careless."

"Falls happen."

"I was alone."

"How come?"

"Hey, hey—" I stopped and looked at him, my eyes hard. "This an inquisition, man?"

"I just want to know what's weighing you down."

"Look," I said, "I like you. I really do. But my ghosts are mine. Okay?"

John Petras seemed to mull things over. Finally he raised both his hands and said, "Sorry. I surrender."

We continued walking. I suddenly felt like a heel. Petras hadn't deserved my response and I knew it—even as I said it I knew it—but I had been right: my ghosts were mine, after all . . .

I glanced over my shoulder. Donald Shotsky had fallen behind, far enough to be out of earshot. "Andrew's playing the savior," I said, anxious to bring up something other than old ghosts. "He's always been eccentric, but this time his ego's riding him bareback."

"The heck are you getting at?"

I told him about Shotsky and how he owed some bookies in Las Vegas twenty thousand dollars. "Andrew thinks this trip will . . . I don't know . . . build character or kick his gambling habit or some shit. Like a goddamn twelve-step program, he brought Shotsky here to fix him."

"How do you know this?"

"Shotsky told me. And when I confronted Andrew, he told me, too. He's paying Shotsky the twenty grand to take this trip."

If the news surprised Petras, it didn't register on his face. He continued to trudge through the deepening snow, the incline growing increasingly steep.

"So," I went on, "it seems we're all apparently here for a reason . . ."

"What's yours? Or is that too personal?" He smiled warmly to show he was ribbing me.

I offered a resigned grin back. I'd already mentioned the death of my wife to Petras the first night we met when he drilled me about my reasons for coming here. I reminded him of it now, though I kept the details vague. "She left because I wasn't the husband I should have been. I was an up-and-coming artist whose sole focus was on getting beyond the up-and-coming status. She always came second. Always. Until she left."

"The moment they leave," said Petras, "is the moment we realize their true worth."

"After she left, I tried hard to get her back. And after she died, I found I couldn't sculpt anymore. I tried but couldn't do it. Haven't done it since."

"Ah, she was your muse."

"I guess." The notion made me smile. "Regardless, I gave up sculpting for a life on the edge."

Raising one eyebrow and glancing over the ridge, Petras said, "Pun intended?"

I laughed.

"So Andrew believes you coming out here will help you get over your wife's death? Maybe you'll learn to sculpt again?"

I snorted and said, "He mailed me a giant slab of granite; did I tell you that? Had it shipped right to my apartment."

"Did you sculpt anything from it?"

"I tried. But it didn't work out. It wouldn't take."

Petras snickered. "You sound like a surgeon attempting an organ transplant. Operation was a success, but the patient died. Wouldn't take."

"Sometimes I feel that way."

"Like a surgeon?"

"No, like the patient." I reached out and touched his giant shoulder. "We're cool, right? I didn't mean to—"

"Don't sweat it." He winked. "Never been cooler."

Shotsky's voice rang out, startling me with how far away he sounded. I turned to find that he had indeed lagged quite far behind us. He raised one hand and stumbled forward. I anticipated his fall before it actually happened: a stiffening of his limbs followed by a keeling over to one side. He thumped down in a plume of powdered snow.

"Shit," I said. Petras and I dropped our packs and sprinted toward him. I expected to find him unconscious, but as we approached I could see his legs moving back and forth along the ground, carving arcs in the snow. As our shadows fell over him, he moaned.

"What happened?" Petras asked. "What's the matter?"

"Cramped . . . up . . ." He looked like someone in pain attempting to smile.

"Where?"

"Left . . . leg . . ."

Petras bent and felt his calf muscle. "It's tightening up," he said, glancing at me. He then looked back down at Shotsky and told him to straighten his leg while he massaged his calf muscle.

"Jesus!" Shotsky hissed.

I grappled with the walkie-talkie on Shotsky's pack, wiping water off it with the sleeve of my anorak and bringing it to my face. "Andrew, this is Tim. Over."

"I'm okay," Shotsky said. "Tim—"

"You got your talkie on, Trumbauer?" I said into the handheld.

Andrew's voice returned, full of static: "Go. Over."

"Shotsky's down. Leg's cramped up. Over."

"You want help? Over."

"How's he feel?" I asked Petras.

"Guys, I'm . . . I'm fine . . ." But he was still wincing.

Petras nodded. "He's coming along."

I keyed the handheld and said, "You go on ahead. We're gonna sit out with him for a bit."

"Stay in the passage along the black rocks," Andrew returned. I could see him at the crest of the precipice far in the distance. "We'll set up camp at the top. Don't leave the passage, Tim. Over."

"No problem. Over."

I waited for something more—perhaps for him to keep his part of the bargain—but he did not respond.

"Spread your toes and bend your ankle," Petras told Shotsky. "Bring your toes toward your head."

"I can't spread . . . my toes . . ."

"Try."

"Boot's too tight." Shotsky sucked in a deep breath, then blurted, "Fucking boot's been too tight the whole fucking trip!"

Without missing a beat, Petras popped the laces and yanked the boot off Shotsky's foot. Shotsky winced and sucked air in through his clenched teeth. Petras clamped one hand against the bottom of Shotsky's foot and bent it upward. Shotsky's toes spread, expanding the tip of his sock like webbing.

"Get bigger boots," Petras told him after he was done.

Only ten minutes had passed, but Andrew and Curtis had already disappeared over the crest of the passage. Hollinger and Chad were close behind them.

"We lose much time?" Shotsky asked, lacing his boot.

"Not much," I said.

"Goddamn boots. Goddamn cramping leg muscle. Is it getting late?"

"We still have a few hours of daylight left."

"Lousy goddamn boots. I'm sorry, guys."

I waved a hand at him, yet I was anxious to start moving again. My hands were shaking. When I looked up, I noticed Petras watching me. His face held no expression.

Shotsky managed to gather his feet beneath him. He dusted the snow off his clothes, his face red and flushed. I could easily picture him as a bloated Popsicle frozen to the wall of an ice cave, his eyes hardened pebbles recessed into the black sockets of his skull.

By the time we crested the passage, Shotsky was behind again. Petras caught my arm and told me to wait. My heart rate was thrumming; I wanted to keep going and to get my mind off the remaining alcohol in my pack.

"I'm okay," Shotsky called from farther down the slope.

"Asshole's going to break his neck," I commented to Petras.

"Or kill one of us in the process. Listen," Petras continued, lowering his voice. "About what you said before—Shotsky and the twenty grand and all. Let's keep that between us, yeah? No need to let any of the others find out."

"You think they'd be pissed?"

"What I think is we've got a crew of alpha males, each of them like to think they're the one in charge. They find out this is some kind of mind game on Andrew's part, and we may have an all-out mutiny on our hands. And seven headstrong individuals going their separate ways on this mountain is a bad idea. So if it's all the same to you, I think we should keep up the façade. Whatever you've learned doesn't need to leave this passageway."

"Fine by me."

"Guys . . . ," Shotsky called. He leaned against one of the large black stones, breathing hard. The skyline was bruising toward dusk. "Wait up . . ."

Petras sighed and rubbed the side of his face, covering his mouth from Shotsky's view. "Anyway, we got bigger problems, I think."

Petras and I grabbed Shotsky by the arms and hoisted him off the rock. He groaned and said he needed just a few minutes to rest.

"It's getting dark," I said, "and we need to catch up to the others before it gets too late. Wind will come funneling through here from the top of the ridge, freezing the place. It'll be twice as hard to climb to the top."

Shotsky groaned. "You two are a couple of downers—you know that?"

It was dark when we crested the incline and continued down the other side of the passage. The stars were countless and dazzling, the line of mountains a blackened series of waves against an inky backdrop of sky.

The flicker of a campfire trembled in the narrow, cupped valley below.

Two hours ago, Shotsky might have sighed with relief and commented in some quasi-humorous fashion about how glad he was to see the campsite. But that was two hours ago. Now all his strength was reserved for propelling one foot in front of the other. The night had cooled the atmosphere considerably, yet Shotsky's round face was glistening with sweat, his cheeks flushed and quivering, his exaggerated breaths volleying his lower lip back and forth, back and forth, back and forth. It would have been comical had I not been concerned about his heart giving out.

The rest of the crew was uncharacteristically quiet upon our arrival. Instinct told me they were thinking the same thing I was—namely, that there was no way in hell Shotsky was going to be able to complete this journey. Wordlessly, Hollinger handed a cup of hot cocoa to Shotsky, who accepted the cup equally as silent.

"You're fucking kidding me," Chad commented under his breath, coming up beside me. "What'd you do, carry the son of a bitch on your shoulders the whole way?"

There was nothing I could say.

"Seriously," Chad went on, his voice rising, "where's the hidden fucking cameras? Because this has got to be a joke—"

"Cool it. I don't need a goddamn recap." I glanced around. "Where's Andrew?"

"Where do you think? He's praying like a goddamn monk up there." He pointed to a silhouetted outline of jagged rock.

I could just barely make out Andrew's form crouched atop one of the peaks, his face in profile.

"Is it just me," Chad said, "or is everyone losing their fucking minds?"

An hour later, Andrew came down from the peaks. Shotsky was snoring against a stone outcropping, while Curtis, Chad, and Hollinger played cards. Petras had taken my book on George Mallory closer to the fire to read by the light. I'd spent the past hour thinking about the situation with Shotsky but mostly thinking about the bourbon in my canteen. I'd come to the decision that I'd take another swig—just one more—after everyone had gone to bed. Either that, or do push-ups till morning.

"We need to talk," I said to Andrew as he took off his shirt and sniffed his armpits.

"I'm ripe," he said, pulling a face. He tossed the shirt atop his pack and bent to rifle for a fresh one. "What's up?"

"I think you know."

"Do I? Because there are so many things going on at the moment."

"What are you talking about?"

"Well," he began, his voice level, "for one thing, I noticed how collected you were this morning and well into the afternoon. Up until early evening, really, when you started lagging behind. And your hands started shaking again."

I wasn't going to mention the liquor to Andrew—though he'd supplied it, I didn't have to let him know that I'd discovered it—but he was already onto me. This angered me. I guess Andrew could see that it angered me because he looked me up and down and asked if I was going to punch him in the face again.

"Thinking about it," I said.

He selected a fresh T-shirt and pulled it over his head, tucking it into the waistband of his camouflage pants.

"He's going to drop dead out here," I said. "And I'm sure as hell not going to be his babysitter for the rest of the trip."

"You didn't have to be his babysitter today, either."

"We had a deal," I reminded him.

"The deal was if *he* feels like he can't finish. Not *you*."

"He won't quit because he needs the money."

"He'll quit," Andrew said. His eyes were like twin orbs of obsidian reflecting the nearby firelight. "That's the problem with him. He's a quitter. I wish it were different, but that's not the case. You'll see—

you'll come out on top, and you'll get your way."

"I just hope it's not too late. We've got a long day tomorrow."

"Yes," Andrew said, squatting down with his back against his pack and lacing his hands behind his head, "we do. Good night."

Speechless, I climbed into fresh socks and had Chad deal me in for a few hands of poker.

"You suck, Shakes," Chad said after I'd lost my tenth hand in a row.

"Just deal," I told him. Truth was, I couldn't concentrate on the game; I was too busy watching Andrew sleep. Whether it had been subconscious or not, he'd removed himself from the rest of us, setting up his sleeping bag on the other side of the bonfire where, in the flicker of the flames, he was nothing but a dance of alternating shadows.

"You got it," said Chad. "Money on the wood makes the game go good. Ante up, boys."

After everyone had gone to sleep, I crawled over to where Shotsky lay, half petrified against the side of the stone outcropping. His snores were like the buzz of a chain saw. I poked his chest lightly and whispered his name into his ear over and over until his snoring broke up and his eyelids fluttered.

"Wha—?"

"Quiet," I told him. Thankfully Petras's thundering snoring compensated for Shotsky's.

"Tim, wha—?"

"Listen. I spoke with Andrew. He's going to give you the money whether you finish this thing or not. He doesn't want you to know because he wants you to finish, but we need to be honest here, Donald." I used his first name, hoping to appeal to the soul of the man. "This trip is going to get one hundred times worse than today. You're going to kill yourself."

His eyes were large and beseeching. I couldn't tell if he was fully awake.

"Do you understand what I'm telling you?"

"Sure." His voice was calm, relaxed. His breath was warm in my face, smelling of onions and cigarettes. "Thing is, maybe I *do* need to prove this to myself. Maybe Andrew's right. Maybe I *need* this."

"Andrew's out of his mind. He's playing a game with you. You don't need to prove a goddamn thing."

"But I do." His voice was oddly serene; just hearing it caused goose bumps to break out along my arms. "I do."

"Then you might die proving it," I whispered and crawled back to my sleeping bag.

Shotsky was snoring again before my eyes closed.

2

IN THE SCANT MOMENTS BEFORE DAWN, I AWOKE to find Andrew and Shotsky standing above me with their packs on. For a second, I thought I was dreaming. I turned over and saw Curtis's slumbering form wrapped in a flannel sleeping bag. I could hear Petras's snores echoing off the stone walls of the valley.

"What's this?" I muttered, rubbing sleep from my eyes.

"I'm taking Shotsky back to base camp," Andrew said, his voice flat and emotionless.

"That's a full day's hike," I said.

"And another day coming back," he added. "We can do it quickly."

I stared at Shotsky, but he refused to meet my eyes. "You want me to go with you?"

"It's not necessary."

But I was already lacing up my boots. "I'll come."

"Tim—"

"Remember what you said to me when I told you I'd gone caving on my own? That I was a fool and I could have died down there?"

Andrew looked away, rubbing his jaw. He seemed to chew on my words.

"Well, you were right. I'm coming with you." I gazed at the camp, which was still dark in the predawn. "Besides, what the hell am I gonna do? Sit here and lose all my money playing poker with Chad?"

"Quiet," Chad groaned a few yards away. "Still sleeping."

Again my gaze shifted to Shotsky, but he still refused to look at me. Finally Andrew said, "Hurry up and get dressed."

While I dressed, Andrew spoke with Petras and told him to wait here until he and I returned which, with luck, would be in less than two days. Petras accepted his duty as next-in-charge in Andrew's absence without protest; however, when he peered over at me, there was a dubious glimmer in his eyes. I could only roll my shoulders in response.

We set out before the sun had time to rise. Conversation was nonexistent. The only sounds were of our boots crunching in the snow, the top layer having frozen in the night, and the collective sighs of our respiration. The descent was easier than the initial climb, and Shotsky had to stop only a handful of times to catch his breath. Each time, Andrew did not wait for him; he continued descending the passage, tromping through our footprints from the day before, until he was once again a dark speck at the opposite end of the passage.

I remained with Shotsky, but we did not speak to each other. There was nothing to be said, and we both knew it. I could tell he was uncomfortable around me, and I could tell by the distance Andrew created between us that he was upset, too.

"I've gotta take a leak," I told Shotsky during one of his breaks and climbed farther down the passage where I urinated into the snow.

When Shotsky caught up five minutes later, somewhat refreshed and ready to continue, I sighed and said nothing. We continued down the slope until my nagging thoughts got the better of me and I said, "What was all that talk last night about needing to finish? You seemed determined."

"Guess I had time to think about it," he said, his voice small. "You're right. Who am I kidding?"

I said no more about it. We stopped for a late, freeze-dried lunch, and none of us spoke. I found my mind wandering, occupying itself with things other than the descent and the coldness between the three of us. I thought of Hannah and how she—

3

—STUCK HER HEAD UP THROUGH THE FLOOR HATCH of our loft. Soft, tallow light framed her face. She smiled as I set down my hammer and chisel and wiped my hands on my pants, leaving white smears of powder on them.

"You need to see this," she said.

"I need to finish this."

She climbed out of the floor hatch. My studio was actually the attic, accessible only through the small hatch at the center of the floor. Brushing dust off her clothes, she stepped around the sculpture and behind me, placing a hand on my shoulder. "I thought you weren't going to do the memorial."

"I'm not." I traced a thumb along the base of the sculpture. It was far from being finished, the bottom half still an unrefined cube of marble. Three faceless soldiers, their rifles drawn and their helmets covering their heads, rose out of the cube of marble, each of them facing in a slightly different direction. "I just couldn't sleep. I kept seeing this in my head . . . and I knew this chunk of marble was up here, growing cold and ugly."

Hannah reached out and stroked the cold, white stone. "It's beautiful."

"What's so important that I need to see?"

"Outside. They're shooting fireworks over the water from the Naval Academy."

I examined the blank oval heads of the three soldiers beneath their helmets. "I should finish," I said, picking up one of my carving tools.

"You should leave their faces blank," she suggested.

"You think so?"

"Seems to make a bigger statement. Like they could be anyone and everyone. All the young men who died over there."

"I need to finish," I told her. "Please, Hannah . . ."

She kissed my cheek, and I felt her hand slide off my shoulder. The floorboards creaked as she made her way to the floor hatch. "I love you," she called to me.

"Love you, too," I said and watched as she descended through the hatch, under-lit by the shaft of yellow light.

I finished the sculpture, but it wasn't good enough. I sat and stared at it for an undefined time, my stomach cramping with hunger and my bladder swollen with piss. Sometime during the night, I'd decided to submit it to the memorial commission after all. Leaning closer to it on my stool, I scrutinized every detail, every nuance. There was anguish and fear in the soldiers' blank faces, creases and tears in their uniforms, and I could almost convince myself that I could see the grease on their hands from their weapons.

And it occurred to me like a burst of fire in a darkened cave: there was *too much* detail. It was *too much.*

Like they could be anyone and everyone.

One week later, I presented the sculpture to the memorial commission—a donation from an up-and-coming artist who'd done only a meager number of commissioned works. Reviews of the sculpture proclaimed it to be powerful, all-encompassing, otherworldly, yet somehow completely unassuming. It graced the covers of several design and art magazines. I started receiving work from more elite clients.

One man in particular, the publisher of a national newspaper, desired a personalized sculpture for his office, something he could set on the mantel above his fireplace. Upon our first meeting, he pumped my hand vigorously and said, "I fell in love with what you did for the memorial, Tim—can I call you Tim? So simple yet so complex. That's how I live my life, really." He winked conspiratorially and added, "How did you ever think to keep the soldiers' faces blank?"

"Guess I was inspired," was my response.

That night in bed, I kissed Hannah on the shoulder and told her what the newspaperman had said. I felt her smile in the dark.

"So we make a good team, you and me, huh?" she said.

"Marry me," I said.

4

WE WERE NO MORE THAN AN HOUR AWAY FROM base camp when Donald Shotsky died.

It happened just as twilight deepened the sky to a blend of cool purples and pinks, the moon visible in the eastern sky. For the past half hour, I had been conscious of Shotsky's breathing—the rasping, closed-throated labor of it—so when it stopped, I was keenly aware of it.

I snapped my head around and saw him ten feet behind me. His eyes were bugging out of their sockets, his mouth working like a fish out of water. One of his pudgy, white hands fluttered in mid-air. I could almost hear his heartbeat closing the distance between us. I watched as his eyes filmed over, going blind. That fluttering hand clutched his chest. A small, froglike croak issued from his gaping mouth, and a moment after that, he pitched forward face-first into the snow.

I ran to him and dropped to my knees. It took some effort to roll him over on his side, and I knew it wasn't a good sign that his eyes were still open.

"Andrew!" I could see him about to climb down the far end of the snowy passage to the path below. "Andrew!"

I pushed Shotsky over on his back. He didn't blink.

"Come on, Shotsky," I pleaded. "Don't do this."

Pressing two fingers to his carotid, I couldn't make out a pulse. I quickly commenced with chest compressions, but he was wearing too much restrictive gear. I unbuckled his pack and opened his coat, then proceeded with more compressions. My breath whistled in my throat, and my pulse drummed in my ears.

"Come on. Come on. Come on. Come on—"

"What happened?" Andrew barked, running toward us.

"Heart attack!"

Like a runner stealing second, Andrew slid in the snow and slammed against one of my thighs. He braced Shotsky's head and positioned it back on his neck, creating a clearer passageway for air. With one hand, he administered quick little slaps to the side of Shotsky's face, which was quickly turning a mottled shade of purple.

My arms were getting sore. I counted under my breath and continued with the chest compressions. A trail of snot descended from one of my nostrils and lengthened until it pattered on my balled, pumping fists.

"He's not breathing," Andrew said, sitting up. He released Shotsky's head, but it did not recoil back on its neck. "There's no pulse."

". . . seven . . . eight . . . nine . . ."

"There's no pulse. He's dead."

"Come on . . ."

"Overleigh. Tim." Andrew put one hand over both my fists and steadied them on Shotsky's chest. My breath was burning my throat. "He's dead. It's over. It's over."

Not moving, I sat there for several minutes. Andrew's hand remained on top of mine. Once I felt my heartbeat begin to slow and regain its normal cadence, I lifted my hands off Shotsky's chest and dropped onto my buttocks in the snow. I was still breathing heavily, but the cold night air was beginning to freeze the sweat on my face and neck.

"Fuck," I uttered and eased back against my pack. Unbuckling the straps, I worked my shoulders out of them and pitched to my side in the freezing snow. "Jesus Christ, Andrew."

Andrew sat forward on his shins and stared at Shotsky's body.

"Did he have kids?" I asked. "Was he married?"

"No." Andrew's voice was small.

"No family?"

"He spent half the year alone in a tiny apartment in Reno, the other half as a greenhorn on crabbing boats in the Bering Sea. He was a pickup man."

I didn't know what a pickup man was; all I knew was Donald Shotsky, his face no more than three feet from my own, was dead.

"What do we do?" I said, sitting up. The cold was beginning to get to me.

"We leave him here."

"Right here?"

"It's no different than dragging him to base camp. And we certainly can't carry him all the way down to the valley."

"Yeah, but—"

"Get out your flags—the ones I left in your cabin. The blue ones."

I unzipped my gear and produced the set of vinyl flags attached to wire rods. Andrew took off his own gear and stripped Shotsky's pack off his body. He dragged the bag aside, then searched through Shotsky's pockets.

"What the hell are you doing?"

"Making sure we're not leaving anything important behind," said Andrew.

"Like what? His fucking wallet? Let him be."

Andrew slammed a fist into the snow, mere inches from Shotsky's head. "Fuck, Tim—you wanna play Pope, go to the fucking Vatican." He continued searching through Shotsky's pockets.

My eyes locked with Shotsky's. They were already beginning to glaze over. His mouth was frozen in an *O*, as if he were freeze-framed singing an opera. Again I thought of the stories I'd read on the Internet about the bodies found on the Godesh Ridge and all through the Himalayan mountains. I thought of George Mallory, dead somewhere on Everest.

Inevitably I thought of Hannah and David, burning to death in their car after it drove off a cliff. David, Hannah's lover, died on impact in the crash, but the coroner's report identified smoke inhalation as Hannah's cause of death. I imagined her, bloodied and disoriented, slamming a single hand against a window as the car filled with smoke.

"Stay with me, Overleigh."

I snapped out of my daze. Andrew bundled Shotsky's body in his clothes, buttoning his coat and positioning his head at a more lifelike angle.

"The flags," I said, holding them up.

"Find peaks, high places. Plant them in the center, where someone can see from a considerable distance. Somewhere they won't get buried if it snows too hard."

Without a word, I stood and meandered around the snowy passageway, driving flags into mounds of snow and atop stone precipices. When I turned a curve in the slope, hidden behind a mass of white rocks, I removed my canteen and took two healthy chugs. The bourbon seared my throat, which was already abraded from dry, heavy breathing. I wiped my mouth on my sleeve and slipped the canteen back into my pack.

I shook feeling back into my hands, then went through my gear, fishing out a titanium anchor and sliding my pickax from its harness. It took me longer than I expected to carve Shotsky's name into the rock. By the time I finished, I was wiped out.

"We'll sleep here tonight," Andrew said, surveying the vast incline. It was already dark, and we hadn't moved from the spot where Shotsky had died. The snow was illuminated in the moonlight. It would take at least an hour to continue down the passage for base camp and probably longer in the cold and the dark. "There's very little shelter. Let's look around for an open niche in the rocks."

We lit our electric lanterns and searched the crevices for an opening wide enough to accommodate both of us. As if by design, a light snow began to fall, causing Andrew and me to exchange a serendipitous glance.

"Here," I called. We'd been searching for forty minutes without luck until I located a narrow crawl space in the face of the rock farther up the incline. We had to wedge ourselves in sideways and duck our heads to pass through the opening, leaving our packs out in the snow because they wouldn't fit. Three or four feet into the mountainside, the passage opened into a circular cave no bigger than the interior of a Volkswagen Beetle. Both our lanterns were too bright so I shut mine off.

Andrew held his lantern up to the ceiling, which was very near the tops of our heads. "This'll do. Nice work."

I was exhausted. Setting my lantern down, I pitched myself against the wall and pulled off my boots. My toes felt like loose marbles rolling around in the tips of my socks.

"You're not going to believe this," Andrew said, setting his own lantern down, "but I've gotta take a massive shit." He chuckled to himself. The lantern threw his enormous and hulking shadow against the wall, curling up and splaying it across the undulated ceiling.

I looked past him at the vertical sliver of darkness that defined the narrow passage through which we'd entered.

"What is it?" he said. "Shotsky?"

"I don't feel good about leaving him out there."

"Well, we're certainly not dragging him in here."

"And now it's snowing."

"It's not a heavy snowfall. Besides, you put out the flags."

"It just doesn't seem right."

Andrew crouched against the wall opposite me. Half his face burned bright yellow in the light of the electric lantern; the other half was masked in shadows. He looked like the embodiment of good and evil. "You blame me for this, don't you?"

I didn't answer.

Andrew sighed and shucked off his boots. The cave was so small

I could smell his feet as if they were propped right under my nose. "Funny," he said and let the word hang in the air.

"What's that?" My tone was dry, disinterested.

"Funny how he was so quick to throw in the towel. You know, he woke me up in the middle of the night and said he didn't want to be a burden on the rest of you guys. That he knew he wouldn't be able to cut it and he had to quit."

I turned away from him, locking my stare on that vertical sliver of moonlight coming through the rock.

"He would have walked over hot coals to get that twenty grand," Andrew went on, "and yet he surrendered out of nowhere, as if the money suddenly didn't matter to him." He shrugged. "Funny, that's all."

"Funny?" I said, still refusing to look at him.

"You don't think it's a bit strange?"

"If you're accusing me of something, spit it out."

Andrew leaned his head back against the cave, his whole face swallowed by shadows. "We used to be such good friends. Remember?"

"You were Hannah's friend. I just found you interesting."

"And now?"

"Now what?"

"You don't find me interesting anymore?"

I paused to consider my thoughts. "I guess I find you tedious. Maybe it was that tedium I originally found interesting, but now—"

"Now it's just tedious," Andrew finished, and I didn't have to see his face to know he was smiling. "Tell me again what you were doing alone in that cave. We've gone through this before, but I don't think we've actually addressed the issue."

"This," I suggested, "is a perfect example of tedium."

This time Andrew laughed—a low, resonant rumbling that played off the closed-in walls. "Come on. Give it up."

"There's nothing to tell."

"Sure there is." Andrew began slowly and methodically cuffing his pants up to his knees. "It's no different than the guy who walks into a doctor's office and is told he's got one month of dehumanizing, agonizing life left in him, that some virulent disease is ravaging and liquefying his insides. He'll be bedridden and lying in his own shit within the week." He finished cuffing his pants. "No different from that guy leaving the doctor's office and walking right out into traffic."

This sent a cold shiver down my spine. Andrew's words hit too close to home. "Go to hell."

"I wonder how it would have played out," Andrew said, "if you hadn't told old Shotsky about our little behind-the-scenes pact."

My face burned. My fingernails dug into the rock. "What the hell did Hannah ever see in you?"

"Who knows? Maybe she was a fan of tedium." He jerked a thumb at the electric lantern. "Mind if I kill this? I wanna get some sleep."

5

IN THE MORNING, SHOTSKY'S BODY WAS DUSTED in snow. His eyes were hard, sightless pellets, and I silently cursed myself for not thinking to close his eyelids before the snow came. Andrew had folded his hands atop his chest; they had blued overnight, hardened with frost, their fingers like solid links of metal. Only the orange canvas of his pack, propped beside him like a grave marker, stood out against the earthen colors of his wet clothes and whitish skin. The blue flags I'd pegged at various points in proximity to his body flapped in the wind.

Andrew and I did not speak for most of the hike up the pass. We maintained a considerable distance between us, choosing to hike in solitude than in each other's company. At one point midway through the climb, I passed Andrew as he sat on his pack in the snow, eating some Cheerios. He did not bother to look in my direction, and I moved past him as if he were invisible.

Come dusk, as I paused to eat my own freeze-dried meal, I could see Andrew coming up the pass in pursuit. He walked with the slow, dilatory ease of someone walking through a dream. The setting sun cast soft pastels across the hardened crust of snow, making it glow with patches of purples and pinks, oranges and yellows. Beyond Andrew and farther down the pass, I thought I saw a second figure.

At first, I thought it was a trick of the fading light. But as I watched, I could tell it was a man, moving alongside the walls of the pass as if to keep out of sight. I dropped my pack and scrounged for my binoculars, but by the time I located them and glassed the area, the man had disappeared. I decided it was a trick of the light after all.

Andrew approached, and we crossed down the other side of the pass together, still in silence. However, as we climbed the next ridge and the bonfire became visible, Andrew grabbed one of the loops on my pack and brought me to a halt.

"We shouldn't tell them about Shotsky," he suggested. "It'll crush their spirits. Let's say we got him back to base camp and everything was fine."

I hated to agree with him, but he had a point. There was no need to tell the others until after we'd finished. We could even hold a memorial service for Shotsky in the village, if anyone desired it. So I agreed with Andrew, then walked ahead of him toward camp.

I didn't think it would be a big deal lying about Shotsky until Petras asked how things went.

"Fine," I muttered, unable to look the bigger man in the eye. "He's back at camp." But all I could picture was the way his eyes had frozen open and the orange canvas of his pack standing up through the snowdrift.

"We've got a problem," Hollinger said as Andrew approached camp and set his gear down. "It was either a miscalculation back in the village or we've mixed up our bluey with the Sherpas in the valley—"

"Wasn't no goddamn mix-up," Curtis chided.

"What happened?" Andrew asked.

"The food," said Hollinger. "Half the lousy freeze-drieds, the foodstuffs. We're missing half our tucker."

I gaped at him. "The *food*?"

"Half of it's gone missing, mate."

"We must have left some behind in the valley without realizing it," said Petras.

"Pig's arse!" barked Hollinger.

"Then what else happened to it?" Curtis intervened, his gaze volleying between Michael Hollinger and John Petras. "It was a stupid mistake on our parts, not packing up more carefully in the valley."

Hollinger threw his hands up. "Bah!"

"Is it really that bad?" Andrew asked, his voice steady.

"It's roughly half the food, man," said Curtis.

Chad appeared behind him, nodding.

"We're still good," Andrew said. "Half is plenty." What he didn't tell them was we'd pillaged the remaining food from Shotsky's pack and carried it with us. It would be a morbid thing to explain, but we would if it needed to be done.

"Tell 'im what you told us," Hollinger said. He was looking straight at Petras. But before Petras could answer, Hollinger turned to Andrew and said, "He told us all about this sacred land we're crossing. You can call me superstitious, but I don't just leave behind half my food."

"You're making a bigger deal out of this than you need to," Andrew said calmly. "Like I said, we've got enough food. We could survive up here for two months if we had to."

"You're wrong and you're blind," Hollinger said. "This is bad luck, and it'll only get worse. You'll see. You don't fuck around with the spectral."

"No such thing as luck." Andrew dropped his pack off his shoulders, then knelt while he dug around inside. "We're all responsible for our own achievements and our own mistakes. Luck is just a convenient ideology to place our own blame."

Though I didn't necessarily believe in luck, either, I couldn't help but summon the image of Donald Shotsky, dead of a heart attack and frozen on the ground.

"We spent six months together in the outback, Mike, living off the land. Luck didn't land our arrows into the chests of our prey so we could eat. That was our own patience and skill. Just like luck didn't make that one chippie fall in love with you. It was your own confidence that did that—a confidence that's curiously left you for the time being."

Hollinger looked like he wanted to respond. In the end, however, he simply crawled over to his gear and reclined near the heat of the fire. Above us, the overhanging cliffs blotted out most of the sky and had kept much of the snow away from the campsite. The ground was fairly dry and warm and covered in small rocks. Hollinger gathered a handful of these rocks and began absently chucking them into the fire.

I looked over at Andrew. He was seated on the ground scrutinizing a map. He looked up and caught my eye. Surprising me, he winked.

I turned away and stretched my sore legs out by the fire. Chad brought me over a steaming cup of tea. "Thanks," I said, surprised by the gesture.

"No sweat." He sat beside me. "Everything went cool with old Donald?"

"Fine," I muttered, covering my mouth with the rim of the cup.

"You think I can get a quick swig of whatever booze you've been hoarding?"

"The hell are you talking about?"

"Come on, man. I've been watching you, Shakes, been watching the peaks and valleys. I'm just asking for a drop."

"I've got nothing," I lied, taking a large gulp of the tea and burning the roof of my mouth in the process.

"Bullshit," Chad said. There was no real anger to his tone. "Anyway, I'm just bitter because I can't find my other joint."

"You had *two* of those monsters?"

"Three." He grinned like a fiend, his face red in the firelight. "We had a bit of a party last night while you three were gone."

A bit of a party, I thought, *while Donald Shotsky keeled over dead of a heart attack just one hour from base camp. A party while we looted his backpack and left him to freeze to the ground.*

But it wasn't Chad's fault. I couldn't be angry, and I didn't want the disgust on my face to be too apparent. I finished the tea and handed him back the empty cup, thanking him under my breath. Ten minutes later, I curled up and went to sleep, while the bonfire popped and Chad blew sad notes on his harmonica.

CHAPTER 12

1

STRADDLING A MONOLITHIC PLATFORM OF ICE-
covered rock, I paused to survey the world below. The vastness of
the drop was enough to cause my heart to slam against the walls
of my chest, the proximity of the edge—mere inches from my steel-
toed boots—both exhilarating and vertiginous. I leaned over the
edge, and the mountainside vanished into indistinguishable levels of
snow-covered peaks.

My stomach, which in the past twenty-four hours had processed
nothing more substantial than a 3 Musketeers bar, ramen noodles,
steamed rice, and countless cups of black coffee, seemed to grow
heavy and felt as though it wanted to descend deeper into my naval.
I hadn't slept in two days.

We were a full two weeks into the climb, having just crossed
the southern pinnacle of the Godesh Ridge, and it was just over a
week since I had carved Donald Shotsky's name in the mountainside
where his body had given out. The beginning of the second week had
been punctuated by tedious treks through deepening snow and the
careful negotiation of serrated, ice-encrusted peaks. The second half
of the week had presented a dramatic notch in the south face of the

mountain, which we climbed vertically while harnessed together in two groups of threes—Petras, Chad, and myself the first of the two groups to ascend. We'd climbed to the summit and continued up the accompanying face as if we were climbing straight to heaven.

Petras passed behind me, peering over my shoulder. His hand on my shoulder was like an anchor.

"Some view," I said.

"Let's keep moving."

Around the other side of the platform, the mountain abruptly ended. Something like three hundred feet below us ran a narrow, snow-packed pass across the shelf of a glacier. Andrew was poised at the lip of the ridge, overlooking the valley. Beside him, Curtis canvassed the surface of the glacier with a pair of binoculars.

I could see the sun streaking colors along the surrounding mountains and the reflection of sunlight mirroring on the ice. Farther down the pass was the hint of a crevasse—a barely noticeable depression in the otherwise undisturbed snow—which I estimated to be at least twenty yards across, though it was impossible to tell for sure from our vantage.

"You guys see it?" Curtis pointed to what appeared to be the beginning of the snow-hidden chasm that ran beneath a buttress of blue stone. "Can't tell how wide it is, but you can bet your ass it's deep."

"Teams," Andrew said.

I zipped my coat to my chin and rubbed my gloved hands together. Petras bumped his shoulder against mine, and I thought my teeth would shatter in my skull. I attached myself to a fixed rope, while Petras and Chad fed a communal safety line down the face of the cliff. Flexing my fingers, I turned around at the edge of the cliff and gripped the line in both hands.

Petras nodded. "Go."

I pitched over the side and rappelled down, my feet pushing off the cliff face as I descended. Glancing over my shoulder, I could see beyond the crevasse and down the far slope of the glacier where, like a grid of blocks, crumbling seracs the size of automobiles rose from the glacier's surface and cast bluish shadows along the snow.

When I touched down on the glacier, the snow was hard like ice. I tugged at the rope and waved to Petras, who looked down at me.

Once they'd all managed to descend, we trekked across the glacier, heedful of traps or snow bridges bent on deceiving us, until we paused approximately fifteen feet from the edge of the crevasse. This close, it looked wider than I'd originally thought. Forty, maybe fifty feet across. Chad stepped too close to the edge, and Curtis, who was standing beside me rubbing his neck, sucked in air through his clenched teeth.

"Careful," Petras called to him.

Chad raised a gloved hand in response but didn't turn. He kept walking until he reached the edge.

"Fucking idiot don't even have a line tied to him." Curtis flipped up the collar of his parka. "Think he would have learned his lesson back at base camp."

"She's deep, all right." Chad peered down into the crevasse. "Can't even see the bottom." He looked across the surface of the glacier, following the fault-line negotiation of the crevasse through the snow. It disappeared beneath an icefall at the base of the next peak. "She's narrower closer toward the base of the mountain. If we're going to cross her, we've got to do it over there."

"I say we climb the wall," suggested Hollinger. He scrutinized a slab of ice that rose maybe five hundred feet to a spire-shaped pinnacle.

"That'll take all day," Chad said.

"So? You in a rush?"

Chad shook his blond hair over his eyes and rubbed the snow from it. "Cut it out, will you, Holly? We can toss a rope and scale—"

Hollinger took a step toward the wall of ice, then disappeared.

It took my lagging brain several seconds to realize what had happened: a trap had opened up in the glacier directly beneath Hollinger's feet, and gravity had sucked him down. I broke into a sprint as Petras nabbed me by the hood of my anorak, jerking me to a halt.

"No running," he said, his voice impossibly calm. "There may be more traps. Watch your footing."

"Holy fuck," Curtis breathed, moving past me as quickly as I had been moving a second earlier, and approached the hole in the ground without trepidation.

I shrugged off Petras's grip and was at Curtis's side an instant later.

The hole in the ground was no wider than a manhole and equally as dark, an optical illusion to stare into. I couldn't see the bottom— I could only see a narrow shelf perhaps thirty feet down protruding from the wall of the shaft on which Hollinger's body lay slumped and motionless.

"He's there!" I called out to the others. Then I directed my voice into the shaft, shouting Hollinger's name over and over again. But he didn't move. I thought I could see blood on the shelf, and his hair looked matted with dark fluid.

"Keep your voice down." Petras gently set down his pack at his feet. "The smallest vibration might break the ledge out from under him."

"I'm goin' down," Curtis volunteered, sliding off his pack.

"No," Petras told him. "Who's lightest?"

"Me," I said. "I'll go."

"The fuck does it matter?" Flecks of spittle shot from Curtis's mouth as he spoke. He and Hollinger had become good friends during the course of our journey.

"You know it matters," Petras said.

I climbed into a harness, while Chad and Andrew secured anchors in the ice. Curtis lowered a second line into the shaft.

Grabbing me by my waist, Petras spun me around like a rag doll and buckled the harness. "Watch yourself, Tim."

"Hurry," I urged him. Sweat was suddenly cascading down my shirt, soaking the waistband of my underwear.

Holding on to the line, I eased myself backward into the opening as Petras held me by my forearms. The opening was tighter than it looked; I just barely made it through, the shaft seeming to narrow as my shoulders passed through it. As my head sunk into the opening, I looked up and saw Andrew's face blotting out the sun. I slipped into darkness, the shaft closing in all around me like—

2

—BLANKETS FORMING A TUNNEL AROUND US. THE bed creaked as she rolled on top of me and kissed my chin.

"You smell like dust," she whispered into the hollow at the base of my neck. "I can smell the powdered stone all over you."

"I showered twice."

"It's not enough."

I pulled the blankets off our heads so she could smell the salty bay air coming in through the open windows. "Better?"

"Not really."

The fishing boats moored in the harbor underscored our love-making with blasts from their air horns as morning broke and they were piloted out into the bay. Afterwards, my eyes grew heavy, and I danced in the place halfway between dreams and wakefulness—the place where I'd entertained my most vivid dreams ever since I was a child.

Hannah's soft voice in my ear, not quite ready to let me drift off to that vivid dream place: "Will you look handsome tonight?"

Eyes still closed, I smiled. "Hmm."

"Will you wear the tux?"

"Hmm." I could barely remember where I was, whom I was with . . .

"You look so handsome in the tux."

"Yes . . ."

"And you look so peaceful when you sleep. Do you dream of sculpting?"

Strangely I didn't. I was dreaming of just the opposite—of smashing things, letting the debris shower me while I stood in the middle of a vacant highway and laughed and laughed and laughed . . .

"Do you care if I put some of your work on display tonight?"

"I thought you said that would be too malapropos?"

"I did say that, didn't I? Well, I've had second thoughts. You don't think it would be malapropos, do you?"

My eyes still closed, I stroked her hair and said, "I don't even know what *malapropos* means."

"I can't believe I'm finally opening this stupid gallery."

"It's not stupid. You've wanted to do it since before we were married."

"I know it's not stupid. But maybe *I'm* stupid for wanting it. It's a lot of work, a lot of time. We hardly see each other as it is, with you always traveling and sculpting and being famous and all."

"It'll be fine." I kissed her shoulder, then rolled out of bed.

"Where are you going?"

"The studio. I need to get some work done today."

"I thought you weren't going in today."

"Not all day." I tugged on a shirt and watched my reflection in the beveled mirror run fingers through my hair.

"Will you pick me up for the opening?"

"I'll be just down the street from the gallery. I'll meet you there."

Pouting, she sat up in bed, the sheets piled into her lap, her small, white breasts prickled in the cool breeze coming in from the open windows.

I kissed her forehead. "No pouting."

"Just don't be late, Tim."

I promised I wouldn't be, but I was. I'd spent the remainder of the day at my M Street studio working on one of the New York projects—a pricy marble piece commissioned by an actor and devout scientologist—and when it began to get too difficult, I broke into one of my bottles of Compass Box. By 6:00 p.m., I'd gone through half the bottle and accidentally lobbed off the upper portion of the sculpture, a section I'd spent the past three days trying to perfect. The chunk lay at my feet on the powder-covered floor like something incriminating left behind at a crime scene.

At 7:15, the lampposts along M Street blinked on. I had an Elvis Costello CD in the stereo on repeat, and I was lying down on the heater at the back of the studio. In the offices upstairs, I could hear doors being locked, heels and loafers moving down the concrete stairs of the fire exit. Burners of the midnight oil.

There was a pretty good chance I might have fallen asleep if I hadn't happened to turn my head and spot my tuxedo hanging from a hook on a closet door. "Shit."

Hannah had already given her speech and cut the red ribbon by the time I arrived at the gallery. It was a good turnout; a number of heads swiveled in my direction when I made too much noise coming through the doors. My tux dusted with powdered concrete and my flesh reeking of booze, I nodded at my closest admirers and went straight for the rear of the gallery. Brightly colored oil paintings glared down at me, disappointed in my appearance. I staggered over to Hannah, pretty in a red sequined gown and holding a champagne flute, but when I touched her arm and she turned around, it wasn't Hannah at all.

"Shit," I said to the woman who wasn't my wife. "I mean . . . shit, I'm sorry . . ."

The woman seemed to look straight through me.

I pivoted and caught a glimpse of Hannah—this time for sure—talking with a good-looking guy in a black suit and tie. She was stunning in a contoured velvet gown cut just at the knee. She wore black nylons—something that had always driven me wild. She must have sensed my gaze from across the room because she looked in my direction at that moment, our eyes locking.

"Hey." I kissed her cheek. "I'm sorry, Hannah. I got caught

up." I nodded at the gentleman in the suit. "Hi."

"Tim, this is David Moore. David, this is my husband, Tim."

David grasped my hand and pumped it like a car jack. "Good to meet you, Tim."

"David bought your sculpture."

I arched my eyebrows. "Oh yeah?"

David smiled. He was dark skinned with silver streaks in his black hair. Firm chin already darkened by tomorrow's beard stubble. "It's a beautiful piece. I noticed it right away. It really spoke to me."

I cocked a grin at him. "What did it say?"

"Uh," David said and followed it up with a nervous laugh. He looked me up and down. "I should leave," he said, turning to Hannah. He leaned in and kissed her on the cheek. "It was a fabulous evening."

"Thanks for coming, David."

I watched him leave before facing Hannah. "So how did it go?"

Grabbing me by the elbow, she led me away from the center of the room. "Jesus, Tim. You stink of booze." She, too, eyed me up and down. "There's . . . there's shit all over your tux."

"I should have covered it with a trash bag. I didn't think."

An elderly couple waltzed by, raising their hands to my wife. She offered them a broad smile, shoving me farther behind her as if to hide me from the world. I took a few steps back until I stumbled into a wall. There was a speaker directly above my head through which issued a slow jazz instrumental.

"Who is he?" I asked that night in bed.

"Who is who?"

"The guy who bought my piece."

"David? He's a linguistics professor at Georgetown. He's written a few books, and he's very well respected in the arts community."

"He seems to like you a lot."

"He's a lover of art."

"I mean, he seems to like you *personally*."

"What's that mean?"

"I don't know," I said. "He just seemed really friendly."

"He's one of the donors. And he spent a lot of money tonight. Most of it on your sculpture." She rolled over in bed, her back toward me.

"A handsome guy, too," I said, staring at the ceiling.

"You're still drunk," she muttered.

"I'm sorry about tonight," I said.

"Just go to sleep, Tim."

"Can we talk about it?"

"We'll talk about it tomorrow."

"All right."

But we didn't.

We didn't.

3

ANDREW'S VOICE FOLLOWED ME DOWN INTO THE darkness: "Is it too tight? Can you move your arms?"

Except for the shrinking circle of light above my head, my world was black. As they lowered me into the ice shaft, my nose only an inch or so away from the wall of black ice, I couldn't help but think about the accident in the cave. Had it really been two years ago now? Bumbling through constricted tunnels below the earth, lost and blind yet going deeper and deeper. Everything had that coal mine smell. Then, just as it had happened to Hollinger, the ground had opened up beneath me and I'd dropped. My leg snapped when I crashed to the bottom of the trench, the pain so intense I was rendered instantly unconscious.

I recalled now what Andrew had alluded to over a week ago as we huddled together in the cave after Shotsky had died. What he'd said about my reason for wandering around in those caves by myself in the first place. I hadn't been afraid of dying. Lying at the bottom of that pitch-black stone trench, my ass soaking up ancient water that had somehow found a way in through the cracks in the rock, I had surrendered. I'd closed my eyes and surrendered, welcoming it. I was tired and wanted no more of it. And I would have simply bled out and died there if it hadn't been for Hannah.

Not now, I scolded myself. *You want to lament, do it on your own goddamn time.*

Andrew's voice echoed to me again. "Tim, did you hear me?"

Cramped and restricted, I could hardly hinge my head far enough back on my neck to make out the circle of light above. "I hear you." My voice was just a notch above a whisper, yet it echoed from every direction. Below, the shaft appeared to widen just enough to permit my arms movement. I brought them up to my face and wiped away the sweat that was stinging my eyes. If the rope snapped, I wondered how far a drop it would be before I hit the ground.

Andrew's voice floated down to me a third time, but I could no longer understand what he was saying.

"It's opening up," I informed him, not knowing if he could hear me or not. "I can move my arms."

I could crane my neck and peer down the rest of the shaft, too, although the sight only caused my stomach to cramp. Around my groin, the harness was too tight, and I started to feel my feet going numb.

Hollinger was a few feet below me. The platform on which he lay sprawled and unconscious was just a narrow lip jutting from the wall of the shaft—a miracle that it had caught him. My own bulk blocked the daylight from funneling down so I couldn't make out any specific details concerning the severity of his condition, but I could see that he was no longer wearing his helmet, which was not a good sign.

My feet touched down on the ice shelf, and I reached up and tugged at the secondary line to alert the others. The shelf felt solid beneath my weight. I plastered my face and chest against the frozen wall for fear that if I didn't I'd lose my balance and fall off the ledge.

My left foot struck Hollinger's leg.

"Can you hear me, Hollinger?" I whispered into the wall of ice. The warmth of my breath bounced back at me off the ice. "Can you hear me?"

Hollinger groaned but didn't move.

I looked up. The opening was no bigger than the size of a quarter now. Raising my voice the slightest bit, I said, "He's alive."

Undoubtedly fearful their voices would create too much vibration, the others did not respond.

"Okay, Holly," I said, pulling off my gloves and stuffing them into the pouch of my anorak. "Hang with me, man. Hang with me."

Sliding one hand along the wall, I was able to grab hold of the secondary line. I ran it through the karabiners at my waist, then pulled at it to test the strength of the pitons the guys had secured in the surface of the glacier far above. It was strong and would hold. It would have to.

My fingers already beginning to tighten up in the cold, I fumbled with the clasps on the harness, unable to get them undone until my third attempt. Around me, the world seemed to sigh. I paused. There sounded a dissonant, sonorous splintering from somewhere below me, and my heart froze in my chest. Something snapped and fell away; I heard the hollow whistle of its descent but did not hear it hit the ground.

The ledge was crumbling under my weight.

I yanked the buckles from the harness and climbed out of it just like stepping out of a pair of pants, my heart slamming against my ribs, and crouched down, while the splintering, popping sounds resonated throughout the ice. Straddling Hollinger, I worked the harness over his legs and around his waist, where I fastened it with increasingly numb fingers. At eye level, I noticed a lightning bolt zigzagging in the ice wall, creeping higher and higher. A second fissure appeared beside it, peeling up the wall from the base of the ice ledge.

The harness secured, I grabbed Hollinger by his coat and tried to sit him upright. A ghostly moan escaped him. It was futile; he was deadweight.

"Come on . . ."

Sweat stinging my eyes, I tugged at the rope affixed to the harness. A second after that, the slack in the rope went taut. Hollinger's body slid up against the ice wall, his head lolling like a spring-loaded toy on his neck. I could see the gash at his left temple and the black blood already freezing in ribbons down the side of his face and neck. There was blood on the ledge where he'd struck it, too.

The shaft creaked like a flight of ancient stairs. I held my breath as Hollinger ascended the shaft, his hip brushing my face in the confined space. He dangled like a rag doll, his limbs limp as streamers. His body blocked out the light.

I pulled my gloves on, flexing the feeling back into my fingers, and gripped the rope in two hands. Just as I planted one spiked sole against the ice wall, the ledge beneath me broke away. The sound was like a tree keeling over. Gravity forced me down with it, my vision blurring and the rope burning through my palms. I could feel the heat of friction through the wool gloves.

I plummeted maybe ten feet before the rope jerked me like a yo-yo. As I twisted at the end of my rope over the narrow abyss, I glanced over my shoulder, my breath harsh and arid. I saw nothing except darkness. Directly above my head, I could see the gaping wound in the ice wall where the ledge had been just seconds before.

Above, one of the guys shouted my name.

"I'm all right," I called.

Once again, I planted my boot against the wall and proceeded to climb until the shaft grew too narrow for my legs to bend and the others had to pull me up.

I noticed the cracks in the ice wall were climbing steadily with me.

Jesus . . .

"Faster!" I shouted. "The shaft's gonna split!"

But they were pulling me as fast as they could. I shifted enough to see them haul Hollinger's lifeless body out of the shaft. Silver daylight spilled down into the hole. I winced and tried to grab the rope, but the shaft was too narrow. It was like being bound by rope at the shoulders.

The circle of light grew bigger and bigger. The silhouettes of heads appeared. For one terrifying moment, I thought I was going to get stuck coming up through the hole.

"Hurry!" I yelled, my voice cracking.

Spears of ice peeled away from the shaft walls and spiraled into the abyss. Chunks of ice fell in my face.

"Here, here, here." Chad's voice was suddenly in my ear. The burst of daylight stung my eyes as the guys hoisted me out of the shaft. I was weightless when they carried me across the glacier, my heart hammering, my lungs aching to breathe.

"Go," I wheezed. "Get away. It's . . . it's going to . . ."

There came a thunderous clap. I was dropped, my spine absorbing the shock of the fall. I managed to sit up in time to see a channel tear across the surface of the glacier from the shaft's opening, swallowing the snow that covered it. Crazily, I thought of the old Bugs Bunny cartoons and the way Bugs would tunnel underground, creating a channel of disturbed earth in his wake.

"Get up." Curtis grabbed the hood of my anorak and nearly strangled me.

I gathered my legs under me and sprinted across the face of the glacier toward the mountainside, tears freezing in rivulets down the swells of my cheeks. The earth roared at my back. There was a niche in the mountainside—a den hidden beneath a brow of black rock—that we were racing toward. We slammed against the mountainside and rolled into the opening in the face of the rock just as the tensile stresses spread over our wake, separating our trail of footprints on either side of the impromptu canyon.

Everything grew silent. In anticipation of further stresses, we huddled together like foxes in a den and listened for the splitting bark crunch of widening crevasses. But all remained quiet. The world was once again frozen in stasis.

Chad broke the silence. "Jesus Christ, we almost bought the farm on that one." He uttered a pathetic little laugh.

I slung my pack against the wall of the cave, then unbuckled my helmet and set it down beside me. "How's Hollinger?"

"I'm here," he said.

"He's awake," Petras said.

"What happened?" He sounded groggy. "Christ, my head hurts . . ."

"Took a spill, Holly," Chad said. "Dropped down five stories like an elevator with its cables cut."

Hollinger groaned. "My gear."

"It's gone," said Petras. "Swallowed up in the crevasse."

"My goddamn *gear*. My fucking *helmet*. What the fuck am I . . . am I gonna do?"

As my eyes acclimated to the dark, I could make out Hollinger sitting against the opposite wall between Petras and Curtis. He cradled his wounded, bloodied head in his hands.

"I've got an extra helmet," Curtis told him.

A flicker of light filled the cave. Andrew stood, holding his electric lantern in front of him. He walked past the entrance of the cave, his silhouette like that of a lawn jockey, and stood in the center of us. The roof of the cave yawned into eternity. It looked as if half the mountain had been hollowed out.

"Where do we go from here?" Chad said after a moment.

Like someone telling ghost stories around a campfire, Andrew raised the lantern to his face and said, "We go up."

The Ascent

4

BLIND AS BATS, WE SCALED THE WALL OF THE
cave. A difficult and tedious feat, the ascent required faith solely on
our sense of touch—feeling for specific grooves in the rock, fumbling for lines with our hands, threading the ropes through the pitons merely by touch. And the higher we climbed the darker it grew,
the only light down below at the entrance of the cave. But even that
would be gone soon as darkness reclaimed the land.

Time meant nothing; I had no idea how long it took us to reach
the plateau. Winded and muscle weary, half of us nearly dropped to
our knees and shed our gear as if we'd just returned to Earth after a
year of space travel.

Hollinger had the most trouble, what with his head wound and
his overall spirit shaken. The wound itself wasn't too troubling—
Petras and Curtis had examined it in the light of Andrew's electric
lamp before we began the climb and noted it was nothing more than
a flesh wound—but the flame within Michael Hollinger's soul had
been extinguished.

His superstitions appeared to be manifesting before his eyes. The
disappearance of half the food had already rattled him; his plummet
through a covered trap in the glacier only reinforced his superstitions.
(Of course, he did not take into consideration the luck involved in
having that ice ledge intercept him, preventing his death.)

As I passed him while climbing the cave wall, I could hear him
muttering to himself—something about trespassing on the hidden land.

Andrew lifted his lantern and studied our location. Curtis and
Chad followed suit, their own electric lanterns coming alive. A
grand chamber, immense and sprawling, opened before us. Stalactites corkscrewed down from the ceiling perhaps a hundred feet
above our heads, dripping calcareous water into russet pools. The
air was stale and warm, underscored by a nonspecific mineral smell.

"It cuts through," Andrew said, the light from his lantern diminishing as he moved farther down the chamber. He followed a trickling stream of water that snaked through a gouge in the stone floor. Running water meant there was a place where that water *originated*, and that typically meant a way out.

Gathering our gear again, we trailed Andrew through the chamber. It narrowed slightly, forming a tunnel all around us, the ceiling of which resembled the gullet of a whale. I tried to remember the story of Jonah and the whale but found that childhood memory was difficult to summon. In fact, for the past hour or so, my entire train of thought had been jumbled and muddy. At first, I thought it had something to do with the incident at the sinkhole—perhaps my body was still percolating mind-numbing adrenaline—but when it didn't wear off, I began to wonder about our altitude.

"How high up are we?" I whispered to Petras.

Petras deliberately lagged behind and said, "Don't really know. We must have climbed forty or fifty yards back there. Why? What's wrong?"

"I'm not sure. My head's funny."

"Dehydrated?"

"I've been drinking water like it's going out of style."

"You think it's altitude sickness?"

I didn't respond.

Daylight, purplish in its old age, filtered in from an opening in the ceiling farther down the tunnel. Motes as big as tennis balls danced in the beam. It wasn't until we drew closer did I realize they were giant snowflakes spiraling lazily in the air. Above us a fissure in the rock framed a panel of pink sky. The walls curled upward, forming natural staircases in the rock. One staircase led directly toward the opening.

Chad laughed dryly. "It's the fucking Stairway to Heaven."

Andrew doused his lantern and led the way up the backbone of rock toward the opening. We climbed out one by one, Petras and me bringing up the rear. As I poked my head into the fresh, frigid air, I noticed my hands were shaking badly. It wasn't alcohol withdrawal, not this time. Petras's voice still rang clear as a bell inside my head: *altitude sickness.*

Beyond, the horizon was blistering with a spectacular sunset. There were colors in it I had never seen before. The shadows created by the jagged outcrop of rocks caused something to stir inside me. It was the same feeling I used to get when looking at a raw chunk of stone, a hammer and chisel in my hands.

We hiked the outskirts of the ridge until nightfall, then set up camp within a basin that overlooked a snow-covered valley.

After everyone had fallen asleep, I crept out of our communal tent, pulling my coat tight about my goose-pimpled frame. A piton and hammer in tow, I negotiated down the rocky slope until one particular slab of stone caught my eye. It loomed in the moonlight, jutting sideways from the earth like one of the toppled smokestacks from the *Titanic.*

I walked two complete circles around it, admiring how it glowed in the tallow light of the moon, before lifting the piton and placing its spiked tip against the rock. Then I raised the hammer and struck the head of the piton. The sound seemed to echo over the mountain pass, into the atmosphere, and out like a comet into the unending depths of space.

CHAPTER 13

1

"THIS," SAID ANDREW, "IS THE SANCTUARY OF
the Gods."

We stood atop the third and final pinnacle of the Godesh Ridge, surrounded on every side by the rising gray caps of the Himalayas. Towers of stone, stacked like risers in a high school gymnasium, loomed all around us. At the center was a pyramid of stone, glossy with black ice, perhaps forty or fifty feet high. Directly below, an immense icefall ran like a frozen river, the sound of its movement like the shhhhh of static. Boulders of ice the size of automobiles crumbled sporadically from the glacier and tumbled into the icefall. Seracs—enormous pillars of ice—rose like skyscrapers out of the white. They looked solid and immobile, but they could collapse under the slightest weight without predictability.

The gateway to the Canyon of Souls stood across from us at the next plateau, separated by an insurmountable distance of air, a canyon in and of itself whose floor was the vicious, unforgiving icefall. It was like a medieval castle surrounded by a moat. Other than a snow-covered arch of stone that curved like a rainbow and connected to the other side of the canyon, the opposite plateau was as remote as an uncharted desert island.

"This is the farthest point along the Godesh Ridge that any group of climbers has ever been," Andrew continued. "I want you all to take a deep breath and taste how clean the air is. You'll never breathe air this clean again in your lives."

Curtis appeared beside me, looking ashen.

"What's wrong?" I said.

He gnawed at his lower lip. "Friend of mine died at the Khumbu Icefall on his way to the top of Everest three years ago. I was there; I saw it happen." He shook his head. "Forget it. I'm cool."

I clapped him on the back but said nothing. My head was becoming increasingly achy, and I'd developed a dry cough over the past two days that I couldn't shake. When I was able to find sleep, my dreams were fitful and frightening, though I couldn't remember anything of significance about them upon waking.

Chad studied the icefall. Even Chad, who was typically unshaken, looked wary. "So how the hell do we get across?"

"That's the tricky part," said Andrew. He acknowledged the stone arch with a jut of his chin. "We use it as a bridge."

Chad scowled. "You're fucking kidding me, right?"

"We can't climb that thing," Curtis added. "The sides and top are pure ice against rock. The ice will shatter the second we drive an anchor into it."

"You're right. That's been the fatal mistake of every other group that came before us," Andrew said. "They try to scale the arch and walk across its top."

"And we're not going to do that," Curtis responded.

"No, we're not." Andrew grinned, and I was once again reminded of that look he gave me all those years ago in San Juan just before he threw himself off the cliff and into space. "We're going to climb *under* it."

2

THEN NIGHT FELL. WE ERECTED OUR TENT AT THE
site of the stone arch, intent on crossing it early the next morning.
The wind was fierce, hardly blocked by the looming spires of stone
and the pyramid-shaped monolith, and the temperature was unforgiving. Weakened from the cold and the continual treks through the
mountainous passes, we huddled inside the tent.

A hot meal was prepared, and we ate heartily. Only Hollinger didn't
touch the food. Between helpings, I sidled up next to Hollinger and
knocked my shoulder against his. That seemed to snap him briefly
from his daze. He offered me a meager smile, then pulled his knees
up to his chest and hugged them.

"Here," I said, handing him a cup of coffee.

"Thanks."

"How's your head?"

He fingered the bandage at his temple. "It's okay."

"How'd that helmet come off so easy?"

"Don't know. Don't recall much about the fall." He spoke with
the detachment of a car crash victim.

"You doing all right?"

"I have a bad feeling."

"About the climb tomorrow?"

"About the whole thing, mate." Hollinger turned and stared at
me. His eyes were full and black, moist like the eyes of a deer. "I've
been seeing things. Things that play with my head. Ever since you
and Andrew left to take Shotsky back to base camp."

A shiver traced down my spine. "What things?"

"My head's playing funny games. I can't think straight."

"It's the altitude," I said, trying to comfort him. "It's messing
with my head, too."

"No, it's not. It's . . . I don't know . . . Something's not right . . ."

I squeezed his shoulder and told him everything would be fine.

But later that night, with everyone asleep in the tent, I found it impossible to shut my eyes. I couldn't stop thinking of Hollinger's words—*My head's playing funny games. I can't think straight*—and I wondered how much longer it would be until we reached the Canyon of Souls. Andrew seemed so confident we would make it there, despite all the other teams that had attempted to do so in the past and failed.

Unable to sleep, I gathered my piton and hammer, and just as I'd been doing the past two nights, I crawled out of the tent, located the perfect stone, and began to sculpt it. Throughout the past few nights of our journey, I'd left a trail of partially finished statues lining the path to this very spot, each of them a reproduction of the woman I'd lost in a flaming car wreck in Italy with a man—a linguistics professor—named David Moore.

The night air froze the marrow in my bones. I chipped away at my chosen stone with numb hands, a fair distance from our camp so as not to disturb the others while they slept. The moon hung fat and yellow behind the nearest peak, illuminating the snow and causing it to radiate with a dull luminescence.

—*Turn back.*

I couldn't tell if I'd actually heard her voice or if it had been only in my head. Nonetheless, I spun around and stared at the passage between the jagged rocks, the snow flooded with shadow. No one was there.

"Hannah?"

—*Turn back, Tim. Please.*

Of all the things I could do—I uttered a weak, little laugh. Surely I was hallucinating. "My head's playing funny games," Hollinger had said. "I can't think straight." Sure enough, sure enough . . .

—*Tim.* She stepped out into the moonlight, her body naked and pale and glistening with condensation, so real she left footprints in the snow.

"Jesus, Hannah . . ."

It felt as though my heart had stopped pumping. My blood ran cold as ice water. As I watched, she seemed to flicker from existence like bad reception on a television set.

"Don't go," I pleaded. "Hannah, please . . ."

—*Turn back*, she said, her voice ringing in the center of my brain.

Something cold and wet trickled over my lips. I touched two fingers to the wetness. They came away black with blood. A nosebleed.

Hannah turned and walked away from me down the sloping, snowy pass.

I begged her to stop, but she didn't. So I pursued, dropping my piton and hammer in the snow, the nylon hood of my flimsy anorak flapping in the freezing wind. She disappeared around a bend in the pass, hidden by giant fingers of rock, but I followed her footprints like a bloodhound on the scent. On the other side of the bend, I saw her silvery form climbing one of the stone towers. She climbed with ease, as if her body had been specifically designed to do so. I called to her, but she didn't stop or look back at me.

My desire to touch her—to reach out and *feel* her—was suddenly overwhelming. The next thing I knew, I was scaling the stone tower after her, my movements much less steady, my speed no match for hers. Each time I looked up, she was farther and farther ahead of me.

Loose rocks broke free under my footing and tumbled in a small avalanche down the face of the tower. One hand lost its grip on the ledge, and I swung outward, my feet flailing briefly in the air, while I held tight to the handhold with one hand. My fingernails digging into the stone, I swung my other hand around and grabbed the ledge as my legs pedaled for a foothold. My heart restarted in my chest. Glancing up, I saw Hannah's fish white body already mounting the summit.

"Hannah, *please* . . ." I continued to climb, the muscles in my arms quaking, my ankles swelling with sprains inside my boots. I was nearly forty feet in the air when I reached the summit, my muscles destroyed and my lungs straining like old car tires pumped up with too much air. The summit was a slanted platform that overlooked the snowy pass and the rush of the icefall farther below. The icefall glittered like a bed of diamonds in the moonlight.

Hannah stood at the far end of the platform, facing me.

"What is it? What do you want?" It burned my throat to talk.

—*I've told you, Tim. I want you to turn back. You shouldn't be here. None of you should be here.*

"I'm dreaming this. Either that or I'm hallucinating."

—*It doesn't matter.*

"Let me touch you. If you're real, let me touch you."

—*It doesn't matter*, she repeated.

"It does. It matters to *me*."

She turned and lifted her arms like wings. She brought one foot over the edge of the platform—

"Hannah, no!"

—and let herself drop off the edge. Her silvery hair trailing her, the twin hubs of her small buttocks . . . there and then gone.

I rushed to the edge, skidding to a halt just inches from sealing my own fate in the icy rush of the icefall a million miles below. Looking down, I could see no evidence of Hannah. She should have been in midair, those ghostly arms still splayed like birds' wings . . . but she had vanished. Or had never existed in the first place.

When I called out her name, the sound of my voice jerked me awake. I was no longer atop one of the forty-foot spires. Nor was I in the tent. I sat up in the snow, my thermal underwear soaked and stiffening in the cold, my teeth rattling like maracas in my head. Disoriented, I looked around. Farther up the incline, wedged at the base of the towering stone spires, I could discern the black Quonset shape of our tent.

I stood, my knees weak and my hands shaking and numb. There was an inky smear on the palm of my right hand. I touched clean fingers to my nose, and they came away bloody. It felt like someone had been using my head as a steel drum. A wave of spasms shook my bones, and an instant later, having temporarily lost control of certain bodily functions, I urinated in my thermals, the heat blessed and welcome as it spilled down my thighs.

There were no footprints in the snow anywhere. None leading to the spot where I now stood. There were no footprints coming down the slope from camp and none from any other direction. Directly above my head was a rocky gangplank; it was possible I'd been sleep-walking and had walked the plank, for lack of a better term, only to wake up in this very spot. But that didn't explain what the hell I'd been doing sleepwalking in the first place. As far as I knew, I'd never walked in my sleep in all my life.

One step into the snow and I was instantly aware that I could no longer feel my feet. They were wrapped in two thick layers of socks, but both layers had soaked all the way through, and their soles had begun to freeze. How long had I been out here, anyway?

Back in the tent, I was careful to not wake the others as I changed into my day clothes. My hands and feet would not get warm, and there was a painful, needling ball of ice in the center of my stomach, as if all my digestive juices had turned to icy slush. I cleaned my bloody nose with my wet socks, my exhalations stuttering while my inhala-tions were equally as hesitant. Fumbling in the dark, I located the canteen with the remaining bourbon and took two healthy swallows. I clenched the canteen against my chest and felt the alcohol burn a magma path down my gullet and into the saddle of my guts. I couldn't stop shaking.

"I was wondering what happened to you."

The voice jarred me, freezing my insides all over again. It was Hollinger, propped up in the dark beside me.

"Christ," I whispered. "Trying to give me a goddamn heart attack?"

"Can't sleep." His tone was noncommittal.

A million responses ran through my head at that moment. In the end, however, I said nothing. I tucked the canteen of bourbon in my pack and slipped beneath the warmth of my sleeping bag. My limbs hadn't fully thawed, and my stomach still felt tied in a not, but I forced myself to close my eyes and hunt down an hour of sleep before morning.

3

ANDREW STOOD AT THE BASE OF THE GIANT STONE arch, a look of deep concentration on his face. His normally pale skin had been burned by the sun and was beginning to flake away by the dry wind. Over the past couple of weeks, a fine coppery beard had fallen into place, somehow making him look younger.

In fact, the only things that hadn't changed throughout the course of our journey were Andrew's eyes. They remained alert, startling, clear, and blue as Caribbean waters. He still had that way of looking at someone and captivating him, holding him prisoner in his stare . . . until he laughed his loud, obnoxious laugh, and all prior sins were instantly forgiven.

"Here's what we're gonna do," he said, addressing the rest of us as we packed our gear. "We've all played on playgrounds when we were kids, right? Well, we're gonna re-create the monkey bars using this arch."

He slapped the underside of the arch as if testing its solidity. "We'll start off with a rope-and-pulley system. I'll climb out and insert cams every two and a half feet along the underside of the arch. We'll use the cams as handholds, one hand over the other, just like the monkey bars. Of course, I want everyone harnessed with a fixed line. And I'll run a second empty line with me so we can slide our gear across on it. This way we won't have to carry our packs." He clapped. "Sound good?"

In truth, it sounded insane. Even if he was able to insert the spring-loaded camming devices, it was still quite a distance to the other side. Hand over hand was a slow, tedious process, and my body was still run-down from the night before. God only knew how long I'd been out in the snow, but it was long enough for me to develop a slight fever that was currently working its way through my system.

Earlier this morning, I'd gone down the pass and climbed the ridge where I'd woken, expecting to find my footprints. But there were no prints in the snow atop the rocks just like there hadn't been prints in the pass. It was as if I'd been dropped there from the sky.

"Hey," Petras said, "you look like shit."

"That explains why I *feel* like shit," I said, trying to make it sound like a joke. It only managed to come across bitter.

"You ready to do this?"

"Ready as I'll ever be."

"It's crazy," Petras went on. "You know that, right? Andrew's plan, I mean."

"Andrew's out of his mind," I said and nearly added, *And I think I'm beginning to follow.*

"It's a good idea, though," Petras said. "Sliding the packs down to him on a second line so we don't have to carry them."

"I just want to get this all over with."

"This climb?"

"The whole trip."

Petras nodded. That nod said, *I know the feeling.* "I'm worried about Hollinger."

"He'll be okay," I said, not quite sure why I said it. I recalled the way he'd been sitting in the tent across from me last night, his disembodied voice calling to me in the darkness. *I was wondering what happened to you.* It suddenly occurred to me that Hollinger had probably been awake when I'd left the tent. I would ask him about it, but I'd wait until we were safely on the other side of the icefall. The last thing I wanted to do was spook him before the climb.

Twenty minutes later, Andrew had rigged a pretty decent rope-and-pulley system at the base of the arch and was prepared to begin his climb along the belly of the arch. While his plan had sounded ridiculous, watching him execute it only reconfirmed it. Several times he nearly lost his grip, flailing one-handed by a single cam, suspended from the bottom of the arch as his legs dangled over the abyss. A fall from this height would ensure death, and it didn't matter if it was the icefall beneath us or a cushion of mattresses; the sudden stop upon landing would be enough to reconfigure someone's internal organs.

Andrew had also clipped the second safety line to his belt, and Curtis tied it to an anchor on our side of the arch. This would be the line we'd use to send our gear so we wouldn't have to cross with any extra weight on our shoulders.

"Holy shit," Chad commented as Andrew finally touched down on the other side of the canyon. The entire commute had taken him three full minutes. "I can't believe the dickhead pulled it off." He cupped his hands to the sides of his mouth and shouted, "You're a fucking nutcase—you know that, Trumbauer? A fucking *nutcase*!"

"He's also the first person to ever set foot on that side of the canyon," Curtis said, not without some awe in his voice.

Petras began applauding, and we all quickly followed suit. Only Hollinger didn't join in. He remained perched at the base of one of the stone towers, a haunted look in his eyes. The wound at his temple had scabbed over but looked stark and severe against the sudden paleness of his face. His own beard—like mine—had materialized in mangy patches, like miniature crop circles. The frigid Himalayan wind had chapped and split his lips. They were the lips of a leper.

Yet Andrew's success had reinvigorated the rest of us. Petras and Curtis rigged our gear to the second line and shoved the packs over the abyss. On Andrew's end, he'd angled the line so that it stood at a gradual decline. The packs rolled across the line toward Andrew as if on a zip line. After he'd finished collecting our gear, he waved both arms as if signaling an aircraft to land.

Chad was anxious to climb next. He popped in the earbuds to

his iPod and allowed Curtis to boost him up using Andrew's rope-and-pulley system until he was able to grasp the first of the cams. Curtis secured the safety line and fed it out to him as Chad loped like an ape, hand over hand, going twice as fast as Andrew had.

"Let's keep the train moving," Curtis said.

Petras motioned to Hollinger. "Come on, bro. You and me. We're up."

Like a zombie, Hollinger stood and strapped on his helmet. With the enthusiasm of someone walking to the electric chair, he unzipped his parka and stomped his feet in the snow. Petras secured himself to Hollinger with a tertiary line and told Hollinger to go ahead. Without a word, Hollinger mounted the stone parapet that preceded the arch. Curtis clapped his back and told him everything would be cool, man.

"Yeah," Hollinger said, offering Curtis a half smile. "Cool, man." He swung out and gripped the camming device on the first try.

Meanwhile, Chad was nearly all the way across and on the other side of the canyon. He was already shouting praise to himself.

"I'll be right behind you," Petras assured Hollinger as he continued to climb.

"You're up," Curtis said and helped Petras across to the first cam. The moment Petras's feet left the platform and swung out into open space, my stomach cramped and I buckled over.

Curtis must have heard me groan. "You okay?"

"Yeah."

"You're next, Shakes." Over the past two weeks, Chad's pet name for me had caught on.

"Shit," I moaned. "You go ahead."

"You sure?"

"Quite. I gotta make a pit stop."

Curtis laughed, running the safety line through his own karabiners. He genuflected and stepped out onto the parapet. Before reaching for the first camming device, he turned back to me and said, "Can you imagine old Shotsky doing this? Lucky bastard is probably sipping hot chocolate and flipping through girlie magazines back at camp."

"Yeah," I said. "Lucky bastard . . ."

I scurried around the other side of the pass and ducked behind a stand of stone pylons. Unbuckling my trousers and squatting, I groaned as I squirted out a ribbon of hot, brown fluid onto the snow. My stomach growled and felt like a fist clenching and unclenching.

Back at the arch, Curtis was halfway across and moving fast. I untied the safe line at my end and ran Andrew's secondary line through the karabiners at my waist. Then I climbed to the edge of the platform and reached out for the first cam. For a moment, I was hypnotized at the rise and swell of the icefall below. Looking at it too long was like looking into a pocket watch swinging like a hypnotist's pendulum. Tearing my eyes away, I gripped the cam and kicked off the platform. My legs swung over the abyss.

The trick was to not think about it. Hand over hand, I swung from cam to cam, finding it easier as I progressed, fueled by the sheer exhilaration of it. In fact, I was moving so fast I was closing in on Curtis, who was only two or three cams ahead of me.

"Catchin' up to you, big man," I called, laughing.

"No chance, white boy!"

"Shake your ass, Booker—I'm on your tail."

On the other side of the canyon, Chad pumped a hand in the air, egging us on.

"You on vacation up here, Booker?" I chided. "You planning to hang around here all day?"

"Yeah . . . sure . . ." He was running out of breath.

"Yeah . . ." I was running out of breath now, too.

"If you think—," Curtis began. Then there sounded a metallic thunk, and one of Curtis's hands fell away from the camming device. A second after that, gravity pulled him straight down. He did not make a sound; the only sound was the whir of the safety line gathering slack as Curtis dropped.

"Curtis!"

When the slack ran out, Curtis's falling body jerked at the end of the line, his arms still flailing. He should have stopped right there, dangling like bait at the end of the line, but then there was a second sound—*twink!*—as the safety line snapped. The release sent Curtis into a spiral, cartwheeling down, down, down.

Mesmerized, I watched him plummet, his arms and legs suddenly still. He shuttled down until he was a tiny smear in midair, no different than an imperfection on a photograph. A moment later, he was swallowed up by the icefall.

And he was gone . . .

"Curtis!" someone shouted from the other side of the canyon. "Curtis! Curtis, you—"

The only remnant of Curtis was the small, wallet-sized photograph of his daughter that had somehow come loose during the fall and now fluttered like a butterfly out over the abyss until that, too, disappeared.

For a moment, I felt as though I'd blinked out of existence. One minute I was dangling from beneath the stone arch, and the next I was floating in some cottony, colorless orbit. Sound was nonexistent. I could see nothing, nothing at all. Everything was white; everything was black. The only feeling was the needling prick of heat shooting up through my body.

Curtis was dead. Curtis was—

"Shut up!" Petras shouted from across the reach. "We've still got a man out there!"

I clung with both hands to the single cam above my head, staring at the roiling channels of ice at the bottom of the canyon. Curtis was gone, completely disappeared . . .

Petras called out to me, "You've got to get your head back in the game, man! Come on! Forget what you just saw! Climb to me, Tim!

Climb to me!"

I managed to pull my gaze from the spot where I'd last seen Curtis Booker and to the opposite side of the canyon. The others were there, their bodies smeared as my vision refused to clear. But I hardly saw them. What I saw was the loose end of the safety line that had snapped and now whipped in the wind.

Which meant I had no safety line . . .

"Come on, Tim!" Petras hollered. The others joined him. "Come on, man! Get your fucking head in the game!"

Head in the game, head in the game, head in the game . . .

I blinked several times, trying to focus not on the dangling section of rope but on Petras, Andrew, Chad, and Hollinger. Holding my breath, I reached for the next cam. I crossed without difficulty. But when I reached for the next one, I found it wasn't fully there: the spiked base was still fixed to the rock but the head was missing, the titanium having snapped off in Curtis's hand. There was no way for me to grab hold of it; it was just a mere glint of metal jutting from the underside of the arch. And the cam beyond that was four feet away.

"Come on!" Petras urged.

"I can't!" I shouted. "The cam's gone!"

"Grab the next one!"

"It's too far!"

"Tim," Andrew interrupted, "swing out and grab the next cam. You can do it. It's not too far."

"It's too far!" I cried. My feet suddenly felt like they weighed fifty pounds each.

"It's not!" Petras added. "You can do it! It's just an arm's length away."

I strained, trying to reach past the broken cam to the next one in line. It was too damn far. An impossibility. The only possible way would be to start a momentum, to swing out and grab it. But if I missed, the strain on my other arm would be too much. I'd surely suffer the same fate as Curtis.

"Stop! Wait! Don't fucking move, Shakes! Don't fucking move!" Chad hooked himself up to a fresh line, intent on climbing out toward me with a safe line he had looped around his shoulder. "I'm coming! Hang on!"

"Too . . . dangerous," I called, but I doubt anyone heard me. My voice was no louder than a child's sob. And my goddamn feet were weighing me down. I closed my eyes and thought of the comic books I used to read as a kid, the ones with Plastic Man who could stretch to preternatural lengths.

"Tim—"

When I opened my eyes, I saw Chad hanging from beneath the stone arch facing me, no more than four feet away. He hung from one camming device while harnessed to a series of ropes. He shook the wound safe line off his shoulder, down his arm, and into his hand.

"Here," he said. "You gotta fuckin' catch this, dude."

"I'm . . . a horrible . . . shortstop," I responded.

Chad actually chuckled, and had we been on solid land I would have wrapped my arms around him and kissed him right on the goddamn lips.

"You're a wiseass, Shakes," he said and tossed the rope.

I didn't so much as catch it as it got tangled around my arm. Nonetheless, I snatched it, worked it through the karabiners, and cinched it at my waist. The strain in my other hand from hanging from the spring-loaded camming device was causing numbness throughout my whole arm.

"Let go," Chad said.

"No, man. Let me . . . reach for the . . . the goddamn . . ."

"Just fucking let go, Shakes. The rope'll hold."

"I think I can—"

"Do it!"

I closed my eyes and let go. My stomach lurched as I felt myself drop and swing in an arc at the end of Chad's line. I couldn't tell when I stopped swinging, and I wouldn't open my eyes. I wouldn't.

The line strained, sounding like someone twisting a leather wallet in big hands. *Open your fucking eyes, coward,* I thought and opened my eyes. I was turned on my side, twisting horizontally in midair, as the safe line held me suspended over the abyss.

"You're still alive," Chad said.

"I'm gonna puke."

"Climb up."

I was beginning to hyperventilate. My exhalations burned my throat. Suddenly I was positive I was going to die out here. But unlike that day in the cave, lying in the dark with my bone jutting from my leg, I did not want to die. *You might have come out here not caring whether you lived or died,* a small voice spoke up in my head, *but you care now, and you're not going to die. Do you hear me, Overleigh? You're not going to die.*

I rolled over and gripped the safe line. A single tug sent me vertical. Hand over hand, I climbed up until the bottoms of Chad's boots thumped against my helmet. I climbed higher, so intent on Chad's pant legs I could make out the individual fibers woven together in the fabric. When I'd climbed high enough, Chad grabbed my shoulder.

Petras shouted something incomprehensible. He could have been shouting from another planet, for all it mattered to me.

"Up, up," Chad urged. He was running out of breath. "Grab onto me if you have to. Just climb up and grab the cam above your head. Come on, Shakes. You can do it."

Somehow I managed to do it. Using Chad's body for extra support, I climbed the rope until I was able to hook back into the network of cams that ran the length of the arch. I wasn't quite out of the woods yet, and I had serious doubts as to what strength remained in me to climb the rest of the way, but the outcome was suddenly looking much better.

"All right," Chad mumbled, his voice nearly a gasp. He seized the next cam with his free hand. "Not bad for a lousy artist."

"Move . . . your . . . ass," I said. "In . . . my way."

"Let's go, fireball."

It seemed to take an eternity to make it across. I hadn't come down from the final cam before Petras and Hollinger dragged me onto the ledge. Solid ground never felt so good. I staggered a few feet, brushing off all the hands that were eager to hold me up, until I dropped to my knees and vomited in the snow.

4

PETRAS WAITED TILL AROUND MIDNIGHT BEFORE going back for the rest of Curtis's gear. After what happened crossing the arch, there was nothing left in us to continue, so we built camp against the mountain and lit a fire. The wind came moaning through the canyon, so cold it could fillet the skin off our bones.

Petras bundled up in extra layers and trekked to the arch to collect Curtis's pack and the extra line that still flapped in the wind. Twenty minutes later, he returned in utter silence, Curtis's pack over one of his broad shoulders, the broken line wound around the other. He set the items at the farthest corner of our cramped little tent, then sat down heavily, exhaling a sigh that shook the tent fabric.

"We should say something." It was Hollinger, his face mottled. "A fucking prayer or something."

No one said anything. None of us was religious, and what was there to say, anyway?

"Fuck it," Hollinger growled. "He was a good fucking guy. He had a daughter. She was beautiful. Her name was Lucinda."

I thought of the photograph, flapping over the freezing air until it vanished against the backdrop of ice.

"I didn't know him well," Hollinger went on, "but he was a good bloke and he became a good friend." His eyes searched us all, as if daring us to disagree with him. "He didn't deserve to go like that."

"No one does," said Petras.

"Yeah," Hollinger agreed. "No one does."

"I guess we've got to make a decision," I said.

Everyone's gaze shifted toward me except Andrew's. He was peering out one of the plastic windows in the tent, staring at the absolute darkness beyond.

"About what?" Chad said.

"About whether we keep going or turn back."

Hollinger was quick to respond. "We fucking turn back."

Only then did Andrew look at me. "Are you kidding?" There was no aggression in his voice; it was simply a question.

"Our spirits are shot," I said. "We've already come farther than anyone's ever come. Isn't that enough?"

Andrew turned back to the plastic window. When he spoke, his breath fogged up the plastic. "We're only two days away from the Canyon of Souls. Three days at the most. If we turn back now, Curtis died for nothing."

There was nothing any of us could say to that. So we slept, the cold mountain winds bullying our tent and reminding us of our isolation straight until morning.

CHAPTER 14

1

DEATH ON AN EXPEDITION SUCH AS OURS WAS NOT uncommon. Thousands of people climb Everest every year, and people labor under the misconception that it's become as safe as skydiving or running a marathon. They believe that the sheer magnitude of mountains must have diminished in the wake of man's ever-evolving scientific prowess and technical savvy. Yet people still die climbing Everest and its neighboring peaks, and some people, like Curtis Booker, will never be found.

Mountaineering is quite possibly the last remaining extreme sport. Like Andrew had once told me many years ago, "If you jump out of a plane and your friend's parachute doesn't open, you sure as hell can't fly back up into the plane and call it quits."

For the next two days, we were a trail of zombies plodding through a world erased by snow. We climbed the remaining peaks in silence, all joviality gone from us, and descended into bowl-shaped valleys with grim expressions on our bearded, windswept faces. It had become taxing. Not just the climbing but being around one another, like coal miners about to go stir-crazy.

Petras and Andrew stopped speaking to each other completely, though whether this was a conscious decision or not, I had no idea. Likewise, Chad's usual jokes at our expense had ceased altogether. He kicked up tufts of snow as he walked, occasionally humming under his breath while listening to his iPod. When his iPod froze, he chucked it off the side of the mountain, then offered a military salute as it shattered on the biting rocks below.

Michael Hollinger looked the worst. His lips were cracked and bleeding from the cold, dry wind, and I doubted he would physically be able to talk even if he wanted to. With each passing hour, his eyes narrowed more and more until they were nothing more than eyeless slits beneath his brow. He hardly ate, and his clothes began to grow too big for him, like he was swimming in them. Several times while trekking along a straightaway, Hollinger had to stop and catch his breath, though I did not think this had anything to do with physical exhaustion. It was a sure sign of an atrophied spirit.

My own temperament fluctuated with the various positions of the sun. My fever had worsened, and my insides alternated between boiling like stew and freezing to a hard lump of coal in my stomach. I sweated profusely during the warmest parts of the day—so much so that the collar of my shirt and nylon anorak became discolored with sweat. When night came, I would quake and rattle beneath both my own sleeping bag and Curtis's.

I wrapped extra pairs of socks over my hands while my gloves dried by the fire—a fire for which we had difficulty finding fodder to burn. In the end, we ripped pages out of my George Mallory book, crinkled them into loose balls, and set them ablaze.

Since that strange night before crossing the arch, Hannah's ghostly image had not returned. Even at night, when my mind seemed most active, she refused to come. In dark solitude I wondered about Petras's mythical *dakini,* the female spirit of Tibetan lore. I thought of Hannah's quicksilver flesh and the flash of her eyes as she crossed from behind mountainous lees into haunting moonlight. A shiver accompanied each new thought.

Though Hannah's ghost remained elusive, I *did* hallucinate . . . or at least I managed to convince myself that it was all a hallucination. Because surely there was no one else up here. Surely . . .

But climbing the outer rim of the Godesh Ridge on that second day, I paused to tighten the laces on my boots and happened to glance down to the snow-laden, black rock valley below. A man—or what appeared to be a man—stood within the shadow of a massive snow-bound overhang halfway up the valley. It was a place we'd crossed earlier that morning, and I could still see the fresh snow punctuated by our footprints. I stared at the shape, recalling how I'd seen a mysterious figure following Andrew up the slope of the pass after Shotsky had died. Was this the same man? Was it a man at all?

I raised my hand in a wave, but the figure did not respond. At this distance, it was impossible to make out any details, but there was no movement, no acknowledgment of my greeting.

It was then that I realized I was sweating through my clothes. I peeled my collar away from my throat, and a waft of warm body heat exited. All of a sudden, I was breathing in great whooping gasps, my heart rumbling like a freight train.

Something wasn't right. This was more than just the fever I'd been fighting the past couple of days. My clothes started suffocating me, my helmet squeezing my cranium. It was as if I were growing to twice my size in a matter of seconds.

Unsnapping the buckle of my helmet strap, I pulled it off my head and tossed it aside. I dropped my pack and fumbled with the zipper on my parka. Then I took my parka off, whipped it into the snowbank, and lifted my anorak over my head. My flannel shirt and thermals were drenched with sweat. Wasting no time with the buttons, I tore the flannel shirt from my torso, the buttons popping loose and soaring through the air, then sloughed off the sopping wet thermal beneath it.

Petras closed one hand around my wrist. "What the hell are

you doing?"

"Gotta . . . get out of these clothes . . ." My voice was breathless, struggling. "Claustrophobic . . ."

"You're not." Petras grabbed my other wrist. I struggled to get free, but his grip was too tight. "It's onset hypothermia. You're actually freezing to death and dehydrated, but you feel like your body is on fire."

"My heart," I gasped. "Jesus . . . help . . ."

My eyelids fluttered, and the world tilted to one side, knocking my legs out from under me. I collapsed into the snowbank, the world grainy and distant before my eyes. My heart was like a jackhammer trying to drill through the wall of my chest. I actually placed one hand over my heart to steady it and could feel its reverberations against my palm.

"Hey!" Petras shouted to the others. "Man down! Some help here!" Strangely his voice was laden with echo. It took me several seconds to realize I was also hearing it come through the walkie-talkie affixed to my backpack, two feet away from me in the snow.

"I think . . . think I'm having a . . . a heart attack . . ."

Petras's hand fell on my chest. "Be cool," he said in his big bear's voice. "Relax."

I forced my eyelids open. They were gummy, and my vision was blurred. Once it cleared, I could make out the wind-chapped skin stretched taut over Petras's high cheekbones and the flecks of snow caught in his auburn beard.

Suddenly I was a child in bed with a fever, and John Petras was my father, who incidentally was also named John. My father mopped my brow and smiled warmly down to me and told me to relax and stay warm. He told me of the birds roosting in the fig trees in the yard and how the limestone wall by the shore was becoming infested—absolutely *infested*—with lichen. It was nothing to worry about now, but I would have to scrub the wall clean once I was better, scrub that moss and lichen and green slime right off.

And what I wound up doing was chiseling away sections of the wall, carving faces and hands so that it looked like people inside the wall pushing against it and trying to get out. My father was angry and sent me to my room for three days, though by the end of the three days, he came to my room and told me I shouldn't have carved up the wall but that my carvings were very good and that he was impressed that they were very good . . .

I was lifted off the ground, my head cradled in someone's hands, and my shoulders and legs were carried by others. I was wrapped quickly in a warm sleeping bag, while Andrew and Chad created a lean-to to keep the freezing winds at bay.

"You'll be all right," Petras said very close to my face. I could smell his sour breath and feel its warmth along the side of my face and down my neck. "Drink some water."

I sipped water from a bottle. It seared my throat on the way down to my guts. My body was quaking, my teeth chattering. I thought I had gone blind until I realized I had my eyes shut.

Yet when I opened them, it was dark. A small fire burned outside the lean-to. My body had ceased quaking, and my heart had resumed its normal pace. I was alone beneath the lean-to. When I peeked out past the fire, I could see no one.

I pulled on a sweatshirt and edged out into the night. Petras was crouched low to the ground, filling water bottles with snow.

"Where are the others?" I croaked, my throat raw and abrasive.

"Making an advance up the east ridge. Andrew said the Hall of Mirrors is right over the next pass, which is the doorway to the Canyon of Souls." He looked me over, his eyes like black pits in the firelight. "You look better."

"I think my fever broke."

"Gave us all quite a scare earlier." He returned to his work.

"It was no picnic on my end, either. Need help?"

"I'm just about finished here."

"It was like my heart was going to burst out of my chest. I've never heard of hypothermia causing a heart to *race*. In fact, it does the opposite, doesn't it?"

"You were also sick as a dog," Petras added. "Let's not forget that."

"Still . . ."

"Still what?"

"Forget it. My head's been funny lately." What had Hollinger said? *My head's playing funny games. I can't think straight.*

Petras gathered a number of the water bottles in his arms. "Give me a hand with these, will you?"

I helped him load the bottles into our various packs. While we worked, I said, "You want to hear something crazy?"

"What's that?"

"Earlier today I thought I saw a man down in the valley below the ridge. Just before I had my little, uh . . . attack, I guess."

"A man?"

"He was too far away to see very clearly, but I was certain of it."

"Are you certain of it now or just certain of it then?"

"I don't know. Hard to say."

"It could have been a hallucination. You were babbling when I got to you and when we carried you away from the ridge. A couple of times you even called me dad." Petras smiled warmly.

"Strange thing is, I thought I saw someone following Andrew up the pass after Shotsky died."

Petras froze. I didn't realize what I'd said until he very slowly turned to face me. Then it all rushed back, and I felt like hiding my head in the snow.

"Fuck," I groaned.

"Shotsky's dead?"

I sighed. "Yes. The end of the first day taking him back to base camp. Heart attack. We tried to revive him, but it was quick."

"Why didn't you say anything?"

"Andrew and I agreed it would be best not to tell anyone. Morale reasons or whatever. I don't know. It made sense at the time, but now . . . well, shit, everything's fucked up now."

Petras's eyes bored into me, heavy on my soul. I told him I was sorry for deceiving him and the others.

"I guess it doesn't matter. Doesn't bring Shotsky back."

"No," I admitted, "it doesn't."

"And there's no good reason to tell Mike and Chad now. Especially after what happened with Curtis. This whole thing's turned into a fuck-a-row." He handed me one of the fresh bottles. The snow inside had already melted. "Here. Drink this. Stay hydrated."

I gulped down half the bottle, wiping my mouth on the sleeve of my sweatshirt once I'd finished. Out in the snow, I refilled the bottle, while Petras, in contemplative silence, rearranged some of the items in his pack. When he swiveled in my direction, his expression was telling.

"What's the matter?" I said after the silence had become over-whelmingly obvious. "What are you thinking?"

Petras chewed at his lower lip. "Not quite sure yet. Working over some things in my head but nothing that's—"

He stopped as voices floated down to us from the top of the pass. A moment later, three darkened figures sauntered toward the lean-to.

"I'll tell you later," Petras promised and zipped up his backpack.

"Look who's decided to join us again," Chad said, his heavy boots kicking up clouds of snow dust as he approached the fire. "You were babbling like Linda Blair for a while there, Shakes. Was wait-ing for your head to spin around and pea soup to come spewing out of your mouth."

"Lousy company will make people do strange things," I retorted, al-though since the incident on the arch where he'd saved my life, I no longer felt any genuine disdain for Chad Nando. It was all playful shtick now.

"Well?" Petras said. "What'd you guys find?"

Andrew sat on a roll of tarpaulin near the fire and unfolded a map in his lap. "The entrance to the Hall of Mirrors is just where the Sherpas predicted it to be. It's a cave—a mouth—right in the center of the mountain. Maybe fifty yards up the pass."

"The opening's maybe a hundred yards from the ground," Chad added. "We'll have to do a short climb to reach it, but it shouldn't be a problem."

"Do we know what to expect once we're inside the cave?" I asked.

"Legend says it's just a straight tunnel that empties into an ante-chamber called the Hall of Mirrors," Andrew said.

I asked him why it was called the Hall of Mirrors.

Andrew snickered and rubbed two fingers across his creased forehead. "Honestly, I have no idea."

I raised my eyebrows. "Then from there?"

Andrew continued to rub his brow. "There's supposed to be an opening, a doorway of sorts, somewhere in the Hall of Mirrors. It leads directly to the Canyon of Souls."

"But no one's ever seen the canyon," I said. "Right?"

"Well, no . . . but so far everything has been verified—the Valley of Walls, the Sanctuary of the Gods, the stone arch and the icefall, and now the opening to the Hall of Mirrors."

"How wide is this canyon supposed to be?" Petras asked.

Andrew shrugged. "No clue. Two feet wide . . . or two thousand. No one knows for sure."

"Someone must have been there," I suggested, "to know it exists."

"I'm sure that's true," Andrew agreed, "but it's never been officially documented. Could be stories passed down from bands of monks or Sherpas or Yogis. Could be campfire tales told by ancient yak herders who once lived in the valleys around these mountains. Christ, for all we know, it could be the equivalent of the stories from the Bible, Jesus of Nazareth, water into wine, and all that. How do any of these tales survive from one generation to the next? I don't know."

It didn't comfort me any to hear Andrew relate the Canyon of Souls to the stories of the Bible. To think Donald Shotsky and Curtis Booker died chasing some fairy tale did not sit well with me.

Andrew looked at me. His eyes gleamed in the firelight. His face was gaunt, nearly skeletal. "Will you be ready to climb tomorrow morning?"

I said I would.

2

THERE WERE NO DREAMS AT THIS ALTITUDE.

3

IN THE MORNING, BLADES OF ICE SLASHED INTO THE

canvas tent and stuck like spears into the smoldering remains of our campfire. Hail came down like bullets, boring tunnels several inches deep into the packed snow.

We drank cold coffee, and I ate the rest of the stale bread I'd rationed from Shotsky's pack after he died while we watched the hail through the opening in the tent. Chad and Hollinger busied themselves with a deck of cards, and Petras thumbed through the remaining pages of the George Mallory book.

Andrew sat by the tent's open flaps watching the hailstones. "Looks like it's letting up. I'll give it ten seconds. Ten . . . nine . . . eight . . ."

I sat at the rear of the tent, my legs resting on my pack, dragging the blade of Petras's hunting knife across a softball-sized stone.

"Seven . . . six . . ."

I slipped and drove the edge of the knife into the soft mound of flesh just below my thumb. It didn't hurt, but blood surfaced almost instantaneously, running in a single stream down my wrist and soaking the cuff of my flannel shirt. I grabbed one of my socks and—

4

—WRAPPED MY INJURED HAND IN A BANDAGE.
Splotches of blood lay like asterisks on the linoleum floor of my studio, and there were two drops on the half-finished sculpture. Out along M Street, the lampposts radiated an incandescent blue, and the traffic was becoming heavy.

At the sink, I washed the blood off my chisel, which had carelessly jumped from the stone and bit into the tender flesh of my palm. However, the chisel might not have been as careless if its handler hadn't had so many scotch and sodas throughout the afternoon. Tightening the bandage around my hand, I removed my smock and turned the lights off in the studio before locking up for the evening.

Thirty minutes later, I arrived home to our split-level along the waterfront, the house dark in the deepening twilight. I kicked my shoes off in the front hallway and called Hannah's name up the stairs. In the kitchen, I prepared a pot of coffee and set it on the stove, then climbed the creaking stairwell to the second floor.

The house was empty. The bed in the master bedroom hadn't been made this morning, which was unusual, and the towel from my morning shower was still draped over the shower curtain rod. My dirty underwear was still in a ball next to the toilet.

"Hannah?"

I stood inside the bedroom doorway while my mind strummed. The closet doors stood open, and after a second or two, I noticed Hannah's large floral suitcase—the one she took on our honeymoon to Puerto Rico—was missing.

Frantic, I drove back into the city and cruised past Hannah's gallery. There was a Closed sign in the window, but there were lights on inside. I double-parked the car, bounded to the door, and knocked.

Kristy Lynn, Hannah's twenty-two-year-old assistant, answered the door. "Hey, Mr. Overleigh. What's up?"

"I'm looking for my wife."

"Oh. Well, she isn't here."

"No?"

"Nope. Sorry." Kristy Lynn curled a length of her dyed black hair. Her dark blue fingernail polish made the tips of her fingers look like those of a corpse. "Hasn't been in all day."

I looked over Kristy Lynn's shoulder as if expecting to find Hannah hidden behind a desk or a chair or something. "And you didn't hear from her?"

"Not all day." Kristy Lynn sounded instantly bored. "What happened to your hand?"

"Huh?" I'd forgotten about it. Blood had soaked through the gauze bandage.

"You need a clean bandage."

"All right. Good night."

"Later, skater," she intoned and shut the door in my face.

I drove to the houses of our mutual friends, but no one was home.

It was nearly nine when I arrived back home. The house was still dark; there was no indication Hannah had returned in my absence. An acrid, burning smell filled my nose as I crossed the foyer. Swearing under my breath, I realized I'd left the fucking coffeepot on the fucking stove. It had boiled over, coughing up brown sludge from the spout and onto the stove. Thankful the whole house hadn't gone up in flames, I shut off the burner and wrapped my hand in a dish towel, then lifted the pot off the stove, and dumped the whole damn thing in the kitchen sink.

The phone rang. I sprinted to it and gathered it up in my wounded, bandaged hand. "Hannah?"

"I'm leaving you, Tim," she said. Her voice sounded distant. I could tell she had been crying.

"Where are you?"

"It doesn't matter. Did you hear what I said? I'm leaving. I have to leave you."

"Hannah, please—"

"I'll talk to you in a couple of days. I just need some time to myself, some time to cool off. You need that time, too."

"What the fuck are you talking about? Where are you? I'll come get you. We should talk."

"Not tonight." It sounded like she was struggling very hard to stay calm. "Give it a couple of days."

"Like hell." My face was burning, my hands shaking. My toes were curling in my shoes. "Tell me where you are. This is bullshit. What's going on?"

Her defenses fell. She started sobbing. "I can't do this anymore. I can't do this."

"Do *what*?"

"Live like we've been living. I'm second best to your obsession."

"*What* obsession?"

She paused, then said, "Yourself. You're obsessed with yourself. I can't keep doing this. I'll call you in a couple of days. Good-bye."

"Hannah—"

"Good-bye." She hung up.

Injured and furious, I threw the phone on the floor and kicked it clear across the kitchen. I grabbed the next closest thing—a kitchen chair—and swung it against the wall. One of the legs splintered off, and I chucked the rest of it down the hallway. Then I collapsed on the floor, sobbing like a child, the bandage having come undone and trailing from my hand like a party streamer. When I stood ten minutes later, there was blood all over my shirt and pants and a widening puddle of it on the tile floor.

Then something on the kitchen table caught my eye. It was a hardcover book, one Hannah had been lugging around with her for the past several weeks, titled *Foreign Words: The Art and Heart of Language.*

I didn't need to examine the author photo on the back of the dust jacket to know it was written by David Moore, my wife's biggest fan.

David made steady appearances at Hannah's gallery throughout the week, and in the past two months, Hannah had heard him speak at Georgetown University three times. They were evening lectures, and she had invited me to the first one, which I declined in order to meet certain project deadlines, but the subsequent two she hadn't even mentioned to me until after she'd gone to them.

We'd even attended an intimate dinner party at his brownstone last month in celebration of the release of his newest book. He'd had my sculpture on prominent display in his living room, and I'd gotten drunk on expensive whiskey.

I turned the book over anyway and stared at his grinning, handsome face. The pretentious ass, he wore glasses only in his author photos and never in real life. In a fit of rage, I tore the dust jacket from the book and shredded it. When I couldn't tear it up any more, I seized the book itself and relieved it of its pages.

At ten o'clock, I parked outside David Moore's brownstone. It was in a collegiate Georgetown subsection, just one block away from the house where *The Exorcist* had been filmed decades ago. I'd had enough time to sober up and was running on full adrenaline now as I jumped out of the car and mounted the steps to his front door. I didn't even knock until I tried the doorknob and found that it was locked. I heard shuffling and voices on the other side of the door. A light came on in one of the upstairs windows, and I thought I saw the silhouette of a head peeking out.

"Come on!" I yelled, banging on the door.

It opened partway, David's face appearing in the vertical, three-inch sliver. He wore a bathrobe, and his dark hair, gray at the temples, was wet from what I assumed was a recent shower. For whatever reason, this sent me into a rage.

"Tim—," he began.

I pushed the door open and barreled into the house. "Where is she?"

"Calm down. Take a breath and—"

I slugged him across the jaw. It was a good punch, forcing him to stumble backward and lean for support on an end table. The look of shock and fear in his eyes was fuel to my fire. I was cuffing my sleeves when Hannah appeared at the end of the hallway, wearing a pair of blue sweatpants and her old Kappa Delta sorority T-shirt. The sight of her weakened me. I froze in the entranceway.

"Jesus, Tim." David righted himself against the wall, massaging his jaw. "That's assault."

Something snapped inside me. I pounced on the son of a bitch, swinging my fists and pummeling him until Hannah grabbed me from behind and attempted to pull me off him. The feel of her at my back caused the fight to flee right out of me.

David curled into a fetal position against the wall, an arm over his face, one pointy elbow facing me.

"Fucking coward," I spat.

Hannah's fingernails dug into my forearms. When I whirled around to her, she shoved me against the wall. Her hair had fallen in her face, her eyes livid. "Get out."

"Hannah, I—"

"Get out of here."

"You're coming home with me."

David scrambled up the wall, straightening his bathrobe as he rose.

I caught a glimpse of his genitals through the part in the robe, which caused me to lash out at him again. I swung at his eyes and cheekbones—anything my fists could reach—until a sudden strike against my left leg sent me crumpling to the floor. An instant later, white-hot pain raced up my thigh.

Hannah stood over me with a golf club poised like a baseball bat, ready to take a second swing. Reflexively I covered my face.

"Jesus Christ," David groaned. "He's out of his goddamn mind."

My eyes locked with David's. "I'm going to kill you," I growled.

"You're not," Hannah said. She was shaking, her arms like pipe cleaners jutting from her sleeves. I had no doubt she would bring the golf club down on my skull if it came to that. "You're going to get up and get out of here. I told you on the phone that I need a couple of days to get my head together. You've got no right coming here."

"I'm calling the police," David said. He staggered to the kitchen and grabbed a portable phone.

"Hannah," I said.

"I don't want to hear it. Get up. Goddamn you. Get the hell up."

"Please . . ."

"This is assault," the son of a bitch said from the kitchen. "This is breaking and entering and assault."

"Come in here, you fucking weasel, and I'll show you assault," I said, standing. David did not respond, and I looked at Hannah. It killed me to see my wife standing in front of me, a golf club over her shoulder. What killed me even more was she was dressed for bed . . . *in this fucker's house*. "Come home with me. Please. We'll talk things out. I love you. You know that, don't you? I love you."

Tears streamed down her face. "Get the fuck out."

"Sweet—"

"I can't do this right now. You're attacking me when I'm weakest. That's unfair."

"Your *leaving me* is unfair!" I shouted. "I come home to an empty goddamn *house*—that's what's unfair! Goddamn it. Come *home* with me!"

"I can't do this. Please, Tim. If you love me, you'll leave."

David walked in, wielding the portable phone like a handgun.

I wasn't going to win this—the realization fell on me like a piano down a flight of stairs. My face burned; my pride burned. Breathing heavy, I straightened my shirt and shot a glare at David.

He took a step backward into the kitchen, holding up the telephone to prove he was serious about calling the cops.

"Fuck you, dude," I said. I turned to Hannah and my soul softened. "One last time. Please come home with me."

"No," she said, tears spilling down her cheeks. "I can't."

"All right." I went to the door, paused with my hand on the knob, then pulled it open and stomped onto the concrete porch. I left the door open behind me, but the second I stepped out, Hannah slammed it. A moment later, I heard the lock click into place.

My head was filled with butterflies. My vision was as clear as it had ever been—I felt I could see for miles without restriction—and my veins were pumping full of lighter fluid.

I climbed into the driver's seat of my car and sat for what could have been an hour, watching traffic slide up and down the block and tourists dip in and out of bars. Parked in front of me was an old 1928 Mercedes motorcar convertible, with running floorboards and a spare tire on the trunk. It had a vanity license plate—4N WORDS.

"Son of a bitch," I uttered and twisted the door handle. I popped the trunk and grabbed my tire iron, feeling its heft in my hands. A malicious grin spread across my face. I marched over to the motorcar and stared down at the front grille.

"Fucking bastard," I murmured and smashed out one of the headlamps. It exploded in a shower of powdered glass. "Asshole." And I smashed the second headlamp, swinging like Babe fucking Ruth, taking the son of a bitch over the wall. "Home run," I said, grinning. "That one's outta here."

"Tim!" Hannah shouted from one of David's upstairs windows. "Goddamn it. We're calling the police!"

"This one's out of the park," I informed her and swung the tire iron into the motorcar's windshield, shattering it. I brought it down again and again until the interior upholstery was blanketed in triangular shards of glass. Exhausted, I dropped the tire iron in the street and held my hands up in mock surrender.

Hannah poked her head through the window, and I could see David pacing behind her.

"Go home!" Hannah yelled. "Go home!"

"*You* go home," I told her. It wasn't about me; it was about her, all about her. "*You* go home."

The window slammed shut and the light went off.

A car full of college kids cruised by, hollering at me from the windows.

I kicked the tire iron at them—it rebounded off the car's rear bumper, a good kick—and got back into my car. I cranked the ignition, and as luck would have it, the goddamn car wouldn't start. I tried it again to no avail. A third time, though, and it kicked over, the engine just as angry with me as my wife.

What the hell happened here tonight? I wondered. Car horns blared at me as I pulled out into the street and cut drivers off. *Will someone tell me what the hell just happened?*

I sped home, the steering wheel greasy with my sweat. In fact, I ran my hands along the steering wheel, surprised at the amount of perspiration. It wasn't until I stopped at a traffic light that I realized it wasn't perspiration but blood. I held my hand up in the glow of the traffic light. It was covered in blood, the bandage completely gone, having unraveled at some point during the evening's events.

Behind me, car horns honked. I looked up and saw the light had turned green. Gunning the engine, the tires squealing, I raced home, caught somewhere between an agonized laugh and a child's lost cry.

5

"FIVE," SAID ANDREW. "FOUR ... THREE ... TWO ... ONE."

Amazingly, the hail stopped. Not exactly at one but within thirty seconds of it. It was a curious enough feat for Chad and Hollinger to glance over at Andrew.

"It's done," Andrew said, climbing out of the tent. "Let's go."

We packed the gear and headed north along the pass. In no time we came to a flattened wall of rock that rose into the heavens, its peak obscured by cumulus clouds. No less than one hundred yards above us, visible like an eye socket in the face of the mountain, a cave yawned black against the whitish gray stone. Icicles the length of jousting poles hung from the ceiling of the cave, and a grayish tongue of ice lolled out from the floor of the opening.

"That's it," Andrew said. "The entrance to the Hall of Mirrors."

Beside me, Hollinger's teeth chattered. I asked him if he was okay, but he didn't answer. He'd been in his own world since Curtis's death.

"Come on." Andrew began scaling the face of the mountain.

It was more difficult than it looked. It was a sheer vertical climb, dependent on anchors and lines rather than hands and feet. Cleared of my fever, I was overcome by newfound strength, but it was still a strenuous, tedious task.

Surprisingly, Chad struggled. Halfway up the face, he dangled by one hand and gaped at me as I passed him. I saw a mixture of fear and defeat in his eyes.

"I'm beat," he said simply, his voice impossibly small. "I can't keep doing this."

"We're almost there. Follow me."

He groaned but swung his free hand back against the rock. "Okay," he said, shuddering. "Lead the way, Shakes."

Together we climbed through the mouth of the cave, our final anchors planted firmly in the tongue of ice spilling from the opening. Dragging myself up, I felt Chad clasp my ankle. "Shakes," he croaked. I reached down and grabbed his wrist, then hoisted him up. I'd never seen his face so empty before.

It was only a cave—dark, narrow, full of echo. We got out our electric lanterns, but only Hollinger's worked. He was hesitant to lead the way, so Andrew intercepted the lantern from him and moved farther down the throat of the cave. The opening had been fairly wide—a truck could probably drive through it with little difficulty—but just a few yards in, the walls seemed to come in and suffocate us. After a dozen or so steps, I could touch the ceiling. It was covered in ice; snow fell into my face.

"I can't see a damn thing," Andrew said, which was bad because he was the one with the lantern.

It was true; all I could see was the yellow glow of the lantern in Andrew's hands, but beyond that, the walls were virtually invisible. Yet I could feel them closing closer and closer around us like a great bear hug choking the life out of us all . . .

"Keep the lantern close to the ground, Andrew," Petras said from somewhere behind me. "Let's not fall down any cracks in the rock."

Andrew lowered the light. "Good idea."

"This can't be right," Chad whispered. I hadn't realized he was so close to me until he spoke. "Stop." He gripped the waistband of my pants. "Let's tie on together."

We ran a line between the two of us. When Petras passed, I asked if he wanted in.

"I'm bigger'n the two of you put together and multiplied by three," he grumbled, moving past us in the dark, barely visible. "I'll do you more harm tying on if I happen to fall down a hole. I'm good on my own, guys. But thanks."

"This is fucked up," Chad said, expelling breath in my face. He couldn't have been more than three inches from me, but I couldn't see him. His hands snaked around my waist, clipping his line to the clasps at my belt. Up ahead, Andrew's lantern was diminishing.

"Let's keep up," I suggested.

We walked until the opening of the cave was nothing more than a pinpoint of gray daylight behind us. Our footfalls echoed loudly, and our voices were even louder. I didn't even have to fully extend my arms to touch the walls on either side. They had narrowed considerably.

"I see light," Andrew said. It was a whisper, but in the confines of the cave, it boomed back to us. "Up ahead."

A moment later, I could see it, too: a pale aquamarine light seeming to emanate from the opposite end of the cave. As we drew closer, the light appeared to be funneling down, like a balcony spotlight shining down on a stage.

Andrew dimmed the electric lantern. "Careful crossing over." He paused, and his legs hinged with exaggerated pantomime over a jagged ridge of stalagmites. "It's sharp."

Blind, I stepped in a pool of cold water, which immediately soaked through my boot and layers of socks. "Shit." My toes went numb instantly.

Chad's fingers pressed into my forearm, but he didn't say anything. I could just barely make out a ghostly blue hint of his profile as we neared the mysterious light issuing from above.

We crossed into the antechamber and stopped.

"Holy Christ," Chad marveled.

I, on the other hand, was speechless.

It was a banquet hall–sized antechamber, the ceiling mostly comprised of crystalline spires and illuminated stalactites, except for the very center that appeared to be a perfect circle cut through the stone to the outside world, but on closer review, it was covered by several inches of solid ice. The result was a sort of ice-paned moonroof in the ceiling of the cave, the moonlight segregated into variously colored beams of light. The rainbow-colored light cast independent spheres of colored light on the frozen cave floor.

Only in the center of the floor, where a section of each circle of light overlapped all the others and focused like sunlight through a magnifying glass, a perfect beam of white light melted the frozen snow from the cave floor, creating a star-shaped opening in the ice that revealed the blackened rock beneath.

It was this display that initially captivated our attention. Together, we all walked slow circles around the shaft of light. Andrew doused the lantern and set it down, his gaze trained on the spotlight of white light in the center of the floor.

Chad gripped my forearm and stopped walking. "Look around," he said, his voice filled with awe. "Jesus Christ, Shakes, look around."

I looked.

It was called the Hall of Mirrors because that was exactly what it was: an antechamber whose walls were existent only in the form of pure ice, perhaps fifteen inches thick, like great blocks of glass encapsulating the entire room. Light refracted off every wall of ice, a constant lamp, keeping the ice from being coated with frost and causing it to melt and refreeze, melt and refreeze, creating a mirrorlike finish to the walls of ice.

"Holy crap," I muttered, stepping into the center of the antechamber. I walked toward one of the walls, my reflection facing me, as perfect as it would be in a bathroom mirror. I reached out to my image's hand. Our fingers touched.

I looked up at my reflection and into my own eyes. Fear shook me. Cadaverous, sunken eyes, lipless mouth, a dark, patchy beard corrupting the lower half of my face—I was a ghost of the man I'd once been, a hint of the soul I'd once carried within me.

Andrew's reflection floated up behind mine. I felt his hand on my shoulder while watching his reflection place it there. "It's who we really are," his reflection said. "We may not like what we see, but the mirrors don't lie. It's who we are. And we have to accept that."

I dropped my hand away from the mirrored ice.

"Can you believe this place?" Chad howled, a skeletal grin etched across his face. He scanned his own reflection in every wall, every mirror. "It's like something out of a goddamn fairy tale. It's amazing!"

Before me, my reflection briefly blurred. I turned and tugged on the rope at my hip. I was still attached to Chad; he felt the tug and paused, staring down at the line, then in my direction. He looked at me with wide eyes and a creased brow.

"Keep your voice down," I warned him.

"I'm just saying," he went on, ignoring me. "This place is fucking outstanding!"

I wound the rope around my hand, pulling him a few inches in my direction. When I spoke, it was no louder than a whisper. "I said keep your voice down. In case you haven't noticed, the fucking walls are vibrating with every sound that comes out of your big mouth."

"The spires in the ceiling, too," Petras added, looking up. His voice was hardly louder than my own.

Unbuckling Chad's line from my karabiners, I tossed it at his feet and said, "Admire the place in silence."

He called me a dickhead, then wound his rope and slid it to his shoulder. "Place is as solid as a Diebold safe." He tapped one of the glasslike walls.

"It's not a safe. It's a tank," Hollinger said quietly, walking around the circumference of the room. "I used to keep piranha in a ten-gallon tank when I was a kid. Real piranha. Used to feed 'em goldfish once a day, and those buggers would tear them apart in seconds. Less than a minute after I'd drop the goldfish into the tank, there'd be nothing but a jagged little backbone at the bottom of the tank." He paused to examine one of the walls up close, grazing the icy surface with his fingers. A plume of vapor blossomed from his chapped lips. "That's what we're in right now. A tank. A fish tank."

"But are we the piranha or the goldfish?" Petras asked, his question holding more weight than perhaps he intended.

"Well," Chad said, unsnapping his helmet and tossing it on the ground, "it's a badass place, but it's also a dead end." He ran two fingers along the reflective surface of one of the glass walls. "We must have missed something."

"No." Petras pointed across the antechamber to the farthest panel of ice. "Look above it."

The ice wall itself was maybe twenty feet high, the snow-encrusted ceiling coming down low to meet it, enormous icicles hanging over the upper part of the ice wall like fangs. However, it was possible to make out an opening between the ice walls and the ceiling of the cave, wider and more obvious in some places, crisscrossed by a network of interlocking spires of ice. The place Petras had pointed out appeared to be the widest opening along the shelf beyond which a natural ice cave recessed into the wall.

"I see it," I said.

"It's the only doorway out of this room," Petras said. "That's got to be it."

"It goes up," Hollinger said.

I turned to Andrew, but he was no longer standing behind me. He'd migrated to the center of the room and sat cross-legged in the snow directly beneath the skylight of ice. His eyes closed, his hands on his knees, he meditated. His entire body seemed to glow in the magnified light.

"I feel like Neil fucking Armstrong." Chad dropped to his knees and rifled through his backpack. "We should have brought a goddamn American flag."

"There's this," Hollinger said, pulling his Australian flag from his backpack like a magician pulling scarves from his sleeve. "Same colors."

Chad stood, a pickax in his hand, and grimaced at Hollinger. "That's blasphemy. Put the goddamn thing away."

A meager grin broke out across Michael Hollinger's bearded face. It was the first semblance of a smile he'd sported in days. "'Australians all let us rejoice,'" he sang in a low voice, "'for we are young and free! We've golden soil and wealth for toil, our home is girt by sea!'"

Chad groaned and said, "The hell is 'girt'?"

As he sang, Hollinger flapped the flag like a matador would flap his cape and set it down unfurled on the ground. He saluted it and continued singing, while Petras and I chuckled.

Then Petras joined Hollinger, both of them grinning like fiends, and I sidled up between them, saluting. Not knowing the words to the Australian national anthem, Petras and I hummed quietly along to Hollinger's off-key, low-pitched singing.

"Yeah, sure, you guys play your games while I make history." Chad hefted the pickax and dragged it across the snow to the ice wall, staring up at the ledge and the partially hidden ice cave above it. "Guess we'll see how easy these walls are to climb," he said, raising the pickax over his shoulder. "Don't worry about me. You fools keep singing."

He swung the pickax into the mirrored wall of ice. The sound was like a gunshot going off in close quarters, reverberating throughout the antechamber.

From his spot on the ground, Andrew opened his eyes.

A sound like splitting wood came from above.

The three of us stopped singing and gaped upward in time to see a jagged boulder of packed snow and ice roughly the size of a love seat drop from the ceiling. It whistled like a missile as it fell.

Chad screamed, bringing his hands up, not quick enough to jump out of its path. It pounded him to the ground in a spray of ice particles, the sound like two automobiles colliding on the highway. The entire antechamber vibrated—the vibrations raced up my legs and rattled my lungs—and Chad bucked once beneath the weight of the boulder. A gout of blood erupted from his mouth and instantly sprayed the snow around him. His head slammed against the ground as the boulder, driven vertical into the ground, leaned back with a deafening creak and slammed against the ice wall, coming to rest at an angle.

The force of it hitting the ice wall caused a minor avalanche of smaller boulders, and spears of ice planted themselves all around us, upright in the snow.

I tripped over my feet rushing to Chad's side. Unbelievably, he was still alive. His eyes had a distant look to them, and his lips were frothed with blood. He tried to raise his head and speak as I knelt over him.

"Don't talk," I said.

The boulder had landed on his pelvis, no doubt shattering the bone and driving him straight into the frozen ground. There was surprisingly little blood . . . but as I sat there gripping his hand, a deepening red stain spread from beneath him and soaked into the snow.

Petras appeared at Chad's other side. He placed one hand against the boulder. We'd never be able to move it in a million years. And even if we could . . .

"Jesus," Hollinger muttered from across the cave. He was still standing beside his flag. "Jesus, oh, Jesus . . . Jesus . . ."

"Hurts," Chad managed. A fresh gout of blood burped from his mouth, dribbled down his neck, and pooled at the base of his throat.

"Shhh," I told him. "Don't fucking talk, Chad. Don't talk."

". . . urrrr . . . ," he gurgled.

Petras's eyes locked with mine. There was no denying what he was thinking.

"Jesus," Hollinger whimpered. "Oh . . . oh . . . Christ . . ."

". . . urrrrrr . . ."

I could hear the wet gurgle of blood at the back of Chad's throat—

Andrew stood and negotiated around the fallen chunks of ice to arrive behind me. He said nothing as he stared at Chad. One of his hands rested on my shoulder in a gesture I initially mistook as camaraderie. But then he pushed me aside.

I scrambled backward on my ass, the seat of my pants soaking in Chad's blood. I glanced down at my hands and saw my palms were sticky and red.

". . . urrrrrr . . ."

Without expression, Andrew grabbed the pickax Chad had dropped only two seconds before the boulder pinned him to the ground. He raised it above his head—

"No!" Hollinger shouted.

—and drove the spiked end into Chad's head.

RONALD MALFI

Chad's fingers dug into the snow, and one of his legs kicked. Blood sprayed across Petras's face, but he looked too stunned to flinch.

Coming to one knee, Andrew steadied what remained of Chad's skull with one hand and pried out the pickax with the other. There was a wet, sucking sound as the spike pulled free of Chad's head. It was a sound I feared would haunt me until my dying day.

"Are you fucking *crazy?*" Hollinger screamed. "Are you a fucking *animal?*"

Andrew stood and tossed the dripping pickax into the snow. He was frighteningly calm. There was a faint constellation of blood across the front of his coat.

"What did you *do?*"

Andrew slowly turned his head in Hollinger's direction. "Keep your voice down."

"You're fucking mad!" Hollinger cried. "You hear me, Trumbauer? You're fucking mad!"

"I said keep your voice down. The last thing we want is more shit to fall from the ceiling."

"Jesus!" Hollinger bellowed, throwing his hands into the air. His eyes locked on Andrew, he backed against the wall, hugging himself.

Andrew went to his backpack and unsnapped the roll of tarpaulin from a set of straps. He unraveled the tarpaulin and carried it to what remained of Chad Nando and draped it over the corpse. Only Chad's legs and boots protruded from the other side of the boulder, twisted at awkward, unnatural angles. It reminded me of Dorothy's house falling on the witch in *The Wizard of Oz.* I half expected Chad's feet to curl up like deflated party favors at any moment.

Sick to my stomach, I rolled over and spat into the snow. I wanted to vomit but couldn't; there was nothing of substance in my stomach. A frothy string of mucus drooled from my lower lip and froze on the ice.

"You killed him," Petras said. He'd scooted back against one of the ice walls after being sprayed in the face with Chad's blood.

"It had to be done," Andrew responded calmly. "You think he was going to walk out of here? You think he would have lasted more than ten minutes like that? And let's not forget the pain—"

"It's murder," Petras said.

"And I'd hope any of you would do the same for me if it came down to it."

Righting myself against a mound of snow, I grabbed fistfuls of snow and rubbed my hands together, desperate to get Chad's blood off me.

Andrew threw his pack down at the mouth of the cave, mostly hidden in shadows, and unrolled his sleeping bag. He spoke to no one the rest of the night, which was fine by us.

6

"WHAT ARE WE DOING HERE?" HOLLINGER WHIS-pered in the dark. The only suggestion of light spilled from the window of ice above our heads—the milky, dreamlike glow of moonlight.

I hadn't been asleep, but Hollinger's voice startled me nonetheless. Staring at the disc of translucent ice above my head, I said, "We're all going mad. Slowly but surely. All of us."

Andrew was asleep on the other side of the antechamber; his snores echoed off the walls. Petras, Hollinger, and I had bedded down as far away from him as we could get. We huddled together like three rabbits caught in a snare.

"I keep seeing him bring it down into Chad's head," Hollinger went on. "I keep hearing the sound it made when he pulled it out. It was like that last bit of water gurgling down a tub drain."

I closed my eyes. "Stop it."

"Did you hear it?"

"Cut it out."

"He's lost his mind. Things are all fucked up."

"Go to sleep," I told him.

"All fucked up."

"Go to sleep."

"Go to hell."

I grabbed Hollinger's electric lantern and headed for the mouth of the tunnel. Andrew was sleeping at the foot of the entrance. I stepped over him and continued down the corridor, the lantern casting very little light beyond the small halo around itself. After a gradual bend in the tunnel, I could see the moonlight cast along the frozen tongue of ice that clung to the bottom lip of the cave's opening. I set the lantern down and sighed, unzipping my fly and urinating into the wind. My stream seemed to freeze midway down the mountainside; I heard it shatter like glass on the rocks below.

Shaking off, I zipped up my pants and grabbed the lantern. I nearly ran into Andrew when I turned around, his face ghost white, his eyes colorless and void of feeling. I skidded on the tongue of ice and almost dropped the lantern.

"Boo," he said quietly.

"Jesus Christ." I brushed past him, knocking his shoulder with mine (though this wasn't on purpose) and holding the lantern up to guide my way.

"Tim."

I paused, unsure if I wanted to turn around and look at him again.

"It had to be done," he said to the back of my head.

"We're through. Doesn't matter how close we are, doesn't matter what you want. We're turning back tomorrow. With or without you."

Andrew didn't respond. We both stood there in the shimmer of a pale moon, half hidden in the darkness of the cave for several seconds without moving, without speaking another word.

Finally, after what seemed like an eternity, Andrew said, "Do you blame yourself?"

I turned around, holding the lantern in his direction. His face was a mask of shadows. "Chad's death was an accident, a horrible accident.

You were right—he was going to die anyway. I don't blame anyone. Not even you."

"I wasn't talking about Chad," he said.

I stared at him. There was a hot rumble in my guts. I knew what he was talking about. I knew it wasn't Chad.

"Because I want you to blame yourself, Tim," he said. "I want you to blame yourself."

"You're a sick bastard," I told him. "If I live to be a hundred, I'll never know how a woman like Hannah befriended a creep like you."

The hint of a grin seemed to play across Andrew's face.

I lowered the lantern and receded into the dark cover of the tunnel, walking backward and staring at Andrew Trumbauer's silhouette poised at the mouth of the cave. He looked like the fleeting remnants of a nightmare.

7

IN THE MORNING, ANDREW WAS GONE. HE'D LEFT behind Hollinger's electric lantern but took his gear as well as our petrol stove. I used the lantern to search the cave, but I found no sign of him. There didn't appear to be any fresh footprints in the snow outside the cave, down along the pass beyond the hundred-yard drop. He'd simply vanished. As if he'd never existed.

Back in the Hall of Mirrors, Petras and Hollinger tried to force down a light breakfast. I had attempted the same moments ago, but my stomach refused to cooperate. I hadn't kicked the fever like I thought I had, either; I could feel it asleep in the center of my body, hibernating but still very much alive.

Petras looked at me. "Anything?"

"He disappeared."

Across the chamber, the bright blue tarpaulin was a constant reminder of all that had happened and what still lay beneath. It was impossible for my gaze not to drift in that direction every couple of minutes. Too much longer in this reflective chamber and I'd lose my mind. Glancing around, my beaten, filthy reflection stared at me from every wall.

"Have some cold tea," Petras offered. "It tastes horrible but it's *something.*"

I sat with them and held the tin cup of cold green tea between my hands but didn't drink any. My stomach was incapable of keeping anything down. I looked at the panel of ice in the ceiling. Warmed by daylight, it dripped constant streams of water against the exposed rock until nighttime when it would freeze all over again.

"Do we wait around for him, or do we just leave?" Hollinger said finally.

Petras's eyes briefly met mine.

"We wait until dark to leave," I suggested. "If Andrew hasn't returned by then, we go without him."

Hollinger looked incredulous. "In the *dark?*"

"We've got nothing to make a fire, to make heat. Andrew's got the lighter fluid, the petrol stove, the goddamn matches. We need to keep moving at night to keep our blood pumping and our bodies warm; otherwise we'll freeze. We'll rest during the day."

Hollinger stared at the black maw of the cave. "Where do you think he went? Did he climb back down the fucking rock?"

Neither of us answered.

Hollinger turned his gaze on the sheet of tarpaulin. "Christ, I can still see him in my head, you know? And the way Andrew brought the goddamn ax down into his . . . into his head . . ." He shivered. "Any of you guys know much about him?"

"Chad? No," I said.

"No," echoed Petras.

"Like if the bloke had a family or someone waiting for him back home," Hollinger went on.

"I have no fucking idea, Holly," I said. It wasn't his fault, but I was growing irritated by the sound of his voice. "What's it matter?"

"Maybe we should go through his gear," Hollinger said. "Maybe he's got stuff in there that he wouldn't want left behind in this place."

"And where would we take it?" I barked. "We're not exactly on the red-eye out of this place, either, in case you haven't noticed."

Petras placed a steadying hand on my knee. *Cool it*, his glare said.

"Fuck it." Hollinger slid up the wall until he was standing and dusted the snow off his pants. "I need to piss."

Without a word I handed him the electric lantern—the only one that still worked—and he switched it on. His head down, his feet dragging tracks in the snow, he shuffled across the antechamber until he crossed into the tunnel and vanished in the dark.

I eased my head down against my pack and folded my hands across my chest. I tried to shut my eyes, but they refused to cooperate. Instead, they focused on the blue tarpaulin at the other end of the chamber.

"I've been thinking about it," I said quietly. "It's sick, but Andrew was right. Chad wasn't going to make it."

"I know."

"Anyone else could have done it, and it wouldn't have been as bad. It's worse that Andrew did it. Somehow that makes it worse."

"We need to keep watch," Petras said. "We need to take turns watching for him. We shouldn't all fall asleep at the same time."

I looked at him. "You think it's . . . that serious?"

"Let's just stay on the safer side of chance."

"All right."

He nodded. "All right."

My gaze turned back to the blue slab of tarpaulin and trailed up the snow-packed boulder that leaned at an angle against the nearest ice wall. My eyelids felt stiff and heavy, my body sore from head to toe.

Beside me, Petras began snoring like a lumberjack, his nostrils flaring with each powerful exhalation.

I caught a glimpse of Hannah's reflection in one of the mirrored walls of ice and sat up. Her image glided along the wall, undulating with the imperfections in the ice, and disappeared behind the solid white pylon of snow and ice that had crushed Chad.

I stood and walked across the chamber, passing under that circular spotlight of light, and over to the finger-shaped pylon that had shattered Chad Nando's pelvis. I stopped walking when I heard an unnatural crumpling sound beneath my boots and realized, with sickening lucidity, that I'd stepped onto the tarpaulin.

Taking a step back, I walked around the tarpaulin to the other side of the massive pillar that canted against the ice wall. I ran one bare hand across it. It was solid ice underneath, coated in just a fine powder of snow, and the thing must have weighed as much as a Volkswagen. *Jesus Christ.* Toward the bottom it was splattered with blood.

Across the floor, Petras snorted and rolled over in his sleep, startling me.

I continued running my hand along the surface of the pylon, pausing only when I noticed what appeared to be the faint impression of a boot heel in the thin crust of snow. Above, the icicle-fanged ledge looked dangerous and foreboding, the narrow little ice cave against the wall hardly negotiable. But still . . .

Like a gymnast preparing to mount a pommel horse, I placed my hands against the bulk of the pylon and, lifting one leg over, pulled myself up. I didn't budge, didn't make a sound . . . although my overactive imagination heard the snapping of Chad's bones, grinding them into powder. *Don't think about it,* I told myself. *Stop thinking about it.*

I lifted my other leg and planted both feet flat against the pylon's surface. I attempted to dig my fingernails into the ice, but it was no good. I slid one boot up the length of the incline, but the moment I put all my weight down on it in order to raise my other leg, I started to slide back down.

"Shit."

I hopped down, rubbing my cold palms together. Pulverized stones and gravel lined the mouth of the cave. I collected two hand-fuls and carried them back to the pylon, showering the surface with grit for traction.

A second attempt at climbing the pylon proved successful; I managed to crawl all the way to the top, where the jagged teeth of broken ice protruded from its base and where the pylon lay against the ledge of the ice wall. Using the crisscrossing spires of ice as hand-holds, I lifted myself onto the ledge and noticed a number of the icicles had been busted away from the opening of the ice cave. There were more boot prints in the snow here as well.

Crouching, I peered into the narrow opening in the chamber wall. It was a tight squeeze for a man of average girth. Petras, I surmised, would have much difficulty crawling through. But I was much slimmer than John Petras. On my hands and knees, I crawled forward and poked my head into the ice cave.

I expected to find a womblike niche punched in the snow . . . but what it turned out to be was a winding wormhole that gradually went up through the center of the mountain. The snow inside was ribbed and made for easy handholds. I climbed through the throat of the snow tunnel, pausing in the crook of its turn to see just how far up it went. It was impossible to tell due to a second bend farther in the tunnel, but I thought I saw faint daylight reflected along the wall.

I continued climbing while the wormhole continued to tighten around me. The impossibility of this tunnel's existence was not lost on me: this was a *man-made* structure, as things this perfectly symmetrical do not exist in the natural world—and a *recently* man-made structure at that. Where had it come from? Who'd been here before us to dig it?

Halfway up, I got stuck. Arms pinned in front of my face like those of a praying mantis, I found I couldn't budge, couldn't struggle and work myself free. My breath made the air stale. Suddenly I was dying in the dark, lost and alone in a cave somewhere in the Midwest.

If I closed my eyes, I was certain I'd smell the moss and dampness of rank soil and stagnant pools of fungal cave water. If I closed my eyes—

8

—I COULD CONVINCE MYSELF IT WAS ALL A NIGHT-mare. But when I opened them again, I was alone in our bed, the achy shades of twilight blues and purples filtering through the bedroom windows.

Downstairs, I heard the front door squeal open.

"Hey," I said, appearing at the bottom of the stairs.

"Jesus, Tim," Hannah said. "You scared the hell out of me. Why aren't you at the studio?"

It had been three days since the incident at David Moore's house and three days since I'd last seen or spoken to my wife. Standing before me now, she looked better than I thought she had any right to look.

"You cut your hair," I said. "It's so short. I like it."

She turned away from me, a hand going to her mouth. "I didn't want to do this with you here."

"Do what? You said we'd talk."

"I know what I said."

"So let's talk."

"We can't."

"We never talk, Hannah."

"I can't do this."

"So why'd you come back?"

She had her floral suitcase with her; the reason was apparent.

"We had our time to talk," she said. "We had our time to try and fix things. But some things can't be fixed."

"No," I said. "That's not true."

"You're a good man and a talented artist. You care about what you do. I love that about you, but I need someone who puts me first.

You don't do that. I've never felt like you've put me first."

"Don't say that. It's not true. You've always been first. Always."

"You say it, but you don't show it. You say it, but then you get drunk, and you forget about me and what's important to me. Your art makes you drink, and your drinking makes you put me in second place." She shook her head, tears rolling down her face. Her hair *did* look beautiful. "I'm tired of being second place."

"Hannah—"

"No." She carried her suitcase toward the front door. "Never mind. I don't need to pack anything. I shouldn't have come here."

"Let's have dinner tonight." It sounded petty, but it was the first thing that came to my mind.

"No—"

"Then tomorrow night."

"No, I can't."

"I don't see why—"

"I'm leaving tonight," she said. The way she said it was like a confession, and I knew that it hadn't been her initial intention to tell me. "I'm going to Europe. There's a collector there who's interested in a few pieces from the gallery. I thought it would be good to take some time to myself away from this place."

"Are you going with *him*?"

"That doesn't matter."

"Just answer the question. Are you?"

"It doesn't change what's happened between you and me."

"Do you love him?" I asked.

"Tim—"

"Do you love *me*? Did you ever?"

Her tears had stopped, and there was a look of disappointment on her face now. "Why are you doing this to yourself?"

"I'm not," I said. "You're doing it to me."

"That's unfair."

"It's true."

"No, it's not. That's just more proof of how you don't understand me. You don't understand any of this."

"Then explain it to me," I said calmly. I felt myself going numb right there in front of her.

"There's nothing to explain," Hannah said, "and I don't have the patience anymore."

"How long will you be gone?"

"I don't know yet."

"Can I see you when you get back?"

She closed her eyes. I could almost hear her thinking from across the room. Finally she said, "Yes. Okay. When I get back."

I stepped aside and leaned against the wall. "You can get some of your things. I'll stay out of your way."

"No. It doesn't matter."

"I love you, Hannah."

"I know you do."

"Be careful."

She left without a response. And since her funeral was closed casket, it was technically the last time I saw her.

9

I WAS JARRED BACK TO REALITY WHEN THE TUN-nel loosened and I slid down several inches. The heat from my body had widened the opening while I hung there, daydreaming. Reaching above my head, I worked my fingers around one of the ribbed corrugations in the snow. My feet pushed off the ribs below me, and I continued ascending the tunnel.

When I reached the bend, I climbed around it and froze when the tunnel opened to dazzling daylight no more than five feet in front of me.

"Here we go," I said, my breath whistling through my restrictive throat, and began crawling toward the opening.

10

THE TUNNEL OPENED UP IN THE WALL OF A CAN-
yon—the Canyon of Souls. I crawled from the opening onto a narrow ledge of black stone. Above me, the walls of the canyon yawned
to a gunmetal sky. Below, they ran on forever, the canyon's bottom
nonexistent, my eyes surrendering to the optical illusion. The other
side of the canyon was a tremendous distance away. I'd hiked the
Grand Canyon a number of times, and this was no less impressive.

Pebbles pushed against my fingertips. I flicked a few over the edge.
They fell but seemed to float, never landing, as if gravity had no authority
here. It seemed to take whole minutes before they disappeared into the
abyss below.

The ledge I was on ran the length of the canyon, both to my right
and my left. It went on farther than my eyes could follow, and the
ledge never seemed to get any wider. An attempt to walk its length
on foot would be nothing short of suicide, as foolish as walking along
the windowsills of a skyscraper.

Something shimmered behind the ice along the opposite wall. I
winced, staring hard at it, and saw colors swirling behind the ice like
oil on water. They moved as if alive, spiraling and intertwining with
one another, these living snakes of uncataloged hues, commingling
and bleeding together only to separate again.

It was then that I realized the *entire canyon wall* was alive with
these streaks of color, pulsing like blood through veins and arteries,
colors that went straight to the heart of this sacred land. The colors
themselves were nostalgic, like they were solely associated with specific events from my past. Looking at one would cause me to weep;
looking at another would cause me to laugh; yet another projected a
soul-rattling melancholia I associated with childhood . . .

Two red splotches of blood fell on the back of my left hand. I touched my nose and found it was bleeding again. My headache was back, too, and my respiration had grown increasingly labored.

"The Canyon of Souls," I whispered. Even under my breath, my voice carried over the arroyo and hung there suspended like a cadre of angels taking flight.

11

BACK IN THE HALL OF MIRRORS, PETRAS'S SNORING was like the idling of a pickup truck. I clambered down the icy pylon and strode across the chamber, my spirits still lifted from the sight of the canyon. Andrew's intention was to cross it. Crossing it, I knew, was impossible. But moreover, something like that was not *meant* to be crossed, was not *meant* to be overcome. It was just what Petras had said—some hidden lands, some *beyuls*, were not meant to be found and conquered. Quite often they only revealed themselves to those pure enough to see them.

I crawled into my sleeping bag, my eyes slamming shut, my body racked with exhaustion. Then I realized something and sat bolt upright, my eyes flipping open.

Hollinger was still gone.

I leaned over and poked Petras on the shoulder. "Wake up."

"Hmm . . ."

"Hollinger never came back from taking a leak."

Petras's eyes fluttered open. He coughed into one fist, clearing his throat, and sat up against a large stone. We exchanged a glance; the look in his eyes did not make me feel any better.

"How long has it been since he left?"

"Maybe forty minutes," I guessed.

"Come on," Petras said, standing.

We crossed the chamber toward the mouth of the tunnel, passing beneath the pastel light sliding down through the eyelet above our heads. We passed the massive finger of packed snow that sat at an angle against one of the mirrored walls, the crinkly blue tarpaulin spread out at its base. Chad's blood had spread and frozen into the cracks in the ice.

Together we paused before the mouth of the tunnel. Midway through, it banked at an angle so it was impossible to see the opening at the other end. Petras cupped his hands about his mouth and shouted Hollinger's name into the tunnel. The echo seemed to go on forever.

Hollinger did not answer.

Entering the tunnel, I extended both hands to feel my way along the wall. My shins barked against calcified spires of stone rising in various angles from the ground. Petras followed close behind me, the sound of his respiration like sandpaper against concrete. Only a dozen steps into the tunnel and we were in absolute darkness. I held my hand just an inch in front of my face and wiggled my fingers. I couldn't see a damn thing.

"He could have—," I began but cut myself off as my right foot struck something loose and metallic. I froze.

"The hell was that?" Petras whispered.

Crouching, I patted the ground like a blind man. Whatever it was I'd kicked it somewhere ahead of me. I crawled, hearing the knees of my cargo pants chafe against the stone and the distant sound of cave water dripping from rocky overhangs. Finally my hands fell upon the object, causing my breath to catch in my throat. I knew what it was without picking it up. "It's Hollinger's lantern."

Petras said nothing.

"Hollinger!" I yelled. "Michael Hollinger!"

"He's not in here."

"He could have fallen, knocked himself out." I cranked the switch on the lantern, but the light wouldn't come on. "He could have struck his head on something and—"

"He's not in here."

"And—"

"Tim, he's not *here*."

I knew he was right. I stood, leaving the broken lantern on the ground, and continued down the tunnel. As I turned the corner, I could see the fading light of day spilling in through the opening of the cave. The tongue of ice glittered on the floor of the cave as I approached.

"Mike? Hollinger?" My voice was insignificant.

"Tim," Petras said, far behind me. "Careful . . ."

I crept to the edge of the cave, heedful not to slip on the icy tongue. Gripping a protruding rock from the wall of the cave, I peered down the hundred-yard drop to the valley below. "Oh, Jesus, fuck," I groaned.

"What is it?"

"Hollinger," I said. "He's dead."

Petras shuffled toward me through the darkness. He stopped behind me, and I could feel his breath along the sweaty nape of my neck.

Hollinger's body was shattered on the rocks below. He'd taken his helmet off, and his head had split open like a cantaloupe.

"Christ," I stammered. "Jesus Christ, man . . ."

Petras dug his fingers into my shoulder. "Come on."

"He's dead. He's fuckin' dead."

Those fingers pressed harder. "Let's go."

12

I MUST HAVE DOZED OFF, BECAUSE WHEN I OPENED my eyes, the quality of the light coming through the hole in the ceiling had changed. I felt groggy and dry mouthed, and a chill rippled through my body. My eyes stung so I closed them again, shivering.

13

PETRAS SHOOK MY SHOULDER. "WAKE UP."

My eyes fluttered. My head was stuffed with cotton. "What happened?"

"We found Hollinger at the bottom of the cliff," he said, and it all came rushing back. "You threw up, then passed out."

Shakily, I sat up. We were still in the Hall of Mirrors, my body sweating beneath a stack of sleeping bags.

"He didn't fall," I said. "Hollinger didn't fall, man."

Petras sighed and said, "I want to show you something." He withdrew a bundle of black rope from his backpack, cinched in a bow by a metal clasp. "It's the line that snapped when Curtis died." He held up the frayed end. It was the first I'd seen of it. I could see that not *all* of it was frayed—just a bit. Petras must have noticed the realization in my eyes. "You see it, right?"

I sat up farther on my elbows. "It's—"

"It's been cut," Petras said. "It's a kernmantle line made of nylon and polyethylene. These lines don't break." He paused. "Just like titanium camming devices don't break."

"I know what you're getting at," I muttered.

"It's awfully suspicious."

Again I turned my gaze on the tarpaulin. The snow had soaked up much of Chad's blood.

"Maybe it's a game," Petras went on. "Maybe it's for some other reason. You said Andrew was going to give Shotsky twenty thousand dollars to come here, that he wanted to help him be a better man or some such shit. But what does that really *mean*?"

"I don't know."

"What better way to get rid of six people without suspicion than to bring them out here?"

245

I stared at the rope in Petras's hands. The partially frayed end appeared to have been cut too perfectly, halfway through the line, just to weaken it enough . . .

"But there are easier ways to do it," I suggested. "It's tedious and dangerous cutting ropes and breaking cams. Why not take a gun out here and blow our brains out? Or poison our food, for Christ's sake?"

Petras's eyebrows arched. "The missing food. The food we were convinced we left back in the valley, remember?"

"Yes . . ."

"Maybe he'd planned to do just that. He gets up in the middle of the night and collects our food, poisons it, puts it back. Only he didn't get a chance to put it back—"

"Because Shotsky interrupted him. Shotsky woke up early that morning, wanted to go back to base camp."

"So maybe Andrew ditches the food, tosses it down a ravine or something. Pretends we left it in the valley."

"Jesus Christ." Something had just occurred to me. A tacky sweat broke out along my forehead.

"What is it?"

"Maybe he only had enough time to put something in just *some* of the food." I added, "Shotsky died of a heart attack."

"Yeah . . . ?"

"What happened to me the other day—my heart racing, sweating and delirious . . ."

"What about it?"

Swallowing a hard lump in my throat, I said, "After Shotsky died, we went through his gear, and I took some of his food. I've been eating his food."

Petras exhaled sour breath. His lips were peeling, and his cheeks were flaking with dried skin. He wound the rope back up and stowed it inside his backpack. "Given all this," he said after a moment, "the question is—why would Andrew do it?"

"I know why," I said. I thought of what Andrew had said to me last night when I'd gone to take a piss and he'd startled me by sneaking up on me in the tunnel. *Because I want you to blame yourself, Tim,* he'd said. *I want you to blame yourself.*

"Tell me," Petras said.

"Because we've all done something to hurt him," I said. "We've all done something he feels we need to be punished for."

Petras could only stare at me. Looking at him for too long, I got dizzy.

"You ready for more bad news?" Petras said.

"What's that?"

"The rest of our food," he said. "It's gone."

"Shit."

"Could have happened while we slept, could have happened when we were stumbling through the cave looking for Hollinger." He rolled his big shoulders. "Doesn't much matter when it happened. Outcome's the same." He narrowed his eyes at me. "Your nose is bleeding."

"It's okay." I kicked the sleeping bags off me. "We need to get the hell out of here."

"Your fever's back."

"Doesn't matter."

"Can you walk?"

"I think so."

"You're going to have to sound more convincing than that."

I managed a weak, spiritless smile . . . which quickly faded as the reality of our predicament settled around me. "We're in the middle of nowhere. What the hell are we gonna do, man?"

CHAPTER 15

1

BEFORE LEAVING THE HALL OF MIRRORS, I REMEM-
bered Chad's Zippo lighter and went over to the display of blue tarp
at the base of the frozen pillar.

Dropping to one knee, I lifted a corner of the tarp to reveal a
rigid paw, fingers curled like the petals of some exotic plant, the tips
of each finger an unnatural purple gray. I rummaged through the
pockets of his coat for the lighter. I could feel the frozen solidness of
his body within his clothes.

Twice, I closed my eyes and counted backward from ten until the
rolling wave of nausea subsided. Then I leaned over to dig through
his other pockets. In the process, I accidentally brushed the tarpaulin
from his face. What was revealed was a darkening, bloodless scowl,
the eyes already dried to crystals, the lips split and receded from the
bloodstained teeth. The gash at the top of Chad's head was ringed
with frozen red crystals, the bone dusted in a frosty film.

In one pocket, my fingers closed around the lighter. I pulled it
out, jostling Chad's body which rocked like a hollow log, and scuttled
backward in the snow.

I flicked the flint and watched the kick of blue flame leap from the wick. "We're going to have to make it last," I told Petras.

Like ancient explorers guided solely by the stars, Petras and I descended the hundred-yard drop to the snow-covered quarry below, leaving the Hall of Mirrors and the Canyon of Souls behind. While we'd packed our gear in preparation for our escape, I'd briefly considered mentioning to Petras about how I'd found the Canyon of Souls. But at the last minute, I decided against it. To speak of it, I thought, would be to cheapen it. If there was one thing of beauty I would remember from this trip, I wanted it to be that and to keep it selfishly to myself.

We hooked ourselves together by a double helix of lines, then looped the lines through friction brakes, which were metal rings in the shape of figure eights. After a simultaneous intake of breath, we descended the face quickly but with caution, our boot nails scraping along the frozen mountainside. The wind was arctic and biting, seeking out and attacking every exposed inch of flesh. My eyes began to tear in a matter of seconds.

I paused only once to glance down at the concavity of frozen earth pocked by snow-crusted boulders. The ice glowed in the dark, the flecks of mica in the exposed stone reflecting the moonlight in a dazzling spectacle. And, of course, there was Michael Hollinger's body, itself a shimmering assemblage of crooked arms and legs, a phosphorescent trail of blood, black like crude oil in the night, snaking from the split in his skull . . .

"Don't look," Petras said. "Keep moving."

At the bottom, our heavy boots crunched through the frozen crust of ice on the snow. Again I peered over at Hollinger's body. There didn't appear to be any footprints in the snow around him.

"I'm guessing he was pushed," I said.

Petras wound his rope around one shoulder. He looked about to say something when he froze, his arms stopping in some semblance of a boxing stance.

"What is it?" I said, following Petras's gaze up the wall we'd just descended toward the mouth of the cave.

"I thought I saw someone."

"Someone?"

"I think he's watching us," he said, his voice lower.

It was too dark to see anything.

At my feet, Hollinger's dead eyes, frozen in their sockets, were white, pupil-less stones.

Petras blew briskly into his palms, flexed his fingers, and tugged his gloves back on. When he turned to me, there were frozen bullets of ice clinging to his beard and eyelashes. His eyes looked as if two steel-colored pitons had been driven deep into the sockets.

"Forget it. Trick of the light," he said, though he sounded like he was trying to convince himself, not me.

Beneath the cover of night, we hiked along the ridge, the snow a glittering carpet of diamonds, until exhaustion and the freezing temperature caused my muscles to seize.

"Petras—" I keeled over against a pillar of stone, clutching my body with stiffening arms.

Petras looked equally exhausted. He slumped beside me, his immense weight pressing me flat against the rock, though I was grateful for his warmth.

"No more," I uttered. "Not tonight."

"Your nose is bleeding again."

I pulled off my glove and attempted to wipe the blood away, but it had frozen in a streak down my lips.

We bivouacked beside the stone pillar, which kept most of the freezing wind from attacking us, and took turns keeping watch. Most of our gear was soaking wet, so it took forever to get a small fire going, which died out halfway through the night. But it was probably for the best: we didn't want to bring any further attention on us.

While Petras slept, I sat wrapped in my sleeping bag with the pickax in my lap. With the fire out, there was nothing but our sleeping bags and our own body heat to keep us warm. The tent was only about ten degrees warmer than outside. The wind screamed down the canyons, rattling like a runaway locomotive. I listened, forcing my eyes wide just to keep them open. They didn't want to stay open. If I drifted too far into my own thoughts, I'd fall asleep, lulled by the numbing calm of dreams and the painlessness of frozen nerve endings. I set the timer on my watch for every three minutes—loud enough to jar me from an unplanned doze yet quiet enough not to disturb Petras.

I was just nodding off when the alarm on my watch made my head jerk up, my eyes blinking repeatedly. Lightning flashed, causing the tent to glow and the plastic windows to fill with brilliant blue light.

My breath caught in my throat.

Backlit by the lightning, stark against the canvas of the tent, a figure briefly appeared.

An electric dread coursed through my body. Gripping the handle of the pickax, I leaned toward the tent flaps. I thrust my head and shoulders out into the freezing night, blindly stabbing the pickax into the darkness in front of me. It had started to sleet, and it was impossible to see beyond the far corner of the tent. A second finger of lightning threw the valley into a wash of pale blue snow and bleak, shapeless shadows.

There was no one out there.

—*Tim* . . .

I shook my head, closed my eyes. "No. Not now, Hannah. Please."

—*Come with me, Tim* . . .

"I can't. You need to go away and let me keep my head straight." Just hearing my own voice out loud caused a tremulous, self-indulgent laugh to rumble in my throat. "Jesus, I'm cracking up."

Retracting the pickax into the tent, I took one final glimpse of the surrounding gully before withdrawing my head and shoulders through the canvas flaps.

In the morning, we continued along the outer ridge on empty stomachs. Beyond the peaks of the Himalayas, the sky looked scratchy and sepia toned, like an old filmstrip. Low-hanging cumulus clouds drew together like brooding eyebrows against the horizon. The sun was thumb smeared and pink. I began to convince myself that Petras and I were the only two men alive on the planet.

At lunchtime, Petras discovered oyster crackers at the bottom of his pack, which we shared while sucking down mouthfuls of snow.

"Andrew's just as dead as we are," Petras said after half a day of silence. His beard was fuller and white with freezing snow. Bits of ice dropped off as he spoke. "There's no hope for him, either."

But he has our food, I thought. *He has the stove to make heat and the means to make a fire that can last through the night. He has the advantage of knowing where the hell we are, while we don't know where he is.* I thought all these things but didn't say them. It hurt my throat to talk, and my nose had started bleeding again: the mound of melting snow in my hand was streaked red.

"It'll take over a week to get back down the way we came." Petras chewed the oyster crackers like a cow chewing cud—working his jaw in a slow rotation. "And that's if we can even manage getting back just the two of us. Of course, that's if we had food, a better source of heat, fire . . ."

"This is all stuff I know," I informed him bitterly. "What are you suggesting? We just lie down in the snow, let it cover us up? Stick a few plastic flags around and hope maybe years from now someone will find us?"

"Is that what you want?" Petras wiped away the larger chunks of ice forming in his beard. His knife-blade eyes jabbed at me. "Remember when you told me about your solo trip into a cave? You broke your leg after falling down a ravine, right?"

I shrugged. It pained my muscles. "So?"

"So are you still that same man? The guy who can't deal with shit and needs to go off by himself in a cave, hoping he won't come out?" He looked down at his fingers, powdered with cracker crumbs. "You still that guy?"

I thought about it. I honestly did. I thought about it for so long that it might have appeared I would never answer his question. But Petras didn't rush me and didn't meet my eyes in order to intimidate me into an answer.

Eventually I said, "No, I'm not that man. I'm a different man now."

"Good."

"So what do we do? You said it yourself we won't make it back the way we came. And we sure as hell don't know any other trails."

"You're right; we don't. But if we go straight down—we take the easiest wall and abseil down the face—we can get to the valley in a day, maybe two. And in the valley—"

"There's food," I finished, suddenly comprehending. "There're trees and streams and animals we could catch. It's not as cold, and we could survive there if we had to. We just have to reach it."

"Remember Hollinger's story about living off the land in the outback for months with Andrew? It's no different. If we can kill enough food, pack it in snow, take it with us . . . we might have a chance out of here."

2

WE FOUND WHAT APPEARED TO BE AN EASY RAP-
pel to a series of jagged peaks, their black pointed hoods cresting through the snow. It was a straight run with what looked like sizable handholds all the way down.

"We'll use one line," Petras suggested. "Go one at a time."

"You go ahead first."

"No," Petras said, "you go. I'm heavier. I'll brace the line for you."

He anchored the line to the ridge and ran it through my harness while I put on my helmet.

Petras breathed into my face: "You strong enough?"

"Guess I've got to be . . ."

"You can do it."

"Yeah . . ." But the intervening days—the intervening hours—had weakened me considerably. My head felt filled with helium, and my eyes would not stop watering. The core of my body felt hollow, my face chafed raw from the unrelenting Himalayan wind.

"All right," Petras said and thumped a hand atop my helmet.

I pitched over the side, Petras's hands briefly on my shoulders, and abseiled the length of the wall to the craggy rocks below. At the bottom, I dropped my gear onto the ground and took off my helmet. Suddenly weightless, I felt as though a strong wind could sweep me right off the ridge.

I gave Petras a thumbs-up, and he proceeded to climb over the side of the cliff. Behind him, the mountains were a mottled matte of pastels, enflamed with the reflection of a setting sun.

Halfway down the ridge, Petras's hand slipped from one of the handholds. He pitched to the right, and one of his boots peeled away a tumble of rocks from the rock face.

I staggered back, mesmerized.

Somehow Petras managed to correct himself, pulling upward on the rope and securing a second handhold. He planted his dangling leg firmly into the side of the mountain. Rocks tumbled down and shattered close to my feet. I felt dirt and grit powder my face.

"Careful!" I shouted.

Without looking at me, he returned my previous thumbs-up.

Andrew appeared on the ridge above.

When I saw him, my blood froze; my heart stopped.

Andrew stared down at Petras, who hadn't yet noticed him. Andrew was a featureless creature, awkward and bent over like a scarecrow come to life. Instantly he was the lunatic who'd stripped out of his clothes and taught me to jump off cliffs in San Juan.

"John! John!"

Andrew disappeared behind the cliff.

Petras paused, swinging lazily, and looked at me over his shoulder. There was a blank expression on his face.

"Get down! Move! Move!"

Petras glanced up just as Andrew's face reappeared over the side of the cliff. His hair was blowing across his face, obscuring all aspects of humanity. He held something I couldn't quite make out until the light from the setting sun glinted across a square, metal head at the end of a long shaft. Andrew raised it while Petras and I looked on. It was his ax.

"John!" I screamed.

Petras was only midway down the cliff. A drop from such a height would prove—

Andrew brought the ax down.

Thwap!

The rope recoiled like a snake after a strike, and Petras dropped like a lead anchor. While in reality the fall could have lasted only a few seconds, it seemed to take forever. It was all in slowmotion. I could make out every detail—the flutter of Petras's clothes in the wind, the way the laces on his boots pointed up at Andrew, the softball-sized rocks that fell beside him at the same speed.

He struck the earth, and the sound was like a house being demolished. I shut my eyes at the last second, not catching the conclusion . . . although I could feel the reverberation through every cell of my body.

"John." My voice was distant, sickly.

His body was a broken, undulating terrain beneath a ski parka and harness, his legs splayed as if caught in the middle of a jumping jack, his arms askew. Petras's gloved fingers slowly curled in toward his palms. His head was at a devastating angle, and I could only make out the back of his shiny yellow helmet.

I raced over to him, shouting his name, and dropped to my knees beside him. He moaned and—thankfully!—turned his head. His eyes were dazed, each pupil a different size, and his lips moved, but no words came out of his mouth.

"Don't talk," I told him. "Don't move."

Yet he tried to move—and winced. There was a tear in the right shoulder of his ski parka, the cotton stuffing soaked through with blood.

"Jesus . . ." Jerking my head around, I caught a glimpse of Andrew retreating once again behind the cliff. "Okay, man," I said, turning to Petras. "Relax for a second . . ."

"My arm," he groaned.

"I see it."

"How . . . bad?"

Pulling off my gloves, I leaned over him and peeled back the tufts of blood-soaked cotton that were protruding from the rip in his parka like bubbles foaming over the top of a boiling pot. A knifelike shard of black shale poked through Petras's shoulder, glistening with blood and what to my untrained eyes appeared to be a meshwork of muscle.

"Fuck," I moaned, sickened.

"Bad?"

"Not too bad," I lied. "It's okay."

"Want to . . . sit up . . ."

I pressed one palm against his chest. His lungs struggled to expand. "Don't move, goddamn it."

"Andrew . . ."

"I know," I said. "Stop talking."

I tore away the bloodied fabric of his parka, exposing the raw and ruined shoulder beneath. The shard of rock hadn't gone straight through the middle of the shoulder; it came up at an angle, splitting through the flesh and muscle like a spike just above his bicep. The thickness of his backpack had broken his fall and kept his back off the ground. Had he not been shouldering his pack, the damage would have been much more severe.

"This is gonna hurt," I warned him.

Petras coughed, then shuddered at the pain.

I bent over him, looping my arms around him in a bear hug, and pressed my face against his chest. His lungs rattled, but his heartbeat was still strong.

"Count . . . of three," Petras managed, aware of what I was about to do.

"No," I said and yanked him off the ground.

Petras howled . . . and there was a sickening sound like someone tearing apart a long strip of Velcro. Petras's good arm swung around my back, his beastly, oversized fingers jamming into my ribs like ice picks. I rolled him over and onto the snow as he began to convulse. There was a manhole-sized stain of blood in the snow where he'd been laying, the jagged shard of shale jutting from its center like the hand of a sundial.

I rushed to my pack and dragged it over to where Petras convulsed in the snow. Rifling through it, I produced a flannel shirt that I tore into ribbons and used them to make a tourniquet to stop the bleeding. The wound itself was a gaping, ragged mouth that bled furiously. I blotted at it with a swatch of flannel.

Petras shrieked and swung a monstrous paw at my face. It was a clumsy, undirected swipe, yet it caught me below my right eye, rattling my jaw and causing tears to dribble down my right cheek.

But his strength drained quickly, and I was able to bandage the wound. It still bled heavily, but it would have to do until I could clear my head and figure out what the hell—

A small avalanche of rocks slid over the side of the cliff and clattered to the ground only a few feet away from me. Andrew was nowhere to be found among any of the ledges above us, but I knew he was up there. Watching.

Petras's convulsions had diminished to a series of spasms. He was still in shock. His eyes tried to focus on me, but they were the rolling, disobedient eyes of a drunkard.

Crawling on my hands and knees, I grabbed the handle of my pickax and stood, brandishing it like a sword.

"Andrew! Where are you, you fuck?" My voice echoed through the canyon. "Show yourself!"

On shaky legs, I backed away from the rock face to get a better view of the cliffs. Andrew was nowhere.

Petras groaned. Blood was already soaking through the swatch of flannel I'd tied around his shoulder. The wound would need to be cleaned and closed if Petras was going to survive.

"Take it easy, big guy." I went to my pack again, setting the pickax down beside me in the snow . . . but close enough to grab at a moment's notice, if needed. I knew exactly what I was looking for, and it took me less than three seconds to find it: the canteen of bourbon.

I rolled over beside Petras, who'd managed to get into a sitting position, his back against the rock wall. In this position he was an easy target for Andrew to drop anything on him. Without saying a word, I tugged on his parka, and he grunted as he slid over until he was hidden beneath a protective outcrop of stone.

His eyes seemed to sober as he watched me unscrew the cap on the canteen. The initial shock had left him, which meant his senses were returning, and the pain would be worsening.

"It's bourbon," I said, dropping to my knees beside him.

"Holding out on us, huh?" he said in one breath. He even uttered a dour little laugh, then winced.

"A gift from our buddy Andrew," I said, peeling away the flannel bandage with one hand. The fabric was soaked with blood and beginning to freeze. After I undid the knot, the flaps fell away, exposing the raw, jagged serration at the top of Petras's shoulder as well as the entry point at his shoulder's back—a wider, oozing chasm.

Not good, I thought. *Jesus. Not good at all.*

"This is gonna hurt, you know," I prepared him.

Petras retrieved the bloodied length of flannel. He stuffed one end into his mouth and bit down, his gaze sliding toward me. He nodded, then looked away.

I poured the bourbon over the wound. It fizzed and bled freely, the cascade of the amber liquor spilling down his shoulder and soaking into the remains of his shirt and the exposed stuffing of his ski parka. While I poured, the amber fluid turned a dark red as it flushed out the wound.

Petras's legs bucked, the nails jutting from the soles of his boots digging through the crust of snow and catching on the stone below. His helmeted head thumped against the stone wall. Tears squirted from the corners of his eyes, rolled down the ruddy swells of his cheeks, and froze in his beard.

Once the canteen ran dry, I tossed it aside and tore a fresh length of flannel from what remained of my shirt. One-handed, I scooped handfuls of snow away from the base of the rock wall, creating a hasty well in the ground. I stuffed the dry cloth inside and created a nest with whatever other bits of dry fabric I could cut away. Petras was breathing heavy and losing a lot of blood.

"Hang in, buddy."

"What . . . ?"

"Gotta close that wound up, man. Just hang in there."

Popping open Chad's Zippo, I cupped the flame and held it to the dry bits of cloth until they caught fire. It was a weak fire, and I feared it would wink out at any moment. Still, there was nothing to fuel it with, so I babied it for perhaps thirty or forty seconds until I had a steady little blaze going. The burning cloth stung my nose and stank of rancidity.

From my backpack, I fished out a metal piton. Petras was still watching me, though with increasingly distant eyes, and he groaned as I placed the piton onto the fire. He knew what was coming.

"You're a tough son of a bitch," I told him. "Probably the toughest son of a bitch I've ever met, John. So for the next ten seconds, you're gonna have to live up to that, okay? Gonna hurt like a motherfucker, but you're gonna have to live up to that."

Petras moaned.

With one gloved hand, I grabbed the end of the piton. I could feel the heat through my glove. Propping my free hand against Petras's chest, I rose to my knees and took a deep breath before pressing the white-hot piton against the wound in Petras's shoulder.

The skin sizzled, and smoke from his scorched flesh ribboned up into the air. Petras screamed and kicked. The smell of burning flesh was sickening.

"Okay, okay, okay, okay," I intoned, dropping the piton back into the fire.

Petras sobbed and slumped forward away from the rock wall.

"Halfway there, man. Hang in there." I repeated the process to the exit wound.

The stench was just as horrible, yet Petras's cries were less energetic this time. He'd lost a lot of blood.

After the wound was sufficiently cauterized, I helped ease Petras against the rock wall. His breathing was trembling and unsteady, whistling through a constricted windpipe.

"It's done," I told him.

I wrapped his shoulder with an extra length of flannel, the muscles in his arm tensing as I tightened the bandage. The odor of the bourbon mixed with his singed flesh created a sickening sweet metallic scent whose potency scorched the hairs in my nose.

"Too tight," Petras mumbled, glancing down at his wounded shoulder for the first time. "Hurts."

"It needs to be tight." The wound was bad, and I didn't want it to split open and start bleeding again.

Sweat rolled down Petras's face. I unsnapped the strap to his helmet and removed it. His hair glistened with sweat, and I could almost see waves of heat wafting off his scalp.

"Where'd he go?" he panted.

I stared at the overhang. The sun having set, it was difficult to see much of anything. A disquieting silence pervaded the valley. "I don't know. He disappeared."

"I'm gonna hold you back." He pushed against me with one hand, but there wasn't any strength in it. "Get going."

"It's too late now. We'll stay here tonight."

"Tim, he's—"

"I don't feel like freezing to death out there tonight, okay?"

Petras held me in his gaze for a few seconds. I could almost read his thoughts. When he looked away, I thought I saw a flash of approval in those lionlike eyes.

Cleaning off my hands in the snow, I nodded toward a small, cavelike opening in the rock wall. "You think you can roll inside?"

He wasn't even looking at it. "Sure. Whatever."

After unsnapping the shoulder straps of his backpack, I helped him wiggle loose from it. He sighed as the weight fell away. Leaning his head back against the wall, clouds of vapor billowed from his chapped lips. His respiration was disturbingly raspy, like a lawn mower struggling to turn over.

That's what they call the death rattle, I thought. *That's not a good sign.* "You're going to have to roll on your side to roll into the cave."

"Okay."

"You can only be so careful. It'll hurt."

He managed a sputtering, motorboat laugh. "It *already* hurts."

"Fair enough." I looped his good arm around my neck. "Come on."

"Uh." He jostled against me, his weight substantial, testing the limits of my own endurance. "Uh . . . Jesus . . ."

"Hang in there," I gasped, dragging him toward the cave. A series of icicles hung like fangs over the opening. I kicked them away with a boot. "Here we go."

Together we eased to a sitting position in the snow. I slid behind

Petras and held him upright as he maneuvered himself down on his good shoulder. I could see the blood soaking through the fresh bandage. The cauterized flesh was splitting open in the cold.

"I'm okay," he said and rolled himself into the mouth of the cave. He moaned as he struck the rear wall and called out, "It isn't very deep."

"It's shelter. It'll have to do."

I dragged his backpack over to the opening, partially obscuring it from view, the zippered compartments facing inside the cave in case Petras needed anything from within. Then I unraveled the canvas tent and pegged it at an angle to the rock wall and drove two pitons into the bottom half, pinning it to the ground. It would keep the wind off us and the cold from infiltrating Petras's womblike cave.

Pulling my own backpack in after me, I climbed beneath the angled canvas and leaned against the rock wall. Like a soldier on night watch, I held the pickax in my lap. It felt heavier than hell. My heart was strumming like an electric guitar, my lungs achy and sore.

Petras's hand appeared from the cave and gripped my thigh. His grip was surprisingly strong. "You done good."

I chuckled. "Oh, Christ . . ."

"Seriously, Tim. Thank you."

"Get some rest. We're gonna head out early in the morning."

"You go on without me."

"Don't be ridiculous."

"Who's being ridiculous? Don't be a fool. Go on without me."

"Let's worry about that in the morning," I told him.

3

THEN IN THE DARKNESS—

Something heavy rolled over in my stomach. I leaned out the tent and retched in the snow. My hands were shaking and my vision blurred. Minutes turned to hours. I prayed I didn't look as bad as

Petras—gaunt, featureless, vaguely misaligned.

4

BEFORE THE SUN HAD FULLY RISEN, I CRAWLED from the lean-to. Halfway up the snow-throated gulley, I leaned against a mound of stone, unzipped my pants, and struggled to urinate. I managed to expel only a few sad droplets, which dribbled onto my pants.

Back at the cave, I packed up the tent and pulled on my gloves. From inside the cave, Petras's raspy breathing was still audible. I bent down to the opening. "Wake up, man."

"I've been awake."

The sheer quality of his voice—or lack thereof—felt like a stick jabbing between my ribs for my heart.

"We should go," I said.

Petras didn't answer.

I tried to peer farther into the crevice. I could see his haunted raccoon eyes, the skeletal whiteness of his face. I wondered how much blood he'd lost during the night.

"I don't know who we're tryin' to kid here. I can't move."

"John—"

"Can't move my arms, can't move my legs, and my head feels about as heavy as an engine block." It sounded as if his voice had been *halved*—had been sliced down the middle and stripped of half the elements that made him who he was.

"I can't just—"

"We don't got time to sit and kid ourselves. Get going. You find food; then you can bring it back to me. You find help; bring them back, too."

I nodded, chewing at my lower lip. Bits of skin flaked off in my mouth. "Right. I will. I'll bring food and I'll find help."

"Go."

"All right." I fished the Zippo from my pocket and placed it in

Petras's freezing hand.

He started to protest, but I wouldn't hear anything of it. If he wanted me to leave him, then I was going to leave him with the means to build a fire, and I wouldn't listen to any protest. Finally he relented. His fingers closed around the silver Zippo and retracted into the darkness of the hollow.

Hooking my helmet to one of the straps of my backpack, I slung the pack over my shoulders and thought my rib cage would collapse. With both hands, I rubbed the ice from my beard and cleared the hardened ice from the spikes in the soles of my boots.

"I'll bring food," I said one last time, though I wondered about his chances of surviving the next twenty-four hours.

"Good luck," Petras said, his voice no more than a rattling croak.

"Good-bye," I said back.

CHAPTER 16

1

ALL PERCEPTION LOST—ALL SEMBLANCE OF NOR-
malcy eradicated—I opened my eyes to a world that no longer existed.

2

BY MIDDAY I WAS OVERCOME BY A CHRONIC
fatigue. Whether it was brought on by simple exhaustion, a lack of suste-
nance, or the middle stages of acute mountain sickness, I did not know.

A deep, angry wind picked up in the north and barreled through
the valley. On either side I was enclosed in tar-colored rocks, glossy with
a coating of ice. My fever had returned full force, my forehead steaming
and bursting with sweat. I stopped and bit down on my gloves, yanking
them off with my teeth. Holding my hands to my eyes, I had twenty fingers. My vision would not clear up. I flexed my fingers and could hear
the tendons creaking like an old rocking chair, the fingers themselves
like hollowed tubing knotted at the joints and knuckles.

Suddenly a low, motorized growl sounded in the distance. I looked
around, but, being at the bottom of a valley, I could see nothing except
the rising black walls around me. Yet the sound grew closer, closer . . .

I jerked my head to the right just in time to see an old motorcar leap over one side of the embankment in a cloud of snow. Its tires spinning, its tailpipe flagging a contrail of exhaust, it gleamed in the sun like a chrome missile.

Breathlessly I watched it careen over the embankment and descend in an arc toward the floor of the ravine. It hadn't been going fast enough to make it to the other side. Nose-first, it slammed into the snow in an expulsion of white powder and crystalline confetti, folding up on itself like an accordion. For a second, it balanced on its front grille, standing perfectly vertical; then the rear end tipped toward the ground.

With a shatter of glass, the vehicle exploded in a bright orange ball of flame. It billowed into the sky, roiling smoke atop a stalk of flame, until it dissipated into streamers of smoke. As the vehicle burned, the snow around it melted until the black rock was exposed.

I dropped my pack and was about to sprint toward the wreckage when it vanished before my eyes.

Sobbing, I collapsed to the ground and pulled my knees up to my chest.

3

SLEET FELL AS THE DAY COOLED TO EVENING AND the warm pastels of the setting sun crouched behind the distant mountains. Shadows elongated and spilled across the valley. I'd spent the day winding through the valley, keeping to the base of the mountain. I walked now to the edge of the cliff and peered over the side. A great distance below was an icefall—perhaps the continuation of the one we'd crossed earlier in the trip, the one that had swallowed Curtis Booker. Seracs split and sluiced through the river of ice to the bottom of the valley. The path they carved instantly altered the geography of the fall.

There was no safe way to cross the icefall, but if I continued winding around the base of the mountain, I would eventually reach the valley floor. Then—

"Hello, Tim."

Andrew stood behind me, backlit by the sunset. *Scarecrow,* I immediately thought. He appeared detached, flimsy, emaciated, skeletal. His clothes hung from him like drapes, his shirt unbuttoned to midchest, exposing the pink, sun-ruined lines of his abdomen. The wind blew his hair across his face, obscuring his eyes . . . but I could make out a partial smirk at the corner of his mouth.

He carried the ax. As he unshouldered his pack, he tossed the ax down at his feet. His too-big clothes flapped in the wind.

"Stay there," I told him, dropping my own pack but grappling with the pickax from the pack's restraint. "Don't move."

Andrew raised his hands, palms up. "We need to share a few words . . ."

I pulled the pickax from the restraint and hefted it like a baseball bat over one shoulder. "You're sick, Trumbauer. You've lost your goddamn mind."

"What I've lost, I've lost long ago. Let's talk." He took a step in my direction.

I swung the pickax to show I meant business. "I said to stay the fuck where you are. You take another step, and I'll come at you swinging."

The rush of sleet increased, pelting my head, my shoulders, my back.

Andrew shivered, his clothes soaked and beginning to freeze in the unforgiving night wind. He ran his hands through his hair. For the first time, I saw his eyes—soulless, remote, vacant. The eye of a needle held more emotion.

"I'm not the monster, Tim."

"Stop playing the game. You brought us all here to kill us."

"I'm just here to make things right," he said. "I've very nearly succeeded."

"Step away from your pack."

Andrew cocked his head at me. "What?"

"I'm taking your pack," I told him. "I'm taking your food."

Andrew laughed . . . or appeared to laugh: he brought his head back on his neck, exposing his enormous Adam's apple, and opened his mouth wide, but no sound came out. When he leveled his gaze on me, there was a gleam of hatred in his eyes.

"It doesn't matter," he said and took three giant strides away from his pack. Away from his ax, too. "It's too late."

With my eyes locked on him, I traversed the sleet-slick ridge until I reached his backpack. Dropping to one knee, holding the pickax out in front of me, I unzipped his pack with one hand. Packets of freeze-dried food spilled out in a tidal wave. A can of mushrooms rolled out and dropped on my boot.

"They each had their reason," Andrew said. He had to shout now above the sleet. Lightning lit the horizon, and I could see the countless purple peaks at his back. "Hell, I flat-out told you about Shotsky!" This time he *did* laugh—a stuttering, mechanical sound. "Everyone's committed an injustice, and everyone must pay for their mistakes." He held his arms out above his head. "Christ, look around! Look where we are! You think a place like this—a sacred, spiritual land as this—exists without divinity? There's divinity all around us. It courses through me, it courses through you, and it pumps life into every living, breathing thing on this miraculous planet."

"You're out of your mind."

"I'm the corrector of *things*," he practically hissed. "I'm the man who fixes your mistakes. Goddamn it, you should be grateful! Because out of everyone on this trip, your mistake was the *biggest*."

My grip tightened on the handle of the pickax. I rose off my knee, wiping the icy water from my eyes. A second flash of lightning illuminated the sky, this one closer than the first.

"I fucking *loved* her, you son of a bitch. But she didn't love me.

And that was okay. It was okay because *she* loved *you*, and you made her happy. Well, for a little while at least . . ."

"Shut your goddamn mouth," I growled, spewing water from my lips. My hands were numb, my heart strumming furiously in my chest. I could taste acidic bile at the back of my throat.

"You weren't man enough for her. You weren't the man she needed you to be. So she left. And because she left, she died. And that's your fault. I loved her more than I've ever loved anyone and she's dead and you killed her."

The head of the pickax, suddenly too heavy for me to hold, swung like a pendulum down into the snow.

"Thing is," Andrew said, "you almost did the honorable thing. Couple years ago, back in that cave, you went there with the intention of never coming out, didn't you? Would have been a noble way to go. But in typical Timothy Overleigh fashion, you chickened out, lost your nerve, and climbed out—the first in a series of events that delivered you from the clutches of death and back to the land of the living."

I tried to lift the pickax but couldn't. I watched Andrew take a step toward me, then another, but I was only *partially* seeing him; I was seeing the motorcar drift off the road and launch over the cliff. I saw it explode at the bottom of a stone quarry. I saw Hannah's palms slamming against the window while the smoke suffocated her and the flames blackened her skin and peeled it from her body . . .

"A beautiful woman," Andrew said, his voice distant like a dream, "who deserved better than you. And now look what happened to her." Startling me, he screamed, "*Now* look!"

He charged me. I went to pull the pickax from the snow, but the sleet had frozen it to the ground; my hands pulled free of the handle, sending me flailing backward, and I fell on my ass. A third charge of lightning lit the sky as Andrew Trumbauer lunged through the air and dropped on me—

4

LIKE A TON OF BRICKS, HANNAH'S BROTHER ON THE
other end of the telephone saying, seemingly over and over again, "Tim, there's been an accident . . ."

5

A CLAWED HAND PRESSED DOWN ONTO MY FACE,
a massive weight from above knocking the wind from my lungs, and a second hand struggled to gain access to my neck.

I bucked my hips, but Andrew had firmly planted his long legs on either side of me, pinning me down. His fingers pressed down on my eyelids, and he pushed my head up and back, grinding it into the ice, while his other hand worked around my neck.

Futilely I continued struggling, banging my hips up and down, up and down, up and down, up—

6

—AND DOWN THE STAIRS, DRUNK OUT OF MY MIND,
the phone broken in two pieces at the bottom of the stairs. Briefly, I felt myself lift up and out of my body until I was able to watch myself from above—the broken, quivering husk I was . . .

7

"YOU . . . *DIE,*" ANDREW SHRIEKED THROUGH
clenched teeth, his face only inches from mine. "You *die* now!"

The hand squeezed around my throat. I shook my head from side to side, but his hold was strong.

Blind, I brought my fists up on either side of Andrew's face and began pummeling him. His grip on my neck relinquished just long enough for him to swat one of my arms away, driving it into the snow. Then he dived back in for my neck, but I brought my chin down on his fingers.

My fingers thumped against something hard in the snow. I grabbed it, made a fist around it, and swung it in an arc toward Andrew's head. It struck with enough force to knock him off me, his entire body going momentarily limp.

I shuffled backward, gasping for air and choking on falling sleet. The object still clenched in my hand, I glanced down to see it was the can of mushrooms.

"Overleigh!" he yelled, scrambling to his feet with one hand to his temple. Black fingers of blood trickled down the side of his head. Dazed, he staggered while trying to charge me.

I threw the can of mushrooms at his head—but missed. Quickly I dropped to the ground and crawled toward the pickax. Just as my hand closed around the handle, one of Andrew's boots stomped on it, impaling the back of my hand with the climbing spikes in the sole of his boot.

I screamed and shuddered, though my hand was too numb to feel the full brunt of the pain.

He ground his foot into my hand, then kicked me on the side of the head with his other boot. Fireworks exploded before my eyes as I rolled over. His boot withdrew from my hand, and I pulled it against my chest and clambered up the snowy embankment.

Andrew pried the pickax from the frozen ground. Swinging it, he raced after me. "Overleigh, you son of a bitch!"

I gripped a handhold and hauled myself up. A second later, Andrew brought the pickax down where my leg had been, splintering the ice and causing a plume of powdery snow to rise from the ground. Ice broke away between my fingers, and I slid down the incline on my side.

Andrew swiped the pickax through the air. I felt it whiz by my face as it planted its nose into the stone. I rushed him, driving my head into his solar plexus and wrapping my arms around his shoulders. He made an oof sound as we collided. I shoved him backward, and he dropped the pickax. He yanked my shirt out of my pants and tried to pull it over my head, but I crushed him against a pillar of stone.

"Bastard!" I shouted and punched him square across the jaw. My fists were frozen clubs of ice. "Goddamn *bastard*!" I split his lip and knocked blood from his nose.

"Tim! Tim!" He waved his hands in front of his face, gagging on blood.

A loud creak resounded from the top of the pillar. A lightning bolt fracture appeared near its top, snaking toward us, dusting us with snow. Andrew's head rebounded off the pillar, and I stumbled backward out of breath just as a deep rumbling echoed somewhere above.

We both looked up to see an avalanche of snow barreling toward us. Andrew pushed off the pillar, which collapsed to a jumble of blocks behind him, and dashed forward. I grabbed him around the neck and dragged him to the ground as the avalanche buried us.

The force knocked me down on top of him. The weight on my back grew heavier and heavier, and it was like being crushed in a giant fist. I took a deep breath and swallowed snow. Still, I refused to release my stranglehold on Andrew. I pressed my cheek hard against his chest while the snow packed on top of my head, adding more pressure. His heartbeat vibrated up through his body.

A sharp, stinging pressure spread along my abdomen, its intensity increasing with the weight of the snow. It blossomed to an agonizing boil until I shrieked and released Andrew from the headlock. My head burst up through the snow. Andrew bucked me off him. He crawled out of the snowbank and rolled down the incline.

I followed him out and staggered a few feet before realizing I was trailing an oil slick of blood from my stomach. Glancing down, I could see ribbons of blood in the snow. My pants were soaked clean through.

I clutched my stomach and doubled over, rolling down the opposite side of the snow mound.

—bloodbloodbloodbloodblood—

Crawling in the snow, heavy with sleet, I hid behind a group of rocks. I struggled into a sitting position and leaned my head against the rocks. My breath seared my throat.

I examined my palms. They were covered in blood—black blood. I coughed and sent a spray of blood into the snow between my feet.

Andrew's voice boomed through the night. "Overleigh! The fuck are you, Overleigh?"

I lifted my shirt and grimaced. My belly was smeared with blood, and at first, I couldn't find the wound. I ran my fingers along the length of my gut and—

"Fuck!" I groaned, squeezing my eyes shut.

In mimicry of my belly button, there was a coin-sized puncture just below my navel. As I exhaled, it squirted a stream of blood down into my crotch. *Goddamn it,* I thought, *it must have been the pickax, caught up in the avalanche. I must have landed on the fucking pickax.*

"Overleigh!" He was closer now.

My throat rattled. I placed both hands over my mouth to silence my breathing.

Movement farther down the ridge caught my attention: it was Andrew, standing like George Washington crossing the Delaware, one foot on a crag. He'd recovered the pickax from the avalanche and held it over one shoulder.

I pressed myself flat against the rocks and held my breath. My mind raced—

—bloodbloodblood—

—and my heart felt like it had crept into my throat. To my right, a narrow ledge wound around the side of the cliff and dipped to a series of climbable rock formations. In the dark it was hard to tell just how steep of a climb it was, but if I could get—

A hand dropped in front of me and balled the front of my shirt in its fist. A moment later, I was heaved over the rocks and slammed down on the other side.

Andrew stood above me, eyes gleaming, blood drooling from his mouth. He said something incomprehensible and raised the pickax above his head.

Without thinking, I lifted one leg and drove my spike-soled boot into Andrew's left knee.

He issued a strangled gah sound, and the pickax fell from his hands and clattered down the slope behind him. Eyes widening, he locked me in his stare. Then he keeled backward, tumbling down the incline. At the bottom, he slid clear across the frozen earth. One of his legs got tangled in the straps of his backpack, preventing him from pitching straight off the cliff.

I leaned against the rocks and stood, wincing at the pain in my gut. It felt like someone holding a hot iron against the lining of my stomach. Trailing one hand along the stone wall for support, I inched my way down the incline. The sleet had started to let up, but what had already fallen had frozen on the embankment. It was a tedious trek to the bottom.

I kept my eyes on Andrew. He didn't move.

—*bloodblood*—

My stomach cramped. I groaned and bent forward, tears spilling from my eyes. The world turned me on my side; I crashed to the ground and slid a few inches on the ice, the brass buckles on my boots scraping the surface.

In a flash, Andrew's face was directly above mine. I tried to breathe but found my throat had closed—he was strangling me with one of the rappel lines from his backpack. I coughed, sputtered, kicked. Spit frothed from his lips; his teeth were clenched so hard they could have shattered under the pressure.

My vision grew spotty and pixilated. Andrew's face broke apart like someone dropping a jigsaw puzzle on the floor. I was aware of my fingers struggling to work their way between the line and my throat . . .

Hannah stood behind Andrew. While Andrew faded from my field of vision, Hannah shone bright like an angel—a *dakini*.

"Ehhh . . ."

I couldn't form words, couldn't breathe.

—*Stay with me, Tim*, Hannah said. She looked down, and I followed her gaze. I spotted the kernmantle rope looped around Andrew's leg, the other end of the rope still fixed to his backpack. As I looked at the pack, it disintegrated into fragments of light, dispersed into darkness. Andrew's face was a flash of disjoined images—a set of teeth, a single eyeball, a dripping strand of hair.

Almost on reflex, I kicked my left leg. My boot struck Andrew's backpack with enough force to send it sliding across the frozen plateau. I could see it as if in slowmotion.

—*bloodblind*—

The backpack slowed as it reached the edge of the cliff and nearly stopped—*did* stop—then went over the side, dropping like the anchor of a steamship. The rope trailed it, eating up slack by the millisecond, also vanishing over the side. Then I saw the rope go taut, watched Andrew's leg jerk out from under him, and felt my throat open up.

"Over—," he began—an attempt at shouting my last name or an attempt at proclaiming his sudden fate, I did not know which—but was cut off after the weight of his pack pulled him over the cliff. One second he was glaring at me with the yellow eyes of a feral cat, and the next he was gone, gone.

Silence fell on me. I sucked in a lungful of air and choked. Bleary eyed, I blinked repeatedly and waited for the pixels of my vision to fully reassemble themselves. Once I caught my breath, I eased myself onto my elbows. The pain in my gut was no less severe, and I couldn't tell if the bleeding had let up any.

I crawled to the edge of the cliff and peered down into the black abyss. I couldn't see the bottom. It was no different than gazing into space.

Exhausted, I rolled over onto my back and turned toward the stars. There were millions of them. Billions. The moon, hooked like a sharp finger curling out of a wisp of gray clouds, glowed above me. As my vision cleared, I could make out the swirled blue craters in its surface. They were like the charcoal-colored veins in an uncut slab of marble.

8

ONCE MY HEART SLOWED, I ROSE. THE PUNCTURE wound in my abdomen throbbed dully. The blood on my hands had dried, my shirt and pants blackened and frozen with it.

A shapeless hump rose out of the snow across the ridge. It was my backpack. I hobbled toward it, wincing with each step. The shiny foil packages of the freeze-dried food that had escaped Andrew's pack before it sailed over the cliff were scattered about the ice. With much effort, I bent and gathered all the packages I could find, which weren't many. I stuffed them into my own pack and shouldered my gear.

It took me several minutes to remember which direction I had come. Finally I found my old footprints, filled now with ice, and followed them to the ridge on my way back to John Petras. There just might be enough food to sustain him until I was able to get help.

If, of course, he was still alive.

9

MIDNIGHT.

Racked by fever, I collapsed in the snow. It took several minutes to worm my way out from under my backpack. Lifting my face, I saw the moonlit curl of the ridge as it wound in gradual ascent around the mountain. I reached out with one hand, pausing to examine how the fabric of my gloves had worn through at the fingertips and in the center of the palm, exposing my raw, pink flesh. I clenched and unclenched my hands over and over but couldn't feel a single thing. Frostbitten.

I rolled over, struggling to breathe. There was blood in the snow; the puncture wound in my navel had opened again as I trekked along the ridge.

I don't know where I am, I thought. *Am I even going in the right direction?*

Pain coursed like adrenaline through my system. Soon my breaths started coming in sizable, whooping gasps. No matter how hard I tried, I couldn't feed enough oxygen into my lungs.

—*You can't stay here,* said Hannah.

It was the sound of her voice that made me realize I had been drifting off into a painless sleep. My eyes opened and the pain returned, roiling like a tropical storm in my guts. "Where are you?"

—*You must get up, Tim. You can't stay here. You'll die here.*

"I'm . . . already dead . . ."

Then—somehow—I was standing and halfway up the ridge. At one point, I paused and rested against a pylon of ice, shivering in the cold. The familiar bulge of my gear against my back was no longer there. I felt for the pack's straps around my shoulders, but they were gone. I'd left my backpack somewhere.

Shit . . .

"No . . . no . . . no . . . no . . ."

Hugging myself, I stumbled out across the plateau and scanned the moonlit passage that wound through the mountainous terrain below. Every stone could have been my backpack. It was everywhere I looked.

—*Up here, Tim.*

Turning around, I saw Hannah standing at the pinnacle of the ridge, her body glowing with a fine, angelic aura. She wore the same white, billowy nightgown she wore that night I followed her from the caves, through the trees, and out to the highway, where I collapsed and was eventually discovered and rescued.

"Hannah . . ."

She descended the opposite side of the pinnacle.

I cast one last glance at the passage before giving up on my gear and following her. I climbed the pinnacle and saw her shimmering visage float around the far side of the ridge. She was not heading back to Petras; even in my unreliable mental state I was able to understand that. Nevertheless, I descended the pinnacle and pursued her around the ridge.

10

"CAN'T," I CRIED. I COLLAPSED IN THE SNOW FACE- first and felt nothing.

—Tim . . .

"No more."

I was standing on the balcony of my Annapolis apartment overlooking the Chesapeake Bay. It was midday, and I could see a fleet of white sailboats motoring beneath the Bay Bridge. I was—I *was*—

—Just a bit farther, Hannah said. *Come up to the ridge.*

"Can't," I insisted, grinding my teeth from the numbing pain. I curled into a fetal position in the snow. I was determined to stay in Annapolis, to watch the sailboats cut through the slate-colored waters of the bay . . .

—Come, she said, *and you can touch me.*

My eyelids fluttered. For a second, I thought I could actually *see* the sailboats, their masts rising like cavalry flags. But it was just snowcaps, countless snowcaps.

Above me, Hannah smiled, her skin radiating a tallow glow, her features pure and clean.

"Your hair . . . is short . . ." I grinned and it pained me to do it. "I . . . like it."

—*Come,* she said and reached for me.

I touched her hand—*her hand!*—and felt her lift me off the ground. I dragged myself farther up the incline until my knees popped and my legs finally surrendered. In a jumble of skin and bones, I collapsed to the snow, panting. My body was freezing but soaked in sweat. I couldn't breathe. With numb fingers, I located the zipper on my jacket, pulled it down. I popped open my shirt, buttons soaring through the black night, and exposed my chest. Beads of sweat coursed down my ribs, my forehead, freezing at the corners of my eyes.

"Can't," I mused. "Hannah . . . *can't* . . ."

11

NO TIME. EARLY MORNING OR TWILIGHT—IT DIDN'T matter. My eyelids gummy and nearly frozen, I pried them open to see a blurry figure advancing toward me. My vision was kaleidoscopic with snow blindness.

"Hannah . . . ," I rasped. My throat burned and I couldn't focus.

The figure doubled, trebled, refused to center itself.

"Hannah . . ." I struggled. Then started coughing.

But it wasn't Hannah. The figure was much bigger and darker than Hannah and walked with a noticeable limp.

Again, my heart began to race. My fingers tried to close into fists, but their tips had frozen to the ground, and I couldn't get them loose.

The figure paused over me. I could smell old camphor and mothballs and stewed meats. I could smell the unmistakable scent of blood, too.

There were a series of tiny pops as I pulled my fingertips, now bleeding, from the ice. My hand shaking, I reached up to touch the bearded face. I tried to speak, although no words came out, and I had no idea what I was trying to say, anyway. It must have had something to do with Hannah because it was Hannah I was thinking about. But I would never know for sure.

"Shhh," the man said, gently taking my quaking hand by the wrist. He placed it on my chest, then reached slowly down toward my face. He had ten, twenty fingers on that one giant hand. My vision refused to clear up.

He covered my eyes and eased my lids down. I didn't bother to fight him.

A moment later, I was unconscious and sailing like Münchhausen between the stars.

CHAPTER 17

1

I WASN'T THERE WHEN IT HAPPENED, BUT I CAN SEE it nonetheless: the Italian countryside, cool in the stirrings of an early summer that promises not to be too overbearing.

The vehicle appears as a glinting beacon over the farthest hill. David is behind the wheel, donning ridiculous driving goggles, racing gloves, and a worn bomber jacket. Hannah is in the passenger seat, wearing a lambskin jacket and a cream-colored jacquard pantsuit.

She laughs, though I cannot hear her. It as if I am watching all this on television with the sound turned all the way down. Her hair is short, curling just at her jaw, and appears the color of new copper in midday.

There is a sound like a clap of thunder as the motorcar's undercarriage collides with a mound of dirt in the road. David looks startled, and Hannah grips the dashboard, turning to David to examine his expression. David senses her unease and turns to her, offers a complacent smile, and perhaps even places a hand on her thigh.

"It's okay, love," he says. "It's not a—"

"David!" she shrieks.

David jerks his head back to the front.

But it is already too late.

2

I OPENED MY EYES TO FIND MYSELF IN A SMALL, ill-lit room in what appeared to be a clapboard hut. I lay on a bed of straw covered with a blanket of cheesecloth. My goose-down pillow was soft to the point of near nonexistence. Candles flickered from every corner of the small room, and a fetid, moldering smell—curdling goat cheese, perhaps—permeated the air. At the opposite end of the room facing my bed, there was a doorway with no door, but aside from a straw mat halfway down the hallway and walls the color of sawdust, I could see nothing.

Above my head and tacked to the exposed wooden rafters hung various *thangkas* painted in bright colors. The one directly above me depicted one centralized, bronze-skinned figure whose black hair was wrapped in a bun and surrounded by a halo. The figure was flanked on either side by smaller figures, one of them white as a ghost and wielding a flaming sword, the other pale blue and multiarmed.

An attempt to sit up sent a red-hot burning sensation through my torso. I pushed aside the cheesecloth blanket and found I'd been dressed in white linens. A tiny red star—blood—stood in the center of the linen shirt. I lifted the shirt to find the puncture wound below my belly button had been sewn shut with stiff-looking black thread. Gingerly I fingered the wound. I felt nothing; it was numb.

Footsteps approached from the hallway. I dropped my shirt as a great looming shadow fell on the wall of the hallway just outside my room. It grew larger as the figure approached. A large man dressed in black robes ducked beneath the low doorway and entered the room. He paused, his surprise at my consciousness immediately evident, then continued over to a small table laden with various vials and instruments spread out on a velvet cloth.

"You're awake," said the man, his back to me.

"I know you," I said. "Your name's Shomas. You were outside my cabin that night before we left for the Godesh Ridge."

Without turning to face me, Shomas said, "Lie back down. You are still healing."

I eased myself down onto the pillow. My eyelids felt heavy, but I refused to fall asleep. Instead, I trained my gaze on the *thangka* above my head.

When Shomas appeared at my bedside holding a vial of amber fluid and a syringe, he followed my gaze to the tapestry. "That is Shakyamuni in the center. He is flanked by two bodhisattva. The one with the sword is Manjusri, and the one with many arms is Chenrezig, also called Avalokiteśvara, the redeemer of samsara."

"What's samsara?"

"Reincarnation." Shomas plunged the syringe into the vial of amber fluid. Once he'd withdrawn a sufficient amount, he withdrew the syringe and gripped my left wrist with his free hand.

"Hey," I stammered, "what's that?"

"This is medicine to help you heal." He jabbed the needle into my arm. "You have suffered the mountain sickness, dehydration, and hypothermia. Also, curiously enough, you were poisoned."

"Poisoned," I echoed, my eyes growing distant.

"Some sort of heart accelerant, apparently. Rather unusual." He steadied my arm, his grip tightening on my wrist. "The cat may have nine lives, but man has only three. Three is the magical number. You have used up one of yours on this trip, my friend."

"Two, actually," I corrected him, thinking of the cave in the Midwest. "I've used up two."

He did not look at me.

"Where am I?"

"Safe," Shomas said. He emptied the syringe into my arm, then pulled the needle out. "You are in the village in the valley of the Churia Hills."

"How . . . how did I get here?"

"We rescued you from the Godesh Ridge."

"But . . . *how?*"

Shomas shuffled over to the table and set the vial and syringe on the velvet mat. From within the folds of his dark robe, Shomas produced what appeared to be a small silver button that he held between his thumb and index finger. It pulsed once with a strobe of white light.

"This," he said, "is the tracking device I put inside your coat. I had just come from your room when you returned that evening."

"A tracking device," I muttered. "Why would you do that?"

"It isn't the first time." He dropped the silver button into one of his many pockets. "Occasionally we get people who wish to traverse the Godesh Ridge in search of the Canyon of Souls. If we fail to sufficiently warn them away, we always take . . . alternative measures."

A young girl dressed all in white with straight black hair appeared in the doorway, holding what appeared to be a bowl of soup. She paused, her head down, and waited for Shomas to address her. I understood none of what they said. The girl nodded and entered the room, her footfalls silent on the wooden floor, and set the bowl on a hand-carved table beside my bed. She stole a glimpse of me from the corner of her eyes. When I smiled, she spun away, her long hair twirling, and disappeared out the door.

Shomas pointed to the steaming ceramic bowl. "You should eat that, even if you are not hungry."

"I'm starving," I said.

"It is hot."

The ceramic bowl was on a cloth. I sat up and leaned against the wall, then used the cloth to transfer the bowl into my lap. The soup was colorless. Barley leaves and cubes of what must have been tofu floated in the broth. I brought it to my mouth and sipped. It was excruciatingly hot and as tasteless as boiling water.

"The Godesh Ridge is a sacred place." Shomas stood at the foot of the bed, his hands folded behind his back. "Many years ago, our measures for ensuring it remained untouched by mankind were much more final than our current methods." He raised one eyebrow to make sure I understood him correctly.

I nodded to express that I did.

"For various reasons, we have adapted to current conditions and now operate in the fashion you see now." He spread his hands to indicate the room as well as the implements on the table with the velvet cloth. "Crossing the Godesh Ridge in search of the Canyon of Souls is no different than a foreigner setting foot in the Vatican only to relieve himself in the entranceway. It is a sign of disrespect for our culture and our beliefs."

"I had no idea. It was never our intention to—"

"Intentions aside, our hidden lands have a way of protecting themselves. They do not show themselves to those they deem unworthy. Also, many are killed in such foolish pursuits—they become injured, stranded, lost, and without communication with the outside world. So we have developed a way to rescue these doomed souls and bring them back from the mountain. Despite our efforts, however, our success rate is quite slim. It is a difficult mountain to cross, and the rescue of individuals from the ridge poses innumerable difficulties. Still, you are among the lucky few."

"I had a friend. John Petras. He was in a cave in the—"

"He, too, has been recovered."

The word *recovered* did little to clarify my friend's condition. "What exactly does that mean?"

"He is growing strong and healthy in this village, just as you are," Shomas said.

My gaze wandered about the room, briefly lost in the flicker of countless candles. "And Andrew?" I heard myself say. "Andrew Trumbauer?"

"You and your friend hidden in the cave were the only two recovered from this mission." Hands together, Shomas nodded in my direction. "I am sorry. But you were warned."

Like a phantom, Shomas drifted across the room. Just as he bowed his head in the doorway, I called to him. He paused and turned toward me, his face expressionless. His eyes glittered in the candlelight like embers sprung from a fire.

"I've seen the Canyon of Souls," I said.

Shomas seemed to smile, but it was such a minute gesture I couldn't be sure. "No," he said quietly, "you only saw what the land *let* you see."

3

THREE DAYS LATER, I WAS STRONG ENOUGH TO venture out to the wooden hut where John Petras recuperated.

He smiled faintly from his bed in a room remarkably similar to mine. "How do I look?"

"The truth? Like you fell off a mountain. How's your shoulder?"

"They bandaged me up pretty good, killed the infection. Your tourniquet saved my life."

"Did they explain to you what happened? How we were saved?"

He nodded. A wave of pain or nausea must have stuck him then, because he closed his eyes and his nostrils flared with each exhalation.

I waited for the moment to pass.

Finally, when his eyes opened, they were glossy and soft. "Andrew? What—?"

"Andrew's dead. This whole thing was a setup, a sick plot of revenge." I was sitting in a wicker chair beside Petras's bed. I rubbed my face and leaned one elbow on his mattress. "We were played. From the very beginning. All of us." Across the room, I glimpsed Hannah's image. But when I looked up, she was gone. It had most likely been a trick of the candlelight. "He wanted me dead because I let someone he loved die," I said in one long, pent-up breath.

"Your wife," he said, the inflection in his voice telling me this wasn't a question.

"He loved her." I smiled. My face went hot. "I did, too."

"*Was* it your fault?" he asked.

I thought about it for a long time. "Some things were my fault," I said finally. "Some of it. I tried to fix things, but I was too late. She went away and never came back. And I can either blame myself for the rest of my life and keep wandering by myself through dark caves waiting to disappear . . . or I can accept my role and move on. Anyway," I said, glancing across the room to the darkened space where I thought I saw Hannah just a moment before, "I think she's forgiven me."

One of Petras's hands slid from beneath the cheesecloth blanket to pat one of my own. He smiled wearily. He looked ancient, a hundred years old.

I cleared my throat and swiped away tears with the heel of one hand. "So why'd he bring you here? What's your sin?"

"Honestly, I don't know." His weak, pained smile widened. Out of nowhere he reminded me of my father.

Ten minutes later, I was back out by the road watching the sun burn behind the mountains while the trees glowed like fiery ember. Shomas approached. He was dressed in a heavy woolen coat that hung past his knees. A wool cap was pulled low over his ears. "Your friend is feeling better?"

"He is, yes. Thank you."

"You both will be leaving soon."

"Right." Behind him, I watched the sun continue to set. In less than a minute, it would be dark. "You haven't asked me what happened up there. Why is that?"

"Because I know what happened."

I looked at him. I tried to read his face but found it an impossible task. It was like trying to sense emotion from a tombstone. "What do you mean?"

"The mountains are a dangerous place. Your friends suffered unfortunate fates. Accidents," he said, his voice lowering, his eyes steady on me, "have a way of happening."

I was about to say something—anything—but he continued before I could open my mouth.

"These lands are sacred lands," said Shomas. "We do not need people coming here to investigate matters. We do not need people coming here to learn what happened. The Godesh Ridge does not need more foolish explorers marking the snow with traitorous footprints."

Expelling a gust of breath, he turned and trudged up the side of the road. Where he went I could not tell; the sun had already set, covering the world in a blanket of darkness, and I lost him somewhere around the bend.

4

ONE WEEK LATER, WE DEPARTED FOR LONDON ON the same flight. Petras slept, and I thumbed through various magazines as well as a newly purchased copy of the George Mallory book I hadn't finished. Mallory and his climbing partner, Andrew Irvine, disappeared while climbing the northeast ridge of Everest in 1924. His body wasn't discovered until 1999, and although the book skimped on description, I could only imagine what would have been left behind after being lost out there in the unforgiving wilds of Everest for seventy-five years.

In London, we boarded separate planes—John Petras to Wisconsin, me to Baltimore-Washington International. Petras's plane left first. At his gate, we embraced, like brothers about to part.

"There's one thing we haven't discussed yet."

I knew what it was. I nodded, rubbing my forehead with aching fingers. "I know. What do you think?"

"I think we can go back and tell the truth," he said. "Call the police, tell them what happened. Tell them everything about Andrew."

"Then there's the other option."

Petras raked his fingers through his beard and down his neck. "It was all an accident, a horrible accident. Just like the Sherpas said."

"I don't have it in me to go through all that right now," I said. "I may *never* have it in me."

"Then it was an accident."

"And Andrew?"

"Another accident, just like the others. Andrew Trumbauer went over the cliff. End of story." One hand on my shoulder, he squeezed my aching muscles and smiled. Then he turned and shuffled through the doors and down the gangway to the airplane.

You only saw what the land let *you see,* I thought.

I remained at his gate until the plane taxied down the runway, my nose nearly pressed against the window, my eyes as vacant as twin chunks of ice.

PART FOUR

THE GHOSTS WE RETURN TO

CHAPTER 18

1

AS THE MOON PASSED BEHIND A DRIFT OF DARK clouds, I turned away from the windows and encircled Marta in my arms. She sighed. Her warm legs intertwined with mine beneath the sheets; she hugged my arms. I peppered her neck with tiny kisses.

"I need to get up," I whispered in her ear.

"Hmm." Warmly.

Five minutes later, dressed in running shorts and Nikes, I took off along the waterfront. To my right, the bay glistened with moonlight, this distant shimmer of the Bay Bridge like something tangible materializing through the fog of a dream. I ran through Eastport and over the small drawbridge, flanked on both sides by the lull of sleeping sailboats. Into downtown, I ran up Main Street and downgraded to a slow jog around Church Circle. The conical spire of St. Anne's looked like a stalagmite rising off the floor of a limestone cave. At this hour, the city was asleep. Only the occasional vehicle rolled past me on the narrow roadways. But other than that, all was silent.

It had been four months since I'd returned from Nepal. A strict regime of exercise and healthy eating had seen to it that I'd fully recovered from the events that occurred on the Godesh Ridge. Now, halfway around the world and a year in the future, it was almost possible to convince myself, particularly on nights such as these, that it had all been a nightmare.

Almost possible.

Of course, there were still the *actual* nightmares—waking up slick with sweat and with a scream caught in my throat from some half-remembered dream where I ran through feet of snow as some faceless, heartless creature pursued me down the face of a mountain. Often the chase would end when I turned a sharp corner and found myself at the edge of a cliff. Behind me, my pursuer slowed to a predatory crawl, hidden in the heavy shadows. My choices were simple: either jump off the cliff or face whatever followed me. For whatever reason, I usually woke up before having to make the decision.

Immediately following my return, I was obsessed with researching the background of the men who had died on the Godesh Ridge, including Andrew Trumbauer. And in most cases, I was able to derive some reason why Andrew would have wanted revenge on them . . .

Donald Shotsky was the easiest, as I already had some information to go by. He'd been a fisherman and a deckhand on various crab boats in the Bering Sea. Years ago, he'd been a crewman on a ship called the *Kula Plate*, along with Andrew.

Eventually I tracked down the captain—a grizzled veteran of the Korean War named Footie Teacar—who confirmed the story of how Shotsky had nearly gone over the side only to be saved by a greenhorn named Andy something-or-other. Of course, Teacar's description of the greenhorn matched Andrew Trumbauer perfectly.

As I'd expected, confirming Shotsky's involvement with a group of Las Vegas thugs was much more difficult. But following a phone call to an old college buddy of mine who'd for years worked as a blackjack dealer at a number of casinos on the strip, I learned one piece of interesting information: for the past decade, a New York corporation had reserved a hotel suite at the MGM Grand, although no one could say for certain if the suite had actually ever been used. The corporation was Trumbauer Petrol, the company Andrew inherited from his father after his death.

Chad Nando possessed an extensive arrest portfolio with various police departments throughout the country, mostly petty stuff—possession of dope, minor theft, a couple of DUIs. Undoubtedly, Chad's biggest claim to fame, at least on the police blotter circuit, had been his arrest in participation with a cocaine-smuggling operation.

Under the Freedom of Information Act, I requested and received documents pertinent to the case, and, although the names and specific identifiers had been blocked out by a black Sharpie, I was able to discern Chad's role in the whole ordeal with little difficulty: he'd been the snitch. Arrested right up front, he agreed to cooperate in exchange for leniency by the courts, which was granted to him in the form of three years' probation.

When police followed the cocaine's money trail, a number of high-profile businesses were mentioned in the report, though they were never able to make anything stick, and the business owners were quickly dropped as targets. One business was a small American entrepreneurial company called CliffDiver, Inc. An Internet search yielded very little information about CliffDiver, which had immediately gone out of business following the investigation. I found no records of any of the company's personnel except for one—Drew Bauer, president and CEO.

Only the police report provided any further insight, stating that just prior to their investigation, CliffDiver had given money to a pharmaceutical company that had patented a pill to combat heart failure. Approval by the FDA never came, the pharmaceutical company folded, and CliffDiver faded into the background before disappearing entirely. Vague? Yes. However, I possessed one small bit of knowledge that the police working the case did not: the word *Cliff-Diver* was tattooed on Andrew Trumbauer's upper thigh, something

I would have never noticed had he not stripped out of his clothes and jumped off the cliff that night in San Juan so many years ago.

The rest were more difficult to decipher, knowing so little about their backgrounds and their individual relationships with Andrew. Any parallels would only be supposition on my part. Yet who knew what sort of things happened in the six months Michael Hollinger spent with Andrew and two aboriginal women in the Australian out-back, for instance? The women could never be found, and even if they were, the chances that they knew anything were more than slim.

What had Curtis Booker done to earn his gravestone? I found very little information about the ex-Marine on the Internet, save for an Ohio address. Feeling it necessary, I mailed a letter to that address. The letter mentioned Curtis's death on the Godesh Ridge, although I went into no specific detail, and concluded with my return address and telephone number in case anyone wanted to get in touch with me for more information. I addressed the letter to Curtis's daughter, Lucinda Booker. I'd yet to receive a reply.

And, of course, there was John Petras. Since he'd survived the or-deal, there was no need to conduct any research, but that didn't mean I was able to figure out his connection to Andrew nor why Andrew wanted to kill him. We phoned each other once a month just to keep tabs, and occasionally I'd pester him about it. But Petras would only sigh and say he could think of nothing.

"We'd had one stupid argument years ago in Nova Scotia," he told me. "It was over who'd win the Super Bowl, and we were both tanked up on liquor. I called him a stupid son of a bitch, and he said I was an ignorant imbecile—hardly grounds for wanting someone dead."

"Do you believe the *dakini* exist?" I asked him during our last phone call.

"What brought this up all of a sudden?"

"It's just been on my mind since you mentioned it."

"They're Buddhist myths. The word translates to 'sky dancer,' a female spirit who traverses through space. Some faiths say they're vengeful. Others say they function as muses. But overall, they're considered 'testers'—their purpose is to put man through tests to prove his worth."

"His worth for what?"

"To enter paradise," said Petras. "Eternal bliss."

"Eden," I said.

"Shangri-la," Petras added.

"So I guess if you believe in the *dakini,* you'd have to believe in the existence of Shangri-la," I said. "You'd have to believe in paradise."

I could tell Petras was grinning on the other end of the phone. "You can't have God without the devil."

My legs pumping, my respiration as tight as a machine, I headed back down Main Street, cut across one of the darkened, narrow alleys that crisscrossed the City Dock, and emptied onto a cobblestone byway illuminated by an interval of lampposts. I burned by the Filibuster, dark and locked up for the evening.

2

EVERY HONEST STORY HAS ONE GREAT REVEAL.
For me and my life—for my story—it would be no different. Despite the proactive research into the people who'd died on Godesh Ridge at the hands of Andrew Trumbauer, my great reveal happened purely by chance nearly one year after my return from Nepal.

I was sitting on a lounge chair on my balcony reading the Sunday edition of *The Capital* when my gaze fell upon a curious headline.

Regatta Race Accident Victim's Body Finally Found

The article went on to detail how, during the annual Regatta race roughly two and a half years ago, boat owner and race participant Gerald H. Figlio had been struck on the back of the head by the boom and fallen into the bay. A search commenced, but Figlio's body was never recovered until this past weekend when the remains of a corpse washed up at Sandy Point State Park. Figlio was identified through his dental records, the article said. The cause of death was ruled accidental.

Perhaps I wouldn't have made the connection if it wasn't for the brief bio of Gerald H. Figlio at the end of the article where it mentioned he'd once been a professor of English at James Madison University—both Hannah's and Andrew's alma mater.

The following day, I went to the local library and fired up one of the computer terminals. I located the Regatta's official Web site and searched the backlog of race registrants from the past couple of years. After finding Figlio's name, I clicked on the PDF document that was his registration card. Among various other information, Figlio had listed his crew for the race.

Boddington, Joseph
Brunelli, Michael
O'Maera, Sean
Trumbauer, Andrew
Wesley, T.J.
Wheaton, Xavier

It was just what I'd expected to find, yet it still caused an uncontrollable chill to race down my spine. And not so much because I'd come across Andrew's name on the list but because the grand scope of all Andrew had been doing suddenly occurred to me: the trip to the Godesh Ridge had not been Andrew's singular expression of revenge. Rather, Andrew had been seeking his revenge *all over the place*, presumably for *years*.

How many people did you kill? I thought, the monitor casting a sickly blue glow across my face. *How long had you been doing this?*

"Well, you're not doing it anymore," I said and logged off the computer.

3

WHEN I RETURNED FROM THE LIBRARY, MARTA was sitting on the sofa with her bare feet drawn up beneath her, a melancholic look on her face. She faced the television but it was off, the whole room growing dark with the onset of night.

I tossed my keys on the credenza and took off my shoes. "What? What is it?"

"There was a phone call from some lawyer," she said dryly. "Your friend John Petras is dead."

4

IT WAS A FREAK ACCIDENT. DURING A PARTICULARLY nasty storm, a felled power line landed on the roof of John Petras's house, sparking a fire. The coroner's report listed asphyxiation due to smoke inhalation as the cause of death.

A week after I'd received the news, a box was delivered to my apartment stamped with a Wisconsin law firm's return address. I opened the box to discover Petras's pearl-handled hunting knife wrapped in newspaper. There was no letter typed on letterhead, no note.

That evening I went to the Filibuster. It was the first time I'd been back since my return from Nepal. The first thing that struck me was how someone had removed all the newspaper clippings and photos of corrupt politicians from the walls. Ricky was tending bar; his eyes nearly dropped out of their sockets upon seeing me.

I grinned and offered a two-fingered salute as I entered and claimed a barstool.

"Holy crap, Tim," Ricky said.

"Guess you're still working here, huh, kid?"

"What's it been?" he said. "A year?"

"At least," I said.

"Where you been?"

"Nepal. Climbing mountains. And chasing ghosts."

"No shit? Wow. That's badass." He flipped a dish towel over one shoulder. "Can I get you the usual? I still remember how you like it . . ."

"Actually, make it a Diet Coke."

"Seriously?"

"And a menu. I'm hungry."

"Man, that mountain climbing stuff must have rattled your brains around, if you don't mind me saying." Ricky slipped me a menu and a Diet Coke.

I glanced around the place and said, "What's with the empty walls?"

"Yeah," Ricky said. "Guess you wouldn't know. Brom's selling the place."

"No shit? How come?"

"Never really came out and said. My guess is he's getting old and doesn't want the hassle anymore." He jerked a thumb toward the back room. "He keeps a picture of some beach in Pensacola on his desk in his office. Been looking at it more and more whenever he's in here. I bet he's itching to retire while he's still got a few good years left, maybe get a house on the beach in Florida. Just relax, you know?"

I was still staring at the barren walls. *This is what it's like for a building to get Alzheimer's,* I thought. *Taking pictures off the walls and leaving those inky, dark-colored rectangles in the wood is how a building loses its memories, loses what makes it what it used to be.*

"You okay, Tim?"

"Fine." I ordered a crab cake and ate it in silence, while Ricky attended to the other patrons. Behind me, the sound of darts striking the dartboard punctuated each bite of my crab cake. At one point, I heard someone slip coins into the jukebox. An old Creedence

Clearwater Revival song came on.

Something caused me to shiver. I turned around on my stool and looked toward the rear of the bar, straight at the booth where, roughly two and a half years ago now, I'd run into Andrew Trumbauer. What I'd written off as nothing more than a serendipitous meeting was now overshadowed by everything I'd come to know about Andrew. How long had it taken him to find me? How many days had he followed me? Had he been following me straight to the Filibuster? The notion caused my hands to go numb; I set my glass of Diet Coke on the bar before I dropped it.

The booth was currently empty, but if I concentrated hard enough, I could visualize what Andrew had looked like that evening when he'd locked eyes with me from across the room. The way he'd lit a cigarette and grinned at the corner of his mouth, that sly, knowing grin, that perfect *Andrew* grin . . .

Then, for no longer than a heartbeat, Hannah appeared in the corner of the bar. She was nude and glistening as if covered by tiny beads of ice, her skin nearly blue, her lips colorless. She was half shaded in gloom, so I couldn't make out her expression, yet I could see the gleam of her eyes through the shadows. They were wide, staring, heartbreaking eyes.

A hand fell on my shoulder. My heart seized; instantly, I was back on Godesh Ridge, trying to plug up a weeping wound in my abdomen before I bled out into the snow.

"You sure you're all right?" It was Ricky. "You look like you're ready to pass out, man."

I waved him off. "No, no—I'm okay."

"Yeah?"

"Yeah." It had been a year since I'd last seen Hannah's ghost in Nepal on the Godesh Ridge.

"It's just, I mean, you look spooked."

"Forget it, Ricky. Just gimme the check, huh?"

I paid the bill and shoved out into the cool night, positive young Ricky's eyes followed me all the way out the door.

5

PUSHING OPEN THE DOOR TO MY APARTMENT, I was immediately overcome by a cold breeze. I closed the door behind me and groped for the light switch. I flicked the switch, but the light didn't turn on. Across the room, the curtains over the balcony doors billowed out. The doors were open.

"Marta?" I called. She was supposed to be at her place tonight, but maybe she'd changed her mind.

I took a step into the room toward the lamp on the end table when movement caught my eye. I froze. Someone was standing in a darkened corner, partially obscured by the billowing curtain.

"Who's there?" My voice was nothing more than a whisper.

"Hello, Tim." It was Andrew. He stepped out from the corner, briefly silhouetted before the panel of light coming through the open balcony doors.

"Jesus—*Andrew?*" I couldn't fathom it. "How did you . . . ? What are you . . . ?"

"Been a while, Overleigh. Been about a year since we last . . . tangoed."

"You're supposed to be dead."

"So are you," he said and took a step forward. Moonlight washed across a distorted, lumpy face, tracked by numerous scars and dents. He shuffled forward with a limp.

"You went over the edge," I breathed. "I saw you."

"Yes." His voice was gravelly, injured. "It was quite a drop. I'll probably never know exactly how long I was unconscious, but when I woke up, the pain . . . oh, the pain was *exquisite*. I wished death upon me countless times, but it never came. And soon I realized I had to take things into my own hands." His hideous, broken face grinned.

His teeth were chiseled pickets filed to points. "Just like always, I had to take things into my own hands."

I backed up against the door. I could taste bile at the rear of my throat.

"They did the best they could, but what can you expect from a bunch of Tibetan monks?" He laughed. It sounded like a box of glass shaken, shaken, shaken.

"Petras," I uttered. "You killed John Petras."

"Shhh." He brought one crooked finger up to his disfigured lips. Another step closer and I could see one of his eyes was partially swollen, his forehead a mountainous terrain of peaks and valleys.

"Why Petras?" I wanted to know. "I've already figured much of it out but not Petras. He was a good man. What'd he ever do to you?"

Andrew's lower lip dropped—a grotesque expression of awe, which slowly curled into his hideous trademark grin. "You mean you two imbeciles never figured it out?"

"Figured what out?"

"You never recognized each other?" He snickered, a ticking time-bomb sound.

"What are you talking about?"

"John Petras is the reason you were on that mountain. If it wasn't for Petras, you would have died in the desert after crawling out of that cave, and none of this would have ever happened to you. Driver finds unidentified injured man unconscious by the side of the road. Something like that, anyway. Forgive me, but I don't remember the newspaper article verbatim."

"Petras . . . Petras was the one who . . . who found me . . . ?"

"I guess I can understand how you two never put it together. After all, it was quite a while ago. You were going through your long-hair stage, too, if I remember correctly."

I couldn't respond. My mind was reeling.

"See, it was John Petras's own fault for stepping in and redirecting fate. Set all the other wheels into motion."

"You son of—"

"Save it," Andrew growled. "So now he's dead—just one more person you're responsible for killing. You're a dangerous man, Timothy Overleigh. You need to be stopped. For good."

Moonlight gleamed to my right. I glanced over and saw Petras's pearl-handled hunting knife on the credenza.

Andrew took one final step toward me. I heard the click of a gun's hammer being pulled back. "I've waited a long time for this. Good-bye, motherfucker."

"Yes," I said. "Good-bye."

I grabbed the knife off the credenza and, like a bull in a ring, charged Andrew. I heard a deafening, bone-quaking pop ring out, saw the fiery muzzle flash . . . Then, an instant later, I collided with Andrew, driving the blade of Petras's hunting knife straight into his chest.

Andrew cried out and dropped the gun. My momentum propelled us clear across the room. Andrew scrambled to grab hold of the curtains; he pulled one from its rod as we shot out onto the balcony. My hand still wrapped around the hilt of the knife, I drove us across the balcony where we broke through the railing and fell over the edge.

The fall lasted only a second, but the blackness that followed could have been an eternity.

CHAPTER 19

1

—TIM, SHE SAID. OH, TIM . . .

2

AND THE WORLD SWAM BACK INTO TEMPORARY
focus: sodium lights . . . corkboard ceiling tiles . . . the droning beep-beep-beep of electrical heartbeats.

Above me, Marta's face, swimming out of the black. A warm hand against my cold cheek.

"Oh, Tim," she said, her voice like a thousand vibrations.

"Where—?" I began, but my throat burst into flames and I cut myself off.

"You're in the hospital," she said. "You're alive, Tim. You're alive."

Then: blackness.

3

THE BULLET FROM ANDREW'S 9MM ENTERED MY
left leg only to ricochet out, embedding itself in the ceiling of

my apartment. According to the doctors who spent several days fawning over me in the hospital, it was the metal plate screwed into my fibula that caused the bullet's redirection and prevented it from bursting through the other side of my leg. There was no question—I was lucky.

Andrew Trumbauer was not as lucky. He died that night, a combination of severe trauma to the back of his head sustained in the three-story fall from my balcony and the five-inch, pearl-handled hunting knife I'd planted in his chest. Which one was listed as the actual cause of death, I did not know. I'd been apprised of too many coroner reports in my lifetime and did not feel I needed to add another notch to my walking stick.

Once my leg healed, I took to running across Eastport and along the breakwater that overlooked the bay. I timed myself, pushed myself, and checked the rate of my pulse as the miles added up. I lost what weight I'd put on while confined to the wheelchair. My left leg never felt stronger.

The police asked questions, of course. After very little consideration, I came clean about all that had happened in Nepal. The two young officers who took notes during my interrogation stared at me in disbelief. It made me look bad, coming clean a year after it had happened. Why had I lied? My reasons were poor but truthful.

And perhaps they wouldn't have believed me had an insightful detective in Wisconsin not uncovered a curious bit of information. On the night of the mysterious fire that had killed John Petras, a man matching Andrew's description rented a vehicle under the name Victor Rios from the airport. The clerk at the rental car agency described the person with ease, relating how he'd been spooked by Victor's busted, scarred face and limp. The clerk said Victor Rios reminded her of Quasimodo. After that, the police accepted my story and never called on me again. Whether they actually believed all that I had told them, I had no idea . . .

Marta and I continued our relationship for a good eight months after my recovery, although we never truly fell in love. We both knew it, but because we cared for each other, we let things drag out longer than they should, each of us not wanting to hurt the other's feelings. But in the end, after a night of smiles and hugs and tears, Marta packed her stuff and left. We remained friends, but things were never quite the same between us again.

And it seemed all was back to normal, including my inability to sculpt. The passion had left me, the drive had gone out of me—

4

—Until midnight of some random night.

I opened my eyes to the soft moonlight coming in through my bedroom windows. I felt a chill wash over my body, which was covered in a film of sweat. Panting, my heartbeat increasing, I sat up stiffly in bed. Across from me was the bedroom doorway and beyond that the deeper darkness of the hall. As I stared, I thought I saw a whitish shape drift down the hall and disappear.

I flipped the sheets off me and climbed into a pair of running shorts. The soles of my feet, tacky with sweat, peeled off the hardwood floor with each step.

Out in the foyer the door to my apartment stood open. Dull, greenish light spilled in from the communal hallway. My breath catching in my throat, I glimpsed a slight shadow easing along the wall outside.

I followed the shape into the hallway, but the hallway was empty.

I hurried down the flights of steps to the lobby in time to see the lobby door closing. Beyond the doors, a smoky mist had overtaken the parking lot. It was impossible to see anything beyond the apartment building's black canvas awning.

My palms left twin imprints on the glass as I pushed the lobby door open and staggered out into the fog. The air was thick, humid.

Breathing in was like inhaling ghostly vapors. I could hear the tide coming in at the beach but could see nothing until I went around the side of the building, the wet grass turning to sand beneath my feet.

At the foot of the bay, the fog seemed to sail over the water, where it slowly dissipated. Revealed by the clearing of the fog and aglow in moonlight, Hannah's ghost stood on the beach. The foaming surf lapped at her bare feet. She was once again in her willowy, flowing white gown—the gown of an angel—and her hair was the short, sculpted hair she'd had the last time I saw her at our Georgetown home before she ran off to Italy.

"Hannah," I whispered, my voice seeming to carry forever over the dark water.

She smiled warmly and turned. I watched her walk along the surf and down the moonlit beach.

After a moment, I began to follow. My heels dug divots in the wet sand, my feet quickly growing numb.

Hannah disappeared around a bend in the coast, briefly masked by a dark veil of trees swaying in the wind.

I rounded the trees, crossing through the freezing bay water to do so, and materialized on the other side of the beach. It was a stretch of beach I'd been on hundreds of times before, but suddenly it was all completely new to me. The way the moonlight played off the contours of the black stones that rose like giant glossy fingers from the sand, glistening like living creatures, reflecting the countless dazzle of diamond stars . . .

It was breathtaking. Helpless, I collapsed in the sand, my arms quivering. My breath was coming in steady gasps now. My face was beginning to burn.

"It's . . . beautiful," I managed, my voice hitching. To my own amazement, I felt a laugh threaten my throat.

Hannah continued walking down the beach, one hand running along the shimmering, glossy stones along the breakwater, never once pausing to look back. Somewhere farther up the beach, her image began to fade. By the time she reached the next outcrop of shuddering trees, she had vanished completely.

5

WHETHER IT WAS A DREAM, A HALLUCINATION, OR something else, I may never know for sure. But in the morning I awoke in a fetal position in the sand, the surf lapping at my legs, dressed in nothing but running shorts. Peering over my shoulder, I could discern my footprints in the sand from the night before—only my footprints, though, and no one else's.

Later that day, I carried a hammer and a chisel to the black stones along the beach, I started sculpting again. I sculpted for myself. Beneath the burn of a midday sun, I sculpted the rocks that lined the breakwater of the Chesapeake Bay. I carved, leaving in my wake things of sudden and unmistakable awe, of spiritual beauty. I sculpted for John Petras who was so close but never got to see the Canyon of Souls. I sculpted for Hannah, my Hannah, who had returned to me my ability to create artistic paradise, to bring Shangri-la to the world.

And I would show it to the world. I would do it for Hannah, my *dakini,* and I would do it for myself—finally, *myself,* letting go, forgiving myself—because it was what she wanted and what she had been trying to tell me all along. It was a gift of forgiveness.

Finished, hours or days or weeks or years later, I dropped my tools in the surf and wiped the tears from my eyes with shaking, gritty hands. Numb, my body trembling, I began to climb up the beach, pausing at the summit of the embankment to glance over my shoulder at the carved black stones, the white band of beach, and the glistening shimmer of the endless bay.

The view from the top was nothing short of breathtaking.

One More Moment

Check it out! There is a new section on the Medallion Press Web site called "One More Moment." Have you ever gotten to the end of a book and just been crushed that it's over? Aching to know if the star-crossed lovers ever got married? Had kids? With this new section of our Web site, you won't have to wonder anymore! "One More Moment" provides an extension of your favorite book so you can discover what happens after the story.

medallionpress.com

MEDALLION

P R E S S

Be in the know on the latest
Medallion Press news by becoming a Medallion Press
Insider!

<u>As an Insider you'll receive:</u>

· Our FREE expanded monthly newsletter, giving you more insight
into Medallion Press

· Advanced press releases and breaking news

· Greater access to all your favorite Medallion authors

Joining is easy. Just visit our Web site at
<u>www.medallionpress.com</u> and click on the Medallion Press
Insider tab.

MEDALLION
P R E S S

Want to know what's going on with
your favorite author or what new releases
are coming from Medallion Press?

Now you can receive breaking news,
updates, and more from Medallion Press
straight to your cell phone, e-mail, instant messenger, or Facebook!

Sign up now at www.twitter.com/MedallionPress to stay on top of all
the happenings in and
around Medallion Press.

For more information
about other great titles from
Medallion Press, visit

medallionpress.com